Ellie DEAN
With Hope and Love

arrow books

1 3 5 7 9 10 8 6 4 2

Arrow Books
20 Vauxhall Bridge Road
London SW1V 2SA

Arrow Books is part of the Penguin Random House group
of companies whose addresses can be found
at global.penguinrandomhouse.com.

Penguin
Random House
UK

First published by Arrow Books in 2019

www.penguin.co.uk

A CIP catalogue record for this book is available
from the British Library.

ISBN 9781787462786

Typeset in 11/14 pt Palatino
by Integra Software Services Pvt. Ltd, Pondicherry

Printed and bound in Great Britain by Clays Ltd, Elcograf S.p.A.

Acknowledgements

This book would never have been completed if it hadn't been for the wonderful care from my GP, Dr Brierley, the staff at the Eastbourne District General Hospital, and the stroke team who visited me every day once I got back home. Because of their swift reaction and diligence I'm fully fit, and I am extremely grateful for their care.

To my husband and children, for all their love and concern over what had been a traumatic time for us all. Your love helped me through in more ways than you could ever imagine. And to my publishers, Arrow, for their understanding and patience when this book was delivered a little late. This was the first time in over twenty years that I've not met a deadline, and I'm determined not to do it again!

Last, but never least, thanks to my agent, Teresa Chris, for fighting my corner and always being there. We've been down a long, tough road together over the years, and I could never have come so far without you.

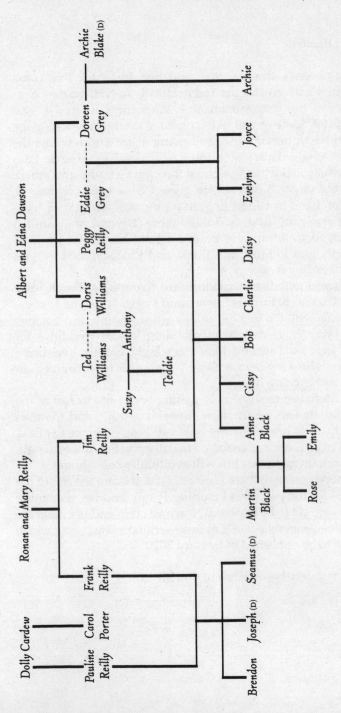

The Cliffehaven Family Tree

Dear Readers,

It has been a strange year, and one in which I've come through with great relief and gratitude to NHS nurses, doctors and the stroke team at Eastbourne District General Hospital. Some of you will have read on my Facebook page that I had a minor stroke following a stressful few months and a long, exhausting journey to Australia and back. I am extremely lucky that I've come through virtually unscathed, and the targets I had set for myself have been conquered. My left hand lost all feeling, so typing was a trial, and cryptic passwords and Sudokus were beyond me until I managed to retrain my brain and my hand! But my first priority was to finish this book, and I'm delighted for you to be reading it now.

As you will discover, things are changing at Beach View now the war in Europe is over, and Peggy is having to come to terms with the fact her chicks are starting to leave home. I've taken huge delight in planning lots of weddings for *With Hope and Love* and, like Peggy and Cordelia, I've shed a tear or two of my own as these young girls have begun their new and exciting lives.

Cliffehaven too, is slowly getting back onto its feet as the holiday makers return, new homes are built, and the men start to come home. But the war is still raging in the Far East, and Peggy is once more forced to call upon her inner strength to maintain hope that Jim will eventually come home.

I hope you enjoy *With Hope and Love*. It is not the end of the series, for the problems besetting Peggy and her remaining chicks are yet to be resolved. Now my brain and my hand are working properly again, I'm busy writing *Homecoming* which is due to be published in January 2020.

With my very best wishes to you all,

Ellie Dean x

They went with songs to the battle, they were young,
Straight of limb, true of eye, steady and aglow.
They were staunch to the end against the odds
   uncounted,
They fell with their faces to the foe.

They shall not grow old, as we that are left grow old:
Age shall not weary them, nor the years condemn.
At the going down of the sun and in the morning
We will remember them.

'For the Fallen' by Laurence Binyon (1914)

1

Burma
8 May 1945

The monsoon heat and humidity had risen swiftly during the day, the rain bucketing down through the jungle canopy in a ceaseless deluge which turned the soft earth to thick, cloying mud that ran in rivers right through the makeshift respite camp. The conditions made the exhausted soldiers' lives a misery, for clothes didn't dry, boots and feet rotted, and there were several instances of men having mould growing in the folds of their skin from being constantly damp.

It was now late afternoon, and although there was a canvas roof and thick matting spread over the floor of steel sheeting in the motor maintenance area, Second Lieutenant Jim Reilly was soaked to the skin with sweat and mud as he lay cursing beneath the three-ton truck. He was struggling to remove its broken exhaust pipe before darkness fell, but the bloody thing seemed to be welded with rust to its moorings, and he couldn't shift it.

The wrench slipped from his wet hand for the third time and, as he dodged to avoid it landing on his face, he cracked his head on the differential – an unforgiving great lump of metal beneath the truck. Spitting out a string of oaths, he impatiently yanked on the thick leather gloves he'd previously discarded because they made him even hotter and, taking a deep breath to keep his temper at bay, started work on the stubborn bolt again.

His task would have been simple enough in ordinary circumstances, but he was in a hurry, and what with the rain and the draining heat, he was beginning to wish he hadn't taken over from the young sapper. However, he'd missed working on the tools, and after the past four months of almost constant fighting with the Japanese, he'd hoped the familiarity of the task would help him banish the memories of what he'd witnessed during the liberation of Rangoon.

Jim blinked away the stinging sweat and brushed the muck off his face which sifted down from the underside of the truck as he attacked the bolt with added vigour, but the images of what they'd encountered in Rangoon still haunted him.

After the battle for Pegu was won in March, Jim and his men had arrived in Rangoon to mop up any resistance, only to discover that the city had been abandoned by the Japanese who'd fled by land and sea, resulting in nine of their eleven convoy ships being sunk by the British Destroyers anchored offshore.

Before the Japanese had left the port, they'd looted and destroyed it, going as far as bombing the convent which had served them as a hospital, killing four hundred of their own men, before locking the Burmese prisoners in their wooden huts and burning them to the ground.

The thousand Allied POWs Jim and his men had found had escaped this terrible fate, for the Japanese had planned to take them with them as slaves, but soon realised that in their desperately weakened state they'd slow them down. As ammunition was in such short supply they didn't want to waste bullets by shooting them, so they'd abandoned them to the lawlessness of the dacoits and a city which was already starving and rife with disease.

The POWs had been held in the city jail for several months and were so emaciated and weakened by starvation, slave labour and disease they were barely living skeletons in their filthy rags. As they waited to be loaded onto a requisitioned sampan to be taken upriver to the safety of an Allied air lift to hospital, Jim had remembered how desperate young Sarah Fuller was for news of her father and fiancé, who'd been captured after the fall of Singapore, so he'd asked if any of them had come across a Jock Fuller or Philip Tarrant.

None of them had, and Jim wasn't really surprised, for he knew there were thousands upon thousands of prisoners in numberless camps spread right across Burma, Malaya and Thailand, to the islands in the East China Sea and even on the Japanese mainland. God only knew what they were going through if these thousand men were an example of how the Japs treated their prisoners.

Jim determinedly turned his thoughts from what he'd seen and heard that day and concentrated harder on his task. He could hear the burbling of the Forces' Radio broadcast coming from the mess tent, and didn't want to miss Prime Minister Churchill's speech, which everyone suspected would come sometime today.

The news from home had lifted the spirits of the Brigade, but the tension had mounted as they waited for confirmation that peace in Europe really was at hand. He'd heard the reports on the radio of people decorating their houses and shops with bunting and flags and pictures of the King and Queen as well as Churchill; and how they were already gathering in their homes and on the streets to cautiously celebrate. He could just imagine Peggy joining in with alacrity. Darling Peggy always did love a good knees-up, and there would certainly be a party to end all parties if the rumours of peace proved to be true.

His smile was soft with love as he thought of how thrilled and excited his Peggy must be to at last be able to believe that the family was to be reunited after so long, and it made him yearn to be with her when they all came home. But he was realistic enough to know it could be months before he saw any of them again. The Japs might be on the run, but there were still thousands of them in Burma, and they'd fight to the death rather than surrender.

He was rewarded with a mouthful of rust and spat it out just as the bolt loosened and the exhaust pipe came free. With a grunt of satisfaction, he tossed it aside and began to attach the replacement.

He was actually on leave for a few days following the liberation of Rangoon, but in less than a week he'd be back in action to rout the retreating Japs from the Mawchi Road. As good as it was not to be shot at or ambushed, or have to witness the blood and guts of the suicidal Japs that were lying everywhere, he'd soon become restless and bored at being confined to this jungle camp on the Indian border where there was little to do but swim in the river, play endless games of cards, drink and watch the rain teem down.

The fact was, he missed Big Bert who'd been killed in action during the battle for Hill 170, and not a day had gone by when he hadn't thought of him. The other blokes in the Brigade were good company, but none of them – apart from Jumbo McTavish – had the large presence or personality that Bert had possessed, and his absence left a gaping void in Jim's life.

Jim finished attaching the exhaust and thankfully rolled from beneath the truck, grabbed his ever-present carbine, and got to his feet. It was almost five-thirty and the sun would soon set, plunging them all into darkness with the swiftness they'd become too familiar with over the past three years. He stretched and yawned before heading to the tent he shared with five others to fetch his wash-kit.

He collected his washbag, took off his watch and emptied his pockets onto the truckle bed, and went back out into the rain and the gloom. With the rain drumming on his hat, he sloshed through the mud past the cookhouse and mess tent, which was already filling up with men eager to hear what the day's news would bring. Jim reckoned that, with the time difference, they wouldn't hear the three o'clock news from London until about eight-thirty that evening, so he had plenty of time to wash, eat, and down a few very welcome beers.

He hurried down to the river, took off his slouch hat and leaned his carbine on a nearby rock before throwing himself in, boots and all. The mud and sweat were washed away and he scrubbed himself thoroughly with a rough flannel and bar of Wright's Coal Tar soap that Peggy had sent from home. The water was almost as warm as a tepid bath and therefore not really that refreshing, but he enjoyed feeling clean for once, and because the river was fast-flowing it was free of leeches, so he splashed about at leisure.

He eventually clambered back out, shook himself like a dog, and retrieved his hat and carbine just as the swift tropical night descended. There was no point in trying to dry off or change into clean clothes for the rain was still hammering down in the torpid heat, and his shorts and shirt were already steaming. But his feet would rot even further if he didn't take care of them, so he went back to his tent, drained the water from his boots, wrung out his socks and dried his feet before pulling on fresh socks and his second – relatively dry – pair of boots.

It was only a short dash to the mess tent, and as he shook the rain from his hat and used the scraper to get the worst of the mud off his boots, he could see it was packed solid with men eating, drinking, smoking and talking. But above all the noise and the continuous drumming of the rain on the canvas, the wireless could be heard very clearly. Jim couldn't help but grin when he realised it was transmitting *Woman's Hour*, with its usual mix of singing, comic turns, household tips and fashion advice. No doubt Peggy was also listening to it back home at Beach View, and that thought brought her closer somehow.

It had been ordered that half-rations should remain in place so the transport planes could carry more arms and ammunition into the battle zones, and although there was a lot of grumbling about this, every man knew it was sensible. The more firepower they had, the quicker they'd get rid of the Japs and be on their way home.

Without much pleasure, Jim eyed the lump of bully beef and the rehydrated mashed potato the cook had dumped on his tin plate, then took two slices of coarse bread, shoved a bottle of beer in each pocket of his shorts and filled his tin cup from the vast tea urn. At least fags, beer and tea weren't rationed – there would have been a riot if they had, but Lieutenant General Slim was wise enough to realise as much, which was why they all admired him.

The tables and benches in the vast mess tent were placed in sections for the different ranks, and it was only the senior officers who had chairs and a table-cloth. Jim sat down on the bench with his fellow junior officers and greeted his mate, Lieutenant Hamish 'Jumbo' McTavish – an enormous Scotsman with fiery hair and fierce eyebrows, large ears and very blue eyes in a strong-featured, ruddy face.

Jumbo reminded Jim of Big Bert in a way, which was why he'd been drawn to him. But for all his size and colouring, Jumbo was a quietly spoken, even-tempered man who'd worked as a gamekeeper on the remote Isle of Skye before joining up. He always had a well-thumbed book in his back pocket and was easy with his own company – but in battle, he was fiercely com-mitted to wiping out as many of the enemy as he could, and performed this task with icy thoroughness. It was only when he'd been at the whisky that the other side of his personality came through, and he'd become garrulous and the life and soul of every gathering.

Jumbo possessed a small set of bagpipes which went with him everywhere, and when in his cups or feeling homesick for the tranquillity of his island's glens and mountains, he was unfortunately inclined to play them, regardless of the fact no one but the other Scots

7

in the Brigade could appreciate the noise. To Jim it sounded as tuneful as a cat being strangled.

'Any news on Churchill's speech yet, Jumbo?' he asked before stuffing in a mouthful of food.

'Och, he'll not be talking just because we want him to,' the big man replied in his soft Highland accent. 'Ye ken what those English politicians are like – tied down with red tape and paper. He'll be waiting for it all to be signed and sealed afore he lets us lesser folk know what's going on.'

'I hope not,' said Jim. He took a slurp of tea and winced as he burnt his lip on the scalding tin mug. 'We know Hitler's dead, and the Allies are now swarming through Europe, so what's the point of keeping us all in suspense?'

Jumbo shrugged and shovelled in the last of his food, making further conversation impossible.

Jim ate in silence, praying that if it really was the end of the war in Europe, Jumbo wouldn't take it into his head to serenade them all on the bagpipes. But it was a forlorn hope, for there was a quarter bottle of whisky on the table, and he could see the familiar instrument of torture to the ears beside him on the bench.

The tension grew as the time for the broadcast approached, and the level of conversation dropped to a murmur as cigarettes and pipes were lit, beers glugged and games of cards and chess abandoned. All attention became focused on the radio and even the youngest and rowdiest sapper fell silent as the announcement came from London that Churchill was about to address the nation.

Jim stiffened with anticipation as the familiar grav-elled voice echoed into the stillness of that jungle tent.

'Yesterday morning at 2:41 a.m. at Headquarters, General Jodl, the representative of the German High Command, and Grand Admiral Dönitz, the designated head of the German State, signed the act of uncondi-tional surrender of all German land, sea, and air forces in Europe to the Allied Expeditionary Force, and simultaneously to the Soviet High Command.

'General Bedell Smith, Chief of Staff of the Allied Expeditionary Force, and General François Sevez signed the document on behalf of the Supreme Commander of the Allied Expeditionary Force, and General Susloparov signed on behalf of the Russian High Command.

'Today this agreement will be ratified and confirmed at Berlin, where Air Chief Marshal Tedder, Deputy Supreme Commander of the Allied Expeditionary Force, and General de Lattre de Tassigny will sign on behalf of General Eisenhower. Marshal Zhukov will sign on behalf of the Soviet High Command. The German representatives will be Field-Marshal Keitel, Chief of the High Command, and the Commanders-in-Chief of the German Army, Navy and Air Forces.

'Hostilities will end officially at one minute after midnight tonight, but in the interests of saving lives, the Cease Fire began yesterday to be sounded all along the front, and our dear Channel Islands are to be freed today.'

A collective sigh of relief whispered through the gathering, the release of tension palpable as Churchill continued.

'The Germans are still, in places, resisting the Russian troops, but should they continue to do so after midnight they will, of course, deprive themselves of the protection of the laws of war, and will be attacked from all quarters by the Allied troops. It is not surprising that on such long fronts, and in the existing disorder of the enemy, the orders of the German High Command should not in every case be obeyed immediately.

'This does not, in our opinion, with the best military advice at our disposal, constitute any reason for withholding from the nation the facts communicated to us by General Eisenhower of the unconditional surrender already signed at Rheims, nor should it prevent us from celebrating today and tomorrow as Victory in Europe days.'

'Not much chance of that if the Nips decide to attack us 'ere,' shouted a Cockney gunner who earned a severe glare from his Commanding Officer.

'Today, perhaps, we shall think mostly of ourselves,' Churchill continued. 'Tomorrow we shall pay a particular tribute to our Russian comrades, whose prowess in the field has been one of the grand contributions to the general victory.

'The German war is therefore at an end.'

A great cheer went up, to be quickly hushed as Churchill continued speaking.

'After years of intense preparation, Germany hurled herself on Poland at the beginning of September 1939; and, in pursuance of our guarantee to Poland and in agreement with the French Republic, Great Britain, and the British Empire and Commonwealth of Nations, declared war upon this foul aggression.'

Churchill's voice held them all in thrall as he continued. 'After gallant France had been struck down we, from this island and from our united Empire, maintained the struggle single-handedly for a whole year until we were joined by the military might of Soviet Russia, and later by the overwhelming power and resources of the United States of America.

'Finally almost the whole world was combined against the evil-doers, who are now prostrate before us. Our gratitude to our splendid Allies goes forth from all our hearts in this island and throughout the British Empire.'

'Too bloody right,' drawled an Aussie sapper.

'We may allow ourselves a brief period of rejoicing; but let us not forget for a moment the toil and efforts that lie ahead. Japan, with all her treachery and greed, remains unsubdued. The injury she has inflicted on Great Britain, the United States, and other countries, and her detestable cruelties, call for justice and retribution. We must now devote all our strength and resources to the completion of our task, both at home and abroad.'

There were shouts of agreement to Churchill's rallying cry, and even the most senior officers could be heard joining in.

Churchill paused and then his voice rose with great passion. 'Advance, Britannia! Long live the cause of freedom. God save the King!'

They stood as one and saluted as the National Anthem was played. There was barely a dry eye amongst them as thoughts of home and loved ones came to the fore. Jim wasn't ashamed of the tears that blinded him, for he was almost weak with relief that Peggy and his beloved family were finally out of danger.

As the anthem came to an end the joy of the moment could no longer be contained. Cheers went up, hats were thrown into the air, beers were swigged and men began dancing on and around the tables.

Jumbo had finished his quarter bottle of whisky and was halfway down his second. He stood and inflated the bag on his pipes, which emitted a terrible wailing, and then began to play a stirring rendition of 'Scotland the Brave'.

The powerful music stopped everyone in their tracks and they listened in awe, for this old Scottish tune was well known and seemed to fit the occasion perfectly. As the pace of the melody quickened and swelled, one of the young sappers began to accompany it by using wooden spoon handles as drumsticks to beat out a tattoo on tin plates. He was soon joined by others, and further into the tune men began to beat their hands on the tables as if playing the big bass drums, whilst others whistled to stand in for the fifes, and stamped their feet in time. As the volume rose and swelled it sent tingles up Jim's spine, for it was as if an entire marching band was beating to the rhythm of the pipes, and he finally understood the power they held to rouse men into battle.

Jim promised himself that he'd never moan about Jumbo's bagpipes again.

2

Cliffehaven

Ron and Rosie's wedding celebrations had lasted long into the night, so Peggy hadn't had much sleep and was suffering from a bit of a hangover. Still, the anticipation for what she'd hoped would come had been enough to get her out of bed that Tuesday morning, and take a stroll with little Daisy and elderly Cordelia Finch along the seafront, to drink in the atmosphere of the gaily decorated town. Her boss, Solly Goldman, had told her the previous evening that since it looked as if Victory in Europe was about to be declared, the clothing factory would be closed for at least two days as there was very little likelihood of any work being done, so Peggy had decided that all but the most basic of household chores could be set aside too.

As the day had progressed, three-year-old Daisy had got over-excited, even though she didn't understand what was going on, and Peggy became a little tearful at the thought of Jim and the rest of her family being so far away and unable to be with her on this special day. But if peace really had come, then at least her darling Anne and her boys would finally be returning home.

It wasn't long before close friends and family started arriving at Beach View to share in this momentous occasion, each bearing gifts of food and drink – much to Peggy's relief, for her own larder was almost bare. The kitchen was soon crammed so it was decided to decamp into the large dining room where, like an omen of good things to come, the sun broke through the clouds to shine brightly through the bay window.

Peggy's young evacuees, Sarah, Rita, Fran, Danuta and Ivy, had excitedly clattered in and out from their brief forays into town, eventually arriving back with a crate of beer, courtesy of the newlywed Ron and Rosie, who were already very busy behind the bar at the jam-packed Anchor. Fran's husband Robert had come in with Ivy's young fireman, Andy, and they'd been swiftly followed by Jim's elder brother Frank and his wife Pauline, who was smiling for once. And to Rita's joy, her injured Australian fighter pilot, Peter Ryan, turned up having charmed the new matron at the Memorial Hospital into giving him a lift in her car. His head was heavily bandaged still, and although the plaster was long-gone from his leg, he still found walking a trial and had to use crutches to get about.

Peggy's one-time evacuees, Ruby and April, arrived with the stationmaster, Stan, and April's baby, Paula, who would be one this coming August; soon to be followed by Kitty and her sister-in-law, Charlotte, from Briar Cottage with their three babies. Luckily, they'd been asleep so their prams had been parked in the denuded kitchen. Cordelia's friend Bertie Double-Barrelled had come looking very dapper in a tweed suit with a patriotic red rose in his buttonhole, and soon there was very little breathing space to be had even in the larger room.

The mood was happy and expectant as food and drink were dispensed and the volume of laughter and chatter rose. It felt to Peggy as if half of Cliffehaven had turned up to listen to Churchill with her that afternoon, and she was absolutely thrilled. These were the people she loved, and they seemed to understand she'd be missing Jim and the rest of her family on such an auspicious occasion, and wanted to do their best to fill that gap.

With only minutes to spare before the broadcast was due, her elder sister Doris slipped into the room with her fiancé Colonel White and Peggy's daughter Cissy, fresh from Cliffe aerodrome. Peggy's thrill at seeing her after so long was curtailed by the sound of Big Ben chiming the hour, so after a swift hug and kiss, Peggy had to be content with clasping her hand as Churchill's familiar voice told them the war in Europe was over, and now they could celebrate before continuing the task of crushing the Japanese.

Churchill's voice strengthened in triumph as he came to the end of his address. 'Advance, Britannia! Long live the cause of freedom! God save the King!'

'Gawd bless you too, Winnie,' shouted a rather over-refreshed Ivy, raising her glass of elderberry wine. 'We couldn't 'ave done it without yer.'

They all cheered and then stood during the National Anthem, the men saluting, the women blinking against happy, relieved tears while Daisy and Paula watched in wide-eyed confusion as to what all the fuss was about.

When the final note of the Anthem faded everyone clasped the person next to them in the sheer joy of the moment. Peggy hugged and kissed everyone, even Pauline, for this was not a day for old enmities to resurface. The war in Europe was finally and indisputably over and, God willing, her nephew Brendon and all the other Cliffehaven men would soon be coming home along with her loved ones from Somerset. But even in her happiness she couldn't help wondering how long it would be before her beloved Jim could cross the threshold of Beach View to be with her again.

Cissy seemed to read her thoughts and embraced her. 'It won't be long before the Japs are forced to surrender, Mum,' she consoled beneath the hubbub of the surrounding celebrations. 'Dad will soon be on his way back, you'll see – and then we can have another big party.'

'Let's go into town,' shouted Ivy, downing her glass of wine in one. 'Come on, Andy,' she urged, pulling the young fireman towards the door. 'I wanna dance and sing before them clouds roll in again and it starts to rain.'

The young ones didn't need asking twice and shot off with promises to return, although it was not made clear as to when that might be. April left little Paula to her Uncle Stan's tender care and quickly followed them whilst Rita argued with Peter over whether it was wise for him to try and walk all that way with crutches.

'No worries, Rita. I'll be right,' he drawled, brushing her argument aside. 'There's no flaming way I'm missing out on what's going to be the biggest party ever.' He grasped the crutches and determinedly led the way through the kitchen, past the prams and slowly down the concrete steps to the basement back door with Rita fretfully shadowing him in case he had one of his dizzy spells and stumbled.

Peggy watched from the top of the cellar stairs, equally worried that the boy was trying to do too much, but she knew she'd be foolish to say anything for he'd take no notice in his utter determination to have his way – and bless him, he'd certainly earned the right to celebrate after spending so many years flying to defend her country.

She was about to warn Rita to close the back door quietly for a change when the girl banged it shut and woke the babies. Peggy gave a cluck of mild annoyance before breaking into a soft smile. Neither Rita nor Ivy had learnt the art of shutting doors quietly, and they were the noisiest, untidiest imps imaginable. But she couldn't help loving them.

Peggy discovered that all the telephone lines were engaged, so reluctantly gave up the idea of trying to speak to her younger sister Doreen or Anne for now, and went back into the dining room to spend precious time with Cissy. Daisy was playing nicely on the hearthrug with Paula as Frank topped up glasses, handed round plates of sandwiches and got the gramophone going. Seeing him take on his father's usual role as host, Peggy realised with a jolt that now Ron and his dog, Harvey were living at the Anchor with Rosie, their absence had taken a little of the shine out of the day. They would be sorely missed over the coming weeks and months. The only consolation was that Ron would be a regular visitor, for he had to tend his vegetable plot in the back garden, and continue helping her with the repairs to the house.

She took her refilled glass from Frank and sat down next to Cissy. 'I'm surprised you haven't gone into town with the others,' she said.

'I'll go in later. For now it would just be lovely to sit with you for a while, if that's all right.'

'Silly girl. Of course it is.' Peggy put her arm around her daughter's slender waist, noting that she seemed thinner, but did look very elegant in the expensively tailored WAAF uniform that had certainly not been made in any factory. 'It's been so long since we've had more than a snatched hour together,' she said on a sigh. 'Still, it's more than I've managed with Anne and the boys over the past five years.'

Cissy smiled. 'You'll soon have them all home, although Lord knows where you're going to put them all.'

'I'll think of something,' said Peggy. 'It's so lovely to see you, darling, but how did you manage to get away from the airfield?'

Cissy lit Lucky Strikes for them both and tucked the little gold lighter in her jacket pocket. 'Cliffe's all but shut down, and as I'll be out of a job by the end of the week, they've let me come home until I'm officially discharged.'

Peggy regarded her beautiful daughter with some concern, for although she'd spoken lightly, there was a brittle quality to her smile. 'But if Cliffe's closing what will happen to all the planes still over in Europe?'

'They'll go to the bigger airfields along with the troop carriers and bombers.'

'And how do you feel about leaving? I know how much you've loved being a part of the WAAFs.'

Cissy shrugged her narrow shoulders and tried to appear nonchalant. 'I shall miss it dreadfully,' she admitted. 'But there's nothing any of us can do about it – in fact a lot of the other girls have already gone home, so it's a bit dreary up there now.'

Peggy could see that, despite her stoic words, her daughter was concerned about losing touch with the many friends she'd made at Cliffe. And noticing the bulging suitcases by the door, she began to fret about where Cissy would sleep. The house was chock-a-block and Danuta was in her old room. She very much doubted that either girl would happily settle in Ron's abandoned basement bedroom.

'Don't worry about me, Mum,' said Cissy, attuned as always to her mother's thoughts. 'I'll bed down somewhere and try not to get under your feet too much. I might be at a loose end for a bit, but things will work out once Randy's released from that POW camp and we can discuss our plans for the future.' She squeezed Peggy's fingers, her face quite radiant with hope and excitement. 'Of course it will probably mean going to live in America once we're married, and that will be a terrific adventure, don't you think?'

Peggy felt a pang of unease as she saw how her daughter's blue eyes were sparkling. Cissy hadn't seen Randy for at least two years, and distance often made the heart grow fonder and reality a hazy blur – especially during such perilous times. She had no doubt her daughter had been in love with the young American at the time of his capture, but had it been reciprocated, and was it strong enough to endure their long, enforced separation? They'd hardly known each other before he'd been shot down and captured, and Cissy's rose-tinted vision of a future with him worried Peggy intensely. But she kept her concerns to herself, for this was not a day to voice doubts.

'Let's just enjoy today and let tomorrow take care of itself,' said Cissy cheerfully. She picked up Daisy and planted a kiss on her cheek before going across the room to pour another drink and make a special fuss of her adored Cordelia.

Despite her worries, Peggy watched her with a heart full of love and pride. Cissy would be twenty-three at the end of the month, and was so very different to the naïve young girl who'd once danced in the back row of the chorus line on the pier, and dreamed of starring in Hollywood. The war had matured her – perhaps a little too swiftly – and taught her to face danger and tragedy with courage and strength. Her work as a driver at Cliffe had also brought her into contact with a set of young men and women from a much higher social class, and their way of talking and mannerisms had rubbed off on her. Peggy suspected she would find it hard to settle down to the mundane life in Cliffehaven after all the excitement – especially if things didn't go to plan with her young American.

Once the babies had been changed and fed, they were brought in to join Paula and Daisy on the hearth-rug. Daisy, at three, immediately took on the role of 'little mother' by telling them what to do. Much to the child's annoyance, David had ideas of his own and kept trying to crawl away, which made everyone smile.

'He's so like his father,' giggled Charlotte, rescuing him from beneath a chair where he'd got stuck. 'According to the few letters I got from Freddy, it seems he spent most of his time as a POW trying to escape.'

'My brother always was an adventurer,' said Kitty dryly. 'He used to drive poor Mum and Dad quite mad with the way he used to keep disappearing out into the pampas.' She gave a wistful sigh. 'As annoying as he is, I do miss him, and can't wait for him and my Roger to be home again.'

Cissy broke the heavy silence this statement had elicited. 'They'll have to go through all sorts of checks and debriefings, and with the utter chaos over there, it could take a while to round them all up and find transport to bring them home. I'm not really expecting to see Randy before the end of the month at the earliest – but of course I could be wrong,' she added hastily, seeing the gloomy faces.

Peggy got to her feet. 'Right,' she said decisively, 'it's time we went out and joined in the fun. Finish your drinks and get your hats and coats. I for one want to see how our newly-weds are faring.'

The mood brightened. The children were rounded up, hats and coats went on, and within a very short time everyone was trooping out of the front door.

Bertie and Cordelia went slowly arm in arm, Peggy walked with Cissy, and Stan had strapped Paula into her pushchair. Frank carried Daisy on his shoulders as he followed Kitty and Charlotte with their sturdy prams, and Doris and John held hands like young sweethearts. Pauline strolled by Stan's side chattering about all the plans she had for when her son Brendon was released from his duties with the Royal Naval Reserve.

Peggy's heart was full on this victorious day, even though there could be storms ahead – and not just for Cissy. She silently prayed that Pauline's hopes wouldn't be dashed by Brendon following his own dreams. The fall-out would affect everyone – especially poor, stoic Frank.

The shops, offices and factories were closed, and it was way past the usual lunchtime closing hour, but the government had permitted the opening hours to be extended over the next two days as long as they shut at ten-thirty p.m. It seemed everyone was determined to take full advantage of the situation by trying to drink the two Cliffehaven pubs dry. Gloria at the Crown and Rosie at the Anchor had ordered in extra stock as soon as it seemed likely peace was at hand, but even with full cellars, they doubted it would last the week if the previous couple of days had been anything to go by.

Ron swept Rosie into his arms as the packed crowd in the Anchor continued their noisy celebration and the two dogs barked excitedly. He kissed her long and passionately whilst their customers formed a circle around them and began to dance and sing the hokey-cokey, their feet stamping so hard the vibrations rocked the furniture and made the bottles and glasses rattle on the shelves.

'They'll bring the roof down in a minute,' giggled a breathless Rosie. 'Quick, help me get the piano outside so they can dance on the pavement.'

'Leave it to me,' said Ron firmly. He did his best to ignore the raucous comments aimed at his newly married status as he squeezed his way through the happy crowd to the old piano. He finally made it and grabbed hold of one side. But as he attempted to tug it across the uneven floor, a stab of pain shot through his lower back and left him gasping. It was a forcible reminder that, although his injuries from the accident in the tunnel some months ago had healed, hauling pianos about wasn't a good idea.

To hide his chagrin at the loss of the strength he'd once possessed, he quickly collared two of the nearest men and ordered them to get the piano outside. This was achieved swiftly, despite being hampered by the dogs, Monty and Harvey, who thought this was a wonderful game.

Within minutes someone was hammering out a polka on the out-of-tune keys and people were dancing. Then, as if from nowhere, tables and chairs were being brought out into the middle of Camden Road. Carefully ironed white sheets were used as tablecloths and soon hidden beneath plates of sandwiches, bowls of jellies, teapots, and cups and jugs of watered-down orange squash. Every child wore a hat made from sheets of newspaper, and was given a lollipop and balloon by the new manager of the Home and Colonial Store who hadn't proved popular with the housewives and was trying to curry favour.

Ron eased his back surreptitiously. There was no need for Rosie to know he was suffering after all the wedding festivities and the night of love-making, and why spoil the day? Once he'd had a bit of a rest, he'd be right as rain again, or his name wasn't Ronan Reilly.

He checked that Harvey and his pup, Monty, weren't trying to steal food or make a nuisance of themselves, and was about to go back in to help Brenda and Rosie behind the bar, when he saw Rita and Peter coming slowly towards him.

The lad's face was quite grey with pain after the walk from Beach View, and Rita's deep concern for him was etched in her expressive dark eyes. Ron fetched the last chair from inside, placed it to one side of the door and quickly sat down before anyone else could nab it.

'To be sure 'tis grand to see you, Peter,' he boomed as they drew nearer. 'Would you be after a pint to wet your whistle?'

Peter nodded and came to an unsteady halt, his heavy breathing testament to the effort it had taken to get this far. 'I reckon so, Ron,' he managed. 'Me throat's as dry as a lizard's backside.'

'Eloquently put,' said Ron, getting to his feet and pressing the lad into the chair. 'Keep that warm for me, young fella. I'll be back with your beer, and then I must go and help the girls. It's mayhem in there,' he added rather unnecessarily.

'Fair go, Ron, mate,' Peter drawled, struggling to get up again. 'A bloke can't sit and leave his girl standing.'

'You'll do as you're told,' retorted Ron, pressing him down again. To cut off any further protest he ordered Rita to come into the pub to collect another seat. Once inside, he sent her upstairs to fetch the stool from the bathroom. 'Guard it with your life,' he warned. 'Seats are as rare as hens' teeth today, and Rosie will kill me if it goes missing.'

With them both happily ensconced outside with their beers, Ron went back to work. It had been decided the three of them would now take it in turns to run the bar and join in with the celebrations, for it would be a long day and a late night.

A while later the pub had quietened enough for Rosie and Brenda to take a breather and join in the fun outside. Ron was about to take up watch in the doorway with a beer so he could serve if need be and still feel part of the street party when he realised the wireless was on, but at a very low volume. As the King wasn't due to speak to the nation until nine tonight, he went to switch it off to save electricity.

He was just reaching for the knob when he heard the announcer say that Churchill was about to give an impromptu speech in Whitehall before he went on to Buckingham Palace for an audience with Their Majesties. Ron turned up the volume and leaned against the bar as all the chairs and tables were now in use outside.

Churchill's voice came through loud and clear above the happy cheering of what sounded like a vast crowd gathered in Whitehall. 'God bless you all,' he rumbled. 'This is your victory.'

'No!' they shouted back. 'It's yours!'

There was a smile in Churchill's voice as he replied, 'It is the victory of the cause of freedom in every land.'

This elicited a great roar of approval and he waited for it to die down before continuing. 'In all our long history we have never seen a greater day than this. Everyone; man or woman, has done their best. Everyone has tried. Neither the long years, nor the dangers, nor the fierce attacks of the enemy, have in any way weakened the unbending resolve of the British nation. God bless you all.'

He waited for the enormous cheer to die down. 'My dear friends,' he said, his voice strong and triumphant, 'this is your hour. This is not victory of a party or of any class. It's a victory of the Great British nation as a whole. We were the first, in this ancient island, to draw the sword against tyranny. After a while we were left all alone against the most tremendous military power that has been seen. We were all alone for a whole year. There we stood, alone. Did anyone want to give in?'

The crowd yelled, 'NO!'

'Were we down-hearted?'

'NEVER!'

'The lights went out and the bombs came down. But every man, woman and child in the country had no thought of quitting the struggle. London can take it!'

'YES!' they roared.

'So we came back after long months from the jaws of death, out of the mouth of hell, while all the world wondered. When shall the reputation and faith of this generation of English men and women fail?'

'NEVER!' came the fierce response.

'I say that in the long years to come not only will the people of this island but of the world, wherever the bird of freedom chirps in human hearts, look back to what we've done and they will say "do not despair, do not yield to violence and tyranny, march straightforward and die if need be – unconquered."'

The crowd cheered and Churchill struggled to be heard. 'Now we have emerged from one deadly struggle – a terrible foe has been cast on the ground and awaits our judgement and our mercy. But there is another foe who occupies large portions of the British Empire; a foe stained with cruelty and greed – the Japanese. I rejoice we can all take a night off today and another day tomorrow.'

Churchill paused to take a breath as the gathering remained silent. 'Tomorrow, our great Russian allies will also be celebrating victory, and after that we must begin the task of rebuilding our hearth and homes; doing our utmost to make this country a land in which all have a chance, in which all have a duty, and we must turn ourselves to fulfil our duty to our own countrymen, and to our gallant allies of the United States who were so foully and treacherously attacked by Japan.'

Whistles and whoops came from the Americans in the crowd.

'We will go hand in hand with them. Even if it is a hard struggle we will *not* be the ones who fail.'

Ron grunted his approval as the crowd whistled and cheered and began to sing. He switched the wireless off to serve the eight customers who'd been patiently waiting whilst Churchill had been speaking, then fetched more beers for Peter and Rita and headed for the door. It had sounded as if half of London had been massed in Whitehall, and he could just imagine the shenanigans going on in Piccadilly and Trafalgar Square, but there was a party going on here, and he was eager to feel part of it.

He handed over the beers and saw Rosie chattering away with Peggy. Standing in the doorway he watched the two women he loved most in the world. He was a

27

lucky man to have been so blessed, and on this wonderful day he couldn't resist grinning like a schoolboy as he caught sight of his gorgeous granddaughter, Cissy, playing a hectic and very noisy game of Blind Man's Bluff with her little sister Daisy and an over-excited group of small children.

It was amazing, he mused, that after six long, hard years of war, the enduring spirit still lived on in the British people – for despite the terrors, the deaths, the lost homes and deprivations, they could still find the energy to rejoice in their hard-won victory.

The rain that had been forecast held off until late Wednesday night when the thunder rolled in and the heavens opened. But it hadn't dampened the spirits of the revellers, and the parties had carried on in the pubs, clubs, dance halls, hotels and restaurants.

Every street had celebrated with its own tea party for the children, and a huge bonfire had been lit on the recreation ground to accompany a firework display. The local brass band had paraded down the High Street followed eagerly by small marching boys and a pack of barking dogs. The Mayor had given a short speech on the Town Hall steps the first evening, and although he was no Churchill and clearly tiddly, the crowds gave him a huge cheer and dragged him into the street to join a conga line that twisted and turned all through the town.

It was now after ten-thirty on Wednesday night, and having rounded up all their tables and chairs, the bar was looking itself again apart from one glaring absence. The poor old upright piano had finally succumbed to over-enthusiastic playing and woodworm, and had been committed to the flames of one of the many bonfires that had been lit this afternoon.

Ron paid Ruby for the hours she'd put in today, thanking her profusely for coming to help in their time of need, and then gave Brenda a large bonus on top of her wages for being such a brick throughout it all. Having wished them both a goodnight, Rosie locked the door behind them, kicked off her high-heeled shoes and almost fell into Ron's arms.

'I don't know about you, Ron, but I'm dead on my feet. Thank goodness for young Ruby and Brenda. We couldn't have coped without them.'

'Aye,' he rumbled. 'Ruby was a bit of a revelation, wasn't she? To be sure she knows her way about a bar – and how to deal with over-amorous drunks.' He chuckled. 'Did you see her arm-wrestle that chap out of the door when he tried to get fresh with her?'

Rosie regarded him with a frown. 'I'm surprised you didn't know she was working in an East End pub before she came to live at Beach View. And once a girl's done that, she can handle anything.'

Ron smiled and drew her back into his arms until her head nestled into his shoulder. 'She's welcome to work here anytime,' he said. 'Ach, Rosie, wee girl, to be sure me feet are sore and me back's complaining, but it's been a party to end all parties, and we'll remember it for the rest of our lives.'

'It's probably not over yet,' she managed through a large yawn. 'The weekend is still to come.'

'It'll calm down after Saturday night, and we can close the pub as usual on Sunday and take the day off.

To be sure we've earnt the rest, and I feel as if I could sleep for a week.'

She looked up at him with a naughty twinkle in her eyes. 'We'll have to see about that,' she purred. 'This is supposed to be our honeymoon, you know.'

'Aye, that it is, and you'll not be spending it here,' he replied with an air of mystery.

'What about the pub? We can't just lock up and walk away.'

'I had a word with the wonderful Brenda. She's agreed to have Monty and take over next week with the help of Flo if she's still around, and Ruby, who's had her hours cut at the factory. Peggy said she'll have Harvey as Cissy's home and can walk him – and Bert Williams promised to come in to see to the ferrets.' He grinned down at her. 'So we'll be fancy free.'

Rosie giggled as she snuggled against him. 'My goodness, you have been busy. So where are we going?'

'To Brighton. So pack your dancing shoes and your best frocks. I managed to book the honeymoon suite at the Metropole where we'll be waited on hand and foot and thoroughly spoilt.'

'Oh, Ron,' she sighed against his lips. 'That sounds like absolute heaven.'

3

Ivy was not feeling the full ticket this early Thursday morning, and neither was Rita going by the dark shadows beneath her eyes. 'You look as ropey as I feel,' Ivy muttered, half-heartedly dragging a brush through the tangles of her brown hair.

'Thanks for nothing,' grumbled Rita, blearily regarding her reflection in the dressing-table mirror and wincing as the sun shone in her eyes. 'You don't exactly look radiant yourself.'

'It's all right for you. You don't have to go into work until this evening. Gawd knows how they expect me to make bullets when me 'ands are shaking like a leaf and me 'ead's pounding. I'm likely to blow the place up.'

'Perhaps they'll put you on different duties today,' said Rita, turning away from the sunlight streaming in. 'Surely the bosses must realise how dangerous it would be to let you loose with explosives after almost a whole week of overdoing things.'

'They obviously don't,' Ivy retorted, pulling up her dungarees and adjusting the shoulder straps. 'But I think it's daft getting us all back so soon. Why couldn't they've waited until Monday?'

'The war might be over here, but the troops in the Far East still need armaments, Ivy. You can't expect

Uncle Jim to face the Japs with an empty gun just because you've got a hangover.'

Ivy sighed and finished lacing her sturdy boots. 'You're right,' she admitted, 'but that don't help with this 'eadache.'

'You'll feel better once you've had an aspirin and got some breakfast inside you,' soothed Rita, digging about in the piles of clothing strewn across the floor and every other flat surface.

Ivy gave a deep sigh. 'I'll feel better once I've heard from me mum or sister. I know they don't write often, but it's been nearly two months since Mum's last letter, and I would've thought she'd let me know where they've been moved to.'

Rita's eyes widened. 'They've been moved *again*? What for this time?'

'The place they was in got condemned after a V-2 came down a bit too close just after Christmas. Mum's fed up with it all, 'cos this will be the fifth move and Dad never stops moaning about how long it takes 'im to get to his allotment. Me sister don't help, neither,' she added gloomily. 'What with 'er gadding about in the West End with all sorts, and staying out all night. Poor Mum's at the end of her tether.'

Rita gave up her search for something to wear and put her arm around Ivy's shoulder. 'I'm sure she'll write soon,' she comforted. 'You know what the post has been like recently, and with moving house and all the excitement over the past few weeks, she probably hasn't had the time.'

'Yeah, that could be it,' Ivy agreed. 'It's just frustrating that I don't have no address for 'em, 'cos I'd've liked to have gone up there to see 'em.'

Rita bit her lip in thought. 'You could ask Auntie Peg to help you write a letter to the rehousing people, I suppose. But I suspect you'll hear from your mum before you get any answer from them. Government offices take their time to reply to anything.'

Ivy's face suddenly brightened. 'Perhaps there's a letter downstairs just waiting for me, and I've been worrying meself silly over nothing?'

Before Rita could reply, she'd shot out of the room and was thudding downstairs to the hall. The metal cage below the letter box was empty. Thinking Auntie Peggy must have already collected the post, she raced into the kitchen to ask her and tripped over Daisy who was sitting on the floor with a jigsaw puzzle.

'Sorry, darlin',' she said, giving her a cuddle to stave off tears. 'Auntie Ivy was in such an 'urry to get to the post, she didn't see you down there.'

Daisy forgave her by winding her arms round Ivy's neck and giving her a kiss.

'I'm sorry, Ivy,' said Peggy. 'There was nothing for you this morning, but there might be something in the second delivery. The Post Office is all behind because of the public holiday.'

Ivy had no option but to accept the fact. She gently disentangled herself from Daisy's clutches and sat down at the table. 'You 'aven't got an aspirin, 'ave yer? Only I got a blindin' headache.'

Peggy smiled knowingly and fetched a bottle from the dresser drawer. 'It's a good thing I bought an extra supply of these last week,' she murmured. 'I have a feeling you won't be the only one suffering today.'

As if to prove her right, Rita came in looking like death warmed up, and Cissy emerged from the basement still in her dressing gown, blonde hair tousled, and last night's make-up smeared on her wan face.

Peggy doled out the aspirin with cups of hot tea and silently placed bowls of porridge in front of each of them.

With muttered thanks, the three girls tucked in and once the last scrape of porridge was devoured, and the teapot emptied, Ivy felt marginally better. She surreptitiously glanced across at Cissy, who she secretly admired for her looks and rather daunting sophistication, and realised that she was far from her usual glamorous, well-groomed self this morning – in fact she looked disappointingly plain.

'How're you settling in Ron's room, Cissy?'

'It's not too bad,' she replied. 'Although I wouldn't want to be down there in winter.' She gave a delicate shudder. 'But I'm not planning on still being here by then,' she said. 'Once Randy comes back, we'll be moving to California where it never gets cold.'

'Lucky you,' replied Ivy without rancour. 'But if you're finding it a bit lonely down there, you could move in with Rita and me. We talked about it yesterday, and there's plenty of room for another bed up there.'

'That's very sweet of you both,' Cissy replied coolly, 'but I'm actually quite enjoying having a room to myself after sharing with eight others; and being downstairs, I can come and go as I please and not disturb anyone.'

Ivy thought this was very kind of Cissy, but suspected the real reason she didn't want to share was because she'd got so posh from being up there at Cliffe with the toffs that she felt she had nothing in common with the likes of her and Rita. Which, to be fair, was true.

'Right, I'm off to work,' Ivy said, scraping back her chair and making Cissy shudder. 'See you all at teatime.'

'Don't forget your lunch box and thermos,' said Peggy, handing her the small battered tin and thermos in a string bag. 'It's only dripping sandwiches today, I'm afraid, but I've tried to liven them up with salt and pepper.'

Ivy gave her a hug. 'Thanks, Auntie Peg, you're a diamond. I'd forget me 'ead if it weren't screwed on proper.'

'You take care at the factory and come home safe,' said Peggy, hooking the girl's untidy hair behind her ears with motherly affection. 'And don't stop off at the pub on the way. You've had enough drink this past week to sink a battleship.'

Ivy giggled, gave her a hug and then clattered down the cellar steps, slamming the back door behind her.

'I do wish she wouldn't do that,' snapped Cissy. 'Can't you have a word with the wretched girl, Rita? All her crashing and banging about is really beginning to get on my nerves.'

'It's not my place to tell her anything,' said Rita calmly. 'If you don't like it, you talk to her. But I wouldn't take that tone, Cissy,' she warned softly. 'Ivy can be a bit of a scrapper if she thinks you're looking down on her.'

'Good grief,' breathed Cissy, rolling her eyes. 'I'm amazed you've kept her on, Mother, if she's like that.'

Peggy raised an eyebrow at being called 'Mother' and placed the refreshed teapot carefully on the table before folding her arms and giving Cissy a stern glare. 'This is Ivy's home, just as it's Rita's and all the others', and if you're going to stay here, then you'll have to get used to it. Apart from that, I don't like your attitude, and if you're going to be in a rotten mood then I suggest you go back to bed.'

Cissy reddened at her mother's chiding in front of Rita, poured another cup of tea and, with a mulish expression, flounced back downstairs.

Peggy smiled at Rita. 'Cissy might think she's all grown-up and terribly smart, but she's yet to learn not to flounce about when taken down a peg or two.' She gave a sigh and turned back to the range to check on the porridge she was keeping warm for the others. 'Some things don't change, do they?'

'Cissy always did a good flounce, I seem to remember,' replied Rita with a chuckle. 'Very dramatic, she was – but back then she'd been harbouring dreams of becoming the next Ginger Rogers.'

Peggy grunted, thankful that that particular phase in her daughter's life was well and truly over. But if she was going to behave snootily towards the other girls and get in a mood at the drop of a hat, then something would have to be done about it. There had been enough disruption at Beach View when her sister Doris had come to live with them, and she was not going to tolerate Cissy putting on airs and graces.

She stirred the porridge. It was the first day back to work after all the excitement, and no doubt everyone would be feeling a bit down about having to return to the humdrum daily routine. She didn't feel that bright herself and wasn't looking forward to facing a factory full of tired women who'd no doubt take umbrage at the slightest thing.

'So, Rita, what are your plans today?'

'I'm going to tidy our room.'

Peggy nearly dropped the spoon in the porridge. 'Good grief, wonders will never cease.'

'I know,' giggled Rita. 'But it's so bad up there we can't find anything.' She scraped a bit of margarine onto a slice of toast. 'And after that I'm doing our washing before going up to the Memorial to see Peter. He didn't look too good yesterday, and I want to make sure he's okay.'

'He's overdone things, silly boy,' said Peggy briskly.

Rita sighed. 'That's Australian men for you, Auntie Peg – stubborn as mules and determined to prove they're tough.'

Peggy giggled. 'You could be describing men the world over. My Jim's the same.' She caught the sound of people moving about in the bathroom and on the landing, and the hum of Cordelia's stairlift descending to the hall. 'Well, you take care on that motorbike, and don't forget it's your turn to cook the tea with Sarah before you go on duty tonight. Alf the butcher dropped off some mince earlier, so you can fry it with onions and make a shepherd's pie with the leftover veg and a fresh mash topping.'

Rita finished her toast and took Daisy upstairs with her just as Sarah and Danuta came into the kitchen with Cordelia, swiftly followed by Fran and Robert. Fran and Danuta were in their nurse's uniforms and Sarah was wearing a sprigged cotton frock and thick white cardigan for her work at the council offices.

Peggy thought they looked a little less exuberant this morning, which was hardly surprising, but Robert was chirpier, freshly shaved and very smart in a three-piece suit. As for Cordelia, she was looking quite exhausted, and Peggy felt a dart of concern. Cordelia had celebrated her eightieth birthday just before Christmas, and was as small and frail as a bird despite her usual boundless enthusiasm for parties and sherry. Like Peter, she'd clearly been overdoing things.

Sarah settled her great-aunt at the table and poured her a cup of tea. 'Are you sure you wouldn't prefer to have your breakfast in bed this morning?' she asked gently.

'I'm not in the habit of lying in when there are things to be done,' Cordelia replied, twiddling to get the volume right on her hearing aid. 'Besides, I hate getting crumbs in the bed.'

'What things need doing, Cordelia?' asked Peggy. 'If you give me a list, I'm sure I can nip out at lunchtime and do them for you.'

'Just this and that,' she replied airily. 'No need to molly-coddle me, Peggy. I'm perfectly capable, you know.' She looked at Peggy over her half-moon glasses. 'Where are the newspapers? You know I can't eat breakfast without having something to read.'

'They haven't arrived yet,' Peggy replied, placing the porridge in front of her. 'But there are a couple of letters from your son's family in Canada. Why don't you read them until the papers come?'

Cordelia gave a sigh and looked around the silent gathering without much enthusiasm. 'I must say,' she declared, 'you look a very dull lot this morning. What's the matter? Can't you take the pace?' She chuckled. 'I bet that old scallywag Ron is as bright as a button – but then he always could hold his drink.'

There was a general gasp at this sweeping statement as they all remembered scenes of past shenanigans involving Ron and alcohol. 'He could do no such thing,' Peggy spluttered.

'He was always over it by morning,' Cordelia replied stubbornly. 'Breakfast won't be the same without the old rogue to spar with – and although I'd never tell him, our little arguments used to perk me up no end and set me up for the day.'

Peggy was about to reply when the telephone rang. Dashing into the hall, her hopes high that it could be Anne or Doreen, she snatched up the receiver.

'Hello, Mum. It's Anne. I'm so sorry not to call sooner, but the lines have been jammed solid since Tuesday.'

'It's been the same for me,' said Peggy, settling onto the hall chair, ready for a lovely long chat. 'I've lost count of the times I've tried to get through to you and your Aunt Doreen.'

'Isn't it the most marvellous thing to know it's all over at last? We had a brilliant party in the village, with tables going all the way down the middle of the main street, and every house was decorated with bunting and flags. We're so lucky to live down here in farming country. You should have seen the baking all the women did – it was a veritable feast. Of course the boys and I thought of you all at Beach View, but poor Sally was pining for her John, so I think she'll probably leave as soon as the school term finishes – she's really homesick.'

Before Peggy could ask if she was feeling the same about coming home, Anne rushed on. 'I'll be back in the schoolroom today, but to be honest, Mum, I can't really keep my mind on lesson plans for over-excited seven-year-olds when I'm on such tenterhooks waiting to hear if Martin has been released from the POW camp.'

'Neither Kitty nor Charlotte has been notified about Roger and Freddy, and Cissy's heard nothing about Randy, so I suspect the authorities are waiting to confirm their release once they've all been accounted for, given medical checks and been debriefed. It was the same in 1918. Your dad, Frank and Ron had to jump through all sorts of official hoops before they were demobbed, and it was a full three weeks after the Armistice before they came home.'

'I'm rather hoping things will have improved since then,' said Anne with some asperity, 'and that because they've been prisoners of war, they'll be given special treatment.'

'I'm sure the powers that be will see that they do,' Peggy replied, swiftly going on to the question she'd been desperate to ask since peace had been declared. 'When are you all coming home? I can't wait to see you, and Ron is desperate to see the boys and meet his great-grandchildren.'

There was a long silence and Peggy thought they'd been cut off until Anne finally replied. 'I'm sorry, Mum, but it won't be for a while yet. It's the middle of the summer term and the headmaster, George Mayhew, is really struggling to find my replacement. The girl I took over from was sadly killed, and it seems there's a real reluctance to fill teaching posts in such isolated rural areas.'

'But you'll come home at the end of term, won't you?' Peggy persisted. 'I'm sure the school board will have found another teacher by then.'

'Actually, Mum, it's not that simple. I owe it to George to stay on to assist with all the arrangements for getting our evacuee children back home, and in July, the school is being used as a polling station for the general election. As I've become involved in local politics over the past couple of years, I've been asked to oversee things here on polling day and then assist with the count in Taunton.'

Anne took a breath and hurried on. 'Then there's Vi's cows. She can't manage them now the land girls have gone, so I'll have to stay and help until she and Bob can find a reliable chap to take on the dairy.'

Peggy seethed that evacuee children, cows and a general election seemed more important to Anne than returning home. 'What about Martin? Surely you'll want to be here when he's released?'

Anne's voice became brisk. 'I've already contacted RAF HQ and asked them to make sure he's sent straight here. There's plenty of room on the farm, and it's so lovely and peaceful it will do Martin the world of good, and give him time to recover and get used to family life again.'

'Oh, I see.' Peggy's spirits plummeted, for it seemed it could be a long time before *she* had the chance to get used to family life again. 'But what about Bob and Charlie? Surely they can come home?'

There was a silence so tense at the other end of the line that Peggy could feel it, and she braced herself for more bad news.

'Mum, you really haven't been listening to a word I've said, have you?' Anne said with barely concealed impatience. 'Bob's running the farm. He's got the summer harvest and autumn ploughing to organise, and although he's been excused National Service, he still has to attend the local Territorial Army base several hours a week.' Her voice softened. 'But I'm sure he can arrange some time off around Christmas when things on the farm slow down.'

'Christmas?' Peggy squeaked. 'But that's months away and, God willing, your father could very well be home by then. He'll be expecting to see all his family, and will be devastated if Bob's not here.'

'I know how disappointed you must be, Mum, but farming isn't a nine to five sort of job, and Bob can't leave everything to Vi and the German POW who's asked to stay on.'

Anne had absolutely no idea of the depth of her mother's disappointment. Peggy was getting crosser by the minute at being thwarted at every turn. All she wanted was to get her family back to Cliffehaven where they belonged.

'At least none of that will affect my young Charlie – he'll definitely be coming home once school term's over,' she said brightly. 'I suppose he'll travel with Sally, her little Harry and young Ernie?'

'Oh, Mum. I'm so sorry,' sighed Anne, her voice cracking with emotion. 'But he's refusing to leave. Aunt Vi, Sally, Bob and I have tried everything from blackmail to threats to make him change his mind, but he's adamant he wants to stay here and get his school certificate. Although I think his place in the rugby team has more to do with it. You see, he's been asked to join the Somerset Junior Fifteen, which is quite a coup.'

Peggy had the most awful lump in her throat which she couldn't shift. Charlie had only just turned fourteen, which last year would have allowed him to finish school. But the government had raised the leaving age to fifteen only this year. It simply wasn't fair. And it felt as if the world – and her family – was against her.

She wanted to cry, to beg Anne to try again to change Charlie's mind, but she knew that no amount of cajoling, boxed ears or bribing would work on her youngest son, who from an early age had possessed the Reilly stubborn streak. Once he'd decided on something, nothing would shift him. In that way he was very much like his father and grandfather.

'Is he there? Can I speak to him?' she managed.

'He left half an hour ago to catch the school bus,' said Anne.

Peggy swallowed her tears and tried to be brave, but her heart was aching with sorrow and she couldn't think of a thing to say.

'You could always catch a train down here and bring Daisy to meet us all,' said Anne hopefully. 'We'd love to see you, really we would, and it would give you a chance to talk to Charlie face-to-face. He might listen to you.'

'I can't,' Peggy said brokenly. 'I have responsibilities here and at the factory – and the journey is too long to come just for a weekend.'

'Then there's nothing either of us can do until the end of summer,' said Anne rather purposefully. 'I'm sorry to have been the bearer of such disappointing news, Mum, but I promise faithfully that when we do come home, I shall bring Charlie, even if I have to get Martin to carry him kicking and screaming onto the train. He's getting too big for his boots, if you ask me, and although Bob has done his best to keep him in line, he really needs a man's firm hand.'

'Oh dear,' said Peggy on the verge of tears once again. 'He always was a handful.'

'He still is,' said Anne flatly.

Peggy was desperate to end this awful telephone call, so when Cissy wandered into the hall, she saw a way to escape. 'Cissy's here. I'll hand you over.' Before Anne could reply, she thrust the receiver at a startled Cissy and fled upstairs to lock herself in the bathroom.

Grabbing a towel, she pressed her face into it to smother the sound of her wracking sobs. She'd waited so long to have them all home and now her hopes were dashed, and all the lovely dreams she'd had of being a proper family again were shattered.

'What's going on, Anne?' Cissy asked. 'What have you been saying to Mum to make her cry?'

'Oh, no,' sighed Anne. 'I didn't mean to do that.'

'Well, you did, so you'd better explain.'

Anne went into a long explanation to justify her side of the telephone conversation. 'How was I to know she'd take it all so badly?' she said some time later. 'She's well aware of the life we've made for ourselves down here and surely must see that we can't just drop everything at a moment's notice? And the farm really is the best place for Martin to rest after all he's been through. Our tenants in the cottage have another three months on their lease, and with Beach View no doubt still packed to the gunnels, he wouldn't be able to cope with all the noise and comings and goings.'

'I do understand your point of view,' Cissy replied, keeping her tone reasonable despite her rising anger. 'But you should have at least warned her before now that it would be some time before you'd all be home – and not leave it until the last minute to drop your bombshell.'

Anne tried to protest, but Cissy talked over her. 'What you haven't considered in your clearly busy little life, is the fact that Mum has bravely kept going these past six years by holding on to the belief that we'll all come home once the war's over. She's clung to it through thick and thin, even though she's terrified that something might happen to Dad. And I think it's thoughtless of you not to at least try to come home earlier.'

'I did suggest she came down here,' said Anne crossly. 'But it seems her job at the factory and her evacuees are more important than us.'

'Don't you *dare* get on your high horse about her job when you won't give up your teaching, or step back from the political nonsense you've got involved in. If you'd taken just a minute to consider how you'd feel if the boot was on the other foot, and you'd been

45

separated from your children for five years, you might have had some glimmering of what Mum's been through.

'Don't forget, Anne,' she carried on over her sister's protest. 'Charlie was only a few years older than your Rose Margaret is now when he left here – just a little boy – Mum's baby.' She took a shallow breath. 'And Martin would be just as happy here as on the farm. All he really needs to recuperate is to have his family around him. And the same applies to Mum. God knows she's waited long enough.'

'I don't appreciate your tone,' snapped Anne.

'I really don't care,' retorted Cissy. 'It's time you were taken down a peg or two when you're being such a selfish, unthinking cow.'

'It takes one to know one. How often have you been to visit Mum? It's not as if you're a million miles away, is it? But then I suspect you've been having such a high old time with all those pilots to flirt with and parties to go to, you haven't given Mum a thought.'

Cissy gripped the receiver, her temper now at boiling point. 'I came when I was off duty – which wasn't that often – and of course I thought about Mum,' she hit back. 'It wasn't all beer and skittles at Cliffe, you know. Friends died, planes crashed and burned with the crews still trapped inside them. Fire crews had to wait until it was safe to retrieve the bodies as Jerry bombed and strafed us. And when those bodies were brought out, melded together, twisted and blackened, they no longer resembled human beings.'

She took a sharp breath as the horrific images returned to haunt her. 'How was it for you, Anne

– down there in safe Somerset with your brothers and children, where the only threat came from a low-flying seagull with diarrhoea?'

Cissy slammed down the receiver before Anne could respond, and stood there trembling with rage at her sister's unfounded accusation and still tortured by those memories of death and destruction – of the fear and horrors she'd witnessed over the past five years.

She hadn't meant to lose her temper, but goody-two-shoes Anne had always got on her nerves. Just because she was the eldest, she seemed to think she was always right about everything. And being a teacher hadn't made her any less opinionated. There was absolutely no excuse for trying to justify her self-ishness towards Mum. It was almost as if Mum had been an afterthought, and she'd ticked off this conver-sation in her long list of things to do without any notion of how it would affect her. If Anne had been here, Cissy would have slapped her.

Cissy lit a cigarette and paced the hall floor, aware that her mother was still in the bathroom and probably crying her eyes out. The thought of it made her heart ache, but she was in no fit state to be of any comfort, for she was still seething.

'What on earth was that all about?' asked Cordelia. 'It certainly didn't sound pleasant.'

Cissy quickly stubbed out her cigarette and gently wrapped the much-loved woman in her arms. 'Oh, Grandma Cordy,' she sighed. 'I'd forgotten just how much Anne winds me up.'

'She always did,' Cordelia replied, returning her hug. 'Rather like your Aunt Doris used to wind up poor Peggy. It was the same with me and my sister before she went doolally. It's the sibling rivalry, you see. We younger ones always feel we need to prove something – but usually come off worse.'

Cordelia patted Cissy's cheek and sat down on the hall chair. 'Where's your mother?'

'Anne's upset her dreadfully, and she shut herself in the bathroom. I must go to her.'

Cordelia grabbed her hand. 'Peggy won't thank you for seeing her in distress, Cissy. Let her get whatever it is out of her system and give her time to put that brave face back on. It's helped her through six years of war, although none of us will ever admit to knowing that.'

'I didn't realise,' murmured Cissy.

'You were never meant to.' She kept hold of Cissy's hand. 'Your mother has been determined to keep her darkest thoughts and fears from everyone because she didn't want to add to the burden when we were already struggling with the horrors of war. And by the sound of that conversation you've just had, it seems she was right to do so.'

'She could have talked to me, Grandma Cordy. It might have been a release for both of us if we could have shared our fears.'

'It's not your mother's way,' Cordelia said softly. 'Peggy is a strong woman who has her own method of dealing with things.' She glanced up the stairs at the sound of footsteps in the bathroom. 'Yet even the strongest of us can be brought to breaking point, Cissy, and it's only their inner core of steel that will give them the strength to fight on – and your mother has proved time and again that she will not be beaten.'

Cordelia struggled to stand. 'Come on, Cissy. Everyone's left for work and Rita's busy upstairs, with Daisy helping to tidy that tip of a room she and Ivy share. We can have the kitchen to ourselves for a while and you can tell me what that conversation was all about.'

Cissy put the kettle on whilst Cordelia closed the door into the hall so Peggy could slip downstairs to her bedroom without being seen. Once the tea was made, Cissy sat down opposite Cordelia and told her the whole unedifying story.

Cordelia listened with increasing sadness. 'Poor, poor Peggy,' she murmured, dabbing away her tears. 'How cruel life can be. The disappointment must be killing her.'

Neither of them heard the door open so didn't realise Peggy was standing there. 'Hitler didn't manage to finish me off, and neither will a bit of disappointment,' she said, coming into the kitchen, her hair and make-up immaculate and looking very businesslike in a new navy pinstripe costume. 'They'll come home eventually. I'll just have to be patient, that's all.'

She looked around the room. 'Where's Daisy? I have to get to work.'

Cissy wanted to embrace her but knew instinctively that any sign of affection at that moment would break Peggy's brittle veneer. 'I'll go and get her. She's helping Rita with her room.'

'Lord help us,' sighed Peggy. 'She could get lost in the mess and never be found again.'

As Cissy hurried upstairs, Cordelia regarded Peggy over her glasses. 'Peggy Reilly, you're a marvel and an example to us all.'

'No, I'm not, Cordy,' she said, firmly meeting Cordelia's gaze. 'I'm just an ordinary woman who has to accept that her children are grown and making new lives for themselves.' There was a tremor in her voice which she brought swiftly under control. 'They'll come home when they're ready, and even if it's only for a short while, I shall make the most of them while I can, and not make them feel guilty – but free to be the people they were meant to be, and go their own way. After all, Cordy, that's why we've just fought a war, isn't it? For freedom.'

4

Peggy was barely aware of anything as she wheeled the pushchair along Camden Road which was still bedecked with flags and bunting. The gaiety of it all left her numb, for her world had become colourless and without joy, the aching hollow inside her dulling her senses to the point where she could no longer even cry.

However, despite the heavy burden of loss she was carrying, she'd meant what she'd said to Cordelia, and was determined to fulfil her responsibilities to her best ability. Anne and the boys might not need her as they once had, but Daisy and Cissy did, as well as Cordelia and her girls. The ending of the war would see great changes at Beach View, and there would be many challenges ahead – not only for herself, but for her chicks. She needed to stay strong, to be there for them when things went awry – which in some cases, she feared they might – and to continue to be the mother hen they'd all come to rely upon.

'You're looking very smart this morning, Peggy,' said Nanny Pringle, opening the door to the factory's crèche. 'New costume?'

Peggy dredged up a smile and unstrapped an impatient Daisy from the pushchair. 'It's from the first batch of Solly's latest venture,' she replied. 'He saw a gap in the market and decided that as the men are all getting demob suits, the women should have the chance of something smart and cheap and off-the-peg. Rachel designed it, and we've already had some healthy orders from some of the big department stores.'

'Goodness me,' replied the plump, motherly woman, eyeing the pencil-slim skirt and close-fitting jacket with its peplum draping from the waist. 'I don't think I'm the right shape for such a thing,' she said with a smile. 'But I can see it will catch on with you young, slim things.'

If Peggy hadn't been feeling so low she might have been rather flattered to be called young, but as it was she could only manage a slight twitch of her lips. She grabbed Daisy and managed to kiss her before the child wriggled away and dashed into the crèche to be with her little friends.

'Don't take it personally,' soothed Nanny Pringle, who must have caught the wistfulness in Peggy's eyes. 'At this age they're always in a hurry to be off and doing.'

Peggy nodded, vowing that she'd keep her feelings to herself from now on. Nanny Pringle was too sharp-eyed. She stored the pushchair in the bicycle shelter and headed for the factory. Clocking in, she took a deep breath, determined to function as usual, keep her mind on her work and just get through the day.

Climbing the stairs to the offices that overlooked the factory floor, she saw her friend Madge sitting at her desk, lost in thought. 'Penny for them?'

Madge grimaced. 'Not worth a farthing, Peg. I was merely trying to work out what to cook for tea.'

'It's a terrible bind, isn't it? Especially when there are so few choices to be had – and what there is costs an arm and a leg. We can only hope that now the war's over, the rationing will be eased and we can all eat properly again.'

'Amen to that,' sighed Madge, rolling a sheet of paper into her typewriter. 'Solly's been in since six as the place has been shut for two days,' she said, shooting Peggy a warning look. 'Being idle for so long has made him as jumpy as a cat on hot bricks, and he's itching to get production going again. Which is more than can be said for that lot down there,' she added, tilting her head towards the window overlooking the lines of machines.

Peggy saw several empty chairs, and noted the desultory way in which those who had turned up were going about their work. 'How many absentees?' she asked.

'Twenty. And I suspect we'll have more on the night shift.'

'Let's hope it's only temporary,' said Peggy, 'or we'll have to start recruiting again.'

'That shouldn't pose a problem,' Madge replied. 'Some of the other factories are laying people off, and I already have a list of men and women who've applied for their old jobs now they've left the services – and who, by rights, should have priority.'

'I'll make a note of the absentees, and if they don't show tomorrow, then they'll have to be deemed as no longer employed. We can't afford to be let down with so much work on.'

Peggy left Madge to her typing and went into Solly's inner sanctum to find him pacing back and forth, furiously puffing on a large cigar as he stopped to glare down at the factory floor. He was a big man and seemed to fill the room which was already thick with the haze of cigar smoke.

'Good morning, Solly,' she said, opening the other window to get some fresh air in to clear the fug and make it easier to breathe. 'Is there anything in particular you want me to focus on today?'

'You can get that lot down there to earn their keep,' he rumbled, turning from the large window with a scowl. He threw himself into his leather chair, making it groan beneath his considerable weight. 'Two days of production have already been lost, and at the rate they're working, we won't finish the demob suit contract in time.'

'We're still on target,' she soothed. Seeing that he wasn't at all in a good mood, she said nothing about the absent workers, although she was certain he'd spotted the gaps. 'Why don't I ask Madge to make you a pot of your special coffee? That always puts you in a good frame of mind.'

He blew out his cheeks. 'My Rachel has been conspiring with that *mashugana* of a doctor again. They've decided coffee and cigars aren't good for me. It seems they've come to the conclusion that my blood pressure's a bit high, so they've put me on a blasted diet as well.' He mashed the cigar out with some vigour.

Peggy knew better than to say anything, because in this mood the slightest thing would set him off on one of his rages – which certainly wouldn't help his blood pressure.

Solly threw up his hands, his brown eyes beseeching as he looked at her. 'Oy vay, Peggy. What's the world coming to when a man can't enjoy a few pleasures? Have I not earnt them? Do I not work hard enough to give that woman everything she could possibly want? Do I not pay that man a fortune to keep his mouth shut when Rachel interrogates him about my health?'

It was a tricky situation for Peggy who knew all about his health problems from Rachel. She would have to tread carefully – but going by the rising colour in his face and the tremor in his hand as he defiantly lit another cigar, he really was risking a heart attack.

'It's tough, I know,' she said. 'But Rachel's worried about you. And to be honest, Solly, so am I.'

'Ach, you women worry too much,' he said dismissively. 'I'm perfectly healthy, and a fine figure of a man for my age. I don't need either of you fussing over me.'

'It's only because Rachel loves you, Solly, and when the factory's running smoothly again and you're in a better frame of mind, you'll realise that.'

He shrugged. 'Maybe,' he replied, his attention now focused on what Peggy was wearing. 'That costume looks good on you, Peggy. How does it feel?'

'It's a good weight for spring and comfortable to wear,' she replied, 'but I think you need to line the skirt as well as the jacket. The cheap cloth is inclined to lose shape around the seat.'

'A lining will make it more expensive,' he grumbled. 'You should wear a petticoat.'

'I am, and it still sags when I sit down. The weave just isn't firm enough. Besides, lining the skirt will only add about a farthing to the cost, and you can recoup that easily on the price and still keep it afford-able. A lined skirt will give it some class, making the whole costume more desirable.'

'I'll think about it,' he mumbled around the cigar. He glanced down at the workforce. 'You'd better get down there, Peggy. The lack of proper care and atten-tion they're giving to their work this morning is hurting my wallet.'

Peggy nodded and left him simmering over the account books strewn across his desk. If only Solly took as much care with his health as he did his bank balance, Rachel wouldn't need to worry so much.

The Memorial Hospital was set in beautiful parkland five miles east of Cliffehaven and had once been a grand mansion owned by a wealthy family. The patri-arch and his only son had been killed in the trenches of World War I, and when the bereft dowager had passed away, she'd gifted the entire estate to the military in memory of her husband and son, to be used as a hospi-tal for injured servicemen.

Rita arrived on her motorbike at mid-morning to find the hospital extraordinarily busy, and as there was no sign of Peter, she decided he must have gone outside to avoid the chaos.

She found him sitting on a bench on the terrace that ran the width of the building and overlooked the garden. He was bundled up in his air force overcoat, his head still heavily bandaged, gloomily watching a couple of blinded men being led around the perimeter of the sweeping lawn by a nurse. He didn't notice her arrival, so she plonked down next to him and kissed his cheek. 'You look as if you've lost a quid and found a penny,' she teased.

His face lit up on seeing her and he returned her kiss. 'I'm just keeping out of the way of all the bustle, and thanking God I didn't end up like those two poor blokes. Strewth, Rita, it's so good to see you.'

Rita hugged his arm and rested her head on his shoulder, as thankful as he that apart from the crack on the head and a badly broken leg which had taken an age to heal, he'd been extremely lucky. 'What on earth is going on today, Pete? Why all the hubbub?'

'We've had an influx of patients from Dover,' he replied. 'According to Matron, they arrived there late last night from France on hospital ships, and because there are so many of them they've had to be transferred to other hospitals all along the coast.'

'Does that mean our men are coming home from Europe?' she asked hopefully, thinking of her father.

'Only the badly injured ones, love,' he replied, taking her hand. 'Your dad will be home very soon, darlin', and I just hope I'll still be here to meet him. He sounds a bonzer bloke.'

'What do you mean about not being here?' she gasped in alarm. 'They're not sending you back to Australia, are they?'

Peter grinned. 'Not until the Japs have been defeated, love,' he drawled. 'But I reckon it won't be long before I'm turfed out of here to make way for someone worse off.'

'But where would you go?'

'I'm hoping I'll be sent to Cliffe. A mate of mine's just been discharged from there, and he reckons it's better than a posh hotel. But nothing's certain, darlin'. I could be sent miles away to a specialist hospital because they're still worried about my head. But I haven't had a funny turn for a whole two weeks, or been getting as many headaches, so they might just discharge me to some billet somewhere until the Japs surrender and I can catch a ship home.'

'Then let's hope you get sent to Cliffe so I can keep you close for a while longer,' Rita said. She looked down at their entwined fingers and found the courage to voice her fears which had been growing ever since peace looked likely.

'I can't bear the thought of you leaving,' she said in a rush. 'Australia's so far away and once you've gone I'll probably never see you again.' She looked up at him through her brimming tears. 'It's horribly selfish, I know, but I can't help it.'

'It's not at all selfish, and although it'll be good to see my family again and get into the Outback, I hate the thought of leaving you behind.' He twisted round to face her, taking both hands. 'But I've been thinking, Rita. Maybe ... if you'd like to ... and you're not put off by my head not being quite right yet ... We could get married – and then you could come with me,' he finished in a rush.

Rita looked into his mesmerising eyes and thought she'd burst with happiness. 'Married?' she breathed.

He gripped her hands more tightly, his expression suddenly very serious. 'Yes, Rita, married,' he said firmly. 'I can't get on my knees because of all the flaming metal pins they put in me leg, but if you agree to marry this wreck of a man whose body might not be working quite right, but whose heart is full of love for you, then you'd make me the happiest man alive.'

Rita's thoughts were in a whirl, her heart thudding and the sheer joy of the moment quite overwhelming. She wanted to accept his proposal – wanted to spend the rest of her life with this wonderful man who returned her love so deeply – but the thought of moving to the other side of the world and never seeing her father or Peggy and Ron again, made her hesitate.

'What is it, Rita?' he asked nervously. 'Have I spoken out of turn?'

'No, oh no, Peter,' she swiftly assured him. 'I would love to marry you but ... Australia's so far from home,' she hurried on. 'And I feel torn between you, Dad, Peggy and Ron. They're the only family I have, you see, and I love them too.'

'Just promise you'll think about coming with me,' he urged. 'I do understand how difficult it will be for you to get used to a new way of life in a place that's so very different to Cliffehaven. But my family will be your family, and I will love and cherish you for the rest of my days.'

Rita burst into tears, her heart and head doing battle as she flung her arms around his neck and kissed him. She knew that if she rejected him they would both end up with broken hearts – but how could she choose between him and the only family she'd ever known?

'Queensland is God's own country, Rita,' he murmured, kissing away her tears. 'There's space to breathe in the Outback where the land has remained unchanged since the dawn of time and a man can be free to wander to his heart's content. And on the coast

59

there are tropical rainforests full of exotic birds, and beaches with fine white sand and palm trees, and a sea so blue it dazzles the eyes. You'll love it, Rita,' he whispered, 'and you're just the kind of girl who has the spirit of adventure to settle there.'

'It all sounds wonderful,' she replied, 'and I promise I'll think about it seriously. When Dad comes home, I'll talk it over with him and see how he feels about me going all that way.' She gave him a watery smile. 'I might act as if I'm tough, but I'm really not that adventurous, Pete. I've never been further than the next town, and the thought of going to the other side of the world is quite terrifying.'

'Your dad could come too,' Peter said eagerly. 'There's always work out there for a good engineer who's not afraid of putting in a hard day's labour. My word,' he breathed, 'the sheep and cattle stations are always crying out for someone to mend their utes and farm machinery. He could make a fortune in no time.'

Rita loved his boyish enthusiasm, and felt bad about not encouraging him. 'We'll see what he has to say, Pete,' she murmured against his lips.

'I reckon I'll have to be satisfied with that,' he said, trying hard to dampen down his enthusiasm. 'But in the meantime, darlin',' he pulled a small box from his overcoat pocket and opened it with a flourish, 'would you wear this ring to seal the promise that you'll consider marrying me?'

Rita gazed at the square-cut diamond that blushed the finest pink in the sun. It was the most beautiful token of love, but she couldn't take it. 'It's truly the loveliest thing,' she managed, closing the box. 'But it wouldn't be right to accept it – not yet.'

To her surprise, Peter grinned. 'Don't be such a stick-to-the-rules Pom,' he teased, taking the ring from the box and determinedly slipping it onto the third finger of her right hand. 'This isn't an engagement ring, see – it's on the wrong finger. But it is a token of my love in the hope you'll eventually let me put it where it really belongs.'

Rita didn't know what to say as she gazed back at him.

He lifted her hand so the sunlight flashed pink fire on the ring. 'That's a diamond – a pink one,' he explained, 'and quite rare. I found it in the Kimberley which is way out in the Never-Never of North Western Australia. I was doing a stint of prospecting in between the shearing seasons. The gold is from a mine in Coolgardie. I got it made into a ring for when I found the girl I wanted to spend my life with. And that's you, Rita.'

Wordlessly, her heart too full to speak, she gazed at the stunning ring and watched how the light played on it as she moved her hand.

Peter watched her. 'Beautiful,' he whispered. 'So beautiful you put that diamond in the shade.' He drew her tenderly into his arms and held her close.

'I love you, Pete, really I do. But I'm frightened,' she confessed.

He stroked her hair and continued to hold her. 'I know, love,' he said softly. 'It's a big decision to make. But we'll work something out, no worries.'

The factory estate looked quite naked without the barrage balloons floating above it, but the high wire fences remained in place because the armament factory was still producing its bombs, bullets and shells.

Doris looked out of the office window to the scene below as the workers traipsed back from the canteen after their lunch break. 'They don't look too happy to be here,' she remarked. 'I can't say I blame them, though. I'm still feeling exhausted after two whole days of celebrating.'

John came to stand behind her, his hand discreetly resting on her hip below the level of the window ledge. 'The numbers are right down,' he murmured, 'and there will be fewer next week once they've got their wage packets. The managers aren't surprised, because many of the workforce aren't local, and now the war's over, they'll be eager to go home to their families.'

'But there's still a war in the Far East,' protested Doris. 'They'll need planes and tools and armaments to fight off the Japanese.'

'America is taking over the supply of weapons and machinery,' he said quietly. 'It's easier for them as they have bases all across the Pacific.'

Doris turned to look up at him, her heartbeat quickening as it always did when he was near. 'Does that mean all these factories will close?'

'Most of them.'

Doris bit her lip as she thought about Ivy and Ruby losing their jobs. 'Will this office have to close too?' she asked fearfully.

He smiled down at her, his silver hair glinting in the sunlight, his blue eyes made more so by the love that shone from them. 'Our jobs are safe, dear heart. The rope makers will remain here along with the engineering shop and tool factory – although they will cut down on their hours. And in time, other companies will take over the leases of the buildings. New enterprises will spring up, and there are already plans in place to divide up the largest ones into smaller units to provide workshops for individuals to set up their own trades. It might look gloomy and rather sad now, Doris, but once the men come home and begin to rebuild their lives, this place will be booming.'

They returned to their desks. 'Do you think Michael might want to set up something when he comes home?'

'My son is an army man like me and his grandfather before him. I suspect he'll be keen to get back to his regiment.' He squeezed Doris's hand. 'Don't worry about Michael, my love. He's his own man with a good army career in front of him. And although he might be a bit shocked to find us engaged, he has his own life to lead and is realistic enough to accept that I have mine.'

Doris could only hope so, but she harboured many doubts about this beloved son whom she'd yet to meet. Michael had been taken prisoner shortly after the death of his mother, and before his father had retired from the army and moved to Cliffehaven. He'd certainly have a great deal to get used to after almost five years in a German POW camp. Discovering that his father planned to marry again wouldn't be easy to take, and frankly, Doris was dreading his return.

She knew so little about him except for what John had told her, and a loving father would be biased, so she couldn't really take it as read that he'd accept her, or fathom his true character, until she'd met him. John seemed convinced that Michael would welcome her with open arms, but then he was an optimist and a man in love, so saw everything in a rosy light.

Michael could very well be disapproving, and take an instant dislike to her, for she was nothing like his dead mother in looks or background. If that happened things could get very awkward for all concerned. John's love and loyalty would be torn between her and Michael, and if there was no resolution she'd have only one option open to her. She'd have to walk away.

A shiver ran down her spine at the thought of losing him. She couldn't let that happen, not now she'd found real love and contentment for the first time in her life.

'What's the matter, my love? You're not still worrying about Michael's reaction to our engagement, are you?'

'I am rather,' she admitted.

'Silly girl,' he said fondly, reaching for her hand across the desk. 'I know I foolishly hesitated to make things official between us because I was worried about my son's reaction, but it's the best decision I've made in years and I have absolutely no regrets. Michael might be taken aback at first, but he's mature enough to accept the situation and be reasonable about it. You'll see.' He kissed the tips of her fingers. 'Besides,' he added, 'he'll probably only be here on a long leave before he's returned to his regiment, so whether he approves or not, he won't have to put up with us billing and cooing for very long.'

Doris smiled into his eyes but remained unconvinced.

The mood of the girls working in the armaments factory was far from happy as the rumours circulated and the gossip spread that the entire estate was about to be shut down. In fact, there had been a restlessness in them that had grown all afternoon since it was announced there would be an address from the manager at the end of the shift. It was a miracle that there hadn't been a serious accident.

The afternoon had dragged on and Ivy's headache hadn't been improved by the stench of gunpowder and oil, and the ceaseless music blaring from the loud speakers under the corrugated tin roof. She felt sick with apprehension about the announcement, for she'd heard the rumours and seen for herself that the other factories were winding down in preparation for closing or being relocated. She could only hope that as the war was still going on in the Far East she'd be one of the lucky ones to be kept on, for she needed the money.

Five o'clock finally came and the music was switched off to be replaced by the voice of the manager, Staff Sergeant Wilcox, coming over the tannoy. 'Please put down your tools and switch off,' she said, her voice distorted by the echo-inducing tin roof. 'And then wait by your benches until everyone is here.'

Ivy did as ordered. Digging her filthy hands into her overall pockets, she found a boiled sweet she'd forgotten about, and blew off the fluff before popping it into her mouth. If this was the end, then she'd have to move quickly to find another job. There were over two hundred girls in this factory alone, with hundreds of others spread all over the estate – and although a lot of them would pack up and go home to London or wherever they'd come from, it would still be a fight to find anything decent.

The late shift poured in and immediately knew something was up as they saw everyone still standing by their benches, and within seconds the volume of their worried questions rose.

'Attention, please. Attention!'

Silence fell immediately and every face was lifted towards the imposing figure that stood ramrod straight at the top of the iron staircase leading to the factory office. Staff Sergeant Wilcox was a woman who'd always commanded attention with her strong voice and implacable sense of duty – and today was no exception.

'With our glorious Victory in Europe, the government and the people of Great Britain wish to thank you wholeheartedly for the sterling and tireless work you have given to the cause over the past six long years. The Allied Forces and the people of Britain salute you.'

Ivy rolled her eyes, thinking that all the thanks in the world wouldn't butter parsnips, let alone help her to save up to get married.

'As you know,' continued the Staff Sergeant, 'our own Special Forces are now involved with our American allies to bring about Victory over Japan, and they will continue to need to be armed and supplied. It is to this end that it has been decided that all future armaments should be supplied by America and Australia as they are better placed for transport to the areas of fighting. Therefore, it is my sad duty to inform you that this factory will be closing tomorrow night.'

There was a murmur of disappointment laced with sharp questions about wages, and whether or not there would be a late shift on Friday night.

'Tonight will be the last late shift,' she said above the loud voices. 'But those on days will be expected to come in tomorrow and work as usual. You will all be paid at the end of your final shift, and there will be a small bonus for each of you as a token of the government's gratitude.

'However,' she continued, cutting through the muttering. 'Should you decide not to work your last shift, then your wages will be sent on to you without the bonus.'

'Bloody typical,' muttered Ivy.

'I call it ruddy blackmail,' said the girl next to her in disgust. 'Why not shut down now and pay us all? What's the ruddy point of keeping us on for one more shift?'

'They want the last drop of sweat we got,' said Ivy crossly. She blew out her cheeks and looked around. 'I can't say I'll be sorry to leave this place, but I shall miss earning the good money they pay.'

The other girl shrugged. 'They only paid that because it's dangerous and dirty, and we've all ended up with yellow skin. Personally I can't wait to get back to Coventry. There might not be much of it left, but it's home, and I never felt right being all this way south.'

Ivy fetched her things from the locker room, drew on her jacket and traipsed out of the factory to be met by an equally disgruntled Ruby who was waiting for her. 'I suppose you 'eard all that?' Ivy asked, linking arms with her fellow Londoner and friend.

'Yeah,' Ruby replied as they ambled towards the gate. 'It's rotten luck, ain't it? You ain't gunna find them sort of wages again.'

'What about you? I know they've cut yer hours, and laid off a lot of the workers, but are they closing too?'

Ruby shook her head. 'Nah, they're staying open, but the hours from now on will be nine to five, and no night shifts where there was a chance of a bit of extra money.' She heaved a sigh and adjusted the strap of her handbag over her shoulder. 'People still need tools, war or not, but the cut in me wages means I'll have to give up on Cordelia's bungalow at the end of the month. Me mate what was sharing the rent has already gone 'ome to London, and she ain't coming back.'

'But where will you go?'

Ruby grimaced. 'Uncle Stan's, I suppose, though it will be a terrible squash with him, April and baby Paula already taking up the two bedrooms in that little station cottage. I'll just have to 'ope my Mike gets leave to come down before he's sent back to Canada. He'll sort something out.'

'Auntie Peggy would take you in again like a shot. But she's chock-a-block already, and if 'er family come back from Somerset, we'll all be doubling up – even the snooty Cissy.'

Ivy gave a deep sigh. 'I thought the end of the war would be wonderful and everything would go back to the way it were before. But it ain't like that, is it? The factories are closing, friends are leaving, and with the servicemen and women coming back, there ain't a job to be 'ad nowhere.'

'I thought you'd go back to London with Andy,' Ruby said as they came to a halt outside the factory gates.

'That's what we was planning once we got hitched. But I'm waiting to hear from me mum so I knows where she is, and if the young 'uns are back with 'er from Salisbury. How about you and Mike?'

'Everything's up in the air at the moment. I'm waiting to hear from him to see if he's got permission for us to get hitched while 'e's on leave down here. That's if he does get leave before they ship him home,' Ruby added gloomily.

'Won't that be a bit strange? Getting married and then 'im going off straight away?'

Ruby shrugged. 'Once it's safe for me to travel, I'll be going out there to join 'im,' she said, her eyes shining with excitement. 'It sounds ever so exciting, Ivy. Thick snow and husky dogs pulling sledges, and big deer they call elk – although I don't like the sound of the timber wolves that howl in the night, or the bears what come down into the town scavenging for food.'

She giggled. 'Mike's mum has been writing and sending me pictures of what to expect when I get there. She seems ever so nice, Ivy, and I'm looking forward to meeting 'er and seeing it all for meself.'

'Blimey, Rubes, that's a big change from living in the Smoke.'

'I don't wanna go back to London – too many bad memories – and although I do love it 'ere, I wanna be with Mike – and if he's in Canada, that's where I'll be going.'

'Well, you're braver than me, gel, I tell you that.'

Ruby laughed, gave her a hug and hurried down Mafeking Terrace towards the bungalow she rented from Cordelia.

Ivy watched her go and heaved a sigh. She really didn't have much choice about the sort of job she could do, for she'd worked in factories since she'd left school at thirteen, and knew little else. But she had learnt to make bullets and rockets, and mines, so she might be able to turn her hand to something new.

'Beggars can't be choosers,' she muttered, heading down the hill towards the town. 'I'll see if Peggy can get me some sort of work at Solly's.' The fact that she didn't know one end of a sewing machine from another was neither here nor there – she'd damn well learn.

5

Peggy had just about managed to get through the day, but the weight of her bitter disappointment lingered, and there had been moments when she'd had to fight back the almost overwhelming urge to give in to her pain and cry. And as she left her office she knew that, for the first time in her life, she couldn't yet face going home.

Having collected Daisy from the crèche, she decided to walk along the promenade, in the hope that some brisk exercise in the salty air might bring calm to her troubled heart and restore the strength of purpose she so badly needed to keep her going.

Cliffehaven seafront had always been the main attraction of the town. It was where the holidaymakers had come to frolic in the water, sit in deckchairs, and to enjoy the evening variety shows and dances on the pier and the music at the bandstand on Sunday afternoons. The sight of it now was really depressing, for although the barbed wire, gun emplacements and tank traps had been removed, and the beach cleared of mines, the bandstand was a pile of rubble and the poor old pier still had the rusting remains of a German plane stuck into its fire-blackened ribs.

Peggy let Daisy run free to chase seagulls and throw pebbles into the water as she walked along with the pushchair. According to Sarah, who worked in the council offices, there were already plans to rebuild the bandstand and repair the Victorian shelters that were strung along the promenade, and to bring back the tram which used to run along the seafront and up the High Street to the station. But it would cost a great deal of money to resurrect the pier, which the council simply didn't have, so it would probably be left as it was – just without the German plane.

Peggy took a deep lungful of the fresh air that was so reviving after the dusty atmosphere of the factory and paused for a moment to gaze the length of the promenade which stretched from the steeply sloping hills to the west, where the remains of the Havelock Road houses and park were an ugly testament to the destruction of war – to the white cliffs in the east, which had stood sentinel over the horseshoe bay since time immemorial.

Peggy could see there was a lot to do before the summer season got into full swing, which she was sure it would, for although the Far East was still engaged in war, people would want to forget what they'd just been through and have a seaside, bucket and spade holiday with their families like they used to. There were enormous bomb sites to be cleared before urgently needed new housing could be built; hotels and guest houses would need to be repaired to accommodate the visitors, and the High Street and station buildings could certainly do with an overhaul.

She shivered as a sudden gust of wind chilled her, for although it was early May, it still got cold once the sun dipped low in the sky. 'Come on, Daisy,' she called. 'It's time for tea.'

The little girl threw a handful of pebbles into the water and then ran towards her, her dark curls flying, her cheeks rosy from the cold. 'Have ice-cream now, Mum?'

'Not today, Daisy. It's too close to teatime.'

Daisy slumped into the pushchair, arms folded and pouting. 'Want ice-cream.'

'The shop's shut,' said Peggy firmly, strapping her in. 'We'll have it another day, but only if you're a really good girl.'

Daisy continued to pout and squirm, but Peggy took no notice as she strode along the seafront and then up the steep hill towards home. The bomb site where so many had been killed during the last V-2 attack was a dark reminder of how close they'd all come to death on that terrifying night, and the sight of the missing houses at the back of Beach View merely reinforced the fact that luck had most definitely been on their side.

Out of breath from the climb, Peggy pushed through the scullery door and freed Daisy from her restraints before following her, rather reluctantly, up the concrete steps into the kitchen. They must all have heard about the telephone conversation with Anne by now, and she could only hope they knew her well enough not to say anything, for any sign of sympathy would crack through her defences, and she'd be lost.

Everyone but Danuta was home, sitting around the kitchen table and discussing their day as Rita and Sarah dished up the shepherd's pie. They all looked up and greeted her with smiles as Robert helped her off with her coat, and Cordelia attended to Daisy, but Peggy could see in their eyes that they understood how she felt, and was grateful for their silence on the matter.

'How lovely and warm it is in here after that cold walk,' she said. 'And my goodness, that pie smells delicious.' She noticed the glow in Rita's face and assumed she'd had a lovely visit with Peter, and then realised that Ivy was unusually quiet. Surely she couldn't still be suffering from a hangover? Or had something happened at work today to bring her low? Peggy had heard rumours of the factories closing down, and her heart went out to the girl, for she and Andy were saving hard to get married, and if she had lost her job, it would be an awful blow.

Knowing she'd hear about it all sooner rather than later, Peggy went into her bedroom to change out of her suit into comfortable slacks, slippers and sweater. Her feet were killing her after being in high heels all day, and it was utter bliss to get them off.

Sitting on the bed for a moment, she gazed at the photograph of her darling Jim, and wondered fleetingly what he'd have made of that conversation with Anne, and the ensuing row she'd overheard between the two sisters. Jim had always been very protective of her, and regarded his role of husband and father as one to be respected and obeyed. He would probably have given Cissy a hug for defending her mother, and then ordered the rest of them home – or gone down there and brought them all back whether they liked it or not.

Peggy smiled at the thought, even though such actions would definitely have caused even more trouble. But her Jim had always been a man to react swiftly to situations he didn't approve of without first stopping to think before charging in like a bull in a china shop. Whereas, after that initial bitter blow, she'd had the day to think about Anne's reasons for staying on, and had been forced to admit they were reasonable, and that she'd had no business flying off into hysterics. Perhaps she should try and telephone her after tea to smooth things over between them.

Feeling a little lighter in spirit, she returned to the kitchen to find that Daisy was already hungrily tucking into her meal, so collected her own plate from Rita and sat next to Cissy. It was quite a squash around the kitchen table, and had been for a while, but it felt cosier in here than in the dining room, and it meant she didn't have to have two fires going – which with the current shortage of coal would have been almost impossible.

'Where's Danuta?' she asked once she'd staved off her initial hunger.

'She's still doing her district rounds, so I'm keeping her tea warm in the slow oven,' said Rita. 'She's on call tonight, so if the phone goes, don't be alarmed.'

'It's supper, not tea,' reproved Cissy coolly. 'Tea is a drink or something you have mid-afternoon.'

'Well thanks for educating me, Cissy,' the girl replied with an impish glint in her dark eyes. 'But the evening meal has always been tea in this house, as you very well know.'

'Yes,' said Peggy. 'They might have supper in the mess at Cliffe, but we don't stand on ceremony here. Just eat your tea, Cissy, and be grateful there's any food on the table at all.'

Cissy reddened beneath the heavy make-up, moved the food about on her plate with a fork and then abandoned it. 'I'm really not that hungry,' she said.

'I'll 'ave it then,' said Ivy, and before Cissy could react, she'd scraped the lot onto her own plate, and tucked in. 'Waste not, want not,' she said through a mouthful of meat and mash.

Cissy looked at her askance, saw her mother's warning frown and knew better than to say anything.

Fran broke into the awkward silence, her green eyes alight with pride as the last rays of the sun glinted in her copper curls. 'I've been waiting until you were home, Aunt Peggy, to tell everyone our news.'

Peggy's spirits soared in delight. 'You're having a baby,' she squeaked.

Fran giggled. 'You're jumping the gun a bit, Auntie Peg – but the news is just as exciting.' She saw she had everyone's attention and hurried on. 'Robert had a really important meeting in London today,' she declared before nudging her husband. 'Go on, you tell them.'

Robert had always been rather shy, and went pink as all eyes turned to him. He pushed his horn-rimmed glasses back onto the bridge of his nose and had to clear his throat before he could speak. 'Well, you see,' he began, 'when it was clear the war in Europe was soon to be won, Anthony and I realised we should start planning for the future. So we applied for more senior posts within the Ministry of Defence, and were called up to London today to be interviewed.'

'Anthony was with you?' gasped Peggy. 'Doris's son?'

He nodded, took off his glasses and polished them with his handkerchief. 'It seems we're just the sort of men they're looking for,' he said, going a deeper scarlet, 'and so, on the first of June, Anthony will be going to the Cambridge office, and I'll be off to Whitehall. It's a plum posting, and I'm sure I only got it because of my grandfather's long and distinguished career in the Diplomatic Corps.'

'You did not,' Fran furiously protested. 'It was because you've earnt it.' She turned to Peggy. 'To be sure, Aunt Peg, he's too modest by half.'

A chorus of congratulations drowned her out, and although Peggy was delighted for the young couple, and joined in with the congratulations for the new and exciting venture they were about to embark upon, she couldn't imagine Beach View without Fran, who'd been with her for years and was as loved as a daughter.

She smiled across the table at Robert. 'Very well done, Robert. I'm sure you'll have a wonderful career – but what exactly will you be doing in Whitehall?'

'I'm afraid I'm unable to tell you, Peggy,' he said regretfully. 'The Secrets Act I signed at the beginning of the war still holds, you see – for both me and Anthony,' he added with a twinkle in his eye. 'So there's no point in trying to pump him about his work either.'

Peggy chuckled. 'You know me too well, Robert, but you've both been so mysterious about what you do for the MOD that you can hardly blame me for being curious.'

She turned to Fran. 'I shall be so sorry to see you go, my dear. Beach View won't be at all the same without you, but it sounds as if you have exciting times ahead in London. I suppose you'll have to put in your notice at the General pretty soon if you're leaving at the end of the month?'

'I handed it in the minute Robert got home and told me his news,' she replied, grasping Peggy's hand. 'To be sure I'll miss you, Peg, for you've been a mother to me all these years, especially when mine disowned me. I'll not be forgetting you, I promise, and will come for a visit as often as I can.'

'But where will you live in London?' asked Peggy. 'By all accounts the city is little more than an enormous bomb site.'

'The MOD will provide us with furnished accommodation until we can get a place of our own, so you're not to be worrying, Aunt Peg,' Fran soothed.

'Will you carry on nursing, Fran?' asked Danuta who'd slipped into the kitchen without anyone noticing.

'Aye, that I will,' Fran replied. 'Even though I'm now an old married lady,' she giggled, hugging Robert's arm. 'I'm hoping to get a place at St Thomas's, or St George's, but I'll not be applying just yet.'

'You'll want to settle in London first and find your way around, I expect,' said Rita.

Fran bit her lip and shared a glance with Robert. 'There is that,' she conceded, 'but first we're going to Ireland to see my family.'

'Oh, Fran, no,' groaned Peggy. 'You know very well how it will be over there, so why put yourself through the unnecessary heartache of being rejected again?'

'Because if I don't, I'll always wonder if going there and facing up to them might have changed things.' She gripped Robert's hand. 'To be sure me heart is already aching, Peggy, but if there's the slightest chance of turning things round, then I must risk hurting it some more.'

'Well, I think you're very brave,' said Peggy, 'and if things don't work out, you know where I am. I'll never close the door on you, Fran, I promise.'

'To be sure, I know that,' Fran said softly.

'So, Fran, when will you be leaving?' asked Danuta, bringing her hot plate to the table.

'Robert will book our ferry and train tickets tomorrow, and we hope to leave on Sunday morning.'

'So soon?' gasped Peggy.

Fran's green eyes glittered with regret. 'I'm sorry, but there's so little time left before the end of the month, and the journey to Ireland will take two days from here. We plan to be in Ireland for a week, and then travel straight to London, leaving us only four days to settle in before Robert has to be in his office. So you see, Aunt Peg, we have no other option but to leave as soon as possible.'

Peggy wished wholeheartedly that she could go with her, but merely nodded, forced to accept that Fran now had Robert by her side to support and guide her through this journey that would undoubtedly be an extremely difficult and emotional one.

'Then we must make the most of you while we can,' she said. 'I'll see if Alf has got a joint of beef or something under the counter so we can have a proper roast on your last night.'

'It's already in hand and paid for, Peggy,' said Robert. 'I'm picking it up on Saturday morning.'

'Bless you, dear,' managed Peggy. 'You didn't have to do that.'

'Oh, but I did,' said Robert stoutly. 'You've loved and cared for my girl ever since she came to Cliffehaven, given us a home to start our married life in, and seen Fran through her darkest days. A joint of meat is nothing in comparison.'

To avoid further protest, and clearly feeling a bit embarrassed by his unusually long and emotional speech, he pushed away from the table. 'We're off to the Anchor to celebrate my promotion, so if any of you feel like joining us, the first drink is on me.'

Cissy, Rita, Sarah and Cordelia immediately set about fetching coats and outdoor shoes whilst Danuta swiftly finished her meal so she could join them, but Peggy was tired and really not in the mood for celebration. 'I'll stay here with Daisy and put her to bed if you don't mind,' she said. 'It's been a long day for both of us, and we have another early start tomorrow.'

Cissy and Cordelia understood her reluctance and chivvied the others out. 'We won't be back late, Mum,' said Cissy. 'And I'll bring you something as a nightcap.'

'Come on, Ivy,' said Rita impatiently. 'I've only got an hour before I'm due at the fire station.'

'I'll catch up with you,' Ivy replied.

'It's not like you to lag behind when there's a free drink on offer,' teased Peggy as Rita crashed the back door shut behind her.

'Yeah, I know, but it don't feel right taking free drinks when I ain't got the money to pay for a round.'

'What is it, Ivy?' asked Peggy gently. 'You've been very quiet all evening.'

'The factory's shutting tomorrow night, so I'm out of a job.' Her hazel eyes were pleading as she looked at Peggy. 'I don't suppose you got anything at Solly's, 'ave yer? I could learn to use them machines, or 'elp with the packing and stores, or even sweep up and clean the lavs if that's all what's going. But I 'ave to find something, Auntie Peg.'

Peggy could see how desperate she was, and hated having to disappoint her. 'Oh, Ivy, I'm so sorry, but I can't help. We've got a long list of returning service people who want their old jobs back, and I have to take them on first. I'll add you to the list,' she hurried on, 'but it could be a long wait.'

'Oh, Gawd,' Ivy groaned. 'I were afraid you'd say that, but I got to find something quick. It ain't fair on Andy if I keep dipping into our savings.'

Peggy wanted to help, but knew the job situation in Cliffehaven wasn't good. It would be extremely tough to find anything that an unskilled girl could do. Then, as Cissy returned with a bottle of beer for her, she had a spark of inspiration.

'Have you ever done bar work, Ivy? Ron and Rosie might need help at the Anchor – or you could ask your Andy's Aunt Gloria if she could give you something at the Crown?'

'You're engaged to Gloria Stevens's nephew?' gasped Cissy. 'Good grief.'

'You can wipe that snooty expression off yer face,' snapped Ivy. 'She's a diamond, is Gloria, and worth two of you.'

'Pound for pound, she probably is,' sniffed Cissy. 'I've never seen so much blubber on display.'

'That's enough, Cissy,' snapped Peggy. 'This is a private conversation, and I'd appreciate it if you'd go back to the Anchor and leave us to it.'

Cissy shrugged nonchalantly and sashayed off back to the pub.

'Has she always been like that, Auntie Peg?' Ivy asked, still bristling.

'Thankfully, no, but I suspect her time at Cliffe with all those toffs has unfortunately made her see things in a different light. I'll have a quiet word with her over the weekend, and trust you not to say anything to her to make the situation more difficult. We don't want a repeat of what happened with my sister, do we?'

'Nah,' Ivy agreed. She fiddled with her hair, thinking hard. 'I might go over and see if Gloria 'as got any work going. Ruby said Rosie 'ad given 'er a few hours at the Anchor, so there won't be nothing there.' Her little face brightened. 'Best to strike while the iron's hot, eh?' She pushed back from the table and reached for her coat.

'It certainly is,' said Peggy, taking a sleepy Daisy onto her lap for a cuddle. 'Good luck, Ivy.'

Ivy slammed her way out, and Peggy relaxed back into the kitchen chair, little Daisy nestled sweetly against her breast. The changes at Beach View were already beginning, more swiftly than she'd expected, and once Fran and Robert had left, others would surely follow.

If Ivy couldn't find work in Cliffehaven, then it was fairly certain that she and Andy would return to the East End of London where there was bound to be lots of work for them both. Danuta had already expressed a desire to return to Poland, and if things went the way Cissy wanted, her daughter could soon be sailing for America. Sarah would stay until the war in the Far East came to an end, and then join her mother and sister wherever the POWs were sent after their liberation.

And what of Rita? That she was in love with Peter was clear to everyone – but did she have the courage to follow her heart all the way to Australia, or would the ties of home be strengthened once her father returned from the battlefields of Europe? Peggy gave a deep sigh. She didn't have all the answers but knew without a doubt that once she and Cordelia were left with Daisy, all those empty rooms would once again echo with the absence of those she loved.

Somerset

Anne left the bedroom door ajar so that motherly Auntie Vi could hear the girls should they wake. Avoiding the kitchen where Vi was in deep conversation with Bob and Claus, she went into the boot room, pulled on her wellingtons and coat, and let herself out of the side door. All was still in the gloaming of a night sky not yet fully dark. The cows were snuffling and shifting in their byre, the occasional bird called sleepily from the surrounding trees, and she could hear the soft hoot of one of the resident barn owls as it set off on silent wings for its night's hunt.

Anne tied her headscarf under her chin and took a deep breath of the clean country air. She was forced to admit that Cissy's barb about it being safe here had hit the mark – in fact, apart from one terrifying incident with a rogue German fighter plane, the war hadn't touched them physically. Emotionally, of course, it was always there in the absence of her husband Martin, and the distance from home.

The conversation with her mother and the unpleasant row with Cissy had unsettled her all day, which was why she'd needed to get out of the house for a while to clear her head and try to think of the best way to make amends. She tramped across the freshly hosed cobbled yard and climbed the gate, then plodded across the field to the fence bounding the swiftly flowing river at the bottom. The sound of it was soothing as it rushed over its stony bed and raced towards the glimmering line of the sea on the horizon.

Leaning on the fence, Anne lit a cigarette and regarded the darkening vista of sprawling fields, drystone walls and lines of softly rounded hills. She'd come to love it here, for the sense of community was strong, and although they'd been strangers when they'd arrived in Barnham Green all those years ago, they'd been made welcome, and now felt very much at home.

Anne turned her back on the view and regarded Owlet Farm. The comfortable, rambling farmhouse was solidly built of the local stone, and was set on a low hill overlooking hundreds of acres of grazing and arable land. The milking sheds and dairy stood a short distance away across a cobbled courtyard, the byres in large barns behind that. The dairy herd had increased over the years, as had the amount of land put to crops.

There were three small cottages nestled beside the main house. One of them housed a couple of old farm-hands who were living out their days by tending their much prized vegetable garden and offering advice on how things had been done in their day when there were only horses to help with the heavy work. The second was inhabited by the last remaining German prisoner of war, and the third was where Sally Hicks had set up home with her little boy Harry, and her younger brother Ernie who was now twelve and growing like a weed.

Anne noticed a faint light glimmering behind the thin cotton curtains. Sally had been Peggy's first evac-uee, who'd arrived in Cliffehaven from the slums of London with six-year-old Ernie who'd had infantile polio and wore a specially made boot and calliper on his leg. At sixteen, Sally had taken on the role of mother as their own had been so neglectful, and through Peggy's warmth and encouragement, had blossomed in Cliffehaven. She'd started her own home dress-making business and ended up marrying the fire chief, John Hicks, with whom she'd had little Harry.

By that time, Anne was married to Wing Commander Martin Black with baby Rose Margaret already prov-ing to be a handful, and the war was in full terrifying swing. It had been Sally's father – Harold Turner – who'd solved the problem of where they should all go when the school had been bombed and it was clearly too dangerous to stay in Cliffehaven with young chil-dren, and he'd arranged for them to live here with his older sister, Violet.

Childless and widowed, Violet had opened her arms, her heart and home to them for the duration, and they'd grown to love and admire her for her patience and wisdom, and the enormous warmth she showed them all. She'd more than fulfilled the role of mother and grandmother, and as time had gone on, Ernie had filled out and grown into a mischievous, healthy boy who no longer had to wear a calliper.

Anne gave a deep sigh and mashed the cigarette out beneath her boot. Her brother Bob would never feel at home anywhere but here now, so at least Violet wouldn't be left entirely alone. But the thought of leaving her – and this place – was something that Anne couldn't yet come to terms with.

'It's going to be 'ard to leave, ain't it?' said Sally, approaching out of the gloom and making Anne jump.

'Where did you come from?' Anne gasped.

Sally brushed some grass from her trousers. 'I was sitting under that tree, but you was clearly deep in thought so I didn't like to disturb you. Sorry if I startled you.'

They turned back to the fence and leaned against it, staring into the darkness as the moon slowly drifted through the tops of the trees and began to gild the rushing water beyond them. 'I was thinking how much I'm going to miss this place, and how lonely Vi will be once we've all gone,' said Anne.

'Yeah, it won't be easy for her. She loves them kids as if they was her own. I wrote to John about it, and he suggested she could come and live with us, but when I talked it over with her, she didn't seem that keen.' Sally pushed back the hair from her face and giggled. 'It's probably 'cos we're so noisy, and to be fair, it would be a real squash in our little place.'

'Vi was born on this farm and has spent her entire life here,' said Anne. 'Moving away from everyone and everything she knows so late in life would be a terrible wrench, and I doubt she'd settle.'

'Yeah, you're probably right,' said Sally on a sigh. 'But I'm ready to go 'ome to John at the end of the school term. We've been apart for too long, and he 'ardly knows our Harry.' She glanced across at Anne. 'I know you're planning on staying 'ere for a bit after Martin comes back, but you must miss yer mum.'

Anne wondered if Sally had overheard any of this morning's conversation and was angling for more information. 'Of course I do,' she replied carefully. 'And in a way I feel disloyal to her for worrying about leaving Vi behind. But it's Martin who's my first priority, and it's my duty to see that he's fully recovered before we go back to Cliffehaven.'

'There was a bit of a to-do when he came last time,' said Sally, glancing towards the end cottage lights. 'Is it really wise to bring him here with Claus still living on the farm?'

'It wasn't Claus he had the issue with,' said Anne. 'It was Max, remember? And as he and Hans are gone, I can't see there should be any problem.'

'I suppose you'll just have to wait and see,' said Sally on a deep sigh. 'Gawd knows what Martin's been through at that camp. He might hate all Germans now – and I can't say I'd blame 'im.' She took a breath. 'Still, it's going to be strange to be with John after all this time – strange but lovely,' she added with a soft smile. 'I can't wait to be back with him again in our own little home.'

Anne had sharp memories of the dreadful row she and Martin had had when he'd come to the farm unexpectedly on leave to find her and the children playing innocently with the German POWs, and how things had only been resolved between them on the last day. And thank God they had, she thought, for within weeks he'd been shot down and captured, and she hadn't seen him since.

'We'll both just have to adapt to being wives again,' she murmured, 'and let them take the lead. It'll be hard for all of us to get used to being a couple again.'

Sally shivered and drew up her coat collar. 'I'm going in for some cocoa – do you want some?'

'No thanks, Sal. I'll stay here and have a last cigarette.'

Sally placed her hand on Anne's arm, her expression serious. 'Don't leave it too long before you phone Peggy and make things up with her,' she advised softly before walking away.

Anne stood by the fence and watched her go, the blush of shame heating her face as the cold wind flapped her headscarf. She should have given more thought to how her mother would take the news, and Cissy's sharp reminder, that as a mother herself she should have known how hard it would be to be denied her family at the very last minute, had brought that home. Her sister was right in so many ways – although she'd never admit it to her face.

She lit a cigarette and turned her back once more on the farm, staring out at the moonlit panorama as she thought about her relationship with her younger sister. Anne had always been the practical one who'd done well at school and training college to achieve her ambition of being a teacher. She'd lived her life carefully, abided by the rules, always very aware of how people might regard her.

Cissy, in contrast, had always been the little girl who loved dancing and dressing up, and couldn't care a fig about homework. She knew how to get round Dad's finger, flirted outrageously with every boy she came across once she'd passed puberty, and didn't take anything seriously except her dreams of dancing in Hollywood.

'Chalk and cheese,' muttered Anne. 'Rather like the war we experienced.'

She shivered, not with the cold, but with the horror of those images Cissy had conjured up of her experiences. Her little sister had witnessed things no young girl should see, and in those few angry words, she'd revealed what Anne suspected was a mere snapshot of what she'd been through. It was no wonder she'd been so angry when Anne had accused her of being a good-time girl and neglecting their mother.

Anne crushed out the half-smoked cigarette and headed back to the farmhouse, determined to put things right even though she couldn't work miracles and return home immediately. But she could ring her mother to apologise, and admit that she'd gone about things in completely the wrong way.

6

Cliffehaven

Peggy had felt so much better after Anne had telephoned back on that Thursday evening that she'd managed to get a decent night's sleep and was consequently brighter throughout Friday. The fact that nothing had really changed and Anne and the others wouldn't be coming home yet was still a bitter disappointment, but that was just something she had to live with.

As suspected, the number of no-shows and resignations at the factory had increased, so she and Madge had sent on the wages owed with a slip informing each person their job was no longer available. This in turn cut down the long list of those waiting to have their old jobs back, and now that work had started in earnest again, Solly was in a much better mood. He'd even begun talking about taking on one of the empty units up on the factory estate to expand the business into maternity and baby-wear, for with the servicemen coming home there was bound to be a baby boom in nine months' time.

This had made Peggy smile. Solly always had an eye for a future enterprise, and this one seemed very promising. It would also mean taking on more staff, which would ease the long waiting list considerably. However, these things took time, and Peggy suspected the new factory wouldn't be up and running until summer.

Fran and Robert had gone to work on the Friday, stayed out very late to say goodbye to all their colleagues and friends, and then spent most of this Saturday morning packing their belongings and restoring order to their room. They kept a suitcase each for their journey to Ireland, but the rest of their things – most of which were wedding presents and clothes – were to be sent by rail to Robert's mother where they would be kept in storage until needed. A friend from the Fort had lent Robert his car so he could cart it all up to the station, but as they had to return it by five this evening, it was all a bit of a rush.

Peggy watched and listened to all the bustle whilst she and Ivy prepared the vegetables for the special roast dinner they would have this evening. Little Fran had become such an intrinsic part of the Beach View family that it would feel like losing a precious daughter, and it was hard to imagine the house without her.

Peggy knew she should be glad for the girl who had such a bright future awaiting her in London, but couldn't help feeling sad at her leaving. Fran's bright smile and joyous delight in playing Doris's violin so beautifully had been the tonic they'd all needed during the dark days, and was the thread that laced together memories of parties at the Anchor, local concerts, and of course family weddings and celebrations.

'I reckon Rita's up to something,' said Ivy, breaking into Peggy's sad thoughts.

'Why do you say that, Ivy?'

'She's quieter than usual and keeps going off into a daydream,' Ivy replied.

'It's probably something to do with young Peter,' Peggy murmured. 'There's definitely been a glow about her recently.' She regarded Ivy fondly. 'I'm surprised you haven't asked her what's going on.'

'I did, and she just said she was happy the war's over, that Peter seems to be recovering, and her dad will soon be home. It was a bit hurtful really, 'cos we're best friends, and I tell 'er everything.'

'Well, she's due back any minute after seeing Peter at the Memorial, so you may be able to satisfy your curiosity then. But don't push it, Ivy,' Peggy warned gently. 'If there's more to tell, she'll do so when she's ready.'

Ivy nodded, but Peggy suspected that the girl's insatiable nosiness would not be curbed by any warning from her, and she wouldn't be satisfied until she knew what was going on with Rita. But there was enough happening today without adding to the emotional stress and she could only hope Ivy and Rita wouldn't fall out.

She returned to peeling the vegetables, the sound of laughter coming from across the hall where Sarah, Danuta and Cissy were being more hampered than helped by Daisy and Cordelia as they decorated the dining room for this very special occasion. It was fortunate that the joint of beef Robert had bought was enormous, for there would be twenty of them around the table to ensure that Fran and he would have a really splendid send-off.

Peggy didn't want to dwell on the thought that this would be Fran's last night under her roof, so she turned her attention back to Ivy. 'I'm so glad Gloria could give you a few hours.'

'I were lucky,' Ivy said, ''cos she'd decided just that day to open the upstairs rooms to guests again and needed a chambermaid, and a waitress for breakfast. She reckons the holiday season will soon get going, so she's roped poor Andy into painting all the rooms and putting down fresh lino in his off-duty time. He offered to do it for free 'cos she's been so good to him, but she wouldn't hear of it, and is paying him really well for his efforts.'

'Well, I'm delighted for you,' said Peggy warmly. 'But being a chambermaid is hard work, Ivy. Guests can get very fussy over the slightest speck of dust, even if their own homes don't come up to the mark, as I know from the experience of running this place.'

Ivy shrugged. 'I'm used to 'ard work, Auntie Peg, and with Gloria's money, the tips and the bonus I got from the factory, me and Andy will have a deposit on a place in no time.'

Peggy carried on dealing with the vegetables, trying not to think about the house slowly emptying, and was saved by the sound of the late afternoon post clattering through the letter box.

'Go and get that, dear, would you? My hands are wet.'

Ivy plonked the saucepan of spring greens on the hob, ran into the hall and came back with a goodly number of letters and cards. Sifting through them, she squeaked in delight. 'I got a letter from Mum at last, and a card each from me brothers saying they'll be back on shore leave by the end of the month, and there's even a postcard from the young 'uns down near Salisbury.'

She placed them in a pile on the table and shuffled through the rest. 'There's one for you from Jim, two for Sarah, one for Grandma Cordy, and a card for Rita from her dad.' She turned it over and shamelessly read it. 'He says he'll be home in about two weeks.' Sitting at the table, she ripped open her mother's letter.

Peggy raised an eyebrow at her cheek and then quickly dried her hands so she could open Jim's airmail. It wasn't very long, and Jim explained that there really wasn't very much to report. They were stuck in a jungle respite camp in the middle of the monsoon with very little to do until they were sent back into the fighting again. But the news that the war was finally over in Europe had definitely been something to celebrate. His mate Jumbo had played the bagpipes until he'd run out of puff and they'd drunk the place dry of beer, which had incurred massive hangovers the following morning.

He continued on to say that he was extremely relieved to know that she and the rest of the family were safe now, and hoped that she'd soon be surrounded by their children and grandchildren. He longed to see all of them again, and to get to know little Daisy and his two granddaughters, and hoped he'd be home by Christmas. With the war over in Europe he truly believed it wouldn't be long before the Japanese were forced to surrender. He'd signed it as usual with a loving kiss, and the hope they'd soon all be together again.

Peggy folded the letter and gave a soft sigh. Let him imagine that all was well here and that their children were on their way home, for if it helped him get through their separation, then so much to the good.

'They're all right, Auntie Peg,' breathed Ivy, folding the single page back into its envelope.

'Oh, Ivy, I'm so glad for you.'

'The letter must have got lost in the post or something, 'cos Mum wrote this back at the very end of March.' Her face was alight with happiness and relief. 'They was planning to stay with some friends for a couple of nights in Stepney before moving into their new place, which is just down the road by the look of the address she give me. It seems this Hughes Mansions is ever so smart, and she'd've liked to stay there permanent like, but it's crammed with refugees from Europe and people like Mum and Dad who ain't got nowhere else to go.'

Peggy thought it rather strange that there hadn't been a second letter after all this time, but the post was erratic, and it would probably turn up tomorrow now the Post Office had caught up on things.

Ivy seemed to be following the same train of thought. 'I suppose they've been busy moving in and such-like,' she murmured. 'But it's odd she ain't written again.'

'Why don't you write to the new address your mother gave you, and ask her to make a reverse charge call? I expect she's been busy settling in at the new place, and if it's a long journey to work and so on, she might not have had time to write, and doesn't realise how worried you've been.'

'Yeah, I'll do that,' Ivy said brightly. 'Is it all right if I leave the spuds to you, Auntie Peggy? Only I don't want to miss the last post.'

Peggy waved her off and returned to the sink, deep in thought as she finished peeling and chopping the potatoes. There was, of course, one other explanation as to why Ivy's mum hadn't written, but that was almost too dreadful to think about – and surely the authorities would have informed Ivy if anything had happened to her family?

She decided she was making a mountain out of a molehill and imagining all sorts because she was in that sort of blue mood. No doubt Ivy's letter would bring about a rapid response, and the mystery would soon be solved.

Peggy finished peeling the potatoes and put them on to parboil, then dried her hands and went into the dining room to see how the others were getting on. Balloons and bunting had been strung across the ceiling, tinsel decorated the beautifully laid table, and a large hand-painted poster edged with more tinsel wished the couple well in their new lives in London. 'My goodness,' she breathed, 'you have been busy.'

'It isn't too much, is it?' asked Sarah with a frown.

'Not at all. It's lovely and earns you all a nice cup of tea to wash away the dust.'

Ivy thudded down the stairs and slammed the back door behind her on the way to the post box at the end of the street, and Peggy silently prayed that everything would turn out all right, and she'd just been over-imagining things.

Fran had been quite overwhelmed by the love, thoughtfulness and hard work everyone had put in to make her last night at Beach View so special. She would miss all of them dreadfully – especially Ron and Peggy, who'd been such stalwart, caring supporters during the eight years she'd been living here. Consequently, she'd had to battle her tears as people began to drift home, and she'd had to say her last goodbyes.

As Colonel White went to fetch Doris's coat, Fran handed her the precious violin. 'Thank you for lending me this,' she said. 'I've made sure it's tuned and given it new strings and a good polish.'

'Bless you, dear,' said Doris, whose eyes were suspiciously bright. 'It was a pleasure to hear you playing it so beautifully.' She handed it back to Fran. 'Please keep it, and when you next play it, think of us and the happy times we've had.'

'But it's a very valuable instrument,' Fran protested. 'I can't possibly accept it.'

'Take it with my blessing, dear. I know of no one else who deserves it more, and it would be a crime to lock it away and never hear it again.' Doris firmly pushed the violin into Fran's arms. 'Just promise me you'll come back and play it for us one day.' She slipped on the coat the Colonel was holding out for her, then softly patted Fran's cheek. 'God speed, Fran.'

Fran laid the violin carefully on the table before flinging her arms around Doris. 'Thank you, thank you,' she managed through her tears. 'I will treasure it always.'

Doris eventually drew from the embrace and turned swiftly away before her emotions got the better of her.

Fran tearfully watched her bustle away. She could hardly equate this soft-hearted Doris with the ghastly, bossy one who'd made everyone's lives such a misery when she'd moved into Beach View and virtually taken over. It was amazing what love could do, she thought, and silently wished Doris and the Colonel all the luck in the world.

''Tis a fine thing to see that woman softened up,' rumbled Ron with a twinkle in his eyes. 'To be sure we have a lot to thank the Colonel for.' He rose from his chair and held out his arms. 'Come, wee girl, and give me a hug. I know how hard this leaving must be for you – to be sure it's hard for me too.'

Fran went willingly into his arms, glad of their strength and the solidity of his broad chest. She didn't have to pretend with Ron, for he knew all her secrets and had been a stalwart father figure from the moment she'd arrived at Beach View all those years before, offering encouragement, love and guidance – and providing numerous moments of great hilarity. 'I'm going to miss you so much,' she said gruffly.

'And I shall miss you, acushla,' he murmured into her hair. 'But you'll always be in my heart, for you have been a daughter – a much loved daughter – and I'm so very proud of you and all you've achieved.' He kissed her cheek, and still holding her hands, gave her the Irish blessing they both knew so well, and which brought tears to them both.

'May the road rise up to meet you. May the wind always be at your back. May the sun shine warm upon your face; the rains fall soft upon your fields and, until we meet again, may God hold you in the palm of His hand.'

'Oh, Ron, I do so love you,' Fran sobbed.

'There, there, wee girl,' he replied, softly kissing her brow. 'Walk into the future with hope, and the assurance that if you ever need me, I'll be here.' He abruptly released her hands, clicked his fingers at Harvey and Monty who were sprawled in front of the fire, and put his arm around Rosie. ''Tis time for this old man to be abed. Sleep well, acushla, and dream happy dreams.'

Fran watched him leave the house, the dogs trailing after him, and knew how lucky they'd all been when it seemed they might have lost Ron through that accident. But he'd overcome his injuries with a strength of purpose and determination. He was a special man, and she would always think of him as a father.

Curled against Robert's warm back later that night, Fran was soothed by his steady breathing, but couldn't fall asleep. The memories of all the years she'd been living here came in swift succession, making her restless. Without wanting to disturb Robert, she carefully eased out of the bed, pulled on her dressing gown and tiptoed down the stairs. The house was silent but for the familiar creaks and groans of old timbers as she went to the kitchen to make a cup of tea.

'I wondered if you'd come,' murmured Peggy, rising from the fireside chair to pour out a cup of tea. 'I couldn't sleep either, and thought tea might help.'

Fran hugged her, realising that Peggy's company was what she'd really been searching for. 'Having you to talk to like old times is more soothing than tea,' she replied. 'It feels as if we haven't done this in ages,' she added, settling into the other chair. 'It's lovely to have you to myself for a wee while.'

'It has been rather hectic lately, and I'm glad we have this chance to say a proper goodbye.' Peggy grasped her hand. 'Do you remember how we sat up half the night when you and Robert got engaged? And the times we spent gossiping into the wee hours about that hateful matron who treated poor Danuta so badly?'

Fran smiled through her tears and nodded. 'And do you remember the night Ron and Frank came home three sheets to the wind after Brendon's send-off? And the time we hid in here when Doris was being such a pain?'

Their reminiscences continued until the clock struck two and reminded them they had an early start. Feeling more at peace and prepared for the emotional day ahead, they hugged and kissed and went to their beds knowing they'd never forget a moment of that quiet and loving exchange and would hold tonight in their hearts like a precious gift.

Now it was Sunday morning and although the church bells were ringing to usher in a bright new sunny day, it felt to Fran as if a shadow had passed over the skies and settled into her heart. She was dreading the moment when she and Robert had to leave Beach View for the last time. But the ticking clock on the mantel seemed to hasten the moment of their departure and it felt as if only moments had passed since waking when it was time to don hats and coats and collect their suit-cases from the hall.

Robert understood how difficult it was for her to say goodbye, and stood at her side as she hugged the other girls and Cordelia, and then drew Peggy into a loving embrace. 'Please don't come with us to the station,' she begged. 'To be sure I couldn't bear it. But this isn't goodbye, Auntie Peg, I promise. I will come back when I can, and I'll write as soon as we get to London to let you know how we are and how things went in Ireland.'

Peggy held her close. 'I'll always be here for you, Fran. Never forget that.' She drew back from the embrace and lovingly tucked a stray lock of Fran's autumnal hair behind her ear. 'Take care, darling girl,' she managed. 'And don't be sad. You and Robert have a wonderful future ahead of you, and whatever happens in Ireland, know you're very much loved.'

Peggy embraced Robert. 'Take care of our girl, won't you?' she whispered.

'Of course I will,' he replied, kissing her cheek before reaching for Fran's hand to give it an encouraging squeeze. 'Come on, darling,' he murmured. 'Or we'll miss the train.'

Fran's heart was heavy as she took charge of the violin case and he picked up their cases. They stepped out of the front door for the last time, and she turned back just before the end of the cul-de-sac, saw them all standing on the doorstep, and realised that no matter what happened in Ireland, this was her true family, and always would be. She slipped her hand through the crook of Robert's arm and gave him a brave, watery smile.

'You'll always have me beside you, Fran,' he murmured against her cheek. 'So hold on tight, and let's begin our adventure with no regrets.'

Fran's heart melted with love as she gazed up at him. And when they reached the corner, she didn't look back, but into the bright promise of the new lives they were embarking upon together.

7

Germany

The forced march from Stalag IV at Gross Tychow had covered between fifteen and twenty miles a day, with much zig-zagging to escape the encroaching Red Army from the east, and had lasted eighty-six days, according to the notches Freddy Pargeter had made on a length of tree branch he'd cut on the first night.

The treatment they'd received from their guards had been brutal, with some prisoners being bayoneted, kicked or hit if they didn't keep up. And should a man drop to the ground and not manage to get back on his feet, he was shot.

Freddy Pargeter and Randolph Stevens had stuck together throughout the torturous death march, sharing blankets and their greatcoats, helping each other to wade through the deep snow, tending their wounds, and then huddling close throughout the bitter nights when the only shelter had been a tumbledown barn, or a stand of trees.

They'd drunk contaminated water from roadside ditches, eaten snow, grass and even rats to stay alive, and when the opportunity had arisen, they'd risked their own and the farmers' lives by trading their watches, rings and cigarettes – and anything else they possessed – for something to eat. They were infested with lice, suffering from dysentery, frostbite and trench foot, but they knew that if they gave in to the deathly weariness of their aching, half-starved and diseased bodies, they would never see home again.

They'd arrived at another Stalag two months later to find there was no food, shelter or bedding, and after a week, they'd been sent on another march east. But the weather was now more clement and liberation was finally at hand, for the POWs and their captors could hear the growing thunder of the approaching Allied artillery, and although this imbued some spirit into the survivors, they simply didn't have the energy to celebrate. Freddy could barely put one foot in front of the other, and although Randolph held him up and forced him onwards, he knew he too was suffering, and if they should stumble, they'd never get up.

Three weeks later they were sprawled in a ditch next to what they'd been told was the River Elbe near Lauenburg. Of the eight thousand that had set out, almost a quarter had perished. Now sick and starving, it was doubtful the survivors could walk any further, and they would die where they lay. The German guards were in no better state, and although many of them had just abandoned their duties, some of them were as weak as their prisoners and remained with them. Rumours of the war's end were rife, but for all of them, the focus was on just staying alive.

Freddy was slipping in and out of consciousness, and Randolph was delirious from fever when there was the sound of heavy gunfire very close by. Freddy blearily forced his eyes open and could hardly believe it when he saw the few German guards being rounded up by a large contingent of British troops.

'Randy. Randy, wake up,' he urged, nudging him. 'Look, look. It really is over. We're going home.'

Randy mumbled something incoherent as he was overtaken by a fit of terrible shivering, and Freddy slipped back into oblivion.

Lubeck, Germany

Air Commodore Martin Black had never felt so weak and useless, despite the reviving hot tea and thick bully beef sandwich he'd just consumed, and the wonderful news that the war was over, and they were all going home. Determined to help his even weaker wingman, Roger Makepeace, who was suffering from trench foot and diphtheria, he gently hauled him to his feet, shocked at how light he seemed to be.

They'd been together since the start of the war, and would remain together now it was over. Waving away the offer of help from one of their American liberators, he put his arm around Roger's waist and steadied him. 'Come on, old chap,' he muttered. 'Mustn't give in now. We're on our way home to Cliffehaven.'

'Jolly good,' mumbled Roger, slumping against him as he tried to walk on his rotting feet, and breathe through the thick phlegm that was filling his lungs.

The Douglas C-47's engine rumbled on in its comfortingly familiar way as it waited on the landing strip. The long line of ex-prisoners of war weaved and hobbled towards it, their rising spirits giving them the energy they needed to forget about how ill and starving they were, for the troop carrier brought the promise of home and loved ones – of freedom, and the end of their ordeal.

There were six crew including the pilot, and the medical orderlies amongst them moved from man to man to assess their injuries and state of health in general before writing down notes, and nodding cheerfully. Martin and Roger slept for most of the journey, waking only when the C-47 landed with a soft bump and the engines screamed as the brakes were applied.

'Welcome home, guys,' yelled the Captain. 'The weather's a bit disappointing, but I guess, as Englishmen, you're all used to rain.'

The long hours of sitting had stiffened Martin's legs and it was a moment before he could ease the muscles enough to walk towards the open door. As he peered through the misty drizzle, his heart leapt with joy, for these were the green fields and familiar trees of home.

There was a host of American GIs to greet them and help them down the short ladder to the tarmac, where they were sprayed thoroughly with some sort of disinfectant to counteract the vermin they carried in their clothes and hair. Patriotic music was playing over a tannoy and they were told there was food and drink aplenty waiting for them in the reception hut.

Martin and Roger stood arm in arm, weaving slightly as they lifted their faces to the soft rain, breathing in the smell of aviation fuel and England as they held on to one another for balance, and gazed at the scenery they'd thought they'd never see again. Then, as one, they got painfully down on their knees and pressed their faces into the wet grass by the side of the runway, giving thanks for their return when so many of their comrades had not made it through.

'Actually, old chap,' muttered Roger a moment later, 'I don't think I can get up again.'

'Neither can I,' chuckled Martin.

They both collapsed into a heap, tears of laughter mingling with the rain as the Americans looked at them askance and scratched their heads at this strange Limey behaviour – which only made them laugh even harder.

8

Despite Ivy's persistent probing and barely disguised curiosity, Rita had kept Peter's proposal secret and only worn his ring when she'd gone to visit him. It wasn't that she was embarrassed by the grandness of it, but she knew it would elicit too many questions which she was not yet ready to answer. At first she'd worn it on a chain around her neck but then, terrified of losing or damaging it as she went about her work at the fire station, she'd hidden it away in a matchbox amongst the paraphernalia she kept in the bottom drawer of her bedside chest.

It worried her that she was unable to talk to anyone about her dilemma – not even Peggy, who was usually the first person she'd turn to in a crisis – but she soon realised she was waiting for her father to come home, because any decision she reached would affect him the most, and it was only right that he should be the first person she would confide in.

Rita had been on duty all day, so she hadn't been able to get to the Memorial to see Peter, and now it was too late for visitors. Perhaps it was for the best, she thought dispiritedly, for the news she'd received today wasn't exactly cheering, and Ivy would probably need a friend tonight if Andy hadn't taken her off to console her elsewhere.

She trudged up the steps into the kitchen that Monday evening to be greeted enthusiastically by a delighted Harvey. The sight of him made her smile, for Beach View hadn't felt the same without him.

'Hello, boy,' she said, making a huge fuss of him whilst trying to avoid her face being licked. 'Where did you spring from?'

'Ron brought him round just after you left for the fire station,' said Peggy, placing a fresh pot of tea on the table in front of Cissy who was painting her finger-nails. 'He and Rosie went off to Brighton on their honeymoon today, remember?'

She eyed Rita with some concern. 'Whatever's the matter, love? You seem to be walking about in a dream just lately.'

'Nothing,' Rita replied quickly. 'I just forgot, that's all. So much has happened lately it's all become a bit of a blur.'

'Sit down and drink a cuppa. Tea's almost ready.'

'I need to wash and change first. I'll be down in a tick.'

Rita escaped the kitchen and Peggy's attentions and took the stairs two at a time. Shoving through the bed-room door she came to an abrupt halt. Ivy was sitting on her bed, holding the matchbox in one hand, Rita's ring in the other, a triumphant grin on her face.

'I knew something were up,' she crowed. 'You sly old thing, keeping this beauty to yerself. If my Andy could have afforded to give me such a whopper, I'd be flashing it about all over town.'

Rita finally found her voice. 'How *dare* you go through my things, you nosy cow,' she stormed. 'If I'd wanted you to see it, I'd've shown you. Give it back.'

Ivy jumped to her feet on the bed, holding the ring aloft and out of Rita's reach. 'Don't call me a cow, you cow,' she yelled. 'You should'a told me you was engaged. I'm yer best mate, and I tell you everything.'

'Mates don't go poking about in other people's things,' shouted Rita, grabbing hold of Ivy's trouser legs and giving them a tug which unbalanced her, making her tumble to her knees on the rumpled bed. 'Give me back my ring before I slap you so hard you won't know what day of the week it is.'

Ivy bunched her fists. 'Oh, yeah? You and whose army?'

Thoroughly riled, Rita went for her, determined to wipe that smug look off Ivy's face. She made another grab for her ring, but was thwarted by a left hook from Ivy which almost knocked her senseless. 'Bitch,' she spat, shoving Ivy so hard, she hit her head on the metal bedframe.

'Manky mare!' Ivy leapt up, intent on punching her again.

They grappled and shouted, slapped, punched, clawed and swore, so didn't hear Peggy hurrying up the stairs, or the excited barking of Harvey who followed closely behind.

'What on *earth* is going on in here?' demanded Peggy from the doorway. 'Stop this at once.' She strode over to the bed and grabbed a handful of each girl's hair to yank them apart.

Both of them howled with pain. 'What you do that for?' gasped Ivy, rubbing her head. 'It was that barmy bint what started it.'

'It was you going through my things that started it,' barked Rita. 'Now give me back my ring.'

Ivy looked in horror at her empty hand. 'Gawd 'elp me, I ain't got it no more,' she gasped. 'I must've dropped it when you shoved me.'

'I'll do more than shove you if you've lost it,' Rita snapped.

Ignoring a furious Peggy and the spectators that had gathered outside the door, and accompanied by Harvey's excited barking, both girls began to frantically search through the bedclothes.

'I'm so sorry, Rita,' sobbed Ivy. 'I never meant for this to 'appen, really I didn't.'

'Shut up and keep looking,' ordered an equally tearful and desperate Rita as she dropped to her knees to search the floor beneath the bed.

'Is this it?' Peggy stood by the dressing table, the last of the sunlight flashing fire on the large pink diamond.

'Yes, oh yes,' gasped Rita, snatching the ring from her and anxiously examining it to make sure it hadn't been damaged before slipping it onto her finger.

Peggy turned to the others watching from the landing. 'The show's over. Get back to your tea, and take Harvey with you.'

Closing the door, she folded her arms and glared at both girls who were now sitting apart on their single beds. 'Well, I hope you're ashamed of yourselves,' she said. 'In all the years I've lived here, I've never seen anything like it. You aren't alley-cats to be scrapping and screeching like banshees, but young women who should know better – and I will have no more of it. Do you hear?'

'Yes, Aunt Peggy,' they mumbled in unison, their heads bowed.

Peggy struggled to keep a stern face, for both girls were so doleful, they looked like naughty children caught in the act of mischief. But this was not the time to be soft.

She perched on the dressing stool and eyed them both. 'Rita. You'd better explain about the ring – and Ivy, you'll keep quiet until she's had her say, then it will be your turn. Understood?'

Ivy looked mulish, but nodded in agreement.

Rita lifted her chin but couldn't quite manage to meet Peggy's gaze as she explained about Peter's proposal, the dilemma it had caused and the reason she'd kept it all secret.

'But why not confide in me?' Peggy asked, rather hurt that the girl hadn't trusted her to keep her secret, or come to her for advice and guidance on what was clearly an awful conundrum.

'I wanted to talk to you about it, really I did,' Rita said earnestly, 'but I felt it was only right that I should tell Dad first.'

She glanced over her shoulder at a sulking Ivy. 'I might have known that nosy cow couldn't help poking about when I wasn't here. Nothing's secret with her around.'

'That's not fair,' protested Ivy, jumping to her feet. 'I were looking for a match to light me fag, and thought you might have a box stashed away in that junk drawer of yours. How was I to know you'd hidden the bleeding crown jewels in there?'

'I don't smoke, as you very well know,' Rita retorted, 'so why look in my drawer for matches?'

'She has a point, Ivy,' said Peggy, 'and you admitted to me the other day that you were curious as to what was going on with Rita.'

Ivy wrung her hands in distress. 'I weren't being nosy. Not this time, I swear. I really were looking for matches, honest. She's been in such a funny mood these past few days I thought she must have put the box we use to light the gas in her drawer instead of back on the mantelpiece.'

Peggy regarded the woebegone little face and accepted she was telling the truth. Ivy might be nosy and quick tempered, but she wasn't a liar. 'That sounds logical,' she said. 'Rita, will you accept her explanation?'

Rita nodded, although reluctantly. 'If she'd only given me the ring when I asked, I wouldn't have flown off the handle, and none of this would have happened.'

'Then I suggest you stop keeping secrets and Ivy asks before she goes rooting about in other people's things – for whatever reason. Now shake hands, put this behind you and once you've washed your faces and combed your hair, come down for your tea, which must be dried up by now.'

The two girls rather sullenly faced one another and briefly shook hands. Knowing this was the best she could hope for while tempers were still frayed, Peggy got to her feet. 'I suggest you tidy this room as well before you come down, and then I'll put some iodine on that chin, Rita. You'll have a whopping bruise there come morning.'

Smiling to herself, she left the room and went downstairs. Their friendship was strong and would weather this spat, but my goodness, Ivy was a real scrapper, and by the look of that bruise, she could throw a mean punch.

Having tidied the room and themselves in an uneasy silence, they stared in shock at the bruises and scratches they'd inflicted on each other. 'I'm sorry, Rita,' muttered Ivy, gingerly touching the deep scratch on her cheekbone. 'I didn't mean for none of this to 'appen.'

Rita winced as she felt the swelling on her jaw. 'You certainly know how to throw a punch.'

'Yeah, sorry about that. Dad was an amateur boxer, see, and he taught me to defend meself when I was getting bullied as a kid.' She shot Rita a tentative smile. 'I don't know me own strength sometimes. Does it hurt?'

'Yeah, it bloody well does,' Rita retorted with a grimace. 'I'm going to have a right bruise there before the night's out.' She eyed the scratches on Ivy's face and felt deep shame that she could do such a thing to her best friend. 'I'm sorry about them; but you really wound me up, Ivy, and I lashed out without thinking.'

'It were me own stupid fault,' Ivy replied. 'But I were that excited for you, I didn't think neither.' She opened her arms. 'Forgive me?'

Rita hugged her, all anger wiped away by this loving olive branch. 'Of course. We're both guilty of being hot-headed.'

They drew apart and grinned at one another. 'I reckon you've got an announcement to make when we go down. Want me to 'old yer 'and?'

Rita shook her head. 'Thanks, but I can do it. They are family, after all.'

'I can't wait to see that snooty Cissy's face when she clocks that ring,' giggled Ivy. 'It must be worth a fortune.'

Rita thought of Cissy going green with envy. 'Come on, let's do it.' Clasping hands, they ran down the stairs and burst into the kitchen.

Every eye was on them, so Rita swept back her hair, ensuring the light flashed on the ring. 'Pete and I aren't engaged yet,' she said, noting the shock in Cissy's eyes. 'But this ring is a promise between us that we will decide when the time is right.'

'So what was all that ruckus about?' asked Cissy, her gaze still fixed on the ring. 'Surely you weren't fighting over a bit of rather vulgar pink glass he must have got from Woolworths?'

'I'm surprised you don't know a diamond from glass, Cissy,' Rita retorted, stung by her sneering reaction. She waved her hand under Cissy's nose so she got a proper eyeful. 'Big it might be, but it's the real thing.'

Peggy brought Rita and Ivy's supper plates from the warming oven and shot them both a wink, clearly delighted that they were friends again. 'Be careful, Cissy, you're in danger of letting your envy show. Stop staring and get on with your tea,' she reproved mildly.

'It must have cost a fortune,' Cissy breathed, her greedy gaze still glued to the diamond. 'How on earth could some roughneck Australian afford such a thing?'

'That's none of your business, really, Cissy, and I find you calling him a roughneck rather insulting. But to satisfy your curiosity, I'll tell you anyway.' Rita placed her hand flat on the table between them. 'He found the pink diamond and the gold whilst prospecting between shearing and crop-dusting seasons, so all it cost him was to get a jeweller to turn them both into a ring.'

'Gosh,' gasped Cissy.

'Gosh indeed,' piped up Cordelia, eyeing the stunning ring more closely. 'You're a very lucky girl, Rita, for not only is Peter handsome, clever and brave, but he's clearly adept at finding treasure as well.'

'I know I'm lucky,' replied Rita, blushing. 'But according to Pete, treasures like this are lying about in the Outback just waiting to be found.'

'That's true,' said Sarah. 'My grandfather found a nugget of gold that was worth over a hundred pounds when he was planting a new cane field back in the twenties, and another just as valuable when his horse pawed the ground in the home paddock and kicked it up.'

Silence fell whilst they all absorbed this, and Rita waited nervously for the questions that would inevitably follow. And then decided to take the bull by the horns and get in first.

'I haven't made my mind up about anything yet,' she said. 'So there's no point in bombarding me with questions. Dad will be home soon, and it's something I need to talk to him about. Until then, I'd be grateful if you'd keep everything you've seen and heard tonight within these walls. This ring is very valuable, and if word gets out about it, then there's a danger someone might break in to try and steal it.'

'Oh, lawks,' gasped Peggy. 'I hadn't thought of that. Perhaps you should keep it in a safe at the bank?'

'The thought had crossed my mind,' Rita admitted, 'but I do so love wearing it, and Peter would be very hurt if I locked it away.'

'Peter's sensible enough to know what's best,' said Cordelia. 'Talk it over with him, and see what he has to say.'

The conversation was interrupted by the insistent ringing of the telephone.

'That could be Mum,' breathed Ivy, leaping to her feet and dashing into the hall, only to return moments later, her little face a picture of disappointment. 'It's Peter calling from the public telephone at the Memorial.'

Rita squeezed her shoulder in sympathy and hurried out to retrieve the receiver from the chair. 'Hello? Peter? It's not like you to call so late. What's up?'

'They're chucking me out first thing tomorrow morning,' he replied. 'I didn't want you coming here to find me gone and giving you a fright.'

Rita's pulse raced at the thought she might never have the chance to see him again, and she gripped the receiver until her knuckles went white. 'Where are they sending you? Is it local or miles away? Are you being returned to the RAAF base, or some billet near the docks?'

He chuckled. 'If you'd let me get a word in edgeways, I'll tell you. I'm going to Cliffe House, which is even nearer to you than this place. They're pleased with my progress and don't think I need any more treatment for my head injury, but I will have to continue with the physiotherapy for a while longer. Isn't that good news?'

'The best,' she sighed, the tension easing from her shoulders. 'When are the visiting hours at Cliffe?'

'From nine until nine. As I told you before, it's more of a hotel than a hospital and the rules are far more relaxed.'

'I'll come straight over the minute I finish my shift, so it'll be about lunchtime.'

'That's an unusually short shift. What's going on?'

Rita lowered her voice in case Ivy overheard, for it was clear Andy had yet to tell her the news. 'My boss, John Hicks, has had to cut the hours of all the stand-in staff now some of the regulars have returned from their war duties to take up their jobs again. He's keeping me and Ivy's Andy on part-time until the end of the month, but then he'll have to let us go. John didn't like doing it, but we all knew our jobs were only for the duration of the war, so we really can't complain.'

'That's tough,' murmured Peter. 'Especially for Andy and Ivy who were saving up to get married.' His tone lightened. 'Talking of which, it will leave you free to spend time with your dad and give you the chance to make up your mind about marrying me.'

'It certainly will,' she said with a lightness she didn't feel. 'But I am really worried about your very valuable ring, and was wondering if you'd mind me putting it in a safety deposit box. With so many out of work, it could prove too big a temptation if I flash it about, and I don't want Beach View burgled.'

There was a long pause before he spoke again. 'You're right, Rita. I hadn't thought of that. I'll miss not seeing it on your finger, but it's for the best. I'd hate to hear you've been robbed of it.'

'I'll go into town before I come to see you,' she replied just as the pips went.

'Gotta go. No more change. See you tomorrow, darling,' he managed before the line was cut.

Rita returned to the kitchen to find that Andy had arrived and Ivy was in tears.

'I'm sorry, love, but there's nothing I can do about it,' he murmured as he held Ivy close. 'But John has promised to try his best to get me a job with one of the London fire stations. And even if it is only part-time, it'll be better than nothing.'

'It feels as if the end of the war has brought us nothing but bad luck,' she sobbed. 'What we going to do, Andy? We'll never get a place of our own at this rate, and what with your bad 'earing, it ain't likely anyone will take you on in the Smoke.'

'John promised to write a glowing reference, paying particular attention to me 'earing,' he replied stoutly. 'I done five years down 'ere and not put a foot wrong, so I've earnt the right to a decent job with the London fire brigade. It'll all work out, Ivy, I promise. So dry your tears, gel, and give me a lovely smile before I go back to Auntie Gloria's to finish the painting before her first lot of guests arrive.'

'You're going out again?'

His expression was mournful, clearly torn between staying and his duty to his aunt. 'I 'ave to, love. We need the money more than ever now.'

'I'll keep her company,' said Rita. 'Go and finish that painting, and I'll treat Ivy to a pint at the Anchor. After all, we're both in the same boat, and as Ruby's in there tonight, we can have a good old chinwag and put that smile back on Ivy's face.'

'Thanks, Rita. You're a diamond.' He pulled a couple of half-crowns out of his paint-smeared dungaree pocket. 'Have one on me.' He kissed Ivy's forehead and made his escape before she could protest.

Peggy felt sad for both girls as she watched Rita guide Ivy out of the kitchen, and their return some minutes later in their overcoats. Ivy looked a little more cheerful, and the girls were holding hands. Neither of them had had a good day, but their friendship had proved strong enough to overcome what fate had handed out to them. The end of the war had certainly changed things in the most unexpected way.

She drew five bob out of her purse and made Rita take it. 'Buy Ruby a drink while you're at it, and try not to wake us all up when you come home.'

'Thanks, Aunt Peggy,' Rita replied, kissing her cheek. 'I'm sorry about earlier.'

'So am I,' said Ivy. 'You won't stay cross with us for too long, will yer?'

Peggy chuckled. 'You're a naughty pair, but you know very well I always forgive you. Now get out of here, forget all your troubles for a while and enjoy your evening.'

9

Briar Cottage stood at the end of a rutted lane which opened out into fields, and overlooked the town from the northern slopes. Roger, Freddy, Kitty and Charlotte had bought it so the men had a home to come to when not on ops at RAF Cliffe. They'd renovated and extended the rather dilapidated bungalow, and now it provided a cosy home for Freddy's sister Kitty, her baby, Faith, and his wife Charlotte and ten-month-old twins, David and Hope.

The tension had been rising since the declaration of peace, for Roger and Freddy had been prisoners of war for some while, and the young women were on tenterhooks awaiting news of their liberation. RAF Bomber Squadron's Operation Exodus had been up and running since before VE Day when it became clear the Germans were surrendering, and the camps were being emptied of prisoners; now the AAF had joined in to bring the POWs home, so there were numerous flights over the Channel every day.

'My biggest worry is that Freddy might not be picked up,' said Charlotte as they sat knitting in the kitchen by the range fire. 'With his camp being in Poland, the Russians might have got to them first.'

'The Russians wouldn't harm them,' soothed Kitty. 'They're on our side, remember, so they won't hold a grudge against our POWs.'

'But they could have freed them and left them to wander and get lost,' persisted Charlotte.

Kitty put down her knitting and patted Charlotte's arm. 'You're letting your imagination run away with you, love. I'm sure that if the Russians did get to them first, they would have made arrangements for them to make contact with our troops. They're probably on their way home and we haven't heard anything because there are so many prisoners, it takes time to sort them all out.'

Charlotte nodded, but Kitty had known her since their schooldays, and could tell she remained unconvinced. She gave a sigh, dumped her knitting and went to fill the kettle. She was worried about Freddy too, for there had been very little news of him once he and Randy had been moved to Stalag IV. At least she knew Roger was alive, and that he was still with Martin, for there had been a few cards from them before Christmas. It was the lack of communication and information from RAF HQ that was getting to them both, and even with their strong ties to the service – they'd both flown planes as ATA girls – it seemed the powers that be were remaining tight-lipped.

She rubbed the stump of her leg which always played up when the weather was damp, and wondered if winter would ever end. Apart from a very few sunny, pleasant days, it had been overcast with squally showers and gusty winds – not at all like May. The fruit trees they'd planted in the back garden should be in bud by now, and the summer vegetables shooting up, but the ground was sodden and everything was struggling. There was even talk of rationing bread and potatoes because of the terrible wheat harvest at the end of last year, and the potato crops rotting in the ground.

Kitty gave a deep sigh and adjusted the strap on her prosthetic leg in the hope it would ease the ache in her stump. Life was difficult enough without the added strictures of rationing those staples.

'I'll make the tea,' said Charlotte, taking charge of the whistling kettle. 'You've clearly done more than enough today. Why don't you sit down, get that leg off and relax?'

'I think I will,' Kitty replied. 'The walk home from town was too much after standing in the queue at the grocer's for so long.'

'You should have let me do the queuing,' said Charlotte, filling the teapot and giving the leaves a vigorous stir. 'You're too stubborn for your own good at times.'

'You were busy at the clinic with the twins,' Kitty reminded her, sighing with pleasure as she released the final strap and set the prosthetic leg to one side. 'Besides, I'm perfectly capable of doing the shopping,' she added, giving her stump a jolly good rub.

Charlotte was about to pour the tea when the telephone on the dresser began to ring. The two young women looked at one another in dread, and then Charlotte quickly grabbed the receiver.

'Hello? Yes, this is Charlotte Pargeter.'

Kitty anxiously strained to hear what was being said at the other end as Charlotte listened, her face slowly draining of colour.

'Thank you, Air Commodore. We shall be waiting – with the children. So you'd better make suitable arrangements.'

Kitty could hear the loud protest at the other end of the line before it was cut short by Charlotte unceremoniously replacing the receiver.

'It's Freddy,' Charlotte said. 'He's been flown to some place in Buckinghamshire where he's been admitted to hospital.' Her voice wavered and tears shone in her eyes as she took Kitty's hand. 'He's very ill, Kitty, so the RAF are flying us up there from Cliffe.'

The shock hit Kitty so hard she couldn't speak, couldn't move at all.

'We have to be ready in half an hour. Someone's picking us up to drive us to the airfield.' Charlotte was suddenly all motion, moving about the kitchen, dampening down the range fire, putting things away, gathering up coats and hats, and straightening chairs.

Kitty slowly reached for her tin leg, her numb fingers fumbling with the straps. The idea that Freddy was in a really bad way was simply impossible to contemplate. He'd pull through, she was sure of it. He was her brother and like a cat he had nine lives, surviving all sorts of scrapes and disasters. He was the boy who could ride horses and motorbikes with such speed and skill it took your breath away; the boy who'd given her the thirst to learn to fly; the beloved naughty brother who was forever getting into mischief and breaking hearts wherever he went. She could see him now, with his black curly, wayward hair; his dark, flashing eyes in that handsome face which always seemed to be smiling with the sheer joy of being alive.

'He'll be all right,' she mumbled. 'Freddy's never had a day's illness in his life. The RAF is just being very careful because of who he is and our history of flying for them.'

Charlotte knelt down and finished fixing the last buckle. 'Don't you think I pray that's the case?' she asked, the tears streaming down her face. 'But the RAF wouldn't have gone to so much trouble if they'd thought his situation wasn't serious enough to warrant it. Oh, Kitty, he must be in a very bad state indeed. I can only pray we'll get to him in time.'

She collapsed against Kitty, and they held one another tightly for a moment, trying to absorb the awful possibility that they might lose the man they loved so much, and not have the chance to say good-bye to him.

'We must hurry and get the children ready for the journey,' said Charlotte, pulling away and once again becoming a whirlwind of activity. 'We'll need to pack overnight things and changes of clothing for the children as well as ourselves – and then there's nappies and bottles, tins of baby food and blankets. It'll be cold in that plane, so we'll need our warmest coats.'

Kitty determinedly pulled herself together and hurried off to pack an overnight bag for herself and Faith – although she had no idea of how long they would be away. She offered to help Charlotte, but soon realised her best friend needed to keep busy, or she'd fall apart. Leaving Faith to sleep for as long as possible, she went back into the kitchen and telephoned Peggy to let her know what was happening.

Peggy was distraught for all of them, and made Kitty promise she'd stay in touch, but the call was cut short by a discreet knock at the front door. The RAF driver had arrived. It was time to leave.

Both Kitty and Charlotte had flown Oxfords during the war, and it was whilst piloting an Oxford that Kitty had been forced into a crash landing which had resulted in her losing most of one leg. The Ox Box, as it was lovingly known, had been used as an air taxi during hostilities, ferrying personnel back and forth between different airfields and factories, and carrying vital engine parts to where they were needed.

Kitty and Charlotte climbed in to find that three small canvas cots had been firmly strapped into the seats, and although the babies cried a bit when the plane took off, they were soon asleep again, lulled by the steady throb of the engine. 'They're natural fliers,' said Charlotte tearfully, 'just like their fathers.'

Kitty nodded and concentrated on the flight path their pilot was taking. It was pitch-black outside, the rain streaking the windows, with no sign of a moon to guide them. Freddy had to be all right.

They arrived at RAF Oakley at three in the morning, and were driven straight to the military hospital in the Commanding Officer's car. A nurse took charge of the children and whisked them away to the nursery, and then Matron led them along endless corridors to the Intensive Care Ward.

'Wing Commander Pargeter has, amongst many other things, typhoid fever and has had to be isolated in a side room,' she said quietly. 'He's in a bad way, I'm afraid, and mostly in a state of delirium, so don't be too upset if he doesn't acknowledge you.'

'He'll pull through, though, won't he?' asked Charlotte, on the brink of tears.

'We are doing all we can, Mrs Pargeter, but I should warn you that he's extremely weak and it's doubtful whether he has the strength to fight the many infections he's suffering from. You should be prepared for the worst, I'm afraid.' She handed Charlotte and Kitty masks and gowns. 'You must wear these to protect yourselves,' she said gravely.

Charlotte became ashen faced, her hands fumbling with the mask and gown, her eyes haunted as she fought to keep a stoic resemblance of calm. She and Kitty clasped hands to bolster their courage and followed Matron into the dimly lit room. But nothing could have prepared them for the shocking sight that greeted them, and they stood there unable to equate this stranger with the man they knew and loved.

Freddy's handsome face was gaunt, his sunken eyes and cheeks making him look like an old man. His hair had been shaved off, frostbite had attacked his ears, lips and nose, and his skin was the colour of parchment. He lay muttering and rolling his head against the pillow, his eyelids twitching, his almost fleshless hands clawing at the bedclothes.

Charlotte approached the bed and reached for his hand. 'Freddy? It's me, Charlotte. Kitty's here too, so please wake up, darling.'

There was no response, even when Kitty took his other hand.

'You're home, Freddy,' Kitty urged. 'It's all over and we're here to take care of you.' She gripped his bony fingers. 'Come on, Freddy,' she urged. 'You've got to fight this thing and live to see your twins growing up.'

His eyelids fluttered and he took a rattling breath. 'Twins?' he managed.

'Yes, Freddy,' said Charlotte eagerly. 'You never did things by halves, did you, and we've got twins. David and Hope.' She gripped his hand. 'Oh, darling, you must get better. They are so beautiful.'

Freddy was struggling to breathe, his face streaked with sweat as his thin chest rose and fell with the effort. 'Twins,' he rasped again.

'Would you like to see them, Freddy?' urged Charlotte. 'They're here. I could bring them to you.'

'I wouldn't advise it,' said Matron quickly. 'The infections are contagious, and you'd be putting the children at terrible risk.'

'They could have masks,' said Charlotte. 'If Freddy could only see them, it might make all the difference.' The tears were streaming down her face. 'Please, Matron. Please,' she begged.

Freddy's fight to breathe was the only sound in the room as Matron hesitated for a long moment. 'I'll see what I can do,' she said finally and left the room.

Kitty and Charlotte sat down next to Freddy's bed and gripped his hands as they watched him. 'It's so lovely to have you home again, Freddy,' murmured Kitty through her tears. 'I know you're in a very bad way, but you've got to keep fighting. There's so much to live for, and the twins need their father.'

Freddy muttered something incomprehensible as he rolled his head against the damp pillow. Then, without warning, he sat up and stared at something on the other side of the room. 'Randy. Wake up. They're here. They're here. We're going home.' And then he collapsed back onto the pillow and was still.

Charlotte looked at Kitty with tear-filled eyes. 'Does that mean Cissy's Randy could be here too?' she asked.

Kitty shrugged. 'Maybe. Perhaps Matron can tell us if he is.'

All speculation came to a halt as the door opened and Matron appeared. She was pushing two specially adapted bassinets that were normally used to provide oxygen to premature or struggling sick babies, and which were fully covered in Perspex. She wheeled them into the room and closed the door. 'They are a bit of a tight fit, but it was the best I could do in the circumstances,' she said solemnly.

David was yelling fit to bust as he squirmed and fought against the restricting shield, and Hope was working herself up to a screaming fit for having been woken up.

The noise seemed to rouse Freddy, and his eyes opened slightly.

'Your son and daughter have got good lungs,' said Charlotte, taking charge of the bassinets and bringing them to the side of the bed so Freddy could see them. 'Say hello to David and Hope.'

He reached out a bony finger and touched each cot in turn, his drawn face slowly breaking into a soft smile. 'David,' he breathed. 'Hope.' He tore his gaze from them and looked at Charlotte. 'Beautiful, like their mother,' he sighed before closing his eyes.

'We need you to get through this, Freddy,' urged Charlotte. 'Please keep fighting for all our sakes.'

There was no response from Freddy, and it seemed that short moment of clarity had exhausted him, for he lay very still – too still – and Charlotte grabbed his hand. 'Freddy? Freddy?'

Kitty was on her feet at the other side of the bed, pulse racing, fearing the worst – knowing in her aching heart that Freddy could no longer hear anything, but praying she was mistaken and that he'd merely passed out.

Matron pushed through to his side, felt for a pulse both in his neck and his wrist.

Kitty and Charlotte held their breath as they watched her, their silent prayers clear in their eyes.

Matron dipped her chin, and gave a deep, regretful sigh. 'I'm sorry, Mrs Pargeter, but he's gone from us and is finally at peace.'

10

The news of Freddy Pargeter's death had come as a terrible blow to Peggy and the others at Beach View, for they'd all liked him very much and had thought of him as indestructible. Peggy had gone to Briar Cottage on the girls' brief return to offer help and consolation, and discovered that plans had been made to fly Freddy's body home to his parents in Argentina, and Charlotte would be accompanying him with her twins.

Kitty's husband, Roger Makepeace, was making a rapid recovery in a Surrey hospital and once he'd been discharged they would fly out to join the others. They would stay for a while and mourn as a family.

Peggy's son-in-law, Martin, was also making good progress in the same hospital as Roger, and Anne had telephoned in great excitement to tell her that he was expected to travel down to Somerset to join her and the children within the next week.

But of Randolph Stevens, there had been no news, and as the American authorities refused to tell her anything since she wasn't registered as a family member, Cissy became ever more fearful that something must have happened to him. She moped about the house unable to settle to anything and spent half her time talking to her girlfriends from Cliffe on the telephone. Peggy dreaded to think what her bill would be this quarter, but Cissy had promised to pay her share, and as the calls seemed to cheer her, Peggy was willing to accept the arrangement.

A week after Charlotte had left for Argentina, Peggy, Daisy and Cordelia had the kitchen to themselves. It was early Saturday morning, and as it promised to be a fine day for once, Cissy hadn't moaned about taking Harvey for a walk on the hills, and had promised to be back in time to help with the special lunch. Peggy understood that her daughter needed to keep busy during this difficult time, and could only pray that Randy had survived and would get in touch soon.

Ivy was at the Crown serving breakfast to Gloria's first set of holidaymakers before tackling the bedrooms, and would, no doubt, be on tenterhooks all day until Andy returned from his job interview at Walthamstow fire station which John Hicks had arranged. He'd left on the train last night to be sure he was on time for the early interview, and had taken the opportunity to stay with his mother – Gloria's sister – whom he hadn't seen for almost three years. No one knew when to expect him back.

Sarah was already at the bus station awaiting her younger sister Jane's arrival now Jane's mysterious job with the MOD had come to an end and she was free to visit. Rita was dashing about like a headless chicken as she prepared to meet her father's train, and left in a whirlwind of excitement, banging the back door behind her; fortunately not disturbing Danuta who was having a well-earned lie-in after a long night helping to deliver a baby.

'It's certainly going to be a busy day with all the comings and goings,' said Peggy, pouring out a second cup of tea and keeping an eye on Daisy who was playing with her dolls at the other end of the table. 'Jane will, of course, be able to move in with Sarah, but Cissy's being very awkward about moving out of the basement and refuses point blank to go upstairs, so I have no idea where I can put Jack Smith.'

'Cissy seems determined to be awkward about everything,' sniffed Cordelia. 'If she was younger, and my daughter, she'd get a good smacked bottom. Put Jack upstairs on the top floor if he hasn't made other arrangements. He's earned a comfortable billet after what he's been through.'

Cordelia regarded Peggy evenly. 'But I get the feeling it's not where to accommodate everyone that's really troubling you.'

'I'm worried about Ivy,' Peggy admitted. 'It's been over a week since she wrote to her parents, and yet there hasn't been a peep out of them. I'm beginning to wonder if something has happened and they're reluctant to pass on bad news by phone or letter.' She gave a sigh. 'I do wish I knew what was going on up there. It's all very frustrating.'

'I agree it is a worry,' said Cordelia, setting aside her morning newspaper. 'But I do think you're making too much of things, Peggy. By what I've learned about them from Ivy, they seem to be simple, poorly educated people who probably don't find it easy to write letters, let alone know how to use a public telephone to make a reverse charge call. I'm sure that's all it is, so there's little point in getting into a frazzle over it. Today is going to be hectic enough, without the added worry over Ivy and whatever is going on in London. I'm sure Andy will do his best to get over to Hackney after his interview to find out for himself.'

She regarded Peggy solemnly over her half-moon spectacles. 'If my memory serves me correctly, there's a very good train service between the two places.'

'How on earth do you know that?'

'I did some voluntary nursing up there during the first war,' Cordelia replied.

'I never knew that.'

'Well, that just goes to show we all have our little secrets, doesn't it?' Cordelia's eyes twinkled behind her glasses. 'I bet there are a few things you've never told anyone.'

Peggy smiled back, for indeed there were. Yet Cordelia's take on the situation with Ivy was probably correct, even though she knew she'd worry over her until Andy returned home to confirm that all was well with her family in London, and that his interview had been successful. The young couple certainly needed some good news after losing their jobs.

Her thoughts automatically drifted to Kitty and Charlotte who must be going through agonies of grief over Freddy, and then on to Fran and Robert who would be leaving Ireland this weekend – perhaps were already on their way to London if things hadn't turned out well. What the outcome of their visit to Fran's family would be she had no idea, but she prayed that at least one of them would show some Christian feeling and understanding towards her.

'And you can stop fretting over Fran as well,' said Cordelia. 'She's an adult with a husband and has made her choice to visit that uncaring family of hers. She knows the probable outcome but has a strong enough character to overcome any further rejection, and leave them behind with her head held high. Robert will look after her. It's what husbands are for,' she added briskly.

Peggy chuckled. 'My goodness, Cordy, you're being a bit sharp this morning.'

'Well, I have worries of my own,' she replied with unusual tetchiness. 'I've just discovered that Ruby is struggling to pay the rent on my bungalow now her friend has left, and her hours at the factory have been cut. She came round yesterday morning to tell me she'd have to leave by the end of the month.'

Cordelia sighed. 'Of course I offered to lower the rent, but she wouldn't accept what I suspect she saw as charity, and said she'd be moving in with Stan and the others at the station cottage until her Canadian chap came down on leave.' She sniffed and folded her arms. 'Which is utterly ridiculous. That cottage is bursting at the seams as it is.'

'You should have told her she could come here. She must know she'd always be welcome, and I could easily put a third bed in with Ivy and Rita.'

'I did take the liberty of offering that alternative, but she said she didn't want to burden you, knowing how busy you already are.'

'Stuff and nonsense,' snorted Peggy. 'I'll go and see her tomorrow morning and talk some sense into her.'

'Good luck with that,' Cordelia replied dryly. 'Ruby's proud and will see any offers of help as a failure on her part to be able to cope. Besides, she and Mike have now got permission to get married before he's sent back to Canada, so it will be his responsibility to see she's comfortably housed and looked after financially until she can join him, and I've decided not to rent the bungalow out again, so they can move back in after the wedding.'

'Then I really don't understand why you're fretting,' said Peggy, her thoughts already delightfully occupied with wedding plans.

'Your chicks have become mine as well,' Cordelia replied. 'I've come to love them all over the years, and always admired Ruby for her spirit in the way she handled things with her dreadful mother and that rotter of a husband. Of course I fret over all of them. You don't hold the monopoly on worrying, Peggy.'

Peggy chuckled and went round the table to give the old woman a gentle hug. 'Don't ever change, Cordy,' she murmured. 'You're perfect, just the way you are.'

The tender moment was broken by the sound of footsteps on the basement stairs, and stifled giggles outside the kitchen door. Peggy frowned and then broke into a broad smile as Sarah followed Jane into the room.

Jane dropped the large case on the floor with some relief and held out her arms. 'Hello, Auntie Peg. Remember me?'

Peggy almost didn't recognise the sophisticated young woman who stood there with such self-assurance in a beautifully tailored linen suit and high-heeled shoes. 'Oh, Jane, of course I do,' she breathed, rushing to hug her. 'But my goodness – look how grown up and gorgeous you are! What happened to that shy little girl who loved looking after the horses at the dairy and had a pigtail hanging down her back?'

Jane laughed and patted her fair hair which had been fashionably styled and cut into a fetching bob. 'She grew up, Auntie Peg, and learned to live in the real world. Are the horses still there?'

'Indeed they are,' Peggy replied. 'And I'm sure they'd love to see you.'

'I am here, you know,' grumbled Cordelia. 'How about giving your Great-Aunt Cordy a hug too?'

Jane apologised swiftly and gathered Cordelia to her. 'You're just the way I remember you,' she said softly. 'I'm so glad to see you looking so well.'

'It's all the love and care I get from Peggy that keeps me perky,' Cordelia replied. 'Living with these young things makes me forget how old I am.' Her smile was rather smug. 'I'm eighty now, you know.'

Jane laughed. 'And you don't look a day over seventy.'

Cordelia twittered and blushed. 'I wish that were true, but I was always a sucker for a bit of flattery.'

Peggy's heart was warmed by this loving reunion. She swiftly put the kettle on to refresh the pot for the second time, and Jane went to renew her acquaintance with Daisy who'd only been a few weeks old when she and Sarah had arrived at Beach View.

Settling back in her chair as she waited for the kettle to boil, Peggy watched Daisy chattering away to Jane, unfazed by this new arrival in her home, and perfectly at ease. If nothing else, she thought, this war has made my daughter very sociable.

'I suppose Sarah's kept you up to date with all the goings-on here, so I won't go into details,' she said. 'Everyone's out at the moment, but you'll get to see them all at lunchtime. We're celebrating Rita's dad's return as well as yours. Danuta is upstairs asleep, and Ivy, who you've yet to meet, is out at work.'

'It was lovely to hear that Ron and Rosie have finally tied the knot,' said Jane, easing off her suit jacket to reveal a cream silk blouse with a sweetheart bow at the neck. 'I honestly thought they'd never manage it what with all the dramas. But you must miss Harvey now he's living at the Anchor.'

'He's visiting at the moment while they're on honeymoon,' Sarah told her. 'So be prepared to get pounced upon when Cissy brings him back from his walk.'

Jane giggled. 'Perhaps I'd better get changed and take my stockings off before they get ripped to shreds by his claws. I remember how enthusiastic he could get. Where am I sleeping?'

'In with me,' said Sarah cheerfully. 'It'll be quite like old times.'

Jane picked up her case. 'How utterly spiffing,' she said in delight. 'Lead on, Sarah.'

The two girls hurried out of the kitchen. Peggy freshened the teapot and shared a knowing smile with Cordelia. 'I wouldn't mind betting we won't see either of them until lunchtime,' she said.

'They have a lot of catching up to do,' replied Cordelia. 'Letters and cards and the occasional telephone call aren't as satisfying as actually being face-to-face after such a long separation. I wonder if we'll get to hear more about her chap, and the plans she has now she's free of the MOD?'

'We will if she wants us to know,' said Peggy, rather doubting if Jane would reveal anything much, for she wasn't the young, naïve chatterbox who'd left Beach View all those years ago, but a self-contained young woman.

She'd just poured the rather weak tea when the telephone jangled in the hall, so she put the cosy on the pot and went to answer it, thinking it was probably yet another call from London for Cissy.

'Hello, Peggy,' said Miss Gardener from the exchange. 'I have a caller on the line wishing to make a return charge call from a London call-box. She said her name wouldn't mean anything to you, but it concerned Ivy. Do you wish to take it?'

Peggy sat down on the hall chair with a thump, and gripped the receiver. 'Yes, thank you, Vera. I've been expecting it.'

'Putting you through.'

'Hello? Is that Ivy?'

The voice at the other end sounded rather brisk, and Peggy caught the faint hint of a foreign accent which she couldn't place. Whoever it was definitely couldn't be one of Ivy's relatives. 'I'm Mrs Reilly, Ivy's landlady,' she said warily. 'Who is this?'

'My name is Hilde De Vries. I am sorry I have taken so long to reply to Ivy's letter, but I wanted to be sure of all the facts before I made this telephone call.'

Peggy swallowed the lump in her throat, and thanked the Lord that Ivy was out of the house, for the poor little girl had been through enough just lately. 'It isn't good news, is it?' she asked fearfully.

'I'm sorry, but no. Is Ivy there? May I speak with her?'

'She's at work and I think it would be best if you tell me, so I can break it gently to her instead of hearing it from a stranger over the telephone. No offence intended,' she added hastily.

'I understand,' Hilde replied. 'I take no offence.'

There was a long pause and Peggy could hear traffic sounds in the background, mingled with those of children playing with a football in the street. Her heart thudded, and she discovered her hands were shaking as she lit a cigarette.

And then the woman began to speak, more hesitantly now, her voice made unsteady by her emotions.

Peggy listened in horrified silence until the woman finally came to the end of her tragic story. She couldn't begin to imagine how on earth she could tell Ivy – but tell her she must, and then do her very best to comfort and help her through the devastation.

'I am sorry for such terrible news. Please pass on my condolences, and if Ivy wishes to talk to me, then she is welcome to call on me at any time.'

'Thank you, Hilde,' Peggy managed. 'Thank you for taking the time to discover what happened. It can't have been easy for you.'

'I work with displaced persons who have many sad stories to tell, so I have learned to ask questions in the right places and keep strong.' She fell silent for a moment. 'Thank you, Mrs Reilly. I feel you are strong too and will help Ivy with much love and understanding. Now I must go. There is someone knocking on my door.'

Peggy heard the click at the other end and slowly replaced the receiver. Drained of energy, she found she was unable to find the strength to get up from the chair, so when the telephone rang again, she barely managed to lift the receiver.

'I'm so sorry, Peggy,' said Miss Gardener. 'I overheard part of that, but you can rest assured it will go no further. The charge for the call is one shilling and sixpence. Horribly steep, I know, and I'd let you off if it was up to me, but the rules are very strict.'

'That's all right, Vera,' Peggy replied with weary sadness and cut the connection.

She sat there and finished her cigarette, wondering how on earth she could get through the rest of the day without telling the girl and ruining what should be a happy homecoming for Jack and Jane. Had that been Andy knocking on the Dutch woman's door? If so then perhaps it would be better to wait until he came home – but was that simply putting off the evil moment? And with Ivy due back from Gloria's within the hour, could she sustain such a deception on a girl she'd come to love as a member of the family?

Unable to face the others just yet, and needing time to think, she went into her bedroom and sank onto the bed. Jim's photograph stood on the bedside cabinet, and she kissed his handsome face. 'It never ends, does it, Jim? Just when you think it's all over and everyone's safe, something like this happens and knocks you for six.'

She bit her lip, her thoughts on little Ivy who'd already faced such terrors and tragedies throughout the war with enormous courage and fortitude. It simply wasn't fair. And then there were her younger brother and sister billeted down in Salisbury, and her two elder brothers who were with the merchant navy and due shore-leave any day soon. She should have asked Hilde if the authorities would inform them, or if that difficult task was to be left to Ivy.

She sat staring into space until the ticking bedside clock reminded her that time was running away with her, and if she didn't stir her stumps, Ivy would be here and it would be too late to tell her in private.

Rising from the bed, she combed her hair, repaired her lipstick and traipsed back into the kitchen to find Cissy drinking tea while Harvey squirmed at Cordelia's feet, begging to have his tummy rubbed.

'I see nothing came for me in the post this morning,' said Cissy. 'Has Philippa telephoned, or Clarissa?'

Peggy shook her head and took off her apron. 'I have to go out. When you've finished your tea, Cissy, you can make a start on doing the stuffing for the chicken, and finish peeling the last of the winter carrots.'

'I'm too tired and grubby to start cooking,' Cissy replied on a sigh. 'Harvey ran off and wouldn't come when I called, so I had to chase him for absolute miles. I need a long soak in the bath before I'll be fit for anything.'

'Don't be dramatic, Cissy,' Peggy said briskly, reaching for her coat and scarf. 'You know very well that he always comes back to the track you started from. All you had to do was wait for him there. As for long soaks in baths, they're a thing of the past. Two inches of tepid water at this time of the morning is all you'll get if you're lucky.'

Cissy raised a severely plucked eyebrow. 'Gosh, what bit you this morning, Mother?'

'Life in general,' she retorted. 'Now get off your bottom and lend a hand for once. Dinner for nine doesn't appear like magic; someone has to cook it.'

'All right, all right,' Cissy sighed. 'You're clearly in a foul mood this morning, which doesn't bode well for the rest of the day. And what's so important you have to rush off anyway?'

'Cissy, don't talk to your mother like that,' scolded Cordelia who was slicing green beans into a basin at the table. 'You've barely lifted a finger since you came home, and it isn't as if you have anything else to do.'

'There's little point in trying for some boring office job when Randy could turn up any minute,' the girl replied sullenly. 'And I keep my room tidy as well as walking the dog and looking after Daisy.'

Cordelia ignored her and regarded Peggy sharply. 'Where are you off to, Peggy? Has it got something to do with that telephone call?'

'Yes.' Peggy tied her scarf under her chin. 'I don't know how long I'll be, Cordy, but I'd really appreciate it if you could take over here and watch Daisy. Get Jane and Sarah to help you with the lunch.' To avoid further questions, she hurried down the cellar steps and out into the bright sunshine.

Peggy walked quickly towards the Crown, which stood halfway up the High Street, her footsteps faltering as she approached the door. Glancing in the window of the main bar, she saw Gloria standing there staring into space, her expression very solemn. There didn't seem to be any sign of Ivy.

'I were just about to ring you,' said Gloria in a stage whisper, her gaze darting towards the stairs as she opened the door to Peggy. 'I'm guessing you've 'eard from Andy too?'

Before Peggy could reply, Gloria rushed on. 'He phoned about an hour ago and was being very mysterious, ordering me to keep Ivy here until he gets back. Which should be quite soon if the trains are running on time. Do you know what it's all about?'

'Unfortunately, yes, I do.' Peggy took Gloria's arm. 'Where's Ivy?'

'I sent 'er back up to do one of the rooms again, though it didn't need it. Is it her family, Peg?' ·

Peggy nodded and quickly gave Gloria the gist of the conversation she'd had with the Dutch woman.

'Ow, Gawd,' said Gloria, the ready tears threatening to smear her mascara. 'Poor little cow. No wonder Andy were so worried about 'er. He must've been to the house and found out. Should we wait for 'im to get 'ere, or what?'

Ivy solved the dilemma by hurtling down the stairs into the saloon bar to stand squarely before them, arms folded, expression determined. 'Right, you'd better tell me what's going on, 'cos I know something's up. You've had me running about like a blue-arsed fly all morning doing things what don't need doing – and now Auntie Peg's 'ere, it's gotta be serious.'

Gloria's shoulders sagged. 'Oh Ivy,' she sighed. 'You're too sharp fer yer own good, ain't yer?' She took a deep breath and put her arm around the girl, gently drawing her to her side. 'It were Andy on the blower. He's on his way back and wants to meet you here. He's got something to tell yer, see?'

Ivy's face lit up. 'Has he got the job?'

'I dunno, he didn't say,' Gloria replied with a vagueness that didn't ring true to Ivy.

Her hopes rose, convinced now that Andy had been successful, and had ordered Gloria not to say anything because he wanted to tell her himself. But then she saw the solemn expressions on the faces of the two women she most trusted, and knew something was very wrong. 'What is it? What's happened?'

'Ivy, love,' began Peggy, taking her hand. 'There's something …' She got no further, for the pub doors wheezed open and there was Andy looking grim-faced.

All of Ivy's hopes plummeted. 'Oh, Andy,' she breathed, going into his arms. 'There'll be other interviews. It don't matter, love. I didn't want to live in rotten old Walthamstow anyways.'

Andy held her tightly, his face drawn with anxiety. 'That's a shame, 'cos I got the job, and the flat what goes with it,' he said gruffly. 'It seems John Hicks gave me such a glowing reference they'd already made up their mind to take me on even before the interview.'

Ivy squeaked in delight and began to jump up and down, clapping her hands. 'Then why you got a face on like a wet weekend?' she teased before finally realising he wasn't joining in with the celebration.

A cold shiver of dread ran through her as Gloria bolted the door and put up the closed sign. 'What is it, Andy? What's 'appened?'

'Come on, gel, let's go in the private bar and sit you down,' he replied softly.

Ivy shook her head and stepped back from him. 'No. If you've got something to tell me, I'll hear it right here.' She folded her arms tightly about her waist, holding in the rising fear. 'It's Mum and Dad, ain't it?'

He bit his lip and reluctantly nodded. 'Yeah, love. And it ain't good news, gel. You're gunna 'ave to be very, very brave.' He held her by the shoulders and looked into her frightened eyes. 'They're all gone, Ivy. Your mum and dad, and yer sister.'

Ivy felt her legs give way and was saved from falling by Andy's strong grip on her arms. 'How? When?' she managed.

'It were the last V-2 attack on London at the end of March,' he replied softly. 'From yer mum's last letter, we know they was staying overnight on the twenty-ninth with friends at Hughes Mansions.' He took a deep breath. 'I'm sorry, Ivy, but that were the night the mansions took a direct hit.'

Ivy was numb with shock, and she looked from one ashen face to the next, trying to seek answers. 'Then why wasn't I told? How come I've had to wait all this time to find out?'

'Over three hundred were killed in the blast, Ivy, and not all of them could be identified.' He gripped her tightly as if he could imbue her with some of his strength. 'You know what it were like when that terrace went up two streets down from Beach View. There were virtually nothing left of anything.'

Ivy stared at him dumbly, finding it almost impossible to digest this shocking news, as the images of that terrible night flashed vividly in her mind.

Andy held her close, resting his chin lightly on the top of her head. 'I've been to the site, love. There ain't much left of the mansions – just one small section of it is still standing, and all the tenants from there have been accounted for.'

Ivy shuddered as she remembered how the V-2 had devastated the terrace where her mates had been billeted, and who'd escaped only because they'd been on night shift. She began to realise why she hadn't been told. 'I expect Mum and Dad didn't think it necessary to inform the authorities about staying there for just one night. So no one would think of looking for 'em,' she whispered.

'You're right, love. That's exactly what 'appened.' Andy drew her further into his embrace, holding her close in an attempt to ease her trembling as Peggy and Gloria stood helplessly by.

Ivy tried desperately to think straight. 'But why didn't someone get in touch with me when they failed to turn up at their new billet? And how come you know all this, Andy?'

Andy drew a deep, shuddering breath before replying, and Peggy could see how deeply this was affecting him. 'Last night, I went to the address yer mum gave you and met the Dutch lady what's living there with her kids. Mrs De Vries is ever so nice, Ivy, clever too, 'cos she was the one who found out what happened.'

'How?'

'She works with refugees and displaced persons, so knew the right people to ask about the family who never arrived to take up the comfortable billet they'd been offered. Their no-show worried her, and as the timing coincided with the V-2 attack she started asking questions.'

Gloria slipped behind the bar and poured glasses of brandy for them all. 'Drink that,' she ordered. 'It'll stiffen yer nerves.'

Andy swallowed his in one and set the glass aside, but Ivy ignored hers.

'Mrs De Vries started with the rehousing authorities to get their names, and some explanation as to why they weren't concerned at their disappearance. She was told that no-shows often happened, and they assumed they'd found another place to stay that was nearer to their friends, and hadn't bothered to tell them. They hadn't been happy about it, but as so many people were waiting for housing, they didn't have the time or the resources to track them down.'

'That's typical of Dad,' sniffed Ivy, dabbing at her nose with a grubby handkerchief. 'He never trusted the council, and didn't like having to report to them all the time.'

'A lot of people don't,' soothed Andy, stroking her back. 'And the way they'd been shunted about during these last few years, I can't say I blame your dad.'

Ivy swallowed the brandy and grimaced, but it seemed to rouse her spirits. 'So what did this De Vries woman do next?'

'She talked to some of the refugees she was working with who were survivors of the blast. One of their old Hackney neighbours remembered seeing your family in the street outside the mansions with their belongings the day before the blast and thought they were on their way to their new billet which your mum had told her was only four streets away. They'd been planning to meet up, but there was such carnage and chaos following the attack that the encounter slipped her mind entirely.'

'But if they couldn't be identified, and no one knew for sure they'd stayed at the mansions that night, how do we know they're definitely dead?' protested Ivy, still clinging to a last shred of hope.

'When your letter arrived, Mrs De Vries realised she needed to confirm what she already suspected before replying. She discovered where the effects of the un-identified were being kept. Having talked to Mrs Higgins, their old neighbour, who'd described yer dad's watch and your mum's ring and brooch very clearly, she'd known what to look for.'

'Old Ma Higgins always 'ad a sharp eye for Mum's brooch,' muttered Ivy.

Andy gripped her hands very tightly. 'I'm so sorry, love. Mrs De Vries found them, all together in a pad-ded envelope – damaged but identifiable.'

'I gotta go and get 'em,' she rasped through her tears. 'And see where it 'appened and where they've been laid to rest.' She took a shuddering breath. 'Oh, my Gawd,' she gasped as realisation hit. 'I gotta tell the little 'uns and all – and me brothers.' She col-lapsed against him. 'I can't do it, Andy. I just can't,' she sobbed.

'You won't have to, love,' he soothed. 'Mrs De Vries confirmed that the authorities will inform your brothers, and they'll let the little 'uns' foster parents know immediately.'

'I'll have to go and see the kids, she sobbed. 'They'll be ever so upset. But then what? I can't just leave 'em down there in Salisbury, can I?'

'You can bring them to Beach View until you've got things sorted in London,' said Peggy, relieved at last to be able to do something to help. 'That big room on the top floor would be ideal.'

'We'll sort all that out soon enough,' murmured Andy, nodding his thanks to Peggy. 'For now I need to make sure my Ivy is all right.'

Gloria firmly took charge and led the distressed young couple out of the bar and into the private room at the back. 'You're tougher than you think, Ivy gel, and you've always got Andy and me and Peggy to support you. You stay 'ere until you feel ready to go home, love. There's a spare bed if you need to stay the night.'

'Did you know about this, Peggy?' Ivy asked tearfully, settling into one of the deep couches.

'Mrs De Vries telephoned me earlier, which is why I came straight over.'

Ivy reached for her hand. 'Thanks, Aunty Peg, but I'm all right, really I am, and I do appreciate your offer of taking the kids in. But I might stay here tonight, if that's okay. I don't think I can face the others yet.'

'Quite understandable,' murmured Peggy, giving her a soft kiss on the cheek. 'You'll be all right here with Andy and Glo, and I'll tell the others if that would help.'

Ivy nodded, the tears streaming down her face as Andy gathered her to him. A loud, persistent banging on the front door made them all jump.

'I'll have to open up,' Gloria said crossly, 'or they'll have the bleedin' thing off its hinges. Will you two be all right?'

Andy nodded. 'I'll look after her, Auntie Glo.'

'Good lad.' She kissed his brow and with a nod to Peggy they left the pair of them cuddled on the couch.

'I'll pop back later with some nightclothes and so on,' said Peggy, giving Gloria a hug. 'Let me know if there's anything else I can do, won't you?'

Gloria nodded and drew back the bolts as Peggy left through the back way. Life went on and opening hours were set in stone regardless of the tragedies being played out behind closed doors, but Gloria felt her life's experience weighing heavy on her heart. This war had cost the life of her beloved only son and brought untold misery to thousands, and it seemed there was to be no end to it.

11

Jack Smith had fancied himself as quite the toff in the charcoal grey, three-piece demob suit, with its thin chalk stripe, crisp white shirt and smart tie. Highly polished brogues, plain cufflinks and a dark fedora finished off the outfit, and inside the small suitcase provided by a grateful government were a change of underwear, a tin of cigarettes, a bar of chocolate and half a dozen handkerchiefs.

He certainly felt he'd been well set up for civilian life, and he'd swaggered out of the large reception centre in Southampton thinking he was the bee's knees – until he realised that every man there in the milling crowd had been similarly equipped. The suits might be of differing colours, but it was a uniform, nevertheless, which rather took the shine out of the occasion.

However, Jack Smith was not a man to stay down-hearted for long. He was free from the army and the horrors of the battlefield and back on home soil – with a healthy amount of money saved in the Post Office and lots of plans for the future that he was eager to discuss with his daughter Rita. Hoisting his kitbag over his shoulder and gripping the small case, he joined the long line to board the train which would take him home to Cliffehaven.

The carriages and corridors were crammed with men and kitbags, the excited voices managing to blot out the noise of the huffing, puffing and clanking old troop train as it made its slow progress out of the station and into the countryside of Southern England.

Jack managed to wriggle his way to a spot by the corridor window and set down his baggage to watch the rolling hills and sweeping grasslands slowly pass by. He was jammed in, but it didn't matter. These were the green fields of his homeland, and his spirits lightened with every mile that passed.

It was a long, slow journey with many stops at small country halts and market town stations where families waited eagerly to greet their loved ones with flags and bunting. The crush began to ease as men reached their destinations, and Jack was able to stretch out a bit and enjoy a cigarette during the long wait at Hastings, where another carriage was added. He was beginning to get impatient at the delay when the guard blew his whistle and the train slowly started moving again. Only a few more stops and he would see his little Rita again.

The realisation that they would very soon be together brought a mixture of joy and uncertainty which suddenly made him nervous. Jack had only managed to visit Rita during a couple of brief leaves at the start of the war, and once when he was being transferred from the Midlands to the troop ship, but that had only been fleeting – barely long enough to tell her he loved her and not to worry about him, even though he knew he was heading for the beaches of Normandy.

He'd written when he could, and had loved getting her many letters which told of a busy and fulfilling job at the fire station, the goings-on at Beach View, the tragic loss of her first love, Matt, and the blossoming romance with the young Australian flier.

But letters weren't the same as actually being together during the good and the bad times, and he was worried that his daughter had grown away from him during his long absence – after all, he'd been called up in 1940, and a great deal had happened to both of them since. He could only trust that the strong relationship they'd forged during her childhood was still there, and that they wouldn't be like strangers.

Jack threw his half-smoked cigarette out of the window, adjusted the fedora and swung his kitbag over his shoulder. The train was approaching the short spur which would take him into the heart of Cliffehaven.

With the suitcase gripped in his hand, he leaned out of the window, eager to catch sight of his daughter. And there she was, jumping up and down, waving her arms, her dark curls bobbing in the light breeze, her little face alight with excitement.

He fumbled with the door as the train drew to a shuddering halt emitting a great sigh of steam and smoke, and Jack almost fell to the platform in his eagerness to get to her. Barely able to see her in the swirl of fog coming from the engine, he dropped his luggage and was almost knocked off his feet as she threw herself into his arms.

'I'm home, Rita!' he yelled above the noise of the other men disembarking as he swung her round. 'And this time I'm staying!'

'Oh, Dad, Dad. It's so lovely to see you,' she yelled back, the tears streaming down her face as she clung to his neck, 'and to know you're safe at last.'

The fog cleared and Jack set her back on her feet so he could drink in the sight of her. 'You're looking more like your mother,' he managed through a tight throat. 'So beautiful and all grown up too.' He chuckled and gently removed some soot smuts from her face before kissing her damp cheek and hugging her fiercely to him.

'It's been so long, Dad. I can hardly believe you're really here, and for good this time.' She wiped her face with a handkerchief. 'I promised myself I wouldn't cry,' she said. 'You must think I'm daft.'

'Not at all, darling,' he murmured, touching her dark curls which reminded him so much of her mother's. 'You're lucky I'm not bawling like a baby too.'

Rita giggled and clutched his arm. 'Come on, Stan's dying to welcome you home, and then I thought we'd catch up over a cup of tea before we went back to Beach View.'

Jack grinned at Stan who'd been the stationmaster at Cliffehaven for many years and was one of the town's beloved characters. 'Good to see you, my friend,' he said, heartily shaking his hand. 'Goodness, you're looking well,' he added, noting the man's considerable loss of weight.

Stan thumped him on the shoulder. 'That heart attack was a warning, Jack, so I had to do something. Good to see you home safe and sound at last.'

'It's good to be back, Stan. I've seen enough of the world to know where I belong, so I don't reckon I'll be going anywhere for a good long while yet.' He felt Rita's tug on his arm and gathered up his things. 'See you for a pint later, perhaps?'

Stan nodded. 'Aye. I'd enjoy that.'

Rita took charge of the small case, and they slowly walked arm in arm towards the High Street, where workmen were clearing rubble and repairing bomb-damaged buildings. 'I must say, Dad,' she said, eyeing him up and down, 'you do look very smart.'

'Along with the rest of the returning male population,' he replied dryly. 'It seems we've simply swapped one uniform for another.'

'But surely anything must be better than that awful stiff, ill-fitting khaki.'

'You're right. I shouldn't moan,' he said cheerfully. 'So where are we going for this cuppa then? I thought we'd be heading straight to Beach View?'

'I want you to myself for a bit,' she replied, hugging his arm. 'One of Peggy's evacuees came back today and she's organising a special lunch, so it's a bit chaotic. We've all chipped in, and so there's a huge chicken, sausages, stuffing and onion gravy. A meal fit for a returning hero,' she added with a gleam of pride in her eyes.

'I'm no blooming hero,' muttered Jack, 'just an ordinary bloke who got caught up in things too big to ignore or understand. I simply did what I had to do.'

Rita didn't reply, and Jack wondered if she had any inkling of what he'd actually seen and done during those awful months of slaughter that followed the terrifying storming of the Normandy beaches when every day became a battle for survival as they slowly and painfully advanced towards Germany. He firmly set those memories aside, determined to focus on this homecoming and his plans for the future.

They turned into Camden Road to find the majority of the fire crew standing about on the forecourt waiting to welcome him home. He knew John Hicks, but the rest were strangers, yet that didn't seem to dampen their enthusiastic welcome. He shook hands and chatted to John for a little while, asking after his family and his health, and then walked with Rita to the Lilac Tearooms.

'Crikey,' he breathed, as he stepped down into the cosy room with its chintz curtains and matching table-cloths. 'Some things just don't change, do they?' He grinned at the plump middle-aged woman who bustled in from the back at the sound of the tinkling doorbell. He didn't remember her, but guessed she might be the daughter of the woman who'd run the place before he'd been called up.

They settled by the window and Rita ordered a pot of tea with scones and jam. Jack raised an eyebrow at this extravagance and Rita swiftly put him straight. 'Rationing doesn't count in here,' she said in a stage whisper. 'The family own the dairy and have a share in the bakery, so everything's on offer – as long as you're willing to pay for it.' She stayed his hand as he reached for his wallet. 'This is on me, Dad, and I'll have no argument.'

Jack grinned at his daughter's bossiness. She hadn't changed. 'So, when am I going to meet this young fel-low of yours?' he asked once the feast had been paid for and set out on the table in front of them.

'Tomorrow,' she replied. 'He wanted to come today, but I thought it was a bit soon, and besides, I wanted you to myself for a bit.' She poured out the tea and began to slather jam and cream on her scone. 'He's been moved to Cliffe House to recuperate, now he's been given the all-clear on his head injury, so we'll go up there tomorrow on the motorbikes.'

'You've still got the Norton?'

'Of course, and I've got Pete's Royal Enfield too. It was a mess when I took charge of it, but it runs like silk now – much to his annoyance,' she added cheekily before taking a big bite of the scone.

Jack saw how her eyes sparkled and how animated she became when she talked about the Australian, and felt the same pang of unease he'd experienced when reading her letters. Not wanting to spoil the moment, he changed the subject and turned his attention to his own scone.

'So, tell me what's happened in Cliffehaven since peace was declared. I suspect a lot of the factories have closed down on the estate – and have they started building the pre-fabs on our old plot behind the station? I didn't see much work going on from the train on the way in.'

In between mouthfuls of scone, Rita told him about the plans to turn some of the larger factories into smaller units, and that although a few pre-fabs had gone up, and a new school had been built on the plot of the old one, work was slow as the council seemed more concerned with tidying up the town and seafront for the summer visitors, who were already arriving. Then she went on to tell him her job at the fire station was almost at an end.

'I'll be sad to leave,' she said, having finished the last delicious crumb. 'They're a good bunch to work with and John Hicks is a real diamond. But I always knew it was only for the duration, so I can't moan.'

'I'm sorry to hear that, Rita, but it will give us time to catch up on things and talk about the future.' He poured more tea for them both and lit a cigarette. 'As I said in my letters, I want to start up the motor repair shop again,' he said hesitantly. 'There's money in the Post Office because of the government compensation paid out for losing our home and business in the fire bomb attack, so finance won't be a problem when it comes to finding a home and suitable garage premises – and those empty factory units sound ideal for the purpose.'

He paused and then rushed on. 'I was rather hoping you might like to come in with me – as a partner.'

The words hung between them and Jack saw how she couldn't meet his gaze. 'That's of course if you haven't made other plans, Rita,' he added hastily.

Rita finally looked him in the eye. 'It's a wonderful idea, Dad,' she began hesitantly, 'but . . .'

'Look, I know the idea of being a car mechanic isn't every young girl's dream of a career, and of course I'll understand if you fancy doing something else. Besides, I'm sure when Jim Reilly gets back he'd leap at the chance of getting his hands dirty again.'

'That's something you'd have to ask him, Dad,' she replied. She reached across the table. 'I would love to go into partnership with you, but I've had another offer, and it's rather thrown the cat amongst the pigeons,' she said with a lightness that belied the concern in her eyes. 'Now I really don't know what to do for the best. I'm sorry.'

Jack saw the unshed tears glittering in her eyes, felt the slight trembling in her hand and knew immediately what she was trying to tell him. It was what he'd dreaded from the moment Rita had started writing to him about Peter Ryan. 'Peter's proposed and asked you to go back to Australia with him,' he stated.

Rita bit her lip and nodded. 'I haven't accepted yet, because I wanted to talk to you first,' she said softly.

Jack was aware of the other people in the tearoom getting an earful, so stood up and drew Rita to her feet. 'Can I leave the kitbag and case here for a bit?' he asked the waitress.

'Leave them in the corner, but don't forget, we close at one for the weekend.'

Jack thanked her and dumped the kitbag and suitcase out of the way, then left a tip on the table and hustled Rita outside. 'Come on, love. Let's find a private corner so we can talk properly.'

They found a sheltered spot on a bench at the very western end of the promenade, and after Jack's initial shock at the sight of the devastation caused by the V-2 on Havelock Road, he turned his full attention back to his daughter.

'Nothing is ever really set in stone, Rita,' he began. 'We fought this war so youngsters like you could have a better future and the freedom to follow your dreams. So don't ever feel you'll disappoint me or let me down if your plans don't fit in with mine.'

She remained silent and he took her hand. 'But what does worry me is the fact you didn't write and tell me about Peter's proposal, and the implications of it that are clearly worrying you. If you're that unsure, then perhaps it would be best not to rush into anything.'

'Oh, but I am sure. Really sure,' she protested. 'I just wanted to wait until I could speak to you face-to-face. 'I knew how keen you were on us setting up the workshop together, but Pete's proposal means I have a terrible choice to make.' She fell silent for a moment, chewing her lip. 'I love you both, but the thought of going all the way to Australia and never seeing you or Peggy or Ron again ...'

She tailed off and stared out at the sea which was sparkling with sun diamonds. 'I'm so sorry to put all this on you before you've had time to get used to being home. But Pete did suggest something which could solve everything, and I'd really appreciate it if you'd give it some serious thought.'

Jack determinedly buried his disappointment, and although he had a fair idea of what was coming, asked anyway, 'Oh, yes, and what's that?'

'You come to Australia with us,' she said eagerly. 'There's lots and lots of work for a qualified mechanic like you, and Pete says you could be set up like a tall poppy in no time.'

Jack smiled despite his heavy heart. 'A tall poppy, eh?' He'd heard the expression from some of the Aussies he'd met in France, and knew it meant a person of wealth and substance. 'Well, I was counting on being one right here in Cliffehaven where I belong, not in some far-flung corner of Australia.'

'But you'll think about it?' she asked breathlessly, her brown eyes pleading.

Jack didn't have the heart to shatter her dreams, so stayed silent and occupied his restless hands by rolling a cigarette. Having got it alight, he put his arm round her shoulder. 'Why don't you tell me more about Peter Ryan? What is it about this man that makes him so special?'

He listened with a heavy heart as she rattled off all the things she loved about Peter, and how she'd never thought she could care for anyone so much after having lost her first love, Matt. It seemed the young man was not only handsome and clever, but a brave fighter pilot, a gifted mechanic and all-round clever clogs. Peggy and Cordelia had evidently fallen for his charms – along with the nurses and matron at the hospital, and all in all, to Rita he was just about perfect.

'Sounds like he's one in a million,' he murmured when she finally stopped talking. 'But if he cares for you so much, how come he won't stay here and make a life for you both in Cliffehaven? You could both come in with me to run the repair shop.'

'It's not something we've ever really thought about or discussed,' she admitted softly.

'Then perhaps you should,' he replied, thinking that Ryan was being extremely selfish in asking her to sacrifice her home and all she knew for a future on the other side of the world without even considering staying on here.

'Pete made Australia sound very exciting and you have to admit, Dad, it's certainly not that here. It would be an adventure after the dark years we've been through, and a chance to grab new opportunities. Besides, he's been away for years and wants to go home to his family. I'm sure we could make a very good life for ourselves out there.' She glanced at him with a watery smile. 'And so could you, Dad.'

He ignored the prompt. 'So why are you holding back, Rita?'

When she remained silent, he grasped her hand and firmly ignored the pain in his heart. 'If he's the one, then don't give up on him because of me, darling,' he said softly. 'I've lived long enough to know where I belong, and after what I went through in Europe, I want nothing more than to be back here and spend the rest of my days just doing what I do best. Australia's for the young and adventurous, and I really can't see myself settling there.'

He sat away from her and lifted her chin so he could look into her face. 'If you love this man and can't imagine being without him, then you must follow your heart – just as I did with your mother. Life is for living, Rita, and far too short to be beleaguered by regrets.'

'But it would mean leaving you and Peggy and ...'

'Peggy and I will keep each other company, and I'm sure Ron will too. Of course we'll miss you – but we want you to be happy. And if that means going to Australia with Peter, so be it.'

'Oh, Dad, I'm so sorry to let you down. If things had been different I would've loved going into partnership with you. I've learned so much these past years looking after the engines at the fire station, and I've passed all my exams.'

'Then use those skills over there,' he urged despite his inner sadness. 'And write and tell me all about it when you and Pete are tall poppies with a brood of kids.'

Rita burst into tears and hugged him fiercely. 'I do love you, Dad,' she sobbed against his lapel. 'Please won't you consider coming with us?'

'Maybe I'll visit when the first grandbaby is born,' he soothed. 'But don't run away with the idea that I'm totally convinced about all this,' he warned. 'I've yet to meet this man who wants to whisk my daughter off to the other side of the world – and he's yet to earn my approval.'

'Oh, Dad, you'll get on with him like a house on fire, I just know you will,' she said, her tear-streaked face alight with happiness.

Jack very much doubted it. Young Peter Ryan sounded far too perfect for his liking, and he meant to get to know him thoroughly before he even considered giving his consent to anything.

Peggy had returned to Beach View to find Jane, Sarah, Danuta and Cordelia putting the final touches to the lunch while Daisy played with her dolls beneath the table. Cissy was in the hall talking animatedly on the telephone as usual, and Harvey was slumped in front of the range getting under everyone's feet. She took off her coat and scarf and quietly told them what had happened to Ivy's family.

Hearing the news so swiftly after the tragic loss of Freddy Pargeter, Cordelia became very upset and was only soothed by a glass of the sherry Jane had brought with her. 'There are times,' she said tearfully, 'when I feel I've lived too long. It's so unfair that those so much younger than I should be cut down, when I just keep on going.'

'Don't you dare even think such a thing,' said Peggy, taking her into her arms for her own consolation as much as Cordelia's. 'We'd all fall apart if we didn't have you to keep us on our toes. I for one hope you live to be a hundred.'

'Hmph. Chance would be a fine thing,' she replied. 'I've had my four score, so I'm living on borrowed time according to popular belief.' She drained the glass and held it out. 'Any chance of a drop more, Jane, dear? It's very good sherry.'

Jane raised an eyebrow but filled the glass anyway. 'I see things haven't changed much around here,' she teased. 'It's good to know you still enjoy a drink now and then.'

'I do indeed,' Cordelia replied. 'It's one of the advantages of age. One can get pickled and no one takes a bit of notice – unless one falls down, of course,' she added with a cheeky grin.

'Who's falling down?' asked Rita as she came up the cellar steps into the kitchen followed by her father.

'Great-Aunt Cordelia if she has much more of that sherry,' said Jane dryly.

Everyone chuckled, Harvey leapt from the rug to welcome them home and Peggy had to fight him off to hug Jack.

'I've put you up in the top room for now,' she said. 'If you're planning on staying a while, then I might have to move you. I'm sorry, Jack, but you know how it is in this house.'

'That's kind of you, Peggy,' he replied, dumping his heavy kitbag on the floor to hug her back and fend off an over-excited Harvey. 'But I'll be starting to look for a place for me and Rita tomorrow. Don't want to be a bother.'

Peggy swiped his arm playfully. 'Since when have you ever been a bother? You'll stay for as long as you need. I'm in no rush to lose either you or Rita.' She grabbed Harvey's collar and ordered him to behave, which had him looking as if the world was against him as he crawled back to the hearthrug and eyed her piteously.

Jack loved Harvey, but knew better than to sympathise with him, for it would only encourage him to bounce about again. Aware of Harvey's soulful eyes watching his every move, he greeted Cordelia with a kiss and a hug, made a fuss of little Daisy, and nodded hello to Sarah, Jane and Danuta whom he'd never met before, but felt he knew through Rita's many letters.

His eyes widened as Cissy dashed through the kitchen, barely pausing to acknowledge his presence, although he'd known her since childhood. 'Crikey,' he breathed as she ran down to the cellar. 'Is that really Cissy? I hardly recognised her.'

'I'm sorry about her lack of manners, Jack,' Peggy flustered. 'Grown up she might be, but she still has a lot to learn.'

Jack nodded thoughtfully, but wasn't really too surprised at Cissy's rudeness. To his mind, she'd always been far too fond of herself. 'I'll take my stuff upstairs and have a bit of a wash and brush-up, if that's all right?' he said. 'Lunch smells good, Peggy. I can't remember the last time I had a home-cooked meal.'

Harvey saw his cue and quickly scooted from beneath the table to follow Jack upstairs in the hope he had something tasty in that large bag.

Looking more closely at Rita, Peggy realised she'd been crying, and wondered if she'd told her father about Peter and they'd had a bit of a falling out. Jack certainly didn't look as jolly as she remembered, but perhaps that was because his homecoming was all a bit of a shock after being away so long. She hesitated over whether she should tell Rita about Ivy's news, but realised it was bound to come up in the conversation over lunch, so drew the girl to one side and explained what had happened this morning.

Rita stared at her in shock. 'I must go to her,' she breathed, slipping her jacket back on. 'She'll be in a terrible state.'

'She's got Andy and Gloria looking after her, and will be fine,' Peggy said firmly. 'You can help her once she comes home again – which will probably be tomorrow. You need to concentrate on your dad now. I assume you've told him about Peter's proposal?'

Rita nodded. 'I felt awful letting him down, but he was very good about it. He's looking forward to meeting Pete tomorrow, and I just know they'll get on.'

Peggy hoped that was the case, but she knew Jack. He was a loving, fiercely protective father who'd raised his daughter single-handedly since she was five, and would regard any suitor with deep suspicion – especially one who was planning to steal his daughter away to the other side of the world.

Peggy gave Rita a kiss and prompted her to help Jane finish laying the table. She would have liked to be a fly on the wall when the two men met – it would be most interesting to see how things unfolded.

12

Cissy knew she was being obnoxious, but it seemed that everyone and everything was getting on her nerves lately, and she simply couldn't get out of the habit of running roughshod over others' feelings. However, as she scrabbled in her handbag for her address book to write down the telephone number Clarissa had just given her, she did feel bad about virtually ignoring Jack Smith who'd become like a favourite uncle during her formative years when she and Rita were close.

With the name and number neatly recorded, she tucked the little book away, accepting that she'd have to make amends, not only to Jack, Cordelia and her mother, but to Rita. There really was no excuse for her being so rude and difficult, even if she was finding it hard to settle back into the humdrum routine of life at Beach View.

It was as if time had stood still here and nothing had changed, whereas she was a very different young woman compared to the naïve girl who'd left this house all those years ago to enlist into the WAAFs. Cissy was aware of the changes that had slowly been wrought on her, and which now set her apart from Rita and the others, and there were times when she wasn't at all sure she liked the self-possessed, rather cold woman she'd become.

The news about Freddy Pargeter had momentarily shaken her, for he'd been a shining light at Cliffe, forever the life and soul of a party, and the bad boy pilot who took delight in doing victory rolls over the airfield, so low it was quite heart-stopping. To think of all that energy and exuberance being snuffed out ... But then so many of the boys she'd come to know and admire hadn't returned, and it was as if her experiences at Cliffe had formed a protective shell around her heart so that nothing could touch her.

Once she'd found her lipstick and applied it to her satisfaction, her thoughts turned to Ivy and the ghastly news about her family. Cissy hadn't taken to Ivy at all, finding her loud and coarse and extremely irritating, but she couldn't begin to imagine what the girl must be going through at the moment. The thought of losing her own mother and baby sister made her shiver. They'd come too close to being killed several times over the last six years, and it was a miracle that Cissy hadn't found herself in Ivy's situation.

She pulled a thick cardigan on over her silk blouse and linen slacks. It was chilly in the basement, but she liked the solitude and privacy it afforded her until things were resolved and she had a clearer sense of where her future lay.

She stared at her reflection in the mirror she'd placed on the battered chest of drawers, not really understanding why she bothered to fuss with her hair and put make-up on every morning, for there was nowhere to go but the Anchor, the Officers' Club, or for a stroll along the seafront or through the few decent shops that were still standing in the High Street. However, as her glamorous friend Clarissa had said, it was a matter of pride to always look one's best at all times for one never knew what was round the corner. And as she admired Clarissa very much and made a point of emulating her sophisticated style, she'd carried on making the effort.

She sank onto the sagging mattress and gave a deep sigh of longing. Despite the terrors of the enemy raids and the seemingly endless losses among the flying crews, life had been exciting and fulfilling at RAF Cliffe, and now that everything had come to a grinding halt and she had no real reason to get up in the mornings, she'd have given anything to have those days back again. With each passing day it felt as if she was stuck in limbo as she heard from the other girls about their exciting new lives and jobs in London, and waited to hear from Randy. It was hugely frustrating that no one in authority would tell her anything, and she was beginning to wonder if Randy was still alive, or if he'd simply forgotten about her.

She lit a cigarette and contemplated both options – neither of which sat easily with her, for she hoped what they'd shared was too special for him to forget, and certainly didn't want him dead. It had been a very long time since he'd crash-landed and been captured, and back then she was in the throes of love, swept away in his enthusiasm and all the dreams he had of a future with her in America.

She'd been enthralled as he'd talked about his wealthy family, and the comfortable life they could have in Los Angeles once he'd completed his interrupted degree and joined his father's law practice.

From his descriptions, she'd been able to imagine the sandy beaches, the palm trees and endless sunshine of that land of opportunity, which had only made her want it even more.

She'd certainly had stars in her eyes then, but the war had brought ugly experiences to them both, which had changed her, and certainly must have changed him. The long separation and lack of communication had undeniably dulled her fervour and caused the dreams to fade, and although she'd determinedly kept those hopes and memories alive, she now wasn't really sure how she actually felt about him. She had no photograph to remind her of what he looked like, and as she tried to conjure him up, the image was hazy – a mere impression of a tall, dark-haired, vigorous figure in uniform.

Was it the same for him? Did he even think about her as he endured the POW camp, or had he been too occupied with trying to stay alive to remember the girl he'd left behind?

Perhaps her mother had been right when she'd gently warned her not to look at the future through rose-tinted glasses – to realise that absence might make the heart grow fonder, but it could also distil the passion and urgency, turning what had been vital and all-consuming into fading, bitter-sweet memories.

Cissy stubbed out her cigarette and, with new-found clarity, wondered if she'd been as foolish as April Wilton who now lived in the station cottage with her daughter, Paula, and worked at the telephone exchange. April had been a Wren before she'd arrived at Beach View, homeless and penniless, and she'd believed the GI's lies and been left literally holding the baby.

'At least I made certain that didn't happen,' she muttered thankfully. 'But I might very well have let my stupid heart rule my head.'

She wrapped the cardigan around herself and leaned against the pillows as she coolly appraised her situation. She'd always dreamed of going to America, especially in the days before the war when her rather ridiculous ambition had been to be plucked out of the chorus line into the starry world of Hollywood films. Had Randy picked up on that, and fed her fantasy just to get her into bed? Or had his heart been true and he'd really meant all the things he'd said?

There again, was it the dream of America that had made her so enamoured with him, or had she genuinely loved him for himself? He'd been very dashing and terrific company as well as an exciting lover, but looking back on those heady days, were those reasons strong enough to tie herself to him for the rest of her life?

Cissy burned with frustration and confusion, and she got to her feet, unable to be still any longer. If only someone would tell her what had happened to him, then at least she'd know where she stood. As it was, she was stuck here, unable to make her mind up about anything. Should he turn up tomorrow – and she really hoped he would – then maybe they could pick up the pieces and go ahead with their plans, but if the silence went on, and it became clear he wasn't returning, then she'd have to swallow her pride and think again.

Clarissa and Philippa had begged her to join them in London where, in partnership with three other girls from Cliffe, they were running a highly successful limousine taxi company that Clarissa's father had helped to set up. It had been decided right from the start that their clients would be exclusively female of the well-heeled sort who needed ferrying about the city.

Cissy had saved enough to buy a share in the company, and although it would leave her almost penniless, Clarissa had assured her she'd soon recoup her investment as the money was pouring in, and Cissy could move into her spare room rent-free until she'd got enough together to find her own apartment. The hours were sometimes very long, and some of the clients could be tricky, but there was always time for parties and dancing with the social set they'd known before the war.

It was enormously tempting, though what her parents would say about it, Cissy didn't dare think. She could leave tomorrow, shake off the dust of Cliffehaven and throw herself into a new life where she could use her driving skills, have a share in a business venture and mix with the sort of people she'd become used to. And yet still she hesitated, for the war had only just ended; Europe was in turmoil, and a great many men were still to come home. She owed it to Randy to stay and wait for him a while longer.

'Stir your stumps, Cissy. Lunch is ready, no thanks to you.'

Peggy's rather brisk command brought her from her muddled thoughts, and she left the basement bedroom determined to mend her ways and be pleasant for the rest of the time she was here, and to be more helpful to her mother, who worked far too hard, worried too much, and deserved better from her.

Doris hadn't slept well and was now in a terrible fluster as she waited for John to return from the station where he was meeting his son off the twelve-thirty train. She'd risen at dawn and cleaned the bungalow from top to bottom before rushing into town to have her hair and nails done at Julie's Salon in the High Street. Now she was anxiously watching the clock as her carefully prepared lunch sizzled away in the oven.

She turned the heat off beneath the vegetables, basted the roasting chicken and wished for the umpteenth time that she hadn't insisted upon cooking here instead of them all going to the Officers' Club as John had suggested. Her fresh hairdo was going limp in the steamy kitchen and her nerves were making her clumsy, so she burnt her finger on the roasting pan.

'For goodness' sake, Doris,' she hissed, dowsing her finger in cold water, 'pull yourself together. It's just a late lunch.'

But it wasn't just any old late lunch – it was a meal to welcome Michael home, and having decided she wanted their first meeting to be a private affair and not conducted in the full glare of the Club bar, she was desperate to make a good impression.

Glancing at the clock again, she saw it was almost two. She'd reckoned on serving the meal at half-past to give them plenty of time to have a quiet drink and chat, before walking home. But if they were very much longer, it would mean dishing up the minute they walked in the door. And that wouldn't do at all. She wanted her first meeting with Michael to be unrushed over a glass of sherry, not while she drained vegetables and made gravy.

Doris checked that the small kitchen table was correctly laid, the cutlery polished and gleaming, the napkins ironed to perfection, and the glasses crystal clean. John had opened the red wine so it could breathe before he'd left for the station, and Doris had placed the new bottle of sherry alongside three glasses on a tray in the sitting room.

It was on occasions like this that she wished she had a proper dining room, for eating in the kitchen felt far too informal – if not rather common. She rapidly dismissed the notion, for it was opinions like that which had caused rifts with her sister Peggy and the rest of the family. Gone were the days of her big house in Havelock Road, with its two elegant reception rooms and uninterrupted views of the sea, and she was damned lucky to have a home at all. Peggy, whose kitchen – like their mother's – was the heart of the home, had set a fine example, and if it was good enough for them, it was good enough for anyone. Should Michael turn his nose up at the idea, then there wasn't much she could do about it.

Doris took off her apron and went into the bedroom to check on her appearance. The pale cream sweater and tweed skirt were of good quality and sensible for such an occasion, and with the fake pearls in her ears and round her neck, she looked quite presentable. She patted her hair and dabbed some powder on her rather shiny nose, then nodded at her reflection and went into the sitting room.

John had lit a fire in the hearth, for although the sun was bright, there was a chill wind, and they'd be cold after the long walk up the hill. She needlessly plumped cushions, checked the water in the vase of irises, then straightened the pile of magazines on the coffee table. Finding nothing else to occupy her, she nervously lit a cigarette and looked out of the window.

There was no sign of them yet and Ladysmith Road was deserted, but on this clear, bright day she could see every detail of the town spread across the valley between the hills, and the horseshoe bay, where a couple of sailing boats leaned with the wind to race across the sparkling sea.

Peggy was down there in Beach View welcoming Jack and Jane home, but Doris suspected that behind her bright smiles and chatter, her heart would be heavy over the recent loss of Freddy, and the tragedy that had struck poor little Ivy. It had come as a terrible shock when Peggy had telephoned earlier to tell her the news, for Doris had come to like Ivy despite her raucous ways and rather suspect sense of humour, and although their relationship had not started well, they'd formed a surprisingly close bond over the past year or so.

Doris had been with the girl during the bombing raid that had flattened a good deal of the factory estate, and learned that Ivy had survived a similar experience earlier on in the war when another raid had entombed her in the vast underground shelter. She'd found love that day when the firemen had come and Andy had pulled her out, and although she'd been through a great deal, Ivy's fighting spirit had never deserted her, and Doris admired her tenacity. But to learn such awful news so long after the event, would surely dampen even Ivy's spirits, and Doris decided she would go and see her tomorrow to offer any help she could to ease that awful burden.

Doris was so deep in thought she didn't hear the key in the lock, and she started as John called out, 'Hello? Doris, we're back.'

Her heart thudded, but she determinedly took a deep breath and went into the narrow hall to find John standing there with a tall, slender young man whose blue eyes regarded her with undisguised curiosity.

'Hello, darling,' murmured John, briefly pecking her cheek. 'This is Michael.'

The blue gaze didn't falter, but his smile transformed and softened his gaunt face as he quickly took off his hat and shook her hand. 'Father's told me a lot about you in the past couple of hours, Mrs Williams. I'm delighted to meet you.'

'It's lovely to have you back safe and sound,' she replied, noting how bony and cold his hand was, and how his clothes couldn't disguise the slenderness of his frame. The years in the POW camp had certainly left their mark.

'Something smells delicious,' he said, releasing her hand. 'I do hope you haven't gone to too much trouble on my account.'

'Not at all,' she fibbed. 'You must think it rather odd that we're eating here and not at your father's, but I know where everything is here, and find his oven difficult to get on with.'

'Doris is a wonderful cook, so you're in for a treat,' said John, hanging up their hats and coats on the rack and shooting Doris a loving smile. 'Come on in, Michael, and warm yourself by the fire while we have a glass of sherry to welcome you home properly.'

Michael regarded the room appreciatively, took the glass from his father and stood awkwardly by the fire as John moved to Doris's side. 'I have to confess that it does feel very strange to be in a real home again after so long in the camp. It's the small things that stand out, like the rugs, the fire in the hearth, and the flowers in vases. All sound seems muted somehow, and the scent of cooking and furniture polish definitely beats the stink of the hut.' His words were spoken lightly, but his eyes told a different story.

'Was it very bad?' asked John anxiously.

Shadows of something raw and indefinable flickered across Michael's face and he dipped his chin. 'Bad enough, Father, but at least we weren't force-marched across Germany like so many of the other poor blighters.'

His hands trembled as he drained his sherry and reached into his pocket for his cigarettes which he passed round and lit. 'If you don't mind,' he added into the difficult silence, 'I'd rather not talk about it.'

John nodded his understanding and then turned to Doris. 'I'm sorry we're a bit late, but the time ran away with us as we caught up on things, and then we popped in next door so that Michael could dump his bag and see where he'll be sleeping. I do hope lunch hasn't been spoilt.'

'It must almost be ready,' she replied, glad of an excuse to escape Michael's continued scrutiny. 'I'll check and give you a shout when I need you to carve.'

She abandoned her sherry and hurried out to the kitchen to stand for a moment to smoke the cigarette and stare out of the window into the garden. She couldn't begin to imagine what Michael had been through, but seeing how thin and sickly he looked and having heard rumours and whispers of what had happened to the likes of Freddy Pargeter and Martin Black, she understood why none of them wanted to talk about their experiences.

Doris shivered despite the warmth coming from the oven. Michael tried to hide it, but he was clearly puzzled and curious about her, and the relationship she had with his widowed father. He would find this homecoming extremely difficult, for not only had his father moved from the family home to a different town and new way of life out of the army, but he was also involved with Doris. It was a lot to take in, and if it had been her son, Anthony, in that position, she'd have moved heaven and earth to help him deal with it.

Thinking of Michael as a son instead of a threat, Doris suddenly didn't feel nervous, for it made her realise that all Michael needed was time to orientate himself and the assurance that although things had changed, his father's feelings for him were as strong as ever. And as long as Doris didn't try and force things, he'd eventually come round to accepting her, and the loving relationship she shared with John.

Doris emerged from her thoughts and concentrated on getting the chicken and roast potatoes out of the oven. The aroma of the food soon drifted down the hall, drawing John and Michael into the kitchen, eager to help. With the meal on the table and wine in the glasses, the awkwardness disappeared, and they began to talk and relax.

Ruby had returned to the bungalow in Mafeking Terrace after her lunchtime shift at the Anchor, determined to give the place a thorough spring-clean before she had to hand it back to Cordelia. Not that it was dirty, for she'd become quite house-proud over the time she'd been living here with her friend Shirley, and had made sure they both kept the place neat and tidy. But the bright sunlight had shown up the smears on the windows, the few cobwebs that had escaped her notice and the fact that the rugs needed a good beating to freshen them up, and the curtains could do with a wash.

Cordelia's bungalow was a haven of tranquillity after the slums of London where everyone lived cheek by jowl and no amount of scrubbing could get rid of the dirt or the stench of the communal lavatories. Set almost at the top of the hill to the north of the town, the front window afforded a magnificent view of Cliffehaven and the sea. It had two small bedrooms, a bathroom, sitting room and kitchen, all of which had been scoured and painted before she'd moved in. The furniture had belonged to Cordelia's sister, so it was old and battered, but she'd polished it to a gleam, and Ron Reilly had mended the leg on the heavy bedstead so she didn't have to keep shoring it up with a pile of bricks.

Ruby changed out of her skirt and blouse into a threadbare jumper and the dungarees she wore to work at the tool factory. Knotting a scarf over her hair, she exchanged her good shoes for her disreputable slippers and then went into the small paved back garden to the brick outhouse to switch on the copper boiler so she had plenty of hot water to do the washing.

With the wireless on to keep her company, she set to and began to collect the lightweight curtains from the bedrooms and bathroom which she dumped into the outside sink to soak. The ones in the sitting room were heavy, faded velvet, and full of dust, and she spluttered and sneezed as she struggled to get them down. Collecting the three small rugs, she carried them all outside to the washing line, where she proceeded to give them a good bashing with the back of a heavy brush.

Half an hour later her arms were aching, dust stuck to her sweaty face and there was grit in her mouth and eyes from beating the rugs. But everything was as clean as she could get it, and once she'd brought it all back in and dumped it on the settee, she felt she'd earnt a cup of tea and a fag before she tackled the washing, the bathroom and the windows.

Ruby drank the hot, strong, reviving tea, smoked a roll-up and then hummed along to the music on the wireless as she washed and rinsed and wrung out the cotton curtains and hung them on the line. There was enough of a wind to get them dry before she had to be back at the Anchor, so she'd iron and re-hang them ready for tonight.

It didn't take long to clean the pocket-handkerchief bathroom and sweep the floors, and having washed the kitchen floor and polished up the back windows, she filled her bucket with fresh water and went out to the front to do the tiny bathroom window and then the big sitting room bay which was exposed to all the elements and needed cleaning at least once a week – which didn't always happen as she was so busy trying to pack up her things in readiness to move to Stan's, do her hours at the factory and her shifts at the pub.

Ruby really didn't want to leave the bungalow and move in with Stan and April, for she felt right at home here, and would happily stay until Mike came home and they got married. But Shirley had gone back to London, and she couldn't find anyone else she wanted to share with to help pay the rent – and she wasn't about to accept charity from Cordelia who'd already been so kind to her.

She attacked the wet glass with added vigour, the crumpled newspaper drying it to a most satisfyingly squeaky-clean shine. Standing back and admiring the effect, she ran a damp cloth over the sill to rid it of bird droppings and general muck and considered the afternoon's effort as a job well done, even if it had left her filthy.

'Now that's what I call a sight to gladden any man's heart.'

Ruby whipped round as Mike strode through the gate, his eyepatch and dress uniform making him more handsome than ever. Her foot caught the bucket, tipping it over so the handle got entangled in her feet, which sent her stumbling to land with a thump on her bottom in the dirty puddle.

'Mike. Oh, Mike,' she gasped, going red with embarrassment. 'This wasn't how I wanted to welcome you home.'

He grinned and dropped his heavy kitbag on the garden path. 'Oh, I don't know,' he drawled. 'That was kinda neat, the way you did that and still stayed beautiful.'

Ruby erupted into giggles. 'Don't talk daft, you silly bugger. I look a right mess and now I've got a wet arse and all.'

He took her hand, pulled her to her feet and into his arms. 'It's a lovely arse, as you so delicately put it,' he murmured, gently cupping her buttocks in his large hands to pull her closer. 'And I look forward to inspecting it for bruises later,' he teased. 'For now, I'd like a kiss.'

Ruby sank against him and kissed him long and hard, not caring what the neighbours thought, or how much damage her dirty, damp dungarees were doing to his pristine uniform. When they finally drew apart they smiled at one another in the knowledge that the magic was still there and nothing had changed between them despite the two-year separation.

'We'd better go in,' she chuckled, catching sight of the neighbour across the road who was avidly watching them around her net curtains. 'Old Ma Henley's nose is glued to her window and if her eyes get much wider, they'll pop out altogether.'

Mike turned, smiling to smartly salute the nosy woman who looked askance at his eyepatch and hastily withdrew from her window. He was still smiling as he took Ruby's hand. 'If she only knew what my plans are for you, she'd probably faint,' he said with a naughty twinkle in his good eye.

Ruby went a deep scarlet, fetched the bucket and led him into the house. Once the door was closed behind them, Mike dropped his kitbag, relieved Ruby of the bucket, swept her up into his arms and, between kisses, asked where the bedroom was.

Ruby pointed, too busy returning his kisses to talk, and he carried her along the hall and closed the bedroom door behind them.

It was a long while later that Ruby sleepily shifted in Mike's arms and peered at the bedside clock. With an exclamation of horror, she leapt from the bed. 'I've got ten minutes to get to the Anchor,' she gasped, stumbling over their discarded clothes strewn across the floor to get to the bathroom for a wash, and to clean her teeth.

'Do you have to go tonight?' he asked, sitting up in bed as she dashed back into the room, minutes later, still as naked as the day she was born. 'I thought we'd spend it together.'

'Ron and Rosie are away on honeymoon and Saturday nights are always busy. I can't leave Brenda to cope on her own.' She found fresh underwear and the skirt and blouse Rosie had bought for her to wear behind the bar. She finished fastening the fiddly buttons on the blouse and slipped her bare feet into her best shoes. 'Besides, I wasn't expecting you back until next week,' she reminded him.

'They let me go earlier than planned,' he replied, the sheet slipping down to expose his torso and the scars of the wounds he'd suffered along with a blinded eye during the disastrous Dieppe Raid back in 1942. 'Telephone Brenda and tell her you'll be a bit late,' he suggested. 'There are important things I need to discuss with you tonight, Ruby.'

'I don't have a telephone,' she replied, reaching for her hairbrush. 'Why don't you come with me, and we can talk during my break?'

He got out of bed, adjusted his eyepatch, and swiftly began to dress. 'I guess I should have sent a telegram warning you I was on my way, but I wanted to surprise you,' he said, his voice muffled by the shirt he was pulling over his head. 'So it's my fault we have to spend my first night back in a crowded pub.'

'I'm so sorry, Mike,' she said, brushing her hair and swiftly pinning it roughly into victory rolls on either side of her head. 'It's not the way I want to spend it either, but Ron and Rosie were good enough to give me some shifts after the factory cut my hours, and I can't let them down.'

'Well, at least we won't have to run all the way down there,' he said, fastening the brass buttons on his brown uniform jacket and buckling the Sam Browne belt. 'I hired a car, so we can arrive in style.'

'A car? But are you allowed to drive with ...'

'I can see just as well with one eye,' he said evenly. 'It's just a case of adjusting to things, and I've had plenty of time to practise.'

Ruby put her arms around his waist and hugged him tight. 'Of course you have, and I was daft to mention it.' She stood on tiptoe and kissed his cheek. 'Come on, or we'll be late, even with the car.'

The Anchor was packed. Brenda was barely coping, and Ruby realised guiltily that there'd be little chance of any intimate conversation with Mike before closing time. It seemed a number of local men had been demobbed and were celebrating their return home, including Rita's father who was introduced to her the minute Rita saw her come in.

Ruby quickly greeted Cordelia, Cissy, Sarah and her sister, introduced Mike, asked after Peggy who was at home with Daisy, and then hurried behind the bar to begin serving. Mike bought them all a round of drinks, and eventually gravitated towards a group of other Canadians.

The time passed swiftly as Ruby and Brenda were kept on the go until closing time, and Ruby's stomach was growling with hunger, for she hadn't eaten since breakfast. Jack Smith was leaning heavily on Rita as he weaved like a sailor towards Beach View, she noted as she closed the door on the last customer, and Mike didn't exactly look sober either.

'I think we'd better leave the car here and walk home,' she said wearily, helping him off the bar stool. 'The fresh air will do you good.'

'Not as much good as you do me,' he said with a soppy smile.

Ruby rolled her eyes and exchanged knowing looks with Brenda, for they both recognised the signs of the drink talking, but at least Mike was gentle in his cups, not like her brutish late husband who liked using his fists. The three of them left by the side door, and Ruby steadied Mike as they circumnavigated the rented Austin parked at the kerb and began the long uphill walk to Mafeking Terrace.

She was tired after the long day and her feet hurt, but the fresh air had the desired effect, and by the time they reached the bungalow, Mike was almost sober and Ruby's head had cleared.

'Do you want a cuppa and a sandwich? I don't know about you, but I'm starving.' She kicked off her shoes and flexed her aching feet before going into the kitchen to find something to eat and put the kettle on.

Her spirits plummeted as she realised her larder was almost bare, but for the end of a stale loaf and a scrap of margarine. 'Sorry,' she said ruefully. 'It looks like we'll have to make do with tea and toast.'

'Do you often go without, Ruby?' Mike came to stand beside her, his brow creased with concern.

'Not at all,' she fibbed, keeping an eye on the bread under the grill while she loaded up a tin tray with cups and plates. 'But things have been tight lately,' she admitted.

'Then you should have written and told me,' he said sternly. 'I offered to send you money to help out, but you always said you were coping okay.'

'I was. I am,' she insisted, not looking at him as she smeared the last of the margarine on the toast and filled the teapot. 'I just forgot it was early closing today and didn't get stuff in for the weekend.'

Mike sighed deeply and took the tray from her, leading the way into the sitting room where the lack of curtains meant the street light shone straight in and they were fully exposed to the neighbours. He placed the tray on a side table, removed the curtains and rugs, and drew her down beside him on the couch. 'We'll eat out tomorrow,' he said firmly, 'and on Monday, I'll go and do the shopping.'

'You really don't have to do that,' she protested through a mouthful of toast. 'I've got money and plenty of ration stamps. Besides,' she added, 'the queues are endless, and you have to know the right one to join because you can't buy anything if you're not registered to shop there.'

He remained silent as he poured out the weak tea, adding just a couple of drops of milk from the half-empty bottle. 'I'm an officer in the Canadian Army and have a tongue in my head, so I'm sure I can navigate my way around rules and regulations,' he murmured.

Ruby felt awful as he sipped the sugarless tea and then bit unenthusiastically into the toast. She'd let things slide, and he must think she was absolutely hopeless at housekeeping. Eyeing the heap of curtains on the armchair and the bare windows, she remembered she'd left the other curtains on the line. If only Mike had warned her he was coming early she'd have made sure everything was perfect – as it was, he had to put up with toast and evil-tasting marge, and tea the colour of gnat's ...

'Stop worrying,' he said, interrupting her thoughts. 'I came home for you, not fancy meals and a place so tidy I'd feel awkward.' He drew her close and kissed the top of her head. 'All I want is time with my girl, to hold her and love her and tell her all the things I've been wanting to say since I got here.'

Ruby realised nothing really mattered but the fact he was here, and that he still loved her despite her failings, and she relaxed against him as he took her hand and looked at the ruby and diamond engagement ring he'd given her before he'd been sent to Scotland.

'It feels like a lifetime since I put that ring on your finger, Ruby,' he said softly. 'Do you still want to marry me and come to Canada?'

'Of course I do,' she breathed. 'I've never stopped loving you, Mike, from the moment we met at the Memorial Hospital.'

'I feel the same way, and today has proved to me that we were meant for one another.' He drew back and smiled down at her. 'I know my turning up today has thrown you a bit, but things have moved on much quicker than I expected, and it means my leave has been cut short.'

She sat up and regarded him fearfully. 'But you wrote and told me you got permission for us to marry before you were shipped home,' she said breathlessly.

'And we will do just that,' he replied firmly. He gripped her hands. 'Just a bit sooner than we expected. We're due at the Town Hall on Wednesday at two o'clock.'

'To arrange our wedding?'

He grinned and shook his head. 'To *have* our wedding.'

She thought she'd burst with happiness as she threw herself into his arms – and then reality hit, and she gasped in shock. 'This Wednesday? But that's only four days away and I haven't got a frock, or sorted out my hours at work or any kind of reception.'

She wrung her hands as her thoughts whirled. 'Then there's the invitations. We can't just get married without Peggy and Cordelia, and Stan, Ron and Rosie. They'd never forgive us.' She was close to tears as she looked back at him. 'It's too much of a rush, Mike. Can't we at least put it off until next week?'

'I'm sorry, honey, it has to be this Wednesday. We leave for Canada on Saturday.'

Ruby almost fainted with shock and could only stare at him. 'Saturday? Canada?' she managed.

He kissed her softly on the lips and cupped her face in his hands. 'I know it's very short notice and that it has come as a huge shock, but the Canadian Wives' Bureau have pulled out all the stops and arranged everything. We go by train to Liverpool, and will be sailing on the hospital troop ship SS *Lady Nelson* for Halifax, Nova Scotia early Monday morning.'

It was all too much to absorb and she could only stare at him helplessly.

'There's really nothing to panic about, Ruby,' he soothed. 'You told me you'd already packed most of your things to leave for Stan's, so we can take it all with us on the ship. As for the reception and invitations, leave them to me.'

Ruby was still stunned, and could think of nothing to say as he reached into his jacket pocket and pulled out an envelope.

Handing it to her, he smiled. 'This is for a frock and flowers and anything else you might want for our special day. Spend it all on yourself, darling. You deserve it.'

Ruby's hand trembled with shock at the speed things were going as she opened the envelope and gasped at the amount of money inside. 'It's too much,' she protested. 'Much too much. And we'll need all the money we can get when we arrive in Canada.'

Mike folded her fingers around the thickly filled envelope. 'This is my wedding gift to you, Ruby,' he said, his tone brooking no argument. 'It's my way of apologising for turning your life upside down in such a rush. Please use it.'

Ruby realised it was useless to protest further so she snuggled into his embrace, her mind in a whirl of excitement that was tinged with fear, and a nub of resentment for being rushed into things. She was about to marry the man she adored, and set sail for a new life in a country where she'd be regarded as different, with her English ways and Cockney accent. She was sure Mike's family were lovely people, but they were strangers to her and she'd be ignorant of how things were done over there. Would they like her? Would she like them – or more importantly, would Canada live up to the high expectations that had been instilled in her by Mike and his mother's enthusiastic letters?

She'd known this moment would come, but had expected time to make reasoned decisions about her wedding day, and to really prepare for the journey. The original plan had been for them to marry and Mike to leave shortly after for Canada, and she would follow him at a later date. But now it had all changed, and she suddenly felt adrift from reality in an ocean of confusion.

Ruby closed her eyes and listened to the drum of Mike's steady heartbeat. She'd have to give in her notice at the tool factory first thing Monday morning and warn Ron and Rosie she wouldn't be doing any more shifts. Cordelia would have to be told she'd be leaving the bungalow earlier than planned, and of course she had to tell Peggy and Stan about the wedding and not leave such important things entirely to Mike.

She didn't know how long she'd been lying against him, but she was getting stiff with cold and the street light had gone out. She became aware that Mike's breathing had changed and realised that the long day of travelling, the beer and the excitement of this home-coming had finally taken its toll, and he'd fallen asleep.

She inched away from him, drew his legs up so he was full length on the couch, eased off his shoes and put a cushion beneath his head. Covering him with the blanket she used on cold nights when the fire had gone out, she stood for a moment looking down at him, her heart full of love, the thrill of their imminent wedding and voyage across the Atlantic overriding her fear of the unknown.

Softly kissing his forehead, she switched off the light and took the abandoned tray of tea and toast into the kitchen, then went to have a bath in the hope it would help her to sleep. However, the few inches of water were tepid and her over-active mind refused to let her relax, and when she finally climbed into bed, she lay there staring into the darkness wondering how on earth they could manage everything in such a short space of time.

13

It was Sunday morning and Peggy made no comment when a smiling Cissy came into the kitchen, kissed her fondly, made a fuss of Harvey and took over the cooking. Her daughter had clearly decided to mend her ways and Peggy was much relieved, for things had reached the point where a quiet ticking-off had definitely been on the cards.

'I've fed the chickens,' said Cissy as she stirred the porridge. 'And there are enough eggs for everyone, so I thought I'd boil them and do toast soldiers. Daisy tells me it's her favourite breakfast.' Cissy looked around the kitchen with a frown. 'Where is Daisy?'

'Upstairs, waiting for Cordelia. Since we lost Queenie, she's taken to sitting on Cordy's lap for the ride down the stairs each morning – although I fear she's getting a little too heavy for such delicate knees.'

'I'm sure Grandma Cordy will say something if that's the case. She's never been one to stay quiet when something doesn't suit her,' said Cissy with laughter in her voice. 'But the stairlift has certainly given her a new lease of life,' she added. 'It's a marvellous thing. Rita and her chap must be very clever to come up with something like that.'

'Indeed they are,' replied Peggy. 'But then Rita was always good with machinery – she got it from her father.'

Further conversation was halted by the arrival of Sarah, Jane and Danuta, who were swiftly followed by Rita, Jack, Cordelia and Daisy. Harvey rushed from one to the other, whining with pleasure, his tail windmilling in delight as he was patted and petted, and a laughing Daisy was almost knocked over in his enthusiasm.

Peggy lifted Daisy out of harm's way and onto a chair, tying a bib around her neck so she didn't dirty her clean clothes. The others sat down, poured out the tea and tucked into the porridge as they discussed their plans for the day.

Danuta was on duty this evening, so she was going to St Cuthbert's Church to attend morning Mass and put flowers on the graves of her brother and stillborn baby. Sarah and Jane were going to visit the horses at the dairy and then have lunch at the Officers' Club, and Cordelia's friend and loyal companion, Bertie Double-Barrelled, was taking her out for afternoon tea at the golf club. Cissy would be walking Harvey for the last time as Ron and Rosie were due back later this morning, and she told Peggy she might also go to the golf club in the afternoon to see what the game involved and if she might enjoy it. Clarissa and Philippa played golf, and Cissy thought it all sounded very jolly.

'Dad and I will be going to visit Pete,' said Rita, 'but first I need to pop over to the Crown and make sure Ivy's coping.'

'There's no need for that,' said Ivy, appearing in the doorway to the basement. 'I'm fine, really I am.'

Rita shot out of her chair and hugged her. 'I would have come the minute I heard,' she said, 'but Peggy told me you were being looked after by Andy and Gloria.'

Ivy returned her hug and nodded, her little face drawn and shadowed by the tears she'd shed. 'I know you would have,' she murmured, 'but I just needed to be with Andy for a while to take it all in and plan what to do next.'

She drew from the embrace and went to kiss Peggy's cheek. 'Thanks for dropping off my stuff, Auntie Peg, and for being there when Andy got back.'

'Do you want some breakfast?' Cissy gave Ivy a sympathetic squeeze on her arm.

Ivy shook her head and gave a wan smile. 'Thanks, but I 'ad something at Gloria's.' She turned back to Peggy. 'I ain't staying fer long, Auntie Peg. I'm just 'ere to pack a few things, 'cos me and Andy are going to London to sort stuff out and thank Mrs De Vries for all she done, and then I'm going on to Salisbury to see Georgie and Elsie, and make sure they ain't too upset.'

'But you can't go all that way alone,' protested Peggy. 'Andy should be with you.'

'He's got shifts to do at the fire station, and although John Hicks offered to give him some time off, we can't afford to lose out on the money, especially now I've got the kids to think about.'

'As I said before, you can bring them back here,' said Peggy. 'It will mean a bit of shifting about with the rooms, but it's no bother, really it isn't.'

Ivy was tearful as she gave Peggy a hug. 'I don't know what I'd do without yer,' she said gruffly. 'But don't go to any trouble just yet, Auntie Peg. I could be away for a while, and I need to see how the land lies down there before I bring 'em home. They might be too upset to travel straight away – and then of course,

194

me brothers could turn up and 'ave different ideas about what to do.' With that she hurried out of the kitchen and ran upstairs, Rita following closely behind her.

The mood in the kitchen had changed with Ivy's arrival, and once the food had been eaten, the table was quietly cleared, and the crockery washed and dried almost in silence until Cordelia suggested they should have a whip-round to help Ivy with the train fares.

Everyone had been touched by Ivy's plight and chipped in generously before drifting off to get on with their day. Cissy took Harvey for his walk, Danuta left for church, and Sarah went with her sister for a stroll up to the dairy while Jack made his excuses and went into the back garden to inspect the Norton motorbike that he and Rita had restored before the war.

Peggy and Cordelia sat in the kitchen, deep in their own thoughts, as Daisy built towers of wooden bricks and knocked them over. The past week had brought so much tragedy and sadness that it was hard to believe the war was over in Europe, for the consequences were still being revealed in all their horror. Charlotte would be raising Freddy's twins without their father; the youngsters in Salisbury would never see their parents again, and Ivy had been thrust into the role of caring for them instead of being free to enjoy her new married life with Andy.

Cordelia's thoughts seemed to be in line with Peggy's, for she looked over her half-moon glasses and asked, 'Do you think he'll stick by her now she'll have the children to look after?'

'I hope he proves to be the man I believe he is,' said Peggy. 'But it will be hard for both of them, and only time will tell.'

Ruby had woken to the delicious aroma of coffee and sizzling bacon and wondered if she was still dreaming. Throwing on her tatty old dressing gown and digging her feet into her slippers, she'd shuffled into the kitchen to find Mike busy at the range.

He'd greeted her with a kiss and then explained that he'd used his initiative and followed the aroma of cooking to the factory estate canteen where the lady in charge had been delighted to sell him the makings of what Ruby called a Full English breakfast.

They'd tucked in hungrily, and Ruby listened in amazement as he'd outlined the plans for the morning. While Ruby went to see Stan at the station and Peggy at Beach View, he would go to the Officers' Club and try to arrange their wedding reception. Being a Sunday it would be impossible to order a cake or flowers, or shop for a dress, as everything was shut, but first thing Monday morning, Ruby was to go into town on a spending spree.

Ruby had smiled to herself as he'd excitedly rattled on, for he made it all sound so easy, and yet she knew it wouldn't be – not at such short notice and with rationing tighter than ever. As for the shopping spree, it would have to wait until she'd given in her notice at the factory and done her final shift so she got her full week's pay. Mike seemed flush with money at the moment, but he'd soon find that weddings were expensive if carried out on such a lavish scale, and

Ruby certainly didn't want them landing in Canada with little or nothing in their pockets to pay their way.

Having eaten her fill and cleared away the dishes, Ruby brought the curtains in from the line and as it was still early, ran an iron over them, and then got Mike to help her hang them back up so the neighbours didn't get an eyeful of what they were up to. Taking this as a hint, Mike tumbled her into bed and they made slow, sweet love until the sound of the church bells reminded them they had other, rather pressing things to do.

Ruby was positively glowing with happiness as she watched Mike stride up the hill towards the Officers' Club. She had never felt so loved, or content with life, and she almost had to pinch herself to believe it was real, and that within days she would be Mike's wife.

She snapped out of her thoughts and hurried into the station to find Stan just as the London train pulled out. Stan had been the first person she'd met when she'd arrived in Cliffehaven, cold and hungry, and still bearing the bruises from her husband's latest beating. He and Ron Reilly had rescued her from the assigned billet where her husband had tried to rape her, and taken her to Beach View. Peggy's loving care had given her strength and courage to face the man who'd made her life such a misery, and when he'd been killed in an accident shortly after the confrontation, she hadn't shed a tear.

Her mother, Ethel, had followed her down to Cliffehaven and made a beeline for the widowed Stan who had a nice railway cottage and a steady income. Against all advice, Stan had married her, but Ethel soon revealed her true nature by being arrested for stealing food from the Red Cross and selling it on the black market. Poor Stan had been devastated to realise how well he'd been fooled, but with the love and support of Ruby and all his friends, he'd slowly recovered and was back to his ebullient self. Ethel was still in prison, and as far as Ruby was concerned, she could stay there.

Ruby saw that April was up in the signal box switching the levers so the departing train ran along the right track. Stan turned and saw Ruby, and with a huge grin, opened his arms in welcome. 'My dear girl. I hear Mike's home at last.'

Ruby stepped into his soft, all-encompassing embrace. 'Nothing gets past you, does it?' she teased.

'It comes with the job. I hear everything on this platform.' He held her away from him and regarded her with affection. 'I don't need to ask how things are with you and Mike,' he rumbled. 'There are stars in your eyes and you're glowing.' He hugged her again and kissed the top of her head. 'So different to the waif that arrived here in the middle of the night half-starved and covered in bruises,' he murmured. 'And thank God for it.'

'Let the dog see the rabbit, Uncle Stan,' said April, pushing in to grab Ruby. 'So when's the wedding?' she breathed.

'On Wednesday,' Ruby replied and then laughed at their shocked expressions before explaining the reason. 'I want you both there, and Paula, of course.' She looked around, but the child was nowhere to be seen. 'What you done with 'er, April?'

'She's with Vera at the telephone exchange being spoilt rotten with biscuits and milky tea, I suspect. I'm picking her up after I've seen off the next train.' April grinned and gave her a swift hug. 'I'm so pleased for you, Ruby.'

'So am I,' said Stan who was quite flushed with pleasure. 'Mike's a good man. He'll look after you.' He grinned down at her. 'Have you told Peggy and Cordelia yet? There's nothing they like more than a wedding and happily crying all the way through it. But we'll all be sad to see you go. You've become part of the Beach View family.'

'I'm going there next,' she replied. 'I'm hoping Ivy will agree to come shopping with me for me dress tomorrow, and to be me bridesmaid.'

Stan's happy smile vanished and he glanced anxiously across at April as if unsure of what to say.

Ruby experienced a stab of alarm. 'What is it? What's happened to Ivy? She ain't been 'urt, has she?'

Stan took her hand and quietly told her all he knew of Ivy's circumstances. 'You missed her by seconds,' he said finally. 'She and Andy were on that train.'

He saw the tears in her eyes and put his arm round her to hold her close. 'I'm sorry to spoil your day, Ruby, but you had to be told before you went to Beach View.'

Ruby's tears dampened his railway uniform jacket as the sadness for Ivy's situation twisted her heart. 'So I probably won't ever see 'er again if she's going to Salisbury,' she managed.

'It's unlikely. The journey there is long and she'll probably stay a while before coming back.' Stan gently held her away from him, giving her a clean handkerchief to dry her tears. 'Ivy's strong like you, Ruby,' he said softly. 'She'll come through this as she's come through everything else – and she has a good man by her side in Andy.'

Ruby nodded, knowing Stan was right, but the sadness for her friend lingered and the thought of not seeing her again hit hard. She would miss Ivy's raucous laughter, her sense of mischief and fun, and the quiet moments in which they'd shared their dreams about their wedding day when each attended the other as bridesmaid.

She gave a deep sigh, finished drying her eyes and plastered on a smile. 'I hope things turn out all right for her,' she said. 'I'll write a letter with me forwarding address and leave it with you to give to 'er when she gets back. I'd love to 'ear from her and all of you, 'cos I expect I'll get a bit 'omesick all the way over there.'

'I'll make sure she gets it,' he assured her. 'Do you want a cuppa before you go to Peggy's?'

Ruby shook her head. 'Thanks, Stan, but I'd better get on. I'm meeting Mike at one, and don't want to be late.' She hugged and kissed both of them, and as the next train slowly emerged around the bend, she took her leave.

Peggy had finally managed to have a long chat with her younger sister, Doreen, and was delighted to hear that she and the girls were very happy and settled, and that Doreen was being courted by one of the masters at the school in Wales where she worked as a secretary. Doreen was hoping to visit Cliffehaven in the summer holidays so she could see the new and improved Doris for herself and meet the man who'd brought about the miraculous change in her.

Peggy's spirits had been lifted no end after that call, and she was on the point of getting Daisy ready to go out for an hour in the recreation playground when Doris turned up asking after Ivy.

On hearing the news that she'd already left for London, Doris gave a deep sigh and settled into a kitchen chair, so Peggy abandoned her plans, told her Doreen's news, and put the kettle on for tea.

Doris listened, but her mind was clearly still on Ivy for she made no comment about Doreen. 'I was hoping to offer Ivy some help – although I don't really know what I could have done in the circumstances, except to pay some of her train fare. The pair of them don't have much money, and travelling all the way to Salisbury will eat into their savings.'

'Don't fret, Doris,' Peggy soothed. 'We all chipped in with enough to cover her journey to Salisbury and back – although it was the devil's own job making her accept it,' she added with a rueful smile.

'I do worry about her,' said Doris. 'It seems she plunges from one disaster to another, and none of it is her fault.'

'I know what you mean, but there is some good news. Thanks to John Hicks, Andy's got a full-time, well-paid job with Walthamstow Fire Brigade, and a nice flat goes with it. He's due to start there at the beginning of June.' Peggy poured the tea and changed the subject. 'How did it go yesterday? And what's Michael like?'

Doris shot her a beaming smile. 'It was a bit awkward at first, naturally, but once the food was on the table, things improved. Michael's a quiet man, but I sense he's in possession of an inner steel which I suspect is what saw him through his imprisonment. He's far too thin, of course, but with some good square meals inside him, he'll soon fill out.'

Doris sipped the tea before carrying on. 'He made it clear he didn't want to talk about his experiences as a POW and John and I respected that and kept the conversation focused on how we met, our work on the factory estate, and some of the funny incidents we've had to deal with. He seemed to accept his father's relationship with me, and told us he was looking forward to rejoining his regiment in a month's time.' Her smile was wry. 'He feels that his promotion to Major went some way towards paying for the years he'd spent in prison.'

She took a breath and hurried on. 'I told him about Anthony and Susan and darling little Teddy, and how proud I am that Anthony has been promoted to a very important position within the MOD.'

'It's going to be a wrench to have to move to Cambridge after settling so well where they are,' said Peggy.

'I'm sure Anthony will see that everything is organised with the least disruption, and of course the MOD is paying their removal costs and providing accommodation until they find a suitable house in Cambridge.' Doris offered her packet of cigarettes to Peggy and once they were alight, she continued.

'Susan will have to give up her nursing, of course, but that's no bad thing. Anthony's rise in salary means there's no need for her to work, and she can be at home where she should be, looking after Teddy. These formative years are so important, and I'm sure Teddy would much prefer to be at home with his mother than being left in a nursery all day.'

Peggy very much disagreed with her sister, but knew better than to say so. The younger generation of women were no longer satisfied with sitting at home and depending on their husband for every last penny. The war had opened many doors previously closed to them, and those with ambition had leapt at the chance to use their talents, earn their own money and cut through the restrictions that had kept their mothers tied to the kitchen sink. And it seemed men like Anthony and Fran's Robert fully encouraged it. Her Jim, of course, was an entirely different kettle of fish, and there would probably be ructions when he finally made it home.

She smoked the cigarette and watched as her sister helped Daisy with her jigsaw puzzle. Daisy certainly hadn't been harmed by being in the crèche every weekday; in fact she was much more advanced than her other children had been at that age – and she'd been at home all the time with them.

Daisy would be four at the end of the year, and because of Nanny Pringle's excellent programme, could already count to ten, recite nursery rhymes, and recognise certain letters of the alphabet. The child was sociable, had learnt to share her toys, be polite to adults and sit quietly when being read to – and although there were temper tantrums, they were becoming fewer, as she'd realised that big eyes and a bigger smile got her much further than a scowl.

Doris broke into her thoughts. 'I know you go to work and leave Daisy in that crèche, so I hope you don't think I was criticising you. After all, you're much older than Susan, and Daisy has been brought up amongst strangers, so she's bound to be more worldly-wise. But it's different with Susan, and Teddy is that much younger.'

Peggy just smiled and offered her a second cup of tea.

Doris checked her watch and then stubbed out her cigarette. 'I'm meeting John and Michael at the Officers' Club for lunch, so I won't, thank you.' She gathered up her handbag and gloves. 'Please keep me posted on Ivy, and if there's anything I can do, then don't hesitate to ask.'

They embraced and Peggy went with her to the front door to see her off. She smiled as Doris waved and disappeared around the corner, for her sister still refused to use the back way like everyone else. It seemed some old habits died hard, but then that was Doris.

Ron was full of the joys of spring as he parked Rosie's car outside the Anchor and leapt out to fetch the cases from the boot. Their honeymoon had been a great success, and being away from Cliffehaven had rejuvenated them both, making them realise how narrow their lives had become, and vowing to take more time off to see other places. They'd walked the long promenade, eaten fish and chips out of newspaper, poked about in the numerous antique shops in the Lanes, and danced every night in the hotel's grand ballroom, so Ron's back was complaining a bit, but being with Rosie was worth it.

He carried the cases up the stairs and dumped them in the sitting room before hurrying back down to check on his ferrets as Rosie headed for the kitchen to make a welcome cup of tea – it had been a long drive from Brighton, and all the tearooms they'd passed had been closed.

Having discovered that his ferrets were in fine fettle, he returned to the sitting room and shed his jacket. He picked up the bankbook Brenda had left on the dresser alongside a sheaf of notes which told him there had been no trouble in the pub, Monty had behaved himself, Bert had been in each day to see to the ferrets, and Ruby had proved to be a godsend behind the bar as Flo had done a moonlight and no one knew where she'd gone.

Rosie came in with the tea tray and looked over his shoulder at the neatly written bank deposits with a chuckle. 'Brenda and Ruby seem to have managed very well without us. Perhaps we should go away more often now we have two such reliable caretakers.'

Ron had picked up the next sheet of notepaper and was deeply immersed in what Peggy had written. When he came to the end, he silently handed it to Rosie, and then reached for the second note Peggy had left, only yesterday according to the date on the top. The bitter sadness struck him hard and he sank into the nearby armchair trying to absorb how much things had changed since they'd been away.

Rosie finished reading the note, perched on the arm of the chair, and put her hand softly on the back of his neck. 'I can't believe Freddy's gone,' she said tremulously. 'Poor Charlotte must be going through absolute hell. How on earth will she cope with two babies all on her own?'

'She'll have Kitty to help, but I suspect she's just as devastated,' Ron replied. 'You know how much she adored her brother. But at least it seems that Roger and Martin have made it through – and that's something to be grateful for.' He glanced down at Peggy's more recent note still clutched in his hand. 'There's more bad news, I'm afraid, darling. It concerns young Ivy.'

Rosie listened as he told her what had happened and then took a trembling breath. 'We've only been away for a week, and yet so many young lives have been changed forever in that short time that it's impossible to take it all in.'

She slid off the arm of the chair and nestled into his lap. 'Oh, Ron, she breathed. 'Just as we thought the war was over and things could only get better, something like this happens, and we're made to realise that it will leave a lasting legacy for so many.'

Ron cradled her in his arms and kissed her forehead. 'Aye, sweet girl, and my Jim's still out in Burma fighting his war against the Japs. I can only pray that he comes home in one piece.'

He held her for a while longer and then stood to place her gently on her feet. 'Pour the tea, darling, then I must fetch Monty from Brenda's and go to Beach View. Peggy will be deeply affected by all this, and I want to make sure she's all right before I take both dogs for a good long run. I doubt Brenda and Cissy managed to go far, and the animals will need to get rid of all that pent-up energy.'

Rosie poured the tea, and handed him the cup and saucer. 'Peggy said nothing about Cissy's American chap in her notes. I do hope there's better news on that front.'

Ron doubted there was, for Peggy would have mentioned it. He took a slurp of tea and then concentrated on lighting his pipe. He'd had enough bad news for one day; whatever was going on with Cissy's American could be put off for a while. 'Will you be all right on your own this lunchtime, Rosie?'

'Brenda's due in, so we'll manage.' She shot him a wan smile. 'Go and see Peggy, give her my love and tell her I'll pop in later. She'll want to hear about our trip to Brighton, and it might help to cheer her up a bit.'

Ron raised a bushy and rather wayward eyebrow. 'Mind what you tell her, wee girl. It was our honeymoon, remember – and some things are private.'

Rosie giggled and blew him a kiss. 'How could I forget? And wonderful it was too. Let's do it again as soon as we can arrange it.'

Ron felt a twinge in his back as he reached across to squeeze her fingers, and rather hoped she wouldn't plan another romantic break for at least a month, as he needed to get over this one first.

14

Jack followed Rita on the Norton, his heart in his mouth as she'd roared away on the Australian's Royal Enfield, taking the bends much too fast as they wound their way up the hill towards the Cliffe Estate. He was suffering a bit from a hangover, and not at all sure how to handle this meeting with Peter Ryan, but the clean, cold air seemed to be clearing his head, and he decided he'd play it by ear and give the man a chance. After all, Rita loved him, and as long as that feeling was reciprocated, he couldn't really find an objection to them marrying. But he'd make damned sure the man was worthy of her.

As they reached a long straight stretch Rita disappeared in a burst of speed, and Jack opened up the throttle to try and catch up with her, appreciating how well the Norton was running. Rita clearly knew what she was doing when it came to mechanics, but did she know enough about men? And was she mature enough to see beyond a handsome face and winning ways to make such life-changing decisions? He'd soon find out, he thought grimly as he reached the stone pillars marking the entrance to the house and gardens.

Rita brought the Enfield to a skidding halt which sent gravel flying to pepper a couple of men in white coats who were standing on the steps of the imposing entrance. They glared at her, and Rita waved an apology. She cut the engine and took off her helmet, laughing as Jack approached more sedately and parked the Norton beside her.

'Was I going too fast for you, Dad?' she teased. 'Lost your nerve?'

He switched off the engine, kicked the stand in place and climbed off with as much dignity as a man in his late forties could muster. It had been years since he'd ridden a motorbike for any length of time, and it took a moment to ease out his creaking muscles.

'I'll have less cheek from you, young lady,' he chided, taking off his helmet and running his hand through his flattened hair. 'You're a menace on that thing, and I'm amazed you haven't come off it the way you take those tight bends.'

She grinned and tucked her hand into the crook of his arm. 'You worry too much,' she said lightly before gripping his arm and looking up at him with pleading eyes. 'Be nice to Pete, Dad. He's a good man, and I love him very much.'

Jack stiffened in defence, hurt to know his daughter didn't trust him to be fair and polite. 'Of course I'll be nice to him,' he retorted. 'I'm not about to play the heavy-handed father, Rita, and am willing to give the lad a chance.'

Rita regarded him for a long moment, her eyes challenging, for they both knew from past experience that his good intentions could fly out of the window if he thought she needed protecting. She finally gave a sigh and looked away. 'Come on then. He'll probably be in the garden having elevenses, and I don't know about you, but I could do with a cuppa after that ride.'

Jack had never been on the estate before, but he'd listened to Ron's tall stories about his poaching expeditions with his sons Jim and Frank, and it all felt surprisingly familiar as she led him along paths shaded by trees and hedges of hydrangeas, and past a long hut where she told him Sarah used to work as a secretary for the Women's Timber Corps. It had clearly been turned into a sort of day room, for several men were sitting in wheelchairs on the veranda enjoying the sun as they chatted and drank beer.

They passed pretty nurses in crisp white caps and blue dresses who strolled alongside their patients or sat with them on the lawns to watch a game of croquet being played by an enthusiastic but inept group of amputees, and Jack wondered if the girls had been picked especially for their looks to boost the men's morale. The atmosphere was certainly easy-going and cheerful – and so very different to the chaos of the makeshift field hospital he'd been sent to in Belgium to get the German bullet out of his thigh – but that was something Rita didn't need to know about.

They eventually found Peter sitting alone in a cane chair at a table laid for morning tea in the shelter of a white-painted gazebo smothered in clambering roses and honeysuckle.

Jack saw the younger man hurry to his feet and stumble slightly before he regained his balance, and realised he still had a way to go in his recuperation. As they approached one another it was immediately apparent to Jack as to why Rita was so enamoured with him. He was tall, well-built and handsome in his RAAF uniform, with the open face and sunny smile that seemed to be the characteristic of all Australians.

'This is Pete,' Rita said needlessly. 'Pete, this is my dad, Jack.'

The Australian's handshake was dry and firm and the two men appraised one another steadily until the moment stretched uncomfortably and they drew apart. 'How do you do?' said Jack rather formally.

'It's good to meet you at last, sir,' Peter replied with equal formality. 'Rita's talked about you a lot.'

'I hope it wasn't all bad,' Jack said jovially. 'And please, call me Jack.'

Peter relaxed visibly and indicated they should all sit and enjoy the tea and biscuits. 'Glad to see you made it, Jack,' he said once they were settled and Rita had poured the tea. 'I was in Europe near the end, so I have a fair idea of what you must have been through.'

Jack was unwilling to discuss his war – especially in front of Rita. 'I'm glad to be back,' he said, glancing at the walking stick propped against Peter's chair. 'How's your leg coming along?'

'She'll be right,' he replied, giving his thigh a slap. 'I still need the stick when I get tired, but I get physio every day and have to walk a lot.' He grinned at Rita and took her hand. 'I reckon me and Rita know every inch of this place with all the walking we've done lately.'

Rita smiled back at him and Jack saw how radiant she was, how her adoration was mirrored in Peter's eyes, and knew then that if Rita truly wanted to follow him to the other side of the world, there was nothing he could do or say to stop her. His little girl had become a woman in his absence – a woman in love who knew her own mind, and had the courage to follow her heart – just as her mother had done by defying her stuck-up family to marry him.

Rita's voice drew him from his thoughts. 'Pete's making terrific progress, but we're both worried that if he's passed fit, he'll be posted somewhere miles away,' she said. 'So we're making the most of the time we have together.'

Peter kissed Rita's wrist and looked lovingly into her eyes. 'I wish things were different, darlin', but with so many injured coming back and needing hospital beds far more urgently than me, I'm beginning to feel like a bludger.'

He grinned at Jack's frown. 'That's a lazy bloke who sits about making excuses for doing nothing,' he explained. 'And that's not me, Jack. It's a fair go if I'm chucked out tomorrow, but I have put in a request to be billeted in Cliffehaven until I'm shipped home. Whether that comes to anything or not only time will tell.' He shrugged. 'You know what it's like in the forces, mate. You're at the whim of some pen-pusher in uniform who thinks of you as a number and couldn't care less if his orders are inconvenient.'

'I certainly do,' murmured Jack, noting with some amusement that he'd gone from sir to Jack to mate in the space of a few minutes. 'But I'm sure that now you and Rita are engaged, the authorities will look kindly on your application.'

'There's the rub, Jack,' Peter replied on a sigh. 'Rita refused to agree to a proper engagement until she'd discussed it with you, so the authorities don't know about us, and I can't make any plans.' Peter regarded him squarely across the table. 'Look, Jack, I know you must have a lot of questions – I certainly would if I was in your shoes – so why don't we go for a stroll round the gardens and clear things up between us?'

'I think that's a very good idea,' Jack replied, impressed by the younger man's straight talking. 'Rita, do you mind us leaving you?'

'Not at all,' she said lightly. 'Take your time. I'll meet you back at the bikes, and then we can all go out to lunch.' She grinned and replied to Jack's unspoken question. 'Pete can ride pillion behind me as usual. It's quite safe.'

Jack wasn't at all sure about that after witnessing the way she rode that bike, but clearly it was something they did frequently without mishap, so he made no comment.

Peter kissed Rita's cheek, retrieved the walking stick, and the two men set off in silence down a meandering path, Jack measuring his pace to Peter's slower one. They passed the pheasant pens and the dark salmon pool that Ron and his sons had used as their larder over the years, and caught sight of the surly game-keeper patrolling with his vicious-looking dog which was thankfully on a short leash.

Eventually the path petered out at the edge of an ancient forest of oak, ash and elm which shut out the sun and made it feel quite chilly until they finally emerged into a sunlit clearing that afforded them a magnificent view over the peaceful valley to the distant hills.

'Those huts back there provided accommodation for the girls who used to cut the timber,' explained Peter, 'and that ruin on the side of the valley used to be a farmhouse until a V-1 got it. Luckily no one was in it at the time.'

Jack spied the bench which had been placed to afford the very best of the magnificent view. 'Let's sit and talk, Peter,' he said quietly. 'I need to get to know more about you if I'm to let her go to the other side of the world with you.'

'Too right you do,' Peter replied cheerfully, sitting down and offering Jack a cigarette. 'So, Jack, where would you like me to start?' he asked moments later, the smoke curling from his mouth.

'From the beginning.'

Peter's smile didn't falter as he raised a questioning brow. 'Strewth, mate, that's a few years to cover, but if it means you'll give us your blessing, I reckon it's got to be done.'

Jack listened as he talked of his childhood on the isolated sheep station in the Outback of Queensland: his older sisters who were now married, and the little brother who'd been tragically killed by a snake bite at the age of four.

'I was only six at the time,' he said, 'but felt his loss as much as everyone. But these things happen out there, and I had a few close calls myself.'

Peter went on to describe the education all Outback children received by two-way radio until they were old enough to attend boarding school in Brisbane, which he'd hated – and then the three-year mechanical engineering course which he'd thoroughly enjoyed.

However, city life was not for him, and he'd returned home as soon as he was qualified to help on the station and learn to fly his father's elderly twin-prop. His ambition was to set up as a roving mechanic and shearer, and when time allowed, he'd prospected for gold and the other treasures which lay beneath the empty red heart of Australia.

'I'm used to the open spaces and big skies of Australia, you see, Jack. There's a freedom out there where a man can breathe and be in touch with the ancient people who once roamed a land that has barely changed since time began.' His smile was wistful. 'We had Aborigines working for us on the property, and as a kid I used to love listening to their Dreamtime stories.'

He crushed the butt of his cigarette under his heel and stared out at the view of green fields and rolling hills. 'I fell in love with flying in Dad's old plane, and once I could afford to buy my own, I was rarely home. There's nothing like the freedom it gives you, Jack, and when you land in the middle of nowhere to camp under the stars and watch the glory of the Milky Way arch across the sky, it's as if you're at one with the earth and the people that came before.'

Jack was mesmerised by his story and the vivid images he'd conjured up with such lyrical skill. It was no wonder Rita had been so taken with the idea of going there to see it for real. But the tale held a thread of warning to Jack, and he knew he had to follow it. 'I hope you're not planning to live the same nomadic life if you marry Rita,' he said mildly.

Peter gave a deep sigh. 'My flying days are over, Jack. The knock I took to my head when I crash-landed means I could black out at the controls – and that's not a risk I'll take after surviving the last time.'

'But you seem perfectly all right,' murmured Jack.

'Oh, yes, I'm fine for everything else.' He stuck out his leg and shot Jack a grin. 'Except for running a marathon, perhaps. But who knows? I might even do that one day.'

Jack smiled back, liking this young man who seemed unfazed by anything, and had a good sense of humour. 'So, if you can't fly, what will you do?'

'I've saved a lot of money over the past few years, so I asked Dad to send me agents' lists of properties for sale on the north-east coast where it stays warm all year round.' He grimaced and tapped his knee. 'The damp here makes my leg crook – probably because of all the metal they used to hold it together.'

'What kind of property are you interested in? Some sort of Outback station?'

Peter shook his head. 'I don't think Rita would settle easily out there. They're usually very isolated.' He shifted his leg into a more comfortable position. 'What I'm hoping to find is a place that isn't too run-down with enough land round it to grow vegetables, and pasture some animals, and to build storage sheds and a large workshop. I thought somewhere near Port Douglas or Cairns would be good, so we'll have the coast, the rainforests, and the Outback almost on our doorstep.'

'I don't know either place,' Jack admitted. 'I'm ashamed to say I didn't pay attention to the geography classes in school.'

Peter grinned. 'You and me both, mate. But Peggy's got an old school atlas, so I'll point the places out for you next time I visit. Port Douglas is a popular winter watering hole for the city people from the colder south, like Sydney, and has a thriving community, many of whom are English ex-pats from the tea and rubber plantations in India and Asia who are used to living in the tropics.'

'I seem to remember Rita telling me about Sarah's mother who fled Malaya to live with her parents up that way,' said Jack.

'Yeah, they've got a large cane plantation south of Cairns by all accounts. Sarah and I talked about it, but I can't say I've ever been there. Cutting cane is one of the toughest, dirtiest and most dangerous jobs a man can do, and I steered well clear of it.'

Peter fell silent for a moment to gather his thoughts. 'Cairns is regarded as the capital of Northern Queensland and is much bigger than Port Douglas. Because of the cane, it has an airfield, busy seaport, shops, cinema, train station and enough cafés to satisfy anyone. There are settlements dotted all the way down the coast which can be reached easily by ute unless the Wet is particularly bad and the tracks are flooded.'

Jack had heard about the heavy rains and the terrible heat from other Australians, and wondered how his daughter would cope after being used to the gentle warmth and soft rain of England. But that was something he'd worry about another time. For now he was more interested in the young couple's plans for making a living.

'So, if you find the right property and build the sheds and workshop, what will you do with them?' he asked.

'Rita and I have talked long and hard about setting up a business, much like yours, mending cars, trucks, bikes, farm machinery, and anything else that has an engine. We'd get a couple of reliable utes so we could travel to the customers if need be, but the bulk of the work would be done on our property.'

He turned to look at Jack. 'There's a big call for good, hard-working mechanics over there, and if you fancy joining us, I can guarantee you won't regret it, Jack.'

'It's thoughtful of you to offer, but I've already told Rita that Australia's not for me,' he replied. He nodded towards the view. 'Those green fields and rolling hills are what gladden my heart, Peter. They mean home, and it's here that I'll stay.'

'I can understand that, Jack. I feel the same about Queensland. But I know Rita's feeling sad and guilty at the thought of leaving you behind. Won't you reconsider? For her sake?'

Jack watched his cigarette smoke blow away on the gentle breeze. 'I could ask you the same question, Peter. Why don't you reconsider?'

Peter frowned. 'I don't get your drift, mate.'

'Why don't you stay and make a life with Rita in Cliffehaven instead of asking her to give up everything she has here?'

'We did think about it, very seriously,' Peter admitted, 'and I was prepared to go along with whatever Rita decided, because it's important that she's happy. But having talked it over for many hours, we both realised there aren't the same opportunities here to buy a large property with enough land to set up the business we dreamed about.'

Peter stretched out his bad leg and shot Jack a rueful smile. 'You've got to admit, mate, poor old England is grey and exhausted from six years of war. She's battered and bruised, and is only just clinging on to that Bulldog spirit as she struggles to recover. Rita and I want to start our lives together in the sun where the colours are vivid, hope is alive, rationing isn't so harsh, and there are few reminders of the war.'

Jack could have argued that Darwin had plenty of reminders after being totally flattened by a series of early morning Japanese air raids, but knew that was just being petty. He had to agree that England had lost her sparkle, and that everywhere you looked there was the dreary evidence of war.

He regarded the peaceful valley and sighed inwardly. It was clear that Rita and Peter had made up their minds – all they needed now was his blessing.

He glanced across at Peter who sat in silence, staring out at the view which Jack realised he wasn't really seeing. It was the dusty red of the Outback, the isolated sheep and cattle stations, the bright blue of the Coral Sea and the palm-fringed beaches of white sand that were in his mind's eye.

Jack could understand that the young man yearned for home and family and all the familiar things he'd been missing for so long. Yet, as the years passed in all that endless sunshine and bright colour, would his Rita feel the same way about England and start to pine for the gentler climate of home? Only time would tell.

Jack braced himself for the task ahead. He stood and put his hand on the younger man's shoulder, feeling the solid muscle and strength of youth. 'If you promise me faithfully to love and cherish my daughter to the end of her days, then I give my permission for you to marry and go to Australia.'

Peter got to his feet, his handsome face alight with joy. He grabbed Jack's hand to shake it enthusiastically and almost lost his balance on the uneven ground. 'You have my promise to love her forever,' he said earnestly. 'Oh, Jack, you have no idea how happy you've made me. I was so afraid you wouldn't approve.'

Jack chuckled. 'She's over twenty-one, Peter, and didn't really need my permission for anything.'

Peter's expression became serious, the dark blue eyes holding Jack's gaze. 'Fair go, Jack, of course she did,' he said. 'Rita loves you dearly and understands how hard it must be to let her go after having her to yourself all those years.' He squeezed Jack's arm. 'You've been a bonzer dad, Jack. I can only hope to be half as good when my turn comes.'

'Let's get all the arrangements sorted before we go that far,' said Jack, shooting him a wry smile. 'For now, I think we should go and tell Rita the news and then head for that country pub to celebrate over lunch.' He grinned. 'I don't know about you, but all that talking has made me very thirsty.'

Peter's smile lit up his face. 'The beers are on me, Jack. I can't have my future father-in-law going thirsty.'

'Too bloody right,' drawled Jack in an appalling imitation of Peter's accent, which made them both laugh.

Beach View was at peace apart from the usual creaks and groans of the old timbers, and as everyone slept, Peggy sat in the deserted kitchen smoking a last cigarette with a cup of tea and missing Harvey who usually slept at her feet by the range. She was tired, and should have gone to bed earlier for she had work in the morning, but her brain was too active and she knew sleep wouldn't come easily. There were too many things to think about and worry over, and although there was absolutely nothing she could do about any of it, that still didn't stop her thoughts from churning.

Ron had clearly been affected by the news of Freddy's death and Ivy's loss, and it seemed his back was playing up too – which was hardly surprising if half of what Rosie had revealed about the more intimate details of their honeymoon was true. Ron had been reticent to tell her very much about their honeymoon, giving her the most minimal descriptions of where they'd gone and what they'd seen and done. If he'd had the slightest inkling of how much Rosie had told her, he'd be so embarrassed that he'd never darken the doors of Beach View again. As it was, he'd promised to finish mending the windows and find a reliable painter and decorator to freshen up the downstairs.

Andy had telephoned from London earlier in the evening to say he and Ivy were staying with his mother overnight before Ivy caught the train to Salisbury. They'd been to see the shattered remains of Hughes Mansions and visited Mrs De Vries, before collecting the woefully few effects that had been stored by the council. Ivy had become very distressed to discover that her parents and sister now shared a grave with other unidentified victims of the bombing, and so

Andy had promised to try and arrange for a plaque to mark their final resting place.

On a much lighter note, Ruby's news had brought great pleasure to Peggy for she loved a good wedding, and was already planning what she would wear, but the thought of the girl going all the way to Canada had always worried her. Ruby was a Cockney born and bred, used to crowded tenements, raucous pubs, smoking chimneys and solid pavements beneath her feet – how she'd cope in the isolation of a Canadian outpost during the winter, Peggy couldn't imagine.

However, Peggy knew that Ivy's news and her absence from the wedding had hit Ruby hard, and her heart had gone out to the girl when she'd realised that Rita was also feeling bereft, and had kindly asked her to take Ivy's place on the day. They were due to go shopping tomorrow, though goodness knew what they'd find with such few choices – and dull ones at that with all the cheap utility clothing filling the racks. If they didn't find anything, perhaps she could ask Solly if he could get his hands on something decent – failing that, she'd try to find some good material and get one of the senior sewers to run up something more suitable at the factory.

Thinking about Rita brought Peggy back to Jack, and the difficult decision he'd had to make that day. She'd fretted over his meeting with Peter, hoping all would go well, and so was delighted when they'd returned home to tell her to prepare for another wedding as Jack had given his blessing to their future plans.

The young couple had gone to celebrate at the Anchor before getting Peter back to Cliffe, but Jack had stayed to confide in Peggy that although he liked the young Australian very much, and trusted his Rita into his care, it broke his heart to think of having to say goodbye to her when the time came.

Peggy had tried to find the right words to say, fully understanding his pain in the suffering she'd experienced after Anne and the two boys had left for Somerset. But at least they hadn't gone to the other side of the world, were in touch by telephone, and would be home again by the end of summer. She gave a deep sigh and stubbed out her cigarette. She might yet lose Cissy to the heady delights of America, so she shouldn't get too complacent.

Cissy was another worry, of course. The girl was clearly fretting at the lack of news from Randy, and after hearing of the experiences Freddy, Martin and Roger had gone through, she was beginning to doubt if he was still alive. And there was certainly enough evidence to justify that fear.

Randy had been with Freddy throughout their imprisonment, and from the information leaking out, it seemed they must have been involved in the death march from Poland down to Germany. The odds against him having survived that were extremely short, and the longer the silence stretched, the more likely it was he'd perished.

Determinedly turning her thoughts to more cheerful things, Peggy started to plan for Ruby's wedding. If Mike couldn't have the reception at the Officers' Club, then she, Rosie and the Beach View girls would do it at the Anchor. It would mean lots of baking and sandwich making, and they'd dig out the D-Day bunting from under the stairs. A telephone call to Stan secured promises from him and April to help with the food stamps, and although it would be the most terrible rush, Peggy was determined to do Ruby proud.

With that happy thought, Peggy dampened down the range fire and switched off the light. She could sleep now and dream of weddings.

15

It had been a difficult journey from Buckinghamshire to Somerset for Air Commodore Martin Black, for it involved several changes of trains and long, tedious waits at small country stations where children stared at him and their mothers pretended not to notice his appearance. He was still underweight and not fully fit, so tired easily, but at least now he was on the final leg of the journey that would take him to his wife and children.

Martin sat in the empty compartment feeling very much alone without Roger and the other men he'd been imprisoned with. He gazed out at the passing scenery as the train busily chuffed its way towards Taunton. There was nothing quite so lovely as the English countryside in the spring, but the sight of those familiar landmarks reminded him of the last time he'd made this journey, and how he'd almost ruined things with Anne by letting the stresses and strains of the war and his commitment to the men at RAF Cliffe cause friction between them. He could only thank God that Anne had understood what he'd been going through, and they'd parted as lovers; the ties that bound them as husband and wife strengthened and renewed.

That leave had been his last before he'd been shot down and captured two years ago, and although the thought of Anne and his children had kept him going in the camp – and on the long, torturous march across Germany – he knew what they would expect of him, and wasn't at all sure if he could banish the horrors that haunted him day and night, and simply step back into family life as if nothing had happened.

Martin opened the window and lit a cigarette, glad that he had the compartment to himself, but wishing he was on his way to Cliffehaven with his wingman, Roger Makepeace. Cliffehaven was home, where everything was wonderfully familiar, and therefore soothing to his soul. He would have liked nothing better than to sit in the warmth of Peggy Reilly's kitchen, tramp the hills with Ron and his dog, or revisit old haunts with Roger to try and dispel the horrific memories which troubled them both. But Roger was in Argentina for a few weeks to support Kitty and Charlotte in their tragic loss of Freddy, and Anne seemed determined to stay in Somerset, so he had no choice but to travel alone and make the best of things.

He'd felt bereft when Roger had been discharged from the hospital, and had withdrawn into himself, preferring to be alone rather than amongst men who could never understand the demons he was fighting. He and Roger had shared the trials of the prisoner-of-war camp and managed to survive the bitter winter trek across Germany; kept each other going when neither thought they could take another step; and shared what little food they could beg, steal or forage. They'd become closer than brothers through their shared experiences, and because of this unique bond, it was to each other they'd turned when the nightmares became overwhelming and they needed to talk.

Martin stared into the darkness as the train clattered through a long tunnel, and wondered how Roger was coping in Argentina. It would be extremely tough for both of them to have no one to confide in, for their problems were certainly not something to share with their wives.

He gave a deep sigh as the train emerged into the sunlight. The thought of Anne being burdened with such horrors was unacceptable, but it would not be easy to bury those memories and pretend he was untroubled. It posed a fearsome challenge, but then he'd met and conquered far more demanding challenges over the past two years. He'd find a way. He had to.

Martin brushed cigarette ash from his blue-grey Air Force uniform jacket as the train began to slow on its approach to Taunton station. He stood and pulled the heavy kitbag from the luggage rack, dumped it on the seat and, with little pleasure, eyed his reflection in the mirror set in the partition.

He was certainly no oil painting, he thought ruefully, for his eyes and face were still hollow, the flesh the colour of old parchment; the overall effect worsened by the fact his head had been shaved to rid him of lice. He'd lost an earlobe and there was a puckered and still livid scar above his right temple where a guard had hit him with a rifle butt. At least he'd been permitted to keep his moustache, but it was a poor thing compared to what it had been.

'It'll be a miracle if Anne recognises me, and the girls don't run screaming,' he muttered. 'I hope she's prepared them well enough after our telephone conversations.'

The thought of frightening his little girls was too painful, so he concentrated on hiding the scar and dark stubble beneath the cap, centring the RAF insignia and pulling the heavily braided peak low over his eyes. Checking that the buckle on his belt was in line with the jacket's brass buttons, he tweaked the end of the braided sleeves to cover his bony wrists. He could do nothing about the fingers he'd lost to frostbite, or the lack of nails on the ones he still had and on his toes, which had blackened and fallen off during the trek – but the doctors had assured him the regrowth would give him normal nails again, so he should be thankful for small mercies.

He slid open the compartment door and limped out into the corridor as the train slowly chugged along the platform and drew to a halt with a great exhalation of steam. His pulse was racing and he was aware of cold perspiration beading on his forehead as he pulled the leather strap to open the window and reach down for the door handle. Feeling quite nauseous with anxiety, he stepped down onto the platform.

Determined not to limp on his damaged feet, he squared his shoulders and headed for the ticket barrier where he could see Anne jumping up and down and waving excitedly.

Martin drank in the sight of her, praying she didn't find his looks too repugnant, but before he could brace himself for the reunion, she'd barged through the barrier and was running towards him to fling herself against him and cling to his neck.

'Oh, Martin, Martin,' she sobbed, kissing his face and holding him tight. 'It's been so long. So very long.'

He dropped the kitbag and held her as he kissed her deeply, marvelling at how she'd hardly changed in the two years they'd been apart. The war had been kind to her, for her dark hair was glossy, her skin radiant, and beneath that lightweight coat, he could feel that her figure was still as lithe and firm as the day they'd married.

They finally pulled apart breathlessly, aware they were the focus of everyone else on the platform. 'I can hardly believe you're here,' she said, the palm of her hand tenderly cupping his cheek as her gaze noted the damage to his ear and the sickly pallor of his drawn face. 'Oh, darling man. It's so very good to see you.'

Martin was in a daze, for her welcome had been overwhelming and the noise of the busy station was beginning to echo in his head and confuse him. 'Where are the girls?' he asked, looking towards the barrier.

Anne's gaze slid away, and she opened her handbag to retrieve a handkerchief as if she needed a moment to gather her thoughts. 'I left them with Vi at the farm. I thought it would be best for them to meet you at home instead of a crowded station.' She smiled up at him fleetingly and tucked her hand into his arm. 'Besides, I thought we could spend a bit of time together without them pestering for attention.'

The momentary joy of this reunion was shattered in the suspicion that she meant she didn't want the girls causing a scene at the sight of him, and the knowledge broke his heart. But he said nothing as he hoisted up the kitbag and walked with her to the ticket barrier.

The effects of the long journey were beginning to make themselves felt and he became very much on edge as they joined the bustling, eddying crowds on the concourse. The noise was awful, getting louder in his head and making him giddy.

Anne was chattering away at his side and didn't seem to notice he was struggling, so he gritted his teeth, determined to remain calm and focused on the exit which seemed miles away.

As the exit drew closer he was about to congratulate himself on making it outside without mishap when a sudden echoing announcement came over the loud-speakers and made him freeze. He was back in the camp. The guards were blowing their whistles because someone was missing at roll call, and the Commandant was issuing orders through the megaphone.

'Martin?' Anne tugged his arm. 'Martin? Whatever's the matter?'

Oblivious to Anne, he stayed frozen to the spot. To speak or move would bring about a beating, and it didn't matter how cold he got, or how exhausted, he must stay on his feet with the other prisoners.

Anne tugged his arm harder. 'Martin, what's got into you?' she hissed. 'People are beginning to stare and you're frightening me.'

The sharpness of fear in her voice brought him back to the present, but it felt as if he was sleepwalking. 'It's the noise,' he managed. 'I have to get out of here.'

Anne didn't ask any more questions, but quickly led him outside and across the road to where she'd parked the farm's Land Rover.

Martin threw the kitbag into the back and, resisting her offer to help, shakily slid into the passenger seat. He felt drained of energy and knew then that he shouldn't have insisted upon discharging himself early from the hospital, for he was shivering and sweating profusely, his head still full of the noise and the images of the camp.

'What can I do to help, Martin?' she asked anxiously.

'I'll be all right in a minute,' he said through chattering teeth. 'Please don't fuss.' He dug into his trouser pocket and pulled out the bottle of pills. Swallowing two instead of the prescribed one, he grimaced at the bitter taste and wished he had some water to wash it away.

Anne regarded him with deep concern, but made no comment as she turned the key in the ignition and drove away from the station.

Martin rested his head back and closed his eyes in despair. This was not the homecoming he'd envisioned over the last two years, for he hadn't realised what an utter wreck he would be, of no use to anyone. How wise Anne had been to leave the girls at the farm.

As the train from London rattled its way towards Salisbury and her young siblings, Ivy was too tense to relax or even eat the fish paste sandwiches Andy's mother had made for her this morning. Having never left London before she'd taken the plunge and gone to Cliffehaven in search of work, she was finding this journey a real test of her courage and strength after the dreadful two days she'd just been through.

She unfolded the piece of paper for the umpteenth time – although she knew the list by heart, she just needed to check it again. Andy, bless him, had spent ages last night carefully going through the train time-table and had written down the names of all the stations she would have to pass through. He'd even underlined the two where she'd have to change, and she'd managed to find the right platform on both occasions with the help of a friendly guard.

There was one more stop before she reached Salisbury, so she tucked the slip of paper into her jacket pocket and tried to concentrate on the difficult task ahead of her. Elsie had been three, and George had just turned five when they'd first been evacuated. The family they'd gone to then had been neglectful, feeding them nothing but beetroot sandwiches and making them sleep on mattresses in the attic, so when they'd returned to London during what became known as the phony war, Ivy's mother had vowed to keep them with her.

However, the East End soon became the target for mass bombing during the Blitz, and she'd reluctantly sent them away again. This time, they'd really fallen on their feet, for the middle-aged couple in Salisbury wrote regularly to report on their progress, and even enclosed snapshots of them so their parents could see how well they were doing. Ivy knew that her mother had found great comfort in those small kindnesses, but, like Peggy, still found it very difficult to cope without her little ones.

Ivy stared unseeing out of the window. They weren't so little now, for five years had passed since she and her parents had waved goodbye to them at the station with their name tags hanging on string around their necks, their brown paper parcels of clothes clutched in their small hands. The memory of those tear-streaked and bewildered baby faces had haunted her for days until that first letter had arrived from Mrs Johnson assuring the family that she and her husband would take the very best care of their precious little ones.

Ivy's mother had sent on a couple of photographs she'd received when they'd started school, so she had a fair idea of what they looked like now, but they wouldn't know her from Adam, she realised sadly.

The train stopped and Ivy watched disinterestedly as the passengers poured on, filling the compartments and squashing in along the corridors with their shopping bags and suitcases. She was thinking about Elsie and George and how they might have taken the news that their parents and big sister were gone. Ivy had no doubt that Mr and Mrs Johnson had tried to keep the memory of their parents and scattered family alive, and would have broken the news as gently as possible, but had the children really understood the meaning of their loss, and its consequences?

As the train pulled out of the station and picked up speed, Ivy hauled down her small, heavy case from the luggage rack and placed it between her feet, then sat back down and adjusted the hat Sarah had lent her for the journey to a better position, and buttoned up her navy linen jacket. Her sprigged cotton dress was proving a bit too flimsy for the chilly but bright weather.

Rita had given her a powder compact for Christmas, and she used the mirror to check that her lipstick hadn't been smeared. Snapping it shut, she dropped it into her capacious bag along with the packet of uneaten sandwiches, two comics and a bag of sweets she'd bought at Waterloo station as gifts for the children.

The train was slowing and there was a general bustle as people gathered their things and prepared to alight. Ivy's heart was thudding so loudly she was sure everyone could hear it, and the squash of people was making it hard to breathe, but she edged forward and finally stepped down onto the platform.

Moving away from the tide of passengers hurrying towards the barrier, she paused and took a deep breath, then dug her ticket out of her jacket pocket and slowly rejoined the flow. She'd sent a telegram yesterday, informing the Johnsons of the time of her arrival, but would someone be here to meet her – or would she have to make her own way to the village of Amesbury? Doing a mental calculation of the money she had to last her for the duration of this visit, she handed over her ticket, hoping there was a bus service to Amesbury and she wouldn't have to get an expensive taxi.

'Miss Tucker?'

Ivy snapped out of her thoughts and saw she was being addressed by a pleasant-faced, rather rotund and dapper little man in a three-piece suit and bowler hat. 'Yeah? That's me,' she replied with inbred London wariness.

'Richard Johnson,' he said, swiftly removing his bowler to reveal a head as bald and polished as a billiard ball. 'I'm delighted to meet you, although of course my wife and I wish it was under more pleasant circumstances.'

'Pleased to meet you, I'm sure,' she said, at last remembering her manners. 'It's ever so kind of you to meet me.'

Ivy found she was an inch or two taller than him and as he stuck out his hand, she saw how pale and smooth it was and wondered fleetingly if his hand-shake would be limp and unpleasantly moist. But his grip was surprisingly firm and cool, his gaze direct but kindly. No wonder he'd been the branch manager of the local bank for so many years, she thought. The old ladies must love him.

'It's the least I can do considering the long journey you've had to make – and the reason for it,' he replied, reaching to take her suitcase. 'The children will soon be home from school and Marjorie is preparing high tea, so we'd better get on.'

Ivy smiled inwardly as she followed him outside to the black Austin car, for it was just like him, all round and polished, and as neat as a new pin.

He opened the door for her, then closed it carefully before depositing her case on the back seat. Taking his place behind the steering wheel, he racked the seat as far forward as he could and then drew on a pair of leather driving gloves. 'Just a short drive home,' he said as they set off at a decorous pace into the traffic. 'I expect you're hungry after that long journey.'

Ivy realised she was, but there were questions to be asked first. 'How are the kids? Were they ever so upset when you told them about what 'appened?'

'Marjorie and I told them together, and there were a few tears,' he replied, concentrating hard on the road ahead. 'But I don't think they really understood what had happened and who it had happened to.'

'Yeah, I did wonder if that would be the case. They was ever so young when they left London, and kids that age 'ave short memories.' She clenched her fists in her lap, cursing the bloody war that had made strangers of parents to children who'd had to grow up without them.

'I understand you have two older brothers as well, Miss Tucker.'

'Please, call me Ivy,' she replied. 'I never was one to stand on ceremony.'

He nodded briefly in acknowledgement but didn't ask her to call him Richard.

'Yeah, I got two brothers, Mick and Stanley. They joined the Merchant Navy when I were in junior school, and rarely come home when they was on leave. They've been on the Atlantic convoys, so I were lucky I ain't lost them an' all – but to be honest, I'd be 'ard pushed to recognise either of them.'

He gave a sigh and brought the car to a gentle halt at a T-junction. 'I hear so many stories of families torn apart by the war. It's a real tragedy.'

He checked nothing was coming and slowly pulled away to the left which turned out to be a narrow, twisting country road lined by hedgerows. 'It was one of the reasons Marjorie and I decided to take in evacuees,' he continued. 'We have a large, comfortable home, but sadly no children of our own, and wanted to offer a safe and loving haven to the little ones who needed it.'

'They was lucky to land with you,' said Ivy, 'and I can't begin to tell you 'ow much it meant to all of us to know they was being looked after so well.'

She began to take in her surroundings as they entered a street lined with smart thatched houses of honey-coloured stone. There were flowers in the neat front gardens which were shaded by delicate trees bursting with blossom, and at the end of the road where it branched left and right, sat an ancient church.

'It was we who were lucky,' he replied, bringing the car to a standstill outside one of the houses. 'Elsie and George are wonderful children, with lively personalities and clever, inquisitive minds. Elsie is a little young yet to determine where her strengths lie, but George's headmaster is convinced he'll sail through the grammar school entrance examinations next year.'

Ivy noted how his face glowed with love and pride and felt a prickle of unease. She'd come to stay for a bit to get to know the kids and then take them back to Cliffehaven until the flat was ready in London, but it seemed the Johnsons had other ideas if they were planning George's future at the local grammar school. She had to nip any such plans in the bud – and quickly, before there were any more misunderstandings.

'None of our lot went to school after they turned fourteen,' she said lightly. 'We 'ad to earn a living to help out in the house. And when me and Andy take the kids on, we won't have the money for the likes of grammar school.'

She tentatively touched his sleeve to convey her sympathy and understanding, for he clearly adored the kids and it would break his heart when they left. 'I'm sorry, Mr Johnson, but filling George's 'ead with such things ain't good fer 'im, 'cos where we comes from, things like grammar school are a pipe dream.'

Richard nodded. 'Marjorie and I thought that might be the case,' he said quietly, 'so we were wondering if you'd agree to something we've thought long and hard about since it was clear the war was coming to an end.'

'Oh, yeah, and what's that?' she asked, suspicious that he was about to offer her money to educate George – which of course she'd refuse. She was no charity case, and neither were the kids.

Richard switched off the engine and sat there staring out of the windscreen for a long moment before clearing his throat and squaring his shoulders. 'We've come to love George and Elsie as if they are our own,' he said carefully, 'and can't bear the thought of losing them. So ... so we were wondering if you'd consent to letting us adopt them.'

Ivy could only stare at him.

'I realise it's asking a great deal of you,' he said with an edge of desperation in his voice as he turned to her. 'But I beg you to give the idea your full consideration before you dismiss it.'

Ivy didn't know how to respond and was, for once, lost for words.

16

It was the morning of Ruby's wedding, and Peggy was hugely grateful to Solly for giving her the day off from the factory. As the Town Hall ceremony was a fairly early one, she was dressed and ready for it – bar her hat and gloves – before having breakfast. Rolling her eyes at the mess in her kitchen, she fastened her wrap-round apron over her best dress, then quickly fed Daisy and slurped down a cup of tea with an aspirin as her mind raced with all the things still to be done.

There was little time to deal with the slight hangover from the previous night's party she'd held here, for the next few hours would be extremely busy. Mike hadn't been able to book the Officers' Club or the golf club – or indeed anywhere else for the reception due to the number of weddings taking place that day, and so it had been all hands to the pump to organise it at the Anchor, which Rosie very generously decided to close until the evening session. Everyone had done a sterling job of baking and sandwich making, and Peggy had managed to get enough ingredients together to make a passable wedding cake which she'd topped off with red ribbon and the smart plaster bride and groom that Mike had bought from the bakery.

Peggy had taken the cake to the Anchor the day before, but there were still more sandwiches to make and everything had to be carried over before they went to the Town Hall. Tables would have to be decorated and dressed, chairs shifted, decorations pinned up, and the fresh flowers from Stan's allotment put in vases – as long as he'd remembered to deliver them in all the excitement.

Peggy cocked her head and smiled at the excited chatter coming from upstairs. Danuta had the morning off her district nursing duties, and because she had so few pretty clothes, Sarah and Jane were kitting her out with things from their wardrobe. Cordelia was in her usual flutter trying to decide which hat to wear, and calling upon Ruby and Rita for their opinion, while Cissy was trying to get them to sit still for five minutes so she could use her skills with make-up and hairpins to ensure everyone looked their most glamorous.

Peggy smiled and mopped Daisy's face clean of porridge before the child wrestled away from her to run off and join in the fun. It was lovely to hear Cissy laughing again and being her natural, sweet self, and she hoped this was a sign that she'd come to terms with the silence from Randy, and was beginning to enjoy life again.

She looked at the clock on the mantel and began to clear the table of the unusual mess the girls had left behind in their rush to get ready for the day. Ruby had stayed the night, and she and Rita would soon be leaving for the station cottage to change into their finery before they and Stan were driven to the Town Hall in Bertie's car.

The wedding outfits had been kept a very close secret from the minute the girls had returned from leaving them at Stan's – which had been extremely frustrating for Peggy, who was dying to see what Ruby had chosen, and was a little put out that she hadn't asked her to help her dress for the day. However, she was realistic enough to accept that, unlike her other chicks, Ruby was a mature, independent young woman who'd been married before, and it probably hadn't occurred to her to ask. But it was lovely to have Ruby in the house after so long, even though it was only for a night, and in a matter of days she would be leaving England for her new life in Canada.

Peggy sighed at the thought of her going so far away, but was deeply thankful that she'd had the chance to spend time with her and could share in her special day, for she was still one of her precious chicks.

She finished clearing the table and swiftly washed the dishes, her thoughts on all her other chicks. She'd yet to hear from Fran or Ivy, and could only hope that things had gone well for them. As for Anne and Martin, there had been no word since Anne's excited telephone call on Monday morning to tell her he was due to arrive in Taunton that evening.

Peggy's thoughts returned to Ruby as she began to remove the plates of sandwiches, iced buns and jam tarts from the larder, setting them on the table and checking that the tea towels were still damp over the sandwiches to keep them fresh – which they weren't. Ruby had confided in her that she'd been fretting over who should give her away, for she loved and admired

Stan and Ron equally, and it didn't seem right to pick one over the other. Peggy hadn't really been able to advise her, for it had to be her decision, but in the end it had been Mike who'd solved the problem by asking Ron to be his best man.

Peggy clucked her tongue at the thought as she soaked the cloths again and wrapped them round the sandwiches. The young man was asking for trouble to do such a thing, and goodness only knows what state he and Ron would be in this morning for, according to Rosie, Ron had roped in his son Frank, Stan, Rita's Peter, Jack and Ivy's Andy to help Mike celebrate his forthcoming nuptials. Peter had turned up with a couple of lively Australians from Cliffe, Jack had brought an old pal he'd bumped into earlier, and Andy came with three of the fire crew who weren't on duty – and when a group of Canadian soldiers had come into the Anchor, they'd joined in with full-blooded enthusiasm.

Peggy started on a batch of potted meat sandwiches, wondering how Jack was managing to sleep through the racket the girls were making upstairs. Rosie had rung her earlier to assure her that Mike was safely back at the bungalow; she'd poured Peter and his mates into a taxi to take them back to Cliffe, dropping Jack off at Beach View along the way, and closed the door firmly on the Canadians, the firemen and Jack's pal. Frank was snoring in tandem with Ron on her sitting room floor with both dogs, and the bar looked as if a whirlwind had blown through it.

Peggy had quickly promised to get there as soon as possible to help with the clear-up, but Rosie had replied rather grimly that she'd do no such thing, and that Ron and Frank would see to it once she'd woken them by rubbing cold, wet flannels over their faces.

'I've just woken Dad,' said Rita breathlessly as she came into the kitchen with Ruby. 'He's in a bit of a state after last night so I doubt he'll want breakfast, but I'll make him a strong cup of tea before I leave.'

'I'll do that,' said Peggy, reaching for the kettle whilst admiring the two lovely young women. 'My goodness, don't you both look glamorous?' she said, thinking that Rita actually looked better without all that make-up. 'And how's our beautiful bride this morning?'

Ruby's eyes were bright with happiness. 'Nervous. Excited. All the things I should be.' She gently hugged Peggy. 'Thank you for putting me up last night and for everything you've done for our special day. Mike and I could never have managed it all on our own.'

Peggy hugged her back, careful not to disturb the perfect make-up and glossy hair. 'I always promised I'd do my best for my chicks, Ruby – and it will be the same for you, Rita, when your turn comes. Now be off, the pair of you, and I'll see you at the Town Hall.'

They clattered down the steps to the basement, and as Peggy watched through the kitchen window, fairly skipped along the path and out of the back gate.

She chuckled as she went into the hall to collect the post she'd heard arrive several minutes ago. The sun was shining, the bride was beautiful and the day promised to be a very happy one. She plucked the letters from the hall table and shuffled through them to discover two from Jim. Her day was just getting better and better.

Cissy had followed Ruby and Rita downstairs, meaning to grab a cup of tea before she got dressed and dealt with her own hair and face. Seeing that the post had arrived, she quickly rifled through the letters and cards in the hope there would be a brown forces envelope containing news from Randy.

There were two such envelopes, but they were from her father, and it seemed she'd have to go through yet another day with no news. She was about to take the pile into the kitchen when something fluttered from it to the floor. It was an air letter, and thinking it was most likely for Cordelia or Sarah, she picked it up and merely glanced at the address.

And then she looked again and read it more carefully. The letter was for her, but the writing was unfamiliar and there was no clue on the back as to who had written it. Something cold settled in the pit of her stomach, and she placed the rest of the post back on the table before carrying the air letter up to the bathroom.

Her heart was thudding as she locked the door and sank onto the stool, the thin blue paper clutched in her shaking hand. Praying silently that her fears were unfounded and that this was just from someone she'd known at Cliffe, she drew a pin from her hair and carefully slit through the gummed flap so the single page unfolded. Her gaze flew to the signature beneath the three short paragraphs and all hope died.

It took a while before she could read what he had to say, for her tears were blinding her and her hands were shaking so much, the writing was just a blur.

Dear Cissy,

As we were once very close, I felt it was important to write to you to let you know that I'm now back in the States with my family. I'm sure Freddy Pargeter has told you about the ordeals we shared over the years of imprisonment, and I hope that he's fully recovered – as have I. To my regret, we got separated when we were picked up, half-dead, somewhere in Germany. He was air- lifted to England, and I was taken to an American facility in Holland before being flown home, so I never got to say goodbye.

I have fond memories of the short time we spent together, and hope you do too. But I'm sure you'd agree that wartime romances were brought about by youthful exuberance and the times we were living in when life had to be lived to the full because tomorrow was uncertain. Now the war is over and we're more experienced and mature, we can both look back on those days with affection, see them for what they were and hold no regrets.

I hope you and your lovely family have come through unscathed and that you are with someone who makes you smile that glorious smile which once sent my heart racing. I wish you good health, happiness, and the very best of luck in the future.

Yours sincerely,
Randolph

'Cissy, whatever are you doing in there, girl?' demanded Cordelia from the other side of the door. 'I need to wash my hands before Bertie arrives.'

Cissy swallowed the lump in her throat and dashed away her tears. 'I'll be just another minute,' she replied, stuffing the letter into her trouser pocket and leaping to her feet.

Much relieved that she'd yet to put on her make-up which would have been ruined by her tears, she splashed cold water on her face and then checked for signs that she'd been crying in the mirror. Thankfully her eyes weren't too red or puffy, and a quick pinch of her cheeks brought a bit of colour back to her face. The last thing she needed was for her mother or Cordelia to start asking questions.

Ducking out of the bathroom, she apologised to Cordelia for keeping her waiting, then fetched her make-up case from Rita's deserted room. The house seemed very quiet – too quiet. She glanced at her watch in momentary panic as she hurried down the stairs, and then saw there was plenty of time to sort herself out before she had to be at the Anchor.

A hung-over Jack sat alone at the kitchen table in his demob suit, a strong cup of tea in front of him, and a cigarette burning between his fingers. 'Where is everyone?' she asked.

'Peggy and the girls have taken the food to the Anchor,' he replied, running a finger inside his stiff shirt collar and adjusting his tie. 'They've left me those to carry over once Bertie's arrived to drive Cordelia about,' he added, nodding towards the two large plates of sandwiches on the table.

Cissy left him to his hangover and hurried down to her basement room. She would not let Randy's offhand rejection upset her, she vowed, opening her make-up case and starting on her face. This was Ruby and Mike's wedding day, and no one would ever know of the bitter hurt and disappointment she would hide behind the bright smile that Randy said had once made his heart race.

'Bastard,' she hissed softly, and added a defiant slash of scarlet to her lips.

It was still early when Rosie had banished Ron and Harvey from the pub, making Ron promise he'd get Mike sober and to the Town Hall on time. Arriving at the bungalow, he'd found that the young man was already bathed and shaved and looking very smart in his dress uniform, but his eyes were still bloodshot, he was shaking with nerves, and he'd had to take a couple of aspirin for his headache.

Ron wasn't so bright himself after being roughly woken with a cold flannel and then ordered to help Frank clear up the mess they'd made the previous night. Rosie had provided them both with strong tea but refused to cook breakfast as she had more important things to do, so he was feeling very hard done by.

Finding bread, sausages, bacon and eggs in the larder, he set about making tea and cooking a hearty fry-up, which in his experience was the only cure for a hangover, and they sat down in companionable silence to polish it off as Harvey watched every mouthful in the hope of scraps.

With them both feeling a lot brighter, they went out into the pocket handkerchief back garden to get some fresh air and clear their heads of the last vestiges of alcohol before they had to face the women.

Harvey watered the few plants and nosed about the weeds in search of enticing smells before slumping onto the grass with a deep sigh of disappointment. He'd had no scraps and there was nothing to chase.

'It's a nice day for it,' Ron said, packing his pipe with the good tobacco Mike had given him, and looking up at the almost cloudless sky.

Mike lit a cigarette and chuckled. 'I've learnt not to trust the English weather. It can be like this one minute and pouring down in a howling gale the next. It's even worse in the Highlands of Scotland, and I can't recall ever feeling really warm – even in the height of summer.'

'I imagine it would be cold that far north,' muttered Ron around the stem of his pipe. 'But you must be used to it after living in Canada.'

'The cold back home is crisp and dry, not like the damp cold here that gets into your bones.'

'Well, I don't think it'll change much today,' said Ron, who prided himself on being able to forecast the weather. 'The sky's too blue and what clouds there are don't promise rain.'

Mike nodded distractedly and looked at his watch. 'I guess we ought to start making our way down,' he said. 'I know it's still a little early, but we'll need to park the car outside the Anchor and walk up the hill – and I want to be inside waiting for her when she comes down the aisle.'

Ron recognised a nervous groom when he saw one, and reassuringly patted Mike on the shoulder. 'If we arrive too early we'll get caught up in the wedding already going on, so best to enjoy our smokes and then take our time getting down there.'

'Okay, if you say so,' Mike replied doubtfully. 'But I think I'll just go to the bathroom again and then check the car starts and that there's enough petrol, oil and water in it.'

Ron smiled as Mike hurried back into the bungalow. There was no need to check anything because Mike had done all that yesterday, but he seemed to feel the need to do something, and who was he to stop him?

'Ach, Harvey,' he muttered affectionately to the supine dog. 'Weddings, eh? They make fools of us all.'

Harvey cocked his head, eyed him soulfully and with a soft snort, went back to snoozing in the sun.

Ron knocked the burnt tobacco from his pipe and pondered on the masterful feat of organisation it had taken to make sure today went smoothly – and most of it could be attributed to the women who seemed to have a knack for such things.

He looked at his watch, surprised at how quickly the morning had gone. Rosie, Peggy and the girls would have finished messing about at the Anchor by now, and be getting ready to leave for the walk to the Town Hall. Bertie was under strict orders from Peggy to drop off Cordelia on his way to the station cottage where he would pick up Ruby, Rita and Stan. April would be making her own way to the Town Hall with baby Paula once she'd handed over the day's train schedule to the stand-in railway official, and Rita had ordered a taxi to fetch Peter from Cliffe.

Ron checked the time again. There was just over half an hour to go before the ceremony, so it was probably time to drive Mike down there before his nerves got the better of him.

Peggy had only managed to quickly scan through Jim's letters as the morning's rush had kept her more than occupied, but she was looking forward to reading them properly once the hullabaloo was all over. She saw Ron and Mike already waiting by the steps as she approached the Town Hall with Daisy, Rosie and the girls, and heaved a sigh of relief that they were on time and sober. Mike looked a bit green around the gills, but a nip from Ron's hip flask seemed to put a bit of colour into his face and he managed to flash them a nervous smile before he followed Ron and Harvey up the steps to the entrance hall.

The previous wedding must have just finished, for the bride and groom emerged, surrounded by family and friends in a shower of confetti, reminding Peggy that she'd forgotten to buy any. But it was too late to worry about such things now. Peter was paying off the taxi and she could see Bertie's beribboned car slowly approaching from the top of the hill.

Chivvying the others to get a move on, she eased her way through the happy group on the steps and hurried up the red-carpeted, grand staircase to the large room where the ceremony was to be held.

Cordelia was already there in the front row of chairs, chattering away to Ron and Mike as Harvey flopped down patiently beneath Ron's seat and the female registrar tried to ignore his presence, no doubt having been informed by Ron that the Mayor had given his permission for the dog to be here – which he hadn't, of course, but she wouldn't know that until after the ceremony.

Peggy noted how Cordelia's silver hair gleamed beneath the pretty straw hat trimmed with purple ribbon, and that she looked much younger than her eighty years in her pale lilac dress and coat. But it was a worry that there were so few of them to celebrate this wedding, what with Ruby refusing to even tell her mother about it, and Mike's family being in Canada, and she could only hope the room didn't echo too much during the ceremony.

She nodded her thanks to Ron and kissed Mike's pale cheek. 'There's nothing to be nervous about,' she murmured. 'Ruby's on her way.'

He smiled at her gratefully, sat down, and then stood up again to look anxiously towards the door, clearly still on edge.

Peggy sat next to Cordelia, settled an excited Daisy beside her, and gazed round at the small gathering which barely filled two rows of the many chairs. Sarah, Jane and Danuta looked lovely in their summer dresses and lightweight jackets, as did young April who had just come in with her little Paula.

Rosie was wearing her pale blue going-away costume with her white fox fur slung artfully over one shoulder, and Cissy looked just as sophisticated in a beautifully cut navy-blue dress with a matching broad-brimmed hat and two-tone high-heeled shoes. Peter was in his RAAF dress uniform; Andy was in his fireman's uniform; Frank was in his best suit, and his wife, Pauline, wore a close-fitting dove-grey jacket over a matching pencil-slim skirt and white blouse.

Peggy raised an eyebrow, for she'd never seen Pauline looking so smart before, but she didn't have time to ponder on the reason behind this transformation, for the registrar had switched on the piped music of the wedding march and was indicating they should all stand.

Everyone turned to watch as Ruby entered the room on Stan's arm, looking radiant in a cream silk knee-length dress and matching jacket trimmed with lace. Her simple hat of cream velvet sat neatly on her crown of glossy brown hair, the birdcage netting not quite hiding her shining dark eyes that held Mike's with such adoration. She carried a bouquet of delicate pink peonies that had hearts of a deeper pink which matched Rita's floor-length dress perfectly, and on her feet were a pair of high-heeled gold sandals.

Peggy welled up immediately as she watched Stan proudly lead Ruby towards an awed Mike, and hearing Cordelia sniffling beside her, couldn't help but smile through her tears. Weddings always made them cry, but today's seemed extra special, for Ruby was one of their own who'd lived through hell before she'd found hope and love in Cliffehaven, and Mike bore the scars of that disastrous Dieppe raid with admirable stoicism. They were both survivors in their own way, and had more than earnt the right to be so very much in love.

Ron came to sit beside Rosie and lovingly took her hand as the young couple exchanged their vows, and when Mike placed the ring on Ruby's finger and kissed his bride, there was a general sigh of pleasure and smattering of applause.

Stan was doing his best to hide his tears as he sat next to April, for little Paula was watching him with deep concern, her face puckering up to howl in sympathy. This was swiftly avoided by April moving her to her other side and distracting her with a lollipop.

Daisy spotted the sweet immediately, and looked up at Peggy expectantly. Peggy dug in her handbag and found a toffee, glad she'd remembered to bring something to keep Daisy quiet whilst the register was being signed.

It didn't take too long for the large book to be signed and dated, and the young couple held hands, their faces beaming as they walked back towards the door. Everyone hurried after them, and as they gathered on the Town Hall steps, Stan and April threw confetti, and Bertie used his box Brownie to take a whole roll of pictures.

And then, with Cordelia riding like a queen in Bertie's car, it was a leisurely stroll down the High Street towards Camden Road and the reception at the Anchor. Gloria emerged from the Crown to wish them luck and hand over a bottle of champagne. Housewives in the queues outside the shops turned to congratulate them and men doffed their hats as delivery boys whistled cheekily from their bicycles.

As they passed Solly's factory they were cheered and whistled at by the girls who were taking a break in the courtyard, and Peggy could see Solly standing at the office window with a beaming smile as he waved to them. Andy's colleagues at the fire station were on the forecourt to cheer them on, and the shopkeepers in Camden Road came to their doors to wave and shout their good wishes.

Peggy became tearful again, for the lovely people of Cliffehaven knew the young couple's story and clearly wanted to do them proud and ensure they had the best wedding day possible.

17

Stan had given a fulsome speech; Ron read out all the telegrams of congratulations that had come from Canada before reciting his favourite Irish blessing, and an emotional Mike thanked everyone for the sterling effort they'd made to ensure that he and his beautiful bride had the most perfect day. He went on to thank Rita, Ron and Stan for the part they'd played, and presented each of them with a gift – cufflinks for the men and a pretty gold locket for Rita – and then the small cake was cut with much ceremony, to rousing cheers and numerous toasts.

The drinks were flowing thanks to Mike's generosity, and Rosie's collusion with Gloria over the champagne and spirits which miraculously seemed always to be at hand in Gloria's special cellar cupboard.

'You've done them proud, Rosie,' said Peggy above the loud chatter and laughter. 'I don't know how you and Gloria managed it, but I bet the Officers' Club couldn't have supplied such excellent champagne.'

Rosie winked. 'The Officers' Club don't have Gloria's contacts – and that's all I'm saying.' She glanced across at Cordelia who was giggling, her hat askew, her little face flushed as she sipped from another glass of sherry and tried to keep her balance on the wooden chair. 'It might be wise to keep an eye on her,' she murmured. 'She's going to slide straight off that chair and under the table in a minute.'

Peggy gently propped Cordelia to a more upright position and surreptitiously removed her glass. 'What about a cup of tea, Cordy?' she asked. 'It won't take a minute to put the kettle on.'

Cordelia eyed her blearily. 'Tea? Tea's for old ladies,' she slurred. 'I'll stick to my sherry, thank you, dear.' She frowned and looked round the table. 'Where's my glass?'

'To be sure, Cordelia, your eyesight is not what it was,' said Ron who was equally pie-eyed. 'It's right there.'

'I'll have you know my eyesight is as good as ever,' Cordelia retorted, squinting at the collection of glasses on the table.

Ron reached for the glass Peggy had removed and, ignoring her glare of disapproval, topped it up. 'Bottoms up,' he said, raising his glass of beer and draining it.

'For goodness' sake, you two,' hissed Peggy, trying her utmost to be stern. 'Do try and behave.'

Cordelia giggled, slid sideways, and grabbed Ron's arm to stop herself from falling between the two chairs.

Ron managed to get her upright again. ''Tis a good thing me glass was empty,' he muttered. 'Or we'd both have been awash in beer.' He put his arm about her shoulders. 'I'm thinking, Cordelia, that we've both had enough drink for one day.'

'I'm sinking too,' she replied, slowly sliding down her chair, her hat now over one eye. 'But I agree, it has been fun today.'

Ron managed to stop her from sliding under the table and gathered her in his arms. 'I'll be taking her upstairs to sleep it off,' he said to Peggy who was desperately trying not to laugh.

'I'll come up with you to make sure you don't drop her,' said Rosie as he swayed on his feet and Cordelia's hat finally fell off. 'By the looks of you, Ronan Reilly, you're not fit to be in charge of a knife and fork, let alone an old lady.'

'Ach, woman, it takes more than a few beers to make me incapable of carrying Cordelia. She weighs nothing, and I've been doing it for years.' With that, he weaved his way out of the bar and very carefully carried Cordelia up the stairs, Rosie following nervously at his heels with the hat.

As the afternoon wore on and the noise grew in tandem with the emptying of bottles, Peggy joined in with the sing-song and thought wistfully of Fran and Ivy. It didn't feel right not having Fran here to play her violin and get them all dancing, and poor little Ivy would have loved to be a part of all this instead of being down in Salisbury.

Peggy tuned out of the singing, wondering how both girls were getting on, and why Ivy had delayed bringing her young siblings back to Beach View – but then the children had probably become settled down there, and would find it an awful wrench to be taken away after all those years.

She watched Daisy and Paula dancing along to the raucous singing of 'Little Brown Jug'. According to Ivy, her little sister had been Daisy's age when she'd been sent down there, and her brother only two years older, and Peggy was profoundly grateful that she hadn't sent Daisy away despite the dangers. It had been bad enough seeing her sons leave for Somerset, soon to be followed by her daughter and granddaughter – and look how reluctant they all were to come home. Peggy suspected that Ivy would be having a hard time of it in Salisbury, and her heart went out to her.

Feeling the onset of a headache, Peggy decided she'd make some tea and carefully made her unsteady way upstairs to the kitchen. As she waited for the kettle to boil, she looked in on Cordelia, and finding her snoring happily beneath a blanket on the spare bed, left her to it. She found some aspirins in the bathroom cabinet and swallowed a couple with the hot tea and felt almost instantly refreshed. The noise was still going on downstairs, and the two dogs had clearly beaten a retreat when they discovered there was no food for them and were now sprawled, entwined, along the couch.

Peggy stood by the window and chuckled as she looked down into the street. Ron and the rest of the men were busily tying tin cans to the back bumper of Mike's hired car, fixing bangers under the front wheels, ribbons to the bonnet, and attaching a large sign to the boot, which she guessed proclaimed the occupants as newly-weds.

Watching them staggering about and giggling like schoolboys, Peggy was reminded of Jim doing much the same thing at Anne's wedding. How he would have loved to have been a part of all this instead of being stuck in some horrid Burmese jungle, she thought wistfully. She was reminded then that there were two letters from him still waiting to be read at home – an added treat to be savoured after a lovely day.

She finished her cup of tea and hurried downstairs to join in the fun of seeing the couple off. They wouldn't be going far – just back to the bungalow, where they would probably stay cocooned until Saturday morning. Their proper honeymoon would begin when they set sail for Canada.

Everyone in Camden Road stopped what they were doing to cheer as the couple emerged from the Anchor in a shower of more confetti and a good deal of back-slapping and hugs. Ruby was waving and blowing kisses as Mike started the car, and when it rolled forward the firecrackers beneath the front wheels went off with a volley of sharp bangs, and the cans set up a terrible racket as they were dragged along the road.

Everyone cheered and carried on waving as the car turned out of Camden Road onto the High Street, and the noise of those cans could still be heard in the distance as the car carried on right up the hill to the bungalow in Mafeking Terrace.

Since it was almost opening time, Peggy hitched a sleepy Daisy onto her hip and went back inside to lay her on the padded settle beneath the back window while she helped Rosie clear the tables. The party was already breaking up, for April had taken Paula home to bed; Bertie was on his way to the golf club in search of a game of bridge; Rita had poured Peter into a taxi before reporting for duty with Andy at the fire station, and Danuta had left some time ago for her district-nursing shift.

Stan and Ron were soon pushing the tables and chairs back into place, while Jack swept up the mess from the floor and collected the remains of the fire-crackers and confetti from the pavement. Frank gathered up the empty bottles and carried them down to the cellar where he also tapped a new barrel of beer to replace the empty one. Sarah, Jane and Cissy went upstairs to wash up the plates and cutlery, and Peggy joined Rosie and Pauline to set about washing all the glasses and putting the bar to rights again before the reliable Brenda turned up for the evening session.

Once everything was ship-shape, Ron, Jack, Frank and Stan settled down at the table by the inglenook with fresh glasses of beer and a plate of left-over sand-wiches. It was likely they would stay there until Rosie called time. Peggy refused another glass of champagne and fetched the pushchair from the hall then carefully placed Daisy in it, covering her with a blanket.

'I'm off home,' she said to Pauline. 'You're welcome to come with me and stay the night, but you'll have to share with Rita, I'm afraid.'

Pauline buttoned her tailored jacket and smoothed her skirt over her narrow hips. 'Thank you, but I finally persuaded Frank to get the car out of storage and road-worthy again, so I'll be driving home.' She glanced across at the group by the inglenook and grimaced. 'It looks as if he'll be here for the night again, but at least I won't have to put up with his awful snoring.'

'Yes, it does get worse after they've had a drink, doesn't it?' replied Peggy, rather relieved she wouldn't have to spend the evening with her tiresome sister-in-law. 'I must say, Pauline,' she went on, eyeing the skirt and jacket which had definitely not been made at Solly's factory, 'you do look very smart, and I like the way you've done your hair.'

Pauline patted the neat brown curls. 'I decided to treat myself to a permanent wave,' she said. 'And to a new wardrobe now I've been promoted.'

Peggy raised a questioning brow, for she'd never thought of Pauline as a career woman.

'I'm now senior assistant to the administrator at the Red Cross distribution centre, and as the charity will be remaining in Cliffehaven, it's a full-time, permanent post.'

'Goodness me. Very well done, Pauline. I'm delighted for you,' said Peggy with genuine sincerity. 'They must think a lot of you to do that.'

Pauline looked smug. 'They do indeed,' she replied, gathering up her handbag. 'So much so that when Brendon comes home, they promised to give me a week off on full pay.'

'Have you heard when he's due back?'

'He's already ashore having been demobbed from the Royal Naval Reserve. But he chose to spend his first two weeks with that girl, Betty, down in Devon,' she replied, her lips thinning in disapproval.

Peggy made no comment, for this was typical of her sister-in-law's attitude to Brendan's girl.

Pauline carried on. 'It seems he's planning to bring her home to meet us, and will call in on my mother on the way.' Her lip curled. 'But I doubt she'll be at home as usual, and it will serve her right if she misses her only grandson. Dolly was never much one for family, as you know.'

Peggy was all too familiar with the friction that existed between Pauline and her mother, so didn't ask after Dolly who was actually a very good mother in her way, and had become a close friend over the years. As this conversation was heading into dangerous, rather depressing waters, she decided to take her leave.

'Well, you take care driving home,' she said. 'It's been a long time since you've driven that car, and it's a tricky bit of road to Tamarisk Bay.'

Not waiting for a reply, she turned to the girls who were ensconced at the end of the bar finishing off the last bottle of champagne. 'I'm off home to put Daisy to bed,' she said. 'Try to see that Jack makes it back in one piece.'

'Jack will have to look after himself,' replied Cissy. 'We're going dancing once we've finished this.'

Peggy regarded Sarah, Jane and Cissy, hoping they weren't too squiffy after the afternoon's drinking, for all sorts of shady types hung about the clubs and dance halls looking to take advantage of such girls. 'Just mind you watch out for each other and stay together. And please don't make too much noise when you come in.'

Kissing the girls goodbye, and giving Rosie a hug, Peggy left the Anchor and slowly wheeled the push-chair towards home. It had been a perfect day, and once Daisy was asleep, she would change into her nightclothes, make a cup of tea and snuggle down by the fire to finally read Jim's letters properly.

With a cheerful fire burning in the range to chase away the chill and the curtains drawn against the rapidly darkening sky, Peggy made the cup of tea, wrapped her dressing gown around her and settled down in the armchair with her letters, savouring the moment before opening them again.

They'd been posted a few days apart and bore a new return address ALFSEA which Jim had translated in pencil on the line beneath as Allied Landing Forces in South East Asia. Making a note of this, Peggy carefully prised the letter open and began to read.

My darling Peggy,

We managed to survive our short leave, although it was a close-run thing, what with the heavy monsoon and high winds which blew our bashas to bits so all our kit got soaked. Not that it's ever really dry; it always stinks to high heaven with damp. It's a miserable way to live, and to top it all, we had to contend with rats as big as dogs, and swarms of flying ants.

We set about making traps to catch the rats but they proved worse than useless, so Jumbo rented a good ratter of a dog from one of the Burmese natives which proved far more effective and was worth every rupee and packet of fags he paid for it.

You asked in your last letter how the fighting is going. Well, we're doing our bit in the big push to advance and giving the Japs hell, so I'm convinced it will all soon be over and I'll be packing to come home.

We seem to pack and unpack constantly for we're always on the move, and have only just completed yet another very long march through almost impossible jungle terrain to make camp in the teeming rain. I'm chilled to the bone in soaking clothes, sweating at the same time and aching from head to foot. I'm hoping it's not another bout of malaria coming on because it will mean having to be carted off to a field hospital where the conditions aren't that much better – but at least the dysentery is holding off for the moment.

I shall be so glad to get away from this filthy jungle and sweating rice paddies, and it's at times like this that I long to be back in the cool shade of the Cliffe estate's woodlands, or down by the dark eel pools where Dad used to forage for berries and wild herbs before bringing back a sack of eels. I never really liked jellied eels, but anything's preferable to bully beef.

I can't explain where we are, why we're here or what we're doing, because frankly, Peggy, none of us knows what lies ahead – although we can make a pretty good guess. At the moment it's a waiting game, and although everyone is calm, you can feel the tension building in anticipation of our new orders.

It's stinking hot and because it's so wet underfoot, we're sleeping in our trucks, jammed in like blooming sardines and constantly pestered by great swarms of flies and troops of thieving monkeys – but at least the rats are leaving us alone.

I haven't heard from Anne and the boys since VE Day, but I'm assuming they've been occupied with packing up and coming home to you. Tell them to write, Peggy; the letters and cards I get mean so much to me and they brighten even the darkest monsoon cloud. Cissy has sent numerous postcards which don't say much, and I'm wondering if her American flyer ever did come home to her. I so look forward to reading all the news from home, Peggy, and although I realise you must be extremely busy, please keep writing to me.

With love and the hope we'll soon be together again,
Jim xxx

Peggy folded the letter and stared into the glowing fire, her heart aching for poor Jim who was really going through terrible times, and clearly utterly miserable and depressed. She couldn't imagine how awful it must be to have to put up with those conditions day after day, all the while suffering from the after-effects of malaria and dysentery and never knowing what awaited him.

She gave a sharp sigh of annoyance and reached for her packet of cigarettes. Those in charge of the servicemen out there had to know how appalling the conditions were, for in the past there had been no fighting during the monsoon, and to her mind they were asking too much of men like Jim who'd already given their all – and then more.

But it seemed this latest jungle expedition heralded the final big push to get the Japs out of Burma once and for all – and at least they would be suffering the same deprivations and hardships as Jim and his men, which was some small consolation. Why the hell the Japs didn't just accept they'd lost and call it a day, Peggy didn't know, for it was obvious the war in the Far East was all but over.

She finished her cigarette and threw the butt in the fire before opening Jim's second letter. This proved to have been written in much the same vein, with moans about the weather, the conditions, the half-rations and the terrible, mind-numbing boredom that had set in as they waited for their new orders to come through.

Jim was clearly feeling depressed, isolated and forgotten out there. The men had nothing to entertain them but the drum of the rain and the whine of mosquitoes. The one thing that had cheered them all was the first mention of the official demob plans – but it seemed they would have to wait until his unit had finished their current task and returned to HQ and a well-earned rest. He finished off:

Tell everyone to write to the new address. We're never in the same place for very long, but the mail is delivered with our supply drops and comes regularly unless there's a typhoon or some such weather to hold up the planes.

I hope you're keeping well and that Brendon and the others have made it through. Frank has written often, telling me about Pauline's job and the freedom it has given him to get the boats seaworthy and prepared to go fishing again. I'm glad he's got his compensation from the government, so on my return I'm expecting to see a new fleet anchored under the Cliffehaven cliffs, just as they were when Dad and Grandad were in charge.

The last photograph you sent shows you looking as young and pretty as you were on our wedding day, and I can't believe how much our baby Daisy has grown. It makes me smile every time I look at that snap, for she reminds me of myself at that age. Get Dad to show you the family album, and you'll see what I mean.

I'm physically fitter than I've ever been, and if it wasn't for a hacking cough and nasty cold brought on by being constantly wet, I'd feel even better. But at least I haven't gone down with dysentery or malaria for a while which has to be some sort of blessing.

I love you, Peggy, and think about you every day. I wish with all my heart that I could be with you and our precious family.

Jim xx

Peggy folded the letters and, after dampening down the fire for the night, carried them into her bedroom where she placed them in the latest shoe box for safe-keeping. The number of boxes that had accumulated over the years since Jim had been sent away were a sad and painful reminder of how long they'd been apart, and as she closed the wardrobe door on them, the longing for him made her quite tearful.

Daisy snuffled in her sleep, and Peggy picked up the framed photograph of Jim and kissed it. 'I love you too, and I'm sorry I didn't tell you the truth about Anne and the boys,' she whispered. 'But I'll write tomorrow, I promise. Goodnight, my darling man. Stay safe and come home to us so we can show you just how very much we've missed you.'

18

Ivy had felt uncomfortable and out of place from the moment she'd walked through the door of Dryden House into the wide, panelled hall with its richly coloured oriental rugs on the tiled floor. A highly polished circular table bearing silver salvers and a vase of perfectly arranged flowers stood in the centre, and she couldn't help but notice the antique furniture and sweeping oak staircase that rose grandly to a galleried landing – neither of which would have looked out of place in a mansion. A grandfather clock's mellow chimes announced the half-hour, and she could hear classical music coming from beyond one of the many doors leading out of the hall.

Upon her introduction to Marjorie Johnson, Ivy's sense of being in another world had deepened and she'd become aware of how shabby she must appear to the Johnsons in her cheap clothes and down-at-heel shoes beside the elegance of the soft caramel wool twinset, pearls and tweed skirt. Marjorie was short, dark haired, trim, and vibrant with energy. She was every inch the wife of a successful man, and Ivy had suspected she was probably a stalwart member of the church and WI committees. And yet, despite the disparity between them, Marjorie had welcomed her warmly and with great sympathy for her recent loss before showing her around the house and then up to the lovely room where she would stay for the week.

That week was now almost at an end, and as Ivy sat on the deeply padded window seat in her bedroom and looked out at the riot of colour in the neat back garden, she knew the time for making decisions had come – and once made there could be no turning back.

She opened the window and lit a cigarette, feeling the warmth of the late May day on her face and wishing she could talk to Andy or Peggy – or anyone who might be able to advise her on the best thing to do. As it was, she had to see this through on her own, for there had been no word from her brothers, who she suspected were spending their leave in the local pubs of whatever port they'd anchored in, and she hadn't liked to ask if she could use the Johnsons' telephone to make a long-distance call to Peggy – they might see it as a liberty.

Thinking back to that first evening, she felt a twist of sadness. George and Elsie had been very polite but somewhat wary when they'd come back from school in their posh uniforms, and when she'd enthusiastically called her little brother Georgie, she'd been told rather coolly that he was a bit old for such a babyish name and preferred to be called George.

As they'd all sat down to what Marjorie called 'high tea', Ivy had tried to make conversation with them, asking about their school, their friends, and what they liked doing for fun. It was hard going, for their replies were stilted and short, giving her little idea of what their lives were like. So she'd given up and concentrated on not gobbling down the bread and jam and delicious cake, or slurping her tea. But all the while she ate she'd been conscious of them surreptitiously watching her over their teacups with a certain amount of puzzled curiosity before they decided to ignore her completely and chatter to Marjorie and Richard about their plans for half-term the following week.

Ivy had managed to get through the meal without tasting a thing as she'd watched and listened to them. They talked really posh, she realised, and the way they communicated with Marjorie and Richard showed how confident they were in holding an adult conversation. Their manners were impeccable, asking to leave the table when they'd finished and going straight into Richard's study to do their homework without even being told to.

Ivy had known then that they'd come a very long way from the tenement slums of East London and, despite all efforts, couldn't hide their shock at the sudden appearance in their home of this long-forgotten sister; especially when she opened her mouth and the broad Cockney accent rang out. She'd tried desperately to modulate her tone and not drop her aitches, but it came out all wrong and she'd seen the children exchanging knowing looks as they tried to smother their giggles.

Over the following days Ivy had done her best to get to know them, and regaled them with stories about their old home in London, their parents and the rest of the family. They'd listened politely but shown no real interest or curiosity, and Ivy noticed sadly how little Elsie clung to Marjorie's side as if afraid she'd suddenly be snatched away from her.

Now she stubbed out her cigarette against the outside wall and dropped the remains in the flower bed beneath her window. There really was only one right decision, and although it saddened her to make it, she knew without doubt that it was the best one for Elsie and George.

Leaving the bedroom, she slowly went down the stairs and tapped lightly on the door of Richard's study. At his permission to enter, she stepped inside. 'Mr Johnson,' she began, feeling suddenly awkward in the masculine room that was lined with books and redolent with the scent of leather and pipe tobacco. 'Mr Johnson, I've come to tell yer that I agree to you adopting the kids,' she said in a rush.

He leapt to his feet. 'Oh, Ivy,' he breathed, reaching for her hands, his round face pink with delight. 'You can't possibly imagine how happy and relieved I am that you've come to this decision – and I know that Marjorie would want me to thank you from the bottom of her heart. The thought of losing those children has been a torture for both of us over these past few days.'

Embarrassed by his emotional reaction, she gently withdrew her hands from his grasp and folded her arms. 'Yeah, well, it weren't easy, 'cos they are family, and there's so few of us left it didn't feel like a decision to be made in an 'urry.' She took a shallow breath. 'And I'm only agreeing to it on one condition.'

His delight faded and he frowned. 'What condition?'

'That I can write to them so they don't forget who I am and where they come from. If they want to write back, then so much the better – though I don't expect they will until they get older and can really understand why things turned out the way they have.'

Richard's smile was soft with relief. 'If that is your only condition, then Marjorie and I will be delighted to comply.' He regarded Ivy who was still standing by the door, her arms folded tightly around her waist. 'I know it's been a difficult decision to face, my dear, but you're clearly wise and generous of heart to realise it's the best outcome for George and Elsie.' He smiled. 'Best for you too, I imagine. As a young woman about to be married, it would have been extremely difficult to take on two children you hardly know.'

Ivy admitted silently that it would have been a lot to ask of Andy, but that hadn't been the reason behind her decision. 'I dunno nothing about wise and generous of heart,' she muttered. 'All I know is I been watching 'em all week, and realised they'd never fit in with me and Andy in a poky London flat above a chippy, and would get an 'ard time of it from the other kids at the local state school with their posh talk and ways of doing things.'

She gave a sigh and looked round the room. 'They belong 'ere with you and Marjorie in this lovely 'ouse, not in some back street of Walthamstow. You both done a marvellous job of raising them, Mr Johnson, and you should be proud of that. Them kids love yer, and it wouldn't 'ave been right to take 'em away.'

There were tears glistening in Richard's eyes as he reached once more for her hands. 'Saying thank you feels inadequate, Ivy, but I want you to know that George and Elsie will be loved and cherished until we draw our last breath.'

The moment was broken by the rap of the door knocker.

'Oh dear, Marjorie must have forgotten her front door key again,' said Richard good-naturedly. 'Let's go and welcome her home with the good news.' He bustled out of the study and into the hall leaving Ivy to follow him.

Richard opened the front door and stiffened in surprise. 'I think you must have the wrong address,' he said brusquely.

A deep masculine voice replied, 'Are you Mr Johnson?'

'Yes,' he replied warily. 'Who are you?'

'We're Ivy's brothers, Stanley and Michael. Is she still 'ere?'

Ivy nearly fainted when she saw them standing there in their Navy regulation white short-sleeved T-shirts and bell-bottom trousers, for the last time she'd seen them they'd been skinny boys in their father's hand-me-downs. Now they were over six feet tall and built like brick outhouses with muscled arms covered in tattoos and necks like tree trunks.

'I'm here all right,' she replied, easing past a stunned Richard to block the entrance and fold her arms. 'But how did yer know I was 'ere – and what do yer want?'

'A drink wouldn't go amiss,' said Stanley, who sported a flourishing beard and moustache. 'Mrs Reilly told us you was 'ere. Ain't yer goin' to let us in, gel?'

Ivy looked to Richard for advice and noted he'd gone very pale. He nodded reluctantly and stepped back, indicating silently that she should take them into the kitchen.

'Wipe yer boots,' she ordered her brothers. 'Them's Persian rugs and worth a fortune.'

They dutifully obeyed and, staring agape at the grandness of it all, wordlessly followed her through the hall into the kitchen which overlooked the lovely back garden.

Flustered by this unexpected visit, and still shocked by their appearance, Ivy put the kettle on and hunted out cups and saucers, noticing that Richard had discreetly left them to it – but probably had his ear glued to the door to hear what was being said. She still couldn't believe these giants were the same skinny, spotty youths she'd vaguely remembered leaving home all those years ago – and yet there was a likeness to their father in their size and build, and to their mother in their striking blue eyes.

She braced herself for what was to come, for their timing couldn't have been worse, and if they didn't like what she'd decided about the kids there would be trouble.

'You've changed a bit since I last saw yer,' she said once the tea was poured and a plate of digestive biscuits placed on the table before them. 'The Merchant Navy clearly feeds yer well.'

'You've changed a bit and all,' said Mick, eyeing her up and down as he grinned. 'Last time I saw yer, you 'ad yer drawers half-mast, a snotty nose and scabby knees.'

'Yeah, well, it's been a long time since then,' she replied. 'So what you doing 'ere?

'We come to see the nippers,' said Stanley, dunking a biscuit into his tea and just catching it in his mouth before it fell apart and dropped into his beard. 'Now the war's over, we thought we'd help yer get 'em settled back in the Smoke before we go back to sea.'

'They ain't going to London,' she replied firmly. 'They're staying 'ere with the Johnsons.'

'That ain't right,' muttered Mick. 'They was only supposed to be 'ere temporary like. It's time for 'em to go back 'ome and be with family again.'

'There ain't no 'ome to go to, Mick,' she replied, battling to keep her patience. 'Mum, Sis and Dad was bombed out during the Blitz and lived out of suitcases until they was killed in them flats.' She took a sharp breath. 'As fer family, there's just us – and we're strangers.'

'Yeah, we know about Mum and Dad and Sis,' said Stanley, dunking another biscuit and losing half of it in his tea. 'But Mrs Reilly told us you was getting married to that fireman, and 'e's got a flat what goes with his new job. Walthamstow ain't the East End, but it'll do, I suppose,' he added, chasing the floating bits of soggy biscuit with a spoon.

'Stop doing that,' she snapped, snatching the spoon from him. 'It ain't polite.'

Stanley tipped his chair onto its back legs, making them creak under his weight. 'Get you,' he sneered. 'Since when did you care about what's polite?'

'Since I been living with Peggy Reilly,' she retorted. 'And fer your information, Andy and I ain't taking the kids with us. They're staying 'ere so Mr and Mrs Johnson can adopt 'em.'

Stanley's chair righted itself with a thud and Mick's scraped on the floor as he leapt to his feet and leaned over the table. 'No one's adopting anyone,' he roared. 'Them kids are our blood and we ain't signing them away.'

'Mick's right,' said Stanley. 'And if you know what's good for yer, you'll listen and listen good.' He stabbed a meaty finger on the table to emphasise each word. 'Them kids belong to us. And we're keeping 'em.'

Ivy stiffened her spine and refused to be bullied. 'You mean you want me to keep 'em,' she retorted. 'And I ain't doing it. They ain't bags of spuds to be owned and passed around, and besides, I already promised I'd sign the adoption papers.' She could see the storm brewing in their eyes and leaned forward to make her own point clear.

'I know they're our blood,' she said, forcing herself to speak in a reasonable tone. 'But they ain't really been part of our family for five years. They're not babies no more, and are big enough to know what they want.'

'They're still kids,' muttered Stanley. 'And as such should leave it to grown-ups to decide what's best fer 'em.'

'And what if the grown-ups are wrong?' she countered. 'Them kids are 'appy and settled here and see the Johnsons as their family now.'

She sat back, regarded the two silent, frowning men who had yet to be convinced and decided that only straight talking would do. 'Look around, why don't yer? This is what they're used to. This is where they call home. Do you really want to rip them away from it and 'ave them squashed into a poky flat at the arse end of bleedin' Walthamstow?'

The brothers remained silent as they took in the large, well-equipped kitchen and long back garden with its swing and summerhouse. 'Peggy Reilly did warn us this might happen,' said Mick. 'But I still think we should talk to the kids and explain why they need to be back where they belong.'

Ivy exhaled sharply in exasperation. 'You ain't been listenin' to a bleedin' word I've said,' she snapped. 'But fair enough. You wanna see 'em, now's yer chance, 'cos I can 'ear them comin' back from their posh private schools. Perhaps then you'll see what I've been on about.'

They made to rise from the table, but Ivy stopped them with a glare. 'You'll frighten 'em half to death looking like that, so best you see 'em in 'ere once I've prepared 'em,' she said flatly, eyeing their bulging tattooed biceps and the way the fabric of their T-shirts was stretched over their muscled chests and washboard midriffs. 'Ain't you got jackets or somethin' to cover up them tattoos?'

'We left 'em back at the boarding house in Salisbury,' rumbled Stanley. 'Didn't see no point in them as we're on leave and it's a fine day.'

Ivy rolled her eyes and pushed back from the table. 'It's teatime and the kids will be 'ungry, so the sooner you get this over and done with and on yer way, the better.'

'We ain't going nowhere until we're good and ready,' said Mick stubbornly.

'That's right,' said Stanley with a mulish expression as he folded his meaty arms over his chest. 'They're our blood, and we got a right to find out what's goin' on 'ere.'

Ivy realised it was the best thing possible to let them talk to the children and see for themselves how they'd never fit in to a life with her in Walthamstow. 'I'll go and get 'em then,' she said. 'And don't touch nothing while I'm away.'

She shut the kitchen door behind her and leaned against it for a moment to take a deep breath and calm down. Then she headed for the chintzy drawing room where she found the little family huddled miserably together on the large overstuffed couch.

They all looked up at her with fearful eyes. 'I'm sorry about me brothers turning up like that,' she said. 'They do look a bit scary, I know. Fair gave me a fright when I saw 'em, I can tell you that,' she added, trying to make light of the situation and failing miserably. 'But for all their size, Stanley and Mick are just as soft under all that muscle as our dad was. Gentle giants, all of 'em, and don't mean no 'arm to no one 'ere.'

Her heart went out to George and Elsie who were still in their school uniforms as they clung to Marjorie and Richard. 'They're your brothers too,' she said softly. 'Though they left 'ome long before you was even a twinkle in our dad's eye. They'd like to meet you before they leave 'cos they'll be going back to sea and might never get the chance again.'

'Do we have to, Mummy?' whispered Elsie into Marjorie's shoulder.

George balled his fists in his lap and sat very stiffly next to Richard, saying nothing.

Marjorie looked to Ivy who nodded and tried to silently convey that it was important the meeting took place.

Marjorie seemed to understand. 'I think we should,' she said, kissing the top of Elsie's head and reaching across to put her hand over George's tight fists. 'They've come a long way to see you both, and it would be rude and churlish not to let them.'

She looked at her husband, and together they coaxed the children off the couch and held their hands as they walked into the hall.

'Thanks ever so,' breathed Ivy to Marjorie as they paused outside the kitchen door. 'I expect you 'eard part of that conversation, and I'm 'oping that meeting the kids will convince them I made the right decision.'

Marjorie was pale and drawn, but there was determination in her eyes as she nodded and opened the door.

The two men were standing and seemed to fill the kitchen as Ivy made the introductions and they all shook hands. Their eyes widened at the sight of the smart uniforms, and they suddenly appeared less sure of themselves when Marjorie asked pleasantly in her plummy voice if they'd travelled very far to get here.

'We come ashore at Portsmouth,' Stanley replied bashfully. 'But went all the way to Cliffehaven afore we was told Ivy were 'ere.'

'That must have been quite a journey,' said Richard, carefully avoiding looking at the tattoos. 'But then I expect you're used to a lot of travelling, being in the Royal Navy,' he blustered, clearly intimidated by the brothers' height and width.

'It's the Merchant Navy,' replied Stanley, squaring his broad shoulders. 'And yes, we got to know the Atlantic pretty well over the past five or so years.'

Richard reddened, but Mick broke the awkward moment by advancing on the silent and rather sullen George. 'Wotcha, Georgie,' he boomed jovially, ruffling the boy's hair and making him wince. 'Blimey, you ain't 'alf a big lad. I reckon you take after me and yer grandad and would do well in the ring.' He grinned and faked a few air-punches at the boy's midriff. 'Do any boxing, do yer?'

'I play rugger for the first fifteen at school,' George replied stiffly.

Mick's grin faded and he eyed the boy thoughtfully. 'Good fer you, lad,' he murmured. 'Union or League?'

It was George's turn to be surprised. 'Union.'

'A proper gent's game, that is,' said Mick, nodding. 'I'm prop forward for the Navy team, and we rarely lose a game. What position do you play?'

'Number eight,' he replied reluctantly, looking down at his shoes.

'Back row and fast on yer feet with good 'ands to carry the ball,' said Mick with approval.

George nodded and brought the short conversation to a halt by turning away to stand by his sister and hold her hand as Stanley talked to her.

'There ain't no need to be afraid,' said Stanley, bending down to Elsie's level and keeping his voice low. 'I'm yer big brother, see, and I just come to make sure you're all right.'

'I'm very well, thank you,' she replied, peeking at him through her fringe.

'Ivy says you wanna stay 'ere, and not go back to London with 'er,' he continued. 'Is that right, Elsie?'

Tears trembled on her lashes as she nodded. 'I don't want to leave Mummy and Daddy,' she whispered tremulously. 'Please don't make me go.'

Stanley sighed and would have stroked her cheek if the child hadn't flinched away from his large hand. 'Oh, darling, I ain't gunna make you do nothing you don't want,' he said softly. 'Me and Mick just needed to know you're 'appy 'ere, that's all. So don't cry, please.'

'I think it's time you left,' said Ivy firmly. 'You've seen how things are 'ere, and must realise it was the only decision I could make.'

'Yeah,' sighed Mick. 'Yer right, gel. They fit in 'ere like an 'and in a glove. We won't make no trouble about the adoption.'

'But you'd better look after them,' said Stanley, waving a meaty finger at the startled Johnsons. 'Or you'll 'ave me and Mick to deal with. Understand?'

''Course they will,' snapped Ivy, giving both brothers a push in the back. 'Now get out of 'ere and leave us in peace.'

Stanley roared with laughter as he let her propel him into the hall. 'She's a right little firecracker, ain't she, Mick? Reminds me of Mum. That Andy better watch 'is step or 'e'll never know what 'it him.'

Ivy opened the front door and walked with them down the path to the garden gate. 'When are you going back to sea?'

'In three weeks,' said Mick. 'We got extra compassionate leave 'cos of Mum and Dad.' He looked down at her and smiled. 'I'm sorry you've 'ad to deal with everything on yer own, Ivy, but at least it looks as if them kids are settled all right.'

'When will you two settle down?' she asked. 'Surely you're not planning to be at sea for the rest of your lives?'

Stanley shrugged and pulled at his beard. 'It's a good life, gel. Three square meals a day, girls in every port and we get paid to see the world. What more could a bloke want?'

Put that way, Ivy rather envied them and certainly saw their point. 'Just promise you'll write to me now and then,' she said. 'It's only us now, and Mum and Dad wouldn't have liked it if we lost touch.'

'Yeah, we'll send a postcard when we got time,' said Mick. 'And try to get to see you when we're next on 'ome leave.'

'Don't do me no favours,' she sniffed.

Stanley laughed. 'Touchy little mare,' he said fondly before lifting her off her feet and planting a smacking kiss on her cheek.

'You take care of yerself,' said Mike, holding her in a bear hug which almost squeezed the breath out of her. 'And treat that Andy right. He sounds a nice bloke.'

Ivy felt quite dizzy from their rough affection as she watched them stroll towards the centre of town and the bus station, their rolling gait proof of their years on the high seas. She had no idea when she'd see them again, but prayed she would. They were her brothers – and the three of them were the only ones left out of a family of eight. Their parents certainly wouldn't rest easily in their graves if the survivors became further estranged and lost one another.

19

Peggy had left Daisy sleeping and was up and dressed earlier than usual that Saturday morning for a number of reasons. Cordelia had a nasty cold and needed to be persuaded quite firmly to stay in bed, and she had to wake Ivy, who'd arrived home late last night from her week in Salisbury, so they could be at the station in time to see Ruby and Andy on their way. Rita was already up and about even though she'd finished her last shift at the fire station the previous day, but there was no sign of life from the others yet, which gave Peggy a chance to get breakfast prepared and hang out the few bits of washing she'd done earlier.

Carrying the basket out to the washing line she felt chilled in the shadows of the houses, for although the sky was virtually cloudless and it promised to be a lovely day, the sun had yet to breach the roofs and warm the back gardens. Peggy hung out her bedlinen and underwear, noting that the few remaining chickens looked contented enough in their run as they pecked at the feed she'd thrown down, and Ron's spring vegetables were coming along nicely.

However, Peggy still couldn't get used to not seeing the ugly Anderson shelter huddled against the back garden wall. It had been there – a blot on the landscape, and dubious hideaway during the bombing – since the council workers had set it up in 1939, and now Ron had dismantled it, she rather strangely missed it. But the seed potatoes Ron had planted once he'd dug, hoed and fertilised the dead ground would certainly come in handy, for they cost sixpence for five pounds in the shops, and that could add up over the week with so many to feed.

She shook the creases out of a wet blouse and tethered it to the line with a wooden peg, her thoughts drifting to all that had happened in the three days since Ruby's wedding. Kitty and Charlotte had returned from Argentina to Briar Cottage with Roger and the children on Thursday night, and although Peggy hadn't had the time to go up there to see them, she'd managed to have a long and rather disturbing conversation with Kitty over the telephone.

Kitty had explained Roger's state of mind and health well enough to give her a vivid idea of how much he was struggling both physically and mentally to fit into family life again. According to Kitty he hardly slept, and when he did he was troubled by nightmares which made him shout and sweat and writhe about. During their time in Argentina he'd seemed to prefer being alone and would wander off into the pampas for hours on end until her father had got so worried he'd been on the point several times of getting together a search party.

However, he'd always returned – sadly, quiet and lost in his own world – not at all like the jolly, fun-loving man Kitty had married. Now they were home again, he'd taken to haunting the abandoned airfield at Cliffe, wandering through the empty huts and hangars as if looking for the comrades he'd lost.

Peggy gave a deep sigh. Poor Kitty was terribly worried and rather frightened by the change in her husband, and both she and Charlotte had agreed he needed to be taken out of himself and given something to do – which was why they were now looking into the purchase of a second-hand plane so they could start up the air transport business they'd been planning since the men had been captured.

Peggy suspected that both girls also needed this distraction after losing Freddy, and wondered if the same thing was happening with Martin down in Somerset. She'd heard nothing from Anne since his arrival, and was very uneasy at the thought of her daughter and grandchildren having to cope with such a painful and distressing situation. She'd tried telephoning, but the line was either busy or no one answered, which was most frustrating, and she decided then and there that if she hadn't heard anything by this evening, she'd ring again and keep on ringing until someone picked up at the other end.

Peggy raised the line with the forked wooden prop so any wind would catch the washing, checked the time, and went to lean on the garden gate to smoke a cigarette and ponder on what to do about Cissy.

For all her bright smiles and cheerful chattering on the telephone, Peggy could tell there was something eating away at her daughter – it was in her eyes and clear in the moments when she thought she wasn't being observed – and Peggy knew she had to get to the bottom of it before things went any further. Yet, ever since the wedding, Cissy had avoided being alone with her, staying in bed until she'd left for work, disappearing each evening to the pub and coming home long after everyone was asleep.

What she did and where she went during those hours worried Peggy deeply, and she'd begun to wonder if Cissy had finally given up hope of Randy coming home to fulfil those promises he'd made so long ago, and was now attempting to drown her sorrows in one of the shady clubs that had sprung up in Cliffehaven.

And then there was Ivy whom, she'd soon discovered, she'd fretted needlessly over the whole time she'd been away. The girl had been remarkably cheerful considering the difficult decision she'd had to make, and had related the story of her time with the Johnsons and her brothers' arrival in great detail and with much hilarity.

Peggy chuckled to herself, for the daunting Stanley and Mick had turned up on her doorstep late one night asking for their sister, and although the initial sight of them had alarmed her, she'd nevertheless invited them in and discovered they were actually very nice men who were worried about Ivy and the children in Salisbury. But she could well imagine how they must have frightened the rather smug-sounding, well-heeled Johnsons out of their wits.

She stubbed out her cigarette and went back into the house. Dumping the basket in the scullery sink, she listened at Cissy's door, hoping she might be awake. But hearing nothing, she went up the concrete steps to find her daughter drinking tea and eating toast. Surprised to see her dressed and made up at this time of the morning, she asked her if she was coming to the station to see the newly-weds off.

Cissy shook her head. 'I'll leave that to you,' she said. She dropped the thick crust of toast on her plate and brushed crumbs from her lap. 'Mum,' she began hesitantly. 'There's something I've got to tell you.'

Peggy sat down. 'I thought there might be,' she said calmly. 'Is it about Randy?'

'Yes.' Cissy slid the airmail letter across the table. 'This came on Wednesday.'

Peggy opened the letter and swiftly read through it. 'Oh, Cissy. You didn't have to keep this to yourself all this time,' she gasped. 'Why didn't you tell me?'

'I needed to deal with it on my own,' Cissy replied. 'To make up my mind how I really felt about it and decide what I'm going to do next.' She gave a thin smile. 'Besides, it was hardly the appropriate topic of conversation on Ruby's wedding day, was it?'

'You could still have told me over the past few days,' Peggy chided softly.

Cissy put her hand over Peggy's. 'I know, Mum, and I'm sorry I didn't say anything. But I'm not a child any more, and can't come crying to you every time something upsets me.' She sat straighter in the kitchen chair, her expression hardening as she lit a cigarette. 'Goodness knows, I experienced enough real tragedy during the war to be able to deal with something as minor as my hurt pride and that bastard with his stinking self-righteous, bloody letter.'

'Language, Cissy.'

'Well, I'm angry with him. He's made me look and feel a fool.'

Peggy could understand that after all Cissy's boasting about going to America and living the high life.

'It's best you put him and his letter out of your mind, then,' she said reasonably, folding her hands on the kitchen table. 'So, have you decided what you're going to do now?'

She listened with interest to Cissy's plans to invest all her savings in the London taxi company her smart friends from RAF Cliffe had started up. However, the thought of Cissy being let loose in the city to drive people about at all hours of the day and night worried her. 'Are you sure you'll be safe, Cissy? London isn't like Cliffehaven, you know, and there will be rough elements about.'

'I drove officers about during the worst of the enemy bombing,' she replied a little impatiently, 'so navigating my way around London should be a doddle. Besides,' she added, 'the taxi service is exclusively for women, so you don't have to fret about men causing trouble, and the class of woman we'll be ferrying will not want to go anywhere near the seedier areas of London.'

'But what about accommodation? From what I've heard there's very little of it about now there are so many homeless people in London – and if you're using all your savings to invest in the company, what will you live on?'

'Clarissa has offered me a room in her Mayfair flat until I can afford my own place. There are plenty of nice apartments about if you can afford them. As for money, I have a bit put by to see me through before I start earning.'

'Oh dear,' sighed a fretful Peggy. 'You do seem very determined about all this. I don't know what your father would say if he were here.'

Cissy grinned. 'I expect he'd moan and shout, and try to put up all sorts of daft objections, but in the end he'd give in as always.'

Peggy nodded and smiled back. 'You always knew how to wrap your father around your little finger,' she said. 'And I suspect Daisy will be just the same.'

She paused and regarded her lovely daughter Cissy with deep affection, remembering the time when she'd been dancing in the back row of the revues on the pier, her dreams and high hopes of becoming a star making her just as animated as she was today. Peggy could only hope that, like the dreams of stardom, these new dreams didn't turn to dust.

'I suppose I have no choice but to give you my blessing as you've obviously planned everything so thoroughly. But I want you to promise that if things don't turn out as you wish, you'll come home.'

'I promise,' Cissy replied, reaching once more for her mother's hands. 'Thanks for being so understanding, Mum. Clarissa, Philippa and the other girls are a really spiffing bunch, and this venture excites me. I can't wait to get up there and start this new chapter in my life.'

Peggy looked at her with concern. 'Does that mean you'll be leaving quite soon?'

'I've told Clarissa I'll be catching the three o'clock this afternoon.' At her mother's shocked expression, she stood and gave her a hug. 'I know it's all a bit sudden, Mum, but I've been under your feet for too long already, and I need to get settled there and find my way around the city before I begin driving people about.'

Peggy felt the prick of tears as she embraced Cissy but held them back, not wanting to make her daughter feel guilty about leaving home. 'You'd better go and see your grandfather before you leave,' she managed through a tight throat. 'He'd be hugely hurt if you didn't.'

'Of course I will,' Cissy replied, drawing back from the embrace rather abruptly. 'Honestly, Mum, how could you possibly think I wouldn't?'

Peggy had no reply to this, and stood there feeling helpless as Cissy went down to the basement to finish her packing.

'We'd better go, Auntie Peg,' said Ivy, bursting into the kitchen with Rita. 'It's nearly nine o'clock.'

'Lawks almighty,' Peggy gasped, glancing at the clock. 'And I've yet to get Daisy up.'

'She's just waking now, and Sarah promised to see to her until we get back,' said Ivy.

'I hope she's not sickening for something,' muttered Peggy, reaching for her coat and handbag. 'It's not like her to sleep in for so long.'

'I expect she and Grandma Cordy are still getting over the late nights we've had this week, and the excitement of me brothers turning up to make a fuss of 'em,' said Ivy. 'And don't worry about Grandma Cordy; Danuta's off this morning and will make sure she has everything she needs.'

'Dad's up finally, by the way,' piped up Rita. 'He's planning to see another house this morning, but if it's anything like the last one, he'll be disappointed. I think he's only just realising how difficult it will be to find anywhere decent with so few buildings still in one piece.'

'There are plans in the pipeline to build more homes,' said Peggy, tying her scarf over her hair and leading the way out of the back door. 'But I read in the newspaper that there's a terrible shortage of building materials, as well as skilled men – and those that are available are committed to government contracts.'

'It strikes me,' grumbled Ivy, 'that the government should get its bleedin' thumb out of its arse and get on with giving people decent places to live.'

'Language, Ivy,' Peggy said automatically, and closed the back gate behind them.

The bungalow was as neat and clean as a new pin after the boxes and packing cases had been collected by the carriers, and Ruby had used up all her nervous energy going through it like a dose of salts the evening before. She'd been determined that Cordelia would get her property back in the same state that it had been in when she'd taken on the tenancy.

But now, as she wandered through the almost empty rooms for the last time, she realised sadly that despite the many happy memories she'd made here, she'd left nothing of herself behind.

'Come on, honey,' murmured Mike, moving behind her to put his arms around her and draw her back against his chest. 'Now the car's back at the rental office we'll have to get a move on, or the train will leave without us.'

Ruby nodded, although a small part of her wished the train would leave without them so they could stay here where everything was wonderfully familiar. Dismissing the thought as ridiculous, she turned in his arms to kiss him, and then held his hand as they went to the front door. Taking one last, lingering look at the little home she'd come to love, she closed the door and pocketed the key.

Mike picked up the cases and shouldered the kitbag, then nodded to the nosy parker twitching her net curtains in the bungalow across the road and grinned down at Ruby. 'At least we won't have neighbours like that where we're going,' he remarked. 'The nearest place to us is over three miles away.'

Ruby clutched the strap of her handbag and tried not to think of such distances between neighbours as they walked past the almost deserted factory estate and down the hill towards the station. She came to the conclusion that Mike had to be exaggerating, for his mother had said in her letters that they lived in a large, friendly community with shops – or stores, as she called them – and all the usual amenities modern life called for.

The sun was hot, the hill steep, and although she'd been up and down it hundreds of times over the years without really noticing it, today it felt longer and steeper than ever. She had to almost run to keep up with Mike as he strode along and was relieved she'd packed her high-heeled shoes in the overnight case and was wearing flat pumps, for she'd have broken an ankle in those heels at this pace.

She was soon feeling a bit warm and sticky, but congratulated herself on remembering how sooty and smoky she'd got on her train journey down here all that time ago, so had deliberately chosen dark coloured slacks and a lightweight jacket to go over an old grey blouse. Her lovely pale-blue going-away outfit was packed, and would not be worn until she was on board the ship.

They arrived at the station, and Peggy watched as Ruby was swamped in a hug by Ivy, who gabbled on about how sorry she was to have missed Ruby's wedding, but how glad she was to be back in time to say goodbye and wish her and Mike the very best of luck.

Ruby returned her hug, so relieved and pleased that Ivy had made it back in time to say goodbye, and then drew Rita in so the three of them could tearfully make promises to write. 'I give the address in Canada to Aunt Peg,' she said, finally drawing from the embrace, and drying her eyes. 'So you'd both better send me snaps of your weddings, and I want to 'ear all about Australia, Rita.'

Rita grinned. 'Who'd have thought back in 1940 that we'd all be getting married and off on adventures, eh?'

'It might be an adventure fer you two,' said Ivy with a chuckle, 'I reckon I'm facing a right old challenge. Andy finally told me about the state of the London flat, and he's taking me up there later to 'ave a butcher's and work out 'ow we can make something of it before 'e starts work on Monday.'

'Blimey,' breathed Ruby. 'That's cutting it a bit fine, ain't it?'

Ivy shrugged. 'We couldn't get the key until today because there was some sort of urgent repair work to be done before it was passed as habitable.' She gave Ruby a broad grin and hugged her again. 'Don't worry about me,' she said. 'You look after yerself, and if yer

293

don't like it over there, come 'ome. Auntie Peggy will see you right.'

'I certainly will,' said Peggy, taking Ruby into her arms and kissing her cheek. 'But I really don't expect to. You and Mike make a handsome couple, and I suspect you'll make a very good life for yourselves out there.'

Ruby sincerely hoped so as she watched Stan pumping Mike's hand, but before she could let the thought settle, she was suddenly swamped in a bear hug by Ron. So glad he'd come to see her off, she clung to him, the tears pricking again, as he told her to be good and not do anything he wouldn't do.

'That gives me a fair old scope,' she managed, smiling through her tears. 'You be good too,' she admonished affectionately. 'Rosie's a wonderful woman.'

Harvey bounced about and barked to be noticed, and Ruby made a fuss of him until Stan pulled him away and took her in his arms. 'Good luck, dear girl,' he murmured. 'Although I'm sure you don't need it. But I hope you don't get seasick on that ship. The Atlantic can get very rough at times.'

'I got me special pills,' she replied, the tears now flowing as she heard the train approaching. She turned in some panic to look at all their dear faces, trying to etch them firmly into her mind so she'd never forget them.

Stan hurried off to the signal box, and Peggy handed Ruby an envelope. 'It's from Cordelia,' she explained. 'She told me to tell you good luck, and not to open it until you're on the ship.'

'That's all a bit mysterious, ain't it? Even for Cordelia – and why isn't she here? She ain't ill, is she?'

'She's got a nasty cold and I've made her stay in bed for the day.' Peggy patted Ruby's arm and smiled. 'She'll be back to her old self before you can blink, Ruby, because, as you know, she hates missing out on things and detests being in bed all day.'

Ruby nodded and pocketed the letter, which reminded her about the key. Handing it over, she hugged Peggy again. 'Thanks ever so for taking me in and giving me an 'ome. I shall never forget the love and support you give me when I so badly needed it.'

Peggy was tearful and clearly embarrassed by Ruby's sweet words, and changed the subject to one that could no longer be avoided. 'What should I say to your mother if she turns up? She's due out on parole any day now.'

'Mike persuaded me to write to 'er, so I just told 'er I were married now and going to Canada. I didn't give her no forwarding address,' she added. 'The thought of 'er turning up over there gives me the shivers.'

'Oh dear, poor Ethel.'

'Don't waste yer breath feeling sorry for her, Peggy,' Ruby said fiercely. 'She's brought it on 'erself by lying, stealing, and breaking poor old Stan's heart. Prison won't 'ave changed her, you mark my words.'

The train slowly screeched to a halt with a sigh of steam and a wraith of smoke. Harvey barked and licked Ruby's hand as if he understood she was leaving, and everyone crowded round to say their last goodbyes.

There were only a few passengers alighting at Cliffehaven, and all too soon Mike was taking her arm. 'Come on, honey. It's time to go.'

Ruby didn't have time to pause and take stock of the whirlwind she'd been through these past few days, for she was swamped in a flurry of hugs and kisses. The tears streamed down her face as Mike drew her gently away, and they climbed into a carriage. Dumping her bag on a seat, she opened a window and leaned out to make the most of these last few seconds.

And then Stan blew his whistle and waved his flag and everyone on the platform started walking alongside the carriage, shouting last-minute farewells and waving as Harvey barked and danced on the end of the leash.

The train chuffed and puffed and the wheels turned a little faster so it passed the end of the platform, leaving them all behind, and began to follow the long bend which would take it out of Cliffehaven.

Ruby could no longer see anyone and she slumped into her seat, sobbing and leaning into Mike's comforting embrace. 'I didn't think it would hurt so much to leave them all behind,' she said, her voice muffled against his chest.

'They'll write and send postcards,' he murmured. 'They love you as much as you love them, so you'll never really lose them.'

They sat huddled together as the train rattled its way towards London, and eventually Ruby's tears dried and she felt more composed. Cliffehaven and the lovely people at Beach View would always be in her heart, but now she must look to the future.

She sat straighter and lovingly hugged Mike's arm, silently saying goodbye to the past, and feeling the first tingle of excitement for what lay ahead for them both in their new life adventure.

Rita was anxious to see how her father had got on in his house-hunting, and Ivy was meeting Andy at his lodgings for elevenses before they too left for London, so both girls dashed off as soon as the train was out of sight.

Peggy had waited until she could no longer hear the wheels turning or see the puffs of smoke trailing above the railway line, and was feeling quite low at the thought of having to come back to the station to see Cissy off this afternoon. She slowly walked down the High Street with Ron and Harvey, and could only pray that Ruby would settle happily in Canada. It would be early summer there, too, so at least the weather would be kind, but how she'd manage when the snow was as high as a house, she couldn't imagine.

'Ach, will you stop fretting, wee girl,' said Ron, squeezing her hand. 'Ruby and Mike will be fine – just as Cissy will in London.'

Peggy looked up at him in surprise. 'She's already been to see you then?'

'Aye, that's why I was late to see Ruby off.'

'So, what do you think of her plans, Ron? I'm a bit worried about what Jim will say about it all, to be honest – and I've never met these girls she's going into partnership with. I do hope they're honest and reliable.'

'I'm not entirely sure I approve either,' he admitted. 'Although Rosie thought it was a wonderful idea, and started babbling on about doing something similar here.' He grinned. 'I soon talked her out of it. We've enough to do running the Anchor, and Cliffehaven people have to watch every penny with things being as tight as they are.'

Ron paused to light his pipe while Harvey watered a lamp-post and sniffed in a doorway. 'I don't know anything about the other girls, either,' he said once the tobacco was alight. 'But only time will tell if this scheme will work and they're serious about it.'

He stood and looked down the High Street to the calm blue sea for a long moment and then moved on. 'I could see Cissy had made up her mind about it all and that anything I said wouldn't stop her. So I gave her my blessing and tucked a couple of quid in her bag to tide her over for a bit.'

'That was good of you, Ron,' murmured Peggy.

'She's my granddaughter, Peg, and a couple of quid is neither here nor there.'

Peggy raised an eyebrow, for Ron was not known for splashing his money about – but he'd clearly decided Cissy's new venture was worth it.

They reached the short alley which led to the side door of the Anchor and came to a halt. 'Will you be coming in for a cuppa, Peggy?' he asked as Harvey shot through the door and up the stairs in search of his food bowl.

'Not today, Ron, thanks. I've left the girls in charge of Daisy and Cordelia, and I want to spend what time I have with Cissy.'

'Ach, wee girl, Beach View is emptying fast, and I know how difficult that must be for you.' He gave her a hug. 'We have to let them all go in the end, Peg,' he said quietly. 'But I have a feeling you won't lose them entirely. They'll be back to visit with their husbands and wains before you know it.'

Peggy nodded, though she doubted they would, for making visits from Canada and Australia wouldn't exactly be easy – and once Cissy had tasted city life, she'd be very reluctant to come back. 'I'd better get on,' she said, ignoring the heartache that beset her. 'Will I see you over the weekend? Only you promised to have a look at the loose roof tile.'

'Aye, I'll drop in later when I've walked the dogs and helped Rosie with the midday rush.'

Peggy headed for home to find everyone in her kitchen. 'Cordelia,' she chided wearily. 'I told you to stay in bed.'

'She refused to stay up there,' said Danuta help-lessly. 'I am sorry, Mamma Peggy.'

'You don't have to apologise for me,' said Cordelia, snuffling into a handkerchief. 'I'm old enough to do what I want. Such a fuss over a silly cold,' she added.

Peggy kissed the top of Daisy's head as the little girl sat at the table with her colouring book. The child didn't look as if she was sickening for anything, which was a relief – but she really should be outside on such a lovely day.

As if Jane had read her thoughts, she reached for her cardigan. 'Sarah and I were just about to take Daisy to the playground, and then up to see the horses at the dairy,' she said. 'We thought you'd like some quiet time with Cissy before she leaves.'

'Oh, that is kind,' Peggy sighed, sitting down at the table to watch an eager Daisy wriggle into her outdoor shoes and cardigan. 'Lunch will be promptly at one – although it's not very exciting – just Woolton pie again.'

The sisters left with Daisy skipping along between them, and Peggy gratefully accepted a cup of tea from Ivy. 'What time are you and Andy leaving?' she asked.

'In about five minutes.' Ivy dipped her chin and went rather pink. 'I'm staying up there until Sunday night,' she confessed. ''Cos Andy reckons there's a lot to do to get the place straight, and if both of us set to, we'll get it done quicker.'

Peggy raised an eyebrow. 'How very sensible of him,' she said wryly.

Ivy's blush deepened as Cordelia tutted and rustled the pages of the newspaper to make her feelings clear on this dubious arrangement.

Peggy turned to Jack who was miserably staring into his cup of tea. 'I don't need to ask how you got on this morning,' she said. 'Was it awful?'

He shrugged. 'Not as bad as some I've seen, but it'll take a lot of work and money to put it right and make it habitable.'

'I don't know why you're bothering, Jack,' said Cordelia. 'There's a perfectly good empty bungalow in Mafeking Terrace now Ruby has no more need of it.' She eyed him over her half-moon glasses. 'I can negotiate on the rent,' she offered helpfully.

Jack sat straighter in his chair and regarded her in deep thought for a moment. 'I wasn't planning on renting, Cordelia,' he said eventually. 'But if you're willing to negotiate a price on selling it to me, then we can talk turkey.'

'Chalk and turkey?' she asked in confusion. 'Silly man. Of course we're not having that for lunch. Didn't you hear Peggy saying it was vegetable pie?'

While Rita, Ivy and Cissy smothered their giggles, Jack made winding signals to encourage Cordelia to turn up her hearing aid. 'Would you be willing to sell the bungalow to me?' he asked loudly.

'There's no need to shout,' she said crossly, twiddling with her hearing aid and making it screech. 'I can hear you perfectly clearly.' She sat forward and regarded him sternly. 'Why should I sell when I could rent the bungalow out today and have a good income from it?'

'But I could pay you three hundred quid today and you'd still get income from it if you invest it wisely.'

She raised her brows and then grinned. 'And how do I know that's the market price for such a fine home?'

'Telephone the agent and ask,' he replied, sliding a business card across the table. 'But I calculate that if a three-bedroomed house is worth about six hundred, you'd be quids in at three.'

Cordelia chuckled and read the card before pushing back from the table. 'I'd hate to think you were paying too much – or that I was being diddled,' she said with a twinkle in her eye. 'Better to ask an expert before we go any further.'

'Are you sure about this, Dad?' asked Rita, once Cordelia had left the room. 'It's a lovely bungalow, but that's a lot of money you'd be forking out.'

'It's always better to buy than rent if possible, and I've got the money from the government compensation,' he said. 'Renting just means putting money in the land-Lord's pocket and you're left with nothing to show for it at the end of the lease.'

He lit a cigarette and drummed his fingers on the table as Cordelia conducted what sounded like a long, complicated exchange on the telephone.

'I gotta go,' said Ivy, picking up her case and kissing Peggy. 'Best of luck, Jack. And you too, Cissy. See you all Sunday night.'

Cordelia came back just as Ivy slammed the back door. She rolled her eyes and sat down to dab her nose and adjust her glasses. 'If you up your offer another fifty pounds you've got a deal, Jack,' she said, holding out her hand across the table.

'Twenty-five?' he asked.

'Fifty. Or all bets are off,' she replied, struggling not to giggle at his cheek.

'Done,' he said, shaking her hand.

'And you probably have been,' Peggy laughed. 'I learned long ago never to negotiate with Cordy. She always got the better of me.'

Jack laughed, and Cordelia joined in. 'You'd better go up there and see what you've agreed to buy,' she said. We can sort out the legal paperwork later.'

Jack took possession of the key. Peggy fetched the half-empty sherry bottle and after toasting the purchase, Jack and Rita went off on the motorbikes to inspect the bungalow.

Peggy saw the mischievous gleam in Cordelia's eyes. 'What did the agent really advise you on the price, Cordy?' she asked quietly.

Cordelia tapped the side of her nose and giggled. 'Now that would be telling, Peggy dear. Can I have another sherry?'

Lunch was over and it was almost time for Cissy to catch her train. The kitchen was deserted apart from Daisy who was curled up in one of the armchairs by the fire, pretending to read a picture book. The morning's adventure had clearly tired her, and Peggy was still worried that she might be going down with something.

Jack had been full of beans when he'd returned from the bungalow, and now he'd gone off to see some government official at the factory estate to arrange the rental of one of the small units that were almost ready for occupation. Rita had left to see Peter who'd been discharged from Cliffe and was billeted in a boarding house the other side of Tamarisk Bay. Cordelia had finally been persuaded to go upstairs for a snooze; Jane and Sarah were in their bedroom reading the latest of their mother's difficult letters, and Danuta was out having afternoon tea with Solly and Rachel.

Peggy was curious about the friendship the girl had struck up with the Goldmans, but then it was understandable as they too had ties to Poland. She just hoped they wouldn't encourage Danuta's wish to return to Warsaw, for by the sound of it there was utter chaos throughout the region as refugees and the survivors of those evil camps tried to find their relatives and rebuild the ruins.

She took Cissy's hand as they sat at the kitchen table. 'I'm sorry we didn't manage to have much time to really talk, what with all the comings and goings this morning,' she said as Daisy abandoned her book and clambered onto her lap.

'I'm used to it after all this time,' replied Cissy, giving her fingers a squeeze, and blowing a kiss to Daisy. 'But I'm glad things are working out for Jack. He deserves it after all he's been through.' She glanced up at the clock on the mantel. 'I'd better get a move on, or I'll miss my train.'

'I'll come with you,' said Peggy, lifting Daisy off her lap.

'I'd rather we said our goodbyes here,' Cissy replied gently. 'You've done your bit today with Ruby and Mike, and I don't think I could bear seeing you in tears.'

'I promise not to cry,' protested Peggy. 'It's not as if you're going far away – or that I'll never see you again.'

Cissy enfolded Peggy in her arms. 'I know you'll do your best not to cry, Mum, but if you do, then so will I, and completely ruin all my make-up,' she replied, trying to make light of this emotional parting. 'I'll ring and write and come home to visit when I can, I promise,' she murmured.

'Oh, darling,' Peggy breathed, holding onto her tightly. 'Please be careful up there, and don't let city life go to your head.'

Cissy kissed her cheek before stepping back and hugging Daisy. 'I'll make you proud of me, Mum. You'll see.'

'I'm already proud of you,' Peggy managed through a tight throat. 'I love you, Cissy.'

'I love you too, Mum,' Cissy replied, her eyes suspiciously bright as she set Daisy on her feet, tugged at the hem of her smart suit jacket and then turned away to pick up her two cases and handbag.

Peggy hoisted a clinging Daisy onto her hip and followed Cissy down the concrete steps to stand in the doorway as her beloved daughter walked purposefully down the path and through the gate.

She and Daisy returned her brief wave – and then she was gone down the alleyway with her head high, already focused on the bright lights of London.

20

Somerset

Martin couldn't stay in the farmhouse any longer and strode out across the fallow field, determined to put as much distance as he could between himself and the others. It had come as a nasty shock to discover the German farmhand was still working there, and although he knew he'd had nothing to do with the treatment meted out to him by his countrymen, and not all Germans were evil, he'd done his best to avoid him.

Martin had been at Owlet Farm for three weeks now, and although the calm silence away from house and yard was peaceful, he found that the unfamiliar fields and wide open spaces made him feel more isolated than ever – but at least he could breathe out here, and avoid the hurt and worry in Anne's eyes and his children's wariness.

He reached the rickety wooden bridge which spanned the narrow flow of water that rushed towards the sea, and stood there, lost in thought. This homecoming had been a disaster in so many ways – not least because it wasn't really his home, and he longed to be back in Cliffehaven, close to the airfield and his pal Roger. These past three weeks had been a torture, for he'd found it almost impossible to be a proper husband to Anne, and the noise of the children hurt his head. And yet it was the way they'd begun to avoid him that hurt his heart, for he hadn't wanted to frighten them.

He couldn't blame Rose and Emily, who were still under five and must have heard him crying out from his nightmares, and seen their mother's tears despite all her efforts to hide them. But he simply hadn't been able to form any meaningful relationship with any of them; shooing the children away when they pestered him with their babyish chatter; virtually ignoring Sally, Bob, Charlie and young Ernie; shying from the well-meaning, motherly Violet – and turning his back to Anne as they lay in that bed night after long night. He knew it was wrong, but couldn't help himself, for the nightmare images stayed with him day and night, and filled him with such rage and despair he was frightened that if he let his guard down, he might suddenly explode with it all and terrify the life out of everyone.

Martin stared down into the clear water rushing over the gravel and swirling around the dark rocks, and saw the faces of those who'd shared the horrors of Buchenwald before being liberated by that Luftwaffe officer to the dubious delights of Stalag III, and the consequent forced death march halfway across Germany.

There was Freddy Pargeter with mischief in his eyes; and young Allan Forbes who'd saved his life and gone on the run with him through enemy territory after they'd been shot down; and Roger Makepeace who'd been his wingman – and had remained so throughout their ordeal. Then came the Aussie fliers, Billy Stokes the joker, and Jock Cannon his grizzled mentor and laconic drinking partner. They were followed by the Americans, Andrew Pearce, Randy Stevens and the drawling Willy Hurst who always seemed to be half asleep. And last but not least, the most senior of them all, the Anzac marine, Colonel Fuller, with his bristling beard and the obstinacy of a mule.

Martin's vision blurred as the ghostly parade slowly faded into the water until all that was left was the echo of their voices in his head. The nine of them had formed a tight group in the camp until Freddy and Randy had tried to escape once too often and were imprisoned elsewhere. He'd since learnt from Anne that Randy had survived, but of the original nine there were now only five left, and he wondered if they too were being tormented by the things they'd witnessed.

He thought of those who hadn't made it with a deep sorrow that was laced with intense hatred for those who'd pitilessly snuffed out their lives. Freddy had been laid to rest in Argentina; Colonel Fuller had died from gangrene during their last days in the camp and now shared a communal grave in the woods behind it. Allan Forbes was buried somewhere on their route to the other side of Germany, and First Lieutenant Andrew Pearce had survived the ordeal of that murderous march only to die within hours of being liberated by his fellow Americans.

Martin reached for the brandy flask in his pocket and drank deeply. He'd found that alcohol blotted out the memories if he drank enough of it, but it was a short respite, for when it wore off they flooded back with even greater force. He shoved the hip flask back into his coat pocket and gripped the rough wooden rail until his knuckles turned white in his desperation to talk to someone who could understand what he was going through. But there was no one who knew better than Roger, and he was on the other side of the country.

Martin pushed away from the railing and continued his walk. He'd thought of approaching George Mayhew, Anne's headmaster, who'd been shot down and still bore the life-changing scars of the burns he'd suffered. But he'd shied away from doing so when he realised the man had come to terms with what had happened to him and found love and contentment with his new wife. It would have been unkind to stir up old memories and ruin the man's peace of mind.

Anne had tried to persuade him to talk to the vicar, but upon meeting him, Martin knew immediately that although he seemed kindly enough, the man had little experience of real-life traumas and was incapable of doing more than dish out platitudes and offers of prayer.

Martin gave a deep sigh. It was at times like this that he wished he could speak to his father, who'd come through the last years of the First World War and might have some understanding of what was troubling him. However, he was estranged from his parents, who hadn't approved of his marriage to Anne and hadn't shown the slightest interest in either of them since their wedding – even when his girls had been born.

The bitterness seared through him, making him clumsy so that he almost stumbled as he climbed the stile and had to grab onto one of the posts. His damaged hand sang with pain as he knocked it against the hard wood, but he welcomed it, for it fleetingly overrode his inner torment.

As he stood there on the well-trodden shepherd's track that led down to the next village, he became aware of the beautiful song of a robin, the sough of a gentle breeze fluttering the leaves on the trees, and the clear blue of the early summer sky. He'd barely noticed the weather, or his surroundings, so intent had he been on his thoughts and memories, and now he lifted his face to the welcoming warmth of the sun, feeling it slowly sink into him until his tense muscles eased and the anger and hurt faded.

The persistent bleating of the nearby flock of sheep drew him from that peaceful moment, and he opened his eyes to find he was being watched with some curiosity by a weather-beaten old shepherd. 'What a lovely day,' he blustered in embarrassment.

'Aye,' the old man replied, leaning on a finely carved crook, his clear gaze piercing beneath thick brows. ''Tis a foine day to thank the Lord for being alive, soir,' he added with a rolling local burr.

'It is indeed,' replied Martin awkwardly.

'There be peace to be found by these here meadows,' the old man said as Martin hesitantly made to move on. 'You'll not be finding it in the bottom of no glass, soir, if you don't mind me saying.'

'Thank you for the advice,' said Martin politely, now desperate to escape the old boy. 'But a cold pint on a day like this will go down very well.'

The shepherd nodded and reached into his ragged jacket pocket for his briar pipe, his steady gaze still on

Martin. 'Good day to you, soir. May the Lord go with you and comfort you.'

Martin lifted his hand in acknowledgement and hurried down the track towards the village pub he could see nestled in the fold of the hill. The meeting with the shepherd had unsettled him, for although the old chap had meant well, he was clearly a bit soft in the head to be spouting all that religious nonsense to a stranger. As far as Martin was concerned, the Lord had abandoned him and his comrades at the gates of Buchenwald, and had certainly not been with them on that march. It was only through luck, comradeship and strength of will that any of them had survived, so he certainly wouldn't be seeking comfort from Him when there clearly was none to be had.

He continued down the hill until he reached the rickety fence which marked the boundary surrounding the pub. He'd come across this place during a long walk in his first few days here, and it had become a refuge of sorts, for no one would think of looking for him in what was essentially a farmhands' and shepherds' local.

The Lamb was a crumbling building of ancient heritage, with a leaking thatched roof, and windows so small they barely let any light in. It was surrounded by an untended garden, and its one redeeming feature was the clambering rose that smothered the walls in glorious blood-red blooms as if in defiance of the neglect. There was always a wood fire smouldering in the inglenook which filled the small room with smoke if the wind was blowing down the chimney. However, as Martin discovered, that didn't seem to bother the old boys who took up residence beside it to linger over their beer and smoke their pipes.

He ducked his head to avoid the heavy beam above the low doorway and stepped down into the single room which reeked of spilled beer, dirty clothing, sheep shit, wood smoke and pipe tobacco. Coming from the bright sunlight, it took a moment to get his bearings, and as he stood there on the hard-packed earth floor, he heard the familiar pause in the low rumble of chatter before it started up again.

He was no longer a stranger or a curiosity, he realised, and barely earned a glance as he headed for the bar. They would ignore him from now on, and that was the main reason he liked it here. Digging out his wallet, he ordered his usual pint of bitter with a whisky chaser from the enormously fat landlord whose heavy jowls and bloodshot eyes reminded him of a disgruntled bloodhound.

Carrying his drinks to his preferred seat beneath one of the tiny windows, Martin lit a cigarette and then sipped the beer. For all his looks and surly manner, the landlord kept an excellent cellar, and clearly had contacts on the black market, for there was always a bottle of whisky under the counter. Good whisky, too, he thought appreciatively, and not watered down like in some pubs.

He tuned into the conversations going on around him, but found it hard to understand the thick local accent, so tuned out again and let his thoughts drift back to Anne.

He knew she was struggling to cope with him along with her duties at the school and at home and, instead of confiding in her mother, had pretended everything was fine and thrown herself into the preparations for the forthcoming election. Martin acknowledged that it was probably her way of escaping the bleak reality of their failing marriage, just as his was to find his way here each day. At least he agreed with her choice of candidate, for she was supporting Victor Collins, the Conservative candidate for Taunton.

Politics had never been of much interest to Martin, but he suspected Anne was backing the winning side. The Conservatives were still riding high on Churchill's reputation, and leading the polls by a vast margin despite Labour's promises of a radical departure from the past with a comprehensive social security system, a free national health service and the nationalisation of major industries. To Martin's mind it was all pie in the sky, for the country was almost bankrupt after the war and such ideas would cost millions.

He drained his beer, chased it up with the rest of the whisky and went back to the bar to get the same, but with a double whisky this time. He was set for the rest of the day until it was still just light enough to find his way back to the farm, for the landlord didn't believe in closing his pub as long as he had at least one customer in it.

Peggy was determined to enjoy the sunshine of that late June Saturday as she sat in a deckchair on the promenade to watch Daisy making sandcastles with another little girl of similar age. The tide was out, the sea as calm as a mill pond, and even the gulls seemed to be enjoying the warm thermals as they hovered almost lazily overhead.

However, Peggy found she couldn't dismiss her worries entirely for they kept nagging at her. Cissy had telephoned shortly after arriving in London and seemed to be having such a thrilling time with her smart friends that she hadn't bothered since, and Peggy wondered if she would ever come home again. And then there was her sister Anne who really was a cause for concern.

Peggy had managed to have several unsatisfying conversations with Anne over the past few weeks, and although her daughter insisted everything was all right down in Somerset, Peggy had a suspicion she was keeping back more than she was saying. She knew only too well from her visits to Briar Cottage that Roger was still haunting the airfield and drinking himself into oblivion at the Officers' Club, and unless Martin was made of stone, she suspected it was the same story with him.

Peggy's worries over Anne were more serious than the ones she had over Fran, but that didn't make them less vexing. The fact that Fran had replied only very briefly to her letter and told her nothing about her trip to Ireland was proof to Peggy that the girl had had a rough time of it. She wished she would write again and tell her what had happened, but then she was probably busy settling into the London apartment and her new life with Robert, and needed time to come to terms with things.

Beach View was emptier than ever now that Rita had moved into the bungalow with her father, but she called in most days to tell her how they were getting on with setting up the new motor repair shop on the factory estate. All the units had been leased now to small independent businesses, and she and Jack were quickly building up a good number of customers as cars were being brought out of storage. But the girl was anxiously waiting for Pete's official permission to get married, and was worried that if it took too long in coming, the war in the Far East would be over and he'd be sent home without her.

On the brighter side, there was no such hold-up for Ivy and Andy. Their wedding was to take place next weekend – and none too soon to Peggy's mind, for that had been an extended weekend she'd spent with Andy at the flat and, most unusually, she'd been off her food these last few days.

Pregnant or not, the girl appeared far too calm and relaxed about it all in Peggy's opinion, and apart from going into mysterious huddles with Rita, and dashing back and forth between Doris and Gloria, she didn't seem to have organised anything. And yet she'd flatly refused to let Peggy arrange so much as a small party on the eve of the wedding, and all she could do was hope it didn't end up a total disaster.

Peggy smiled to herself, for life was at last looking up for Ivy, and when she'd returned from that long weekend in London in high spirits, she'd been confident that she and Andy would feel very much at home in Walthamstow. It seemed that, despite the tarpaulins and scaffolding Andy had first seen, the work to be done on the flat wasn't structural at all, but was in fact a complete overhaul and redecoration by the staff at the fire station to welcome their new recruit and his bride.

Dear Ivy had been quite tearful as she'd described the lovely new windows, bright white paint, varnished floors and the pretty curtains one of their wives had sewn. There were even a few sticks of second-hand furniture to start them off, and Peggy had suggested Ivy should write a letter thanking them for their kindness. It had taken a while, she remembered fondly, for Ivy could barely write legibly, let alone spell, and it had ended up looking so much like a dog's dinner, Peggy had copied it out on fresh notepaper before it was posted.

As for Jane and Sarah, they were coping with the long wait to hear about their father and Sarah's fiancé, Philip, who'd been captured shortly after the fall of Singapore. The last they'd heard from their father was a brief note from some prison camp, but it had been written over two years before and made no mention of Philip, so anything could have happened since.

Their mother seemed determined to convince herself and her daughters that they'd both come through, and was already making plans for their return to Australia, where she insisted she would hold Sarah's wedding to Philip, and then they'd all live there happily ever after.

It was a fairy tale fabricated by a woman desperate to ignore reality and cling to her dreams, and although she urged the girls to believe in this fantasy, neither of them could. They'd heard the awful stories coming out of Asia and hope for Jock and Philip had all but died – and they certainly had no wish to settle in Cairns.

As for the wedding plans, they really were a step too far. Peggy knew Sarah was still in love with the

American, Delaney, who'd written to her recently to say he was back in the States unharmed. The girl had sacrificed her future with him through what Peggy considered was a misplaced sense of duty to Philip, vowing she'd marry him if he survived, learn to love him again, and make the best of things.

It was hardly the right way to start married life, thought Peggy sadly, and she could only hope the girl realised in time that she was making a terrible mistake, and call the whole thing off regardless of who she upset.

Emerging from her dark thoughts, she smiled and returned Daisy's wave as the child studiously dug a moat in the damp sand around her castle and both children exclaimed in delight when it magically filled with water. It seemed Daisy had fully recovered from her nasty bout of chicken pox which had left only a couple of small marks on her forehead, but had kept her in a darkened room for over a week.

Peggy poured a cup of tea from the thermos flask and lit a cigarette, listening to the happy noise around her. She glanced across at Frank and Ron working on the fishing boats that were once more drawn up the beach beneath the cliffs. It felt strange to see them there and to hear the lively noise of the holidaymakers again, for it was as if the clocks had been turned back and the war had never happened. Until she thought again of her Jim, so far away in Burma, still fighting his war against the Japs, and all but forgotten by the people of Britain in the sunshine and joy of this new and heady peacetime.

The holidaymakers had returned in force to the sea-side for their annual family holiday now the men had come home, and the town was buzzing with life again despite the bomb sites and the lack of a pier or decent cinema.

It was in moments like this that Jim's absence was most poignant, for she was reminded of how, before the war, they'd come down to the beach with the children, laden with buckets, spades, towels, sun hats and picnic hamper, staying until teatime, and then carrying the tired younger ones home.

She blinked back her tears, feeling foolish and rather cross with herself for being so soppy. There would be other summers, and when Jim came home, they could spend every one of them on the beach with their grandchildren.

'Dad said I'd find you here.'

Startled, Peggy looked up and then scrambled awkwardly out of the deckchair. 'Brendon,' she gasped, throwing her arms around him. 'Oh, my goodness, how wonderful that you're home at last! It's so lovely to see you again.'

He hugged her back and grinned down at her. 'And I didn't come alone, either,' he said, reaching for the hand of the small, fair-haired young woman Peggy had noticed keeping a discreet distance from this loving reunion.

'This is my Betty,' Brendon said with great pride.

Brendon and Betty had met down in Devon whilst he'd been visiting his Aunt Carol, who'd been working as a land girl on a farm. Betty was a primary school teacher who had been raised in an orphanage and had suffered from polio as a child. Peggy looked into her elfin face as they shook hands, taking in her bright, intelligent eyes and wide smile, and instantly liked what she saw. 'I'm thrilled to meet you at last,' she said. 'We've all heard so much about you through Brendon's letters.'

Betty laughed. 'I'm delighted to meet you too. Carol and her mother, Dolly, sang your praises so highly, I almost feel I know you already.'

Aware of the thick boot and caliper on Betty's foot, and studiously avoiding looking at it, Peggy dragged over another deckchair. 'Come and sit down,' she urged. 'I'm bursting to hear all your news. How's Carol? And has Dolly been down to Devon recently? And what about you and Brendon? May I see your engagement ring?'

Betty plumped down into the deckchair as Brendon dragged a third across to join them. 'Gosh, that's quite a list,' she chuckled. 'But first things first.' She held out her hand to show off her diamond and emerald ring and giggled as Peggy gasped at the sight of the gold band nestled next to it.

'We got married on special licence when Brendon was demobbed from the Royal Naval Reserve two weeks ago.'

'Good heavens,' breathed Peggy, the delight quite overwhelming as she leapt from her chair again to grab their hands and kiss them. 'Very many congratulations,' she said warmly, giving Betty's hand a little extra squeeze to show she approved. 'I can just tell you're made for one another.'

She regarded their radiant faces as they looked at each other, and dared to ask the question that was now puzzling her. 'But why all the secrecy and rush, Brendon? Didn't you want to have your wedding here with the family around you?'

The couple exchanged glances and Brendon shifted uneasily in the deckchair. 'We wanted to keep the ceremony private with just a couple of close friends as witnesses,' he replied. 'Mum made it plain in her letters that she resented the time I spent with Betty whilst on leave, and we didn't want her making a scene and spoiling things.'

'Oh dear,' sighed Peggy, thinking how foolish Pauline was to drive her son away with her jealousy and miss one of the most important moments of his life.

'There was another reason,' said Betty, regarding Peggy evenly. 'We have a son,' she said in a rush. 'We named him Joseph in memory of Brendon's brother, and he was born while Brendon was at sea after his last leave.'

'But that's marvellous,' Peggy enthused, giving the girl a hug. 'Oh, my goodness, such wonderful news all in one go. I don't know if I can take it all in.' She looked around in confusion. 'But where is he? Surely you didn't leave him down in Devon?'

They both chuckled, and Betty replied, 'He's barely three months old, but his grandfather and great-grandfather thought it was time he experienced the smell and feel of a fishing boat.' She nodded towards the two men who were now sitting on the deck of the beached trawler. 'We left him over there, guarded by a vigilant Harvey, and probably being thoroughly spoilt.'

Peggy grinned and nodded. 'He's certainly safe with those three. Harvey loves babies, and Frank must be cock-a-hoop at having a grandson.'

Brendon laughed. 'He certainly is, and Ron's tickled pink at the idea of having another boy to lead astray, so it looks as if we'll be hard pushed to get any time with Joseph now the two of them have taken charge.'

Peggy noticed that Pauline had yet to be mentioned and felt a stab of concern, but said nothing, not wanting to spoil this happy moment.

Daisy came to the rescue by running up from the beach with her little friend. 'This is Lucy,' she said solemnly. 'We is hungry again.'

Wondering where Lucy's parents had got to, Peggy said hello and delved into the picnic basket for the bottle of squash and packet of sandwiches. 'This is your Uncle Brendon and Auntie Betty,' she explained, doling out cups of squash and a sandwich each.

The children looked wide-eyed at the boot, and Peggy was about to tell them it was rude to stare when Daisy pointed and asked in her piping voice what that was on Betty's foot.

'I'm so sorry, Betty,' babbled Peggy in an embarrassed fluster.

Betty smiled and shrugged. 'Please don't be. It's only natural for children to be curious,' she said before cheerfully sticking out her foot and waving it about. 'This is my magic boot and only very special people can have one.'

The children's eyes widened further. 'Magic?' whispered Daisy.

Betty nodded and smiled. 'This boot covers my bad foot in a spell to make it all right again so that I can walk just like you and Lucy.'

There were appreciative murmurs, but Daisy was still curious. 'Why's your leg bad?' she asked boldly.

'I got very sick with something called polio when I was a little girl,' Betty explained. 'And it made this leg all thin and weak so I couldn't walk on it. That's when I was given this very special boot.'

'But why ...'

'That's enough, Daisy,' Peggy butted in quickly. 'Go and play before the tide comes in and washes away your lovely castles.'

She could see Daisy was on the brink of disobeying her, so dug in the basket again for something to distract her. 'Here we are,' she said, handing over a couple of rock buns. 'Try not to get too much sand on them.'

The little girls ran off with the buns clutched in their small hands, and Peggy sighed. 'I'm sorry about that, but once Daisy starts with her questions, there's no end to them.'

'Shows she has an intelligent, enquiring mind,' said Betty comfortably. 'I hope there are more like her in my new class. It does make life harder, but it's also much more interesting.'

'I hope that means you're staying here,' said Peggy.

Betty glanced at Brendon and clasped her fingers in her lap. 'That was the plan,' she said quietly. 'While Brendon was at sea I discovered that a new junior school was opening here, and managed to secure a post starting in September. It seemed ideal at the time, but now I'm not so sure.'

Peggy felt the dart of unease again. 'But why? This is a lovely place to bring up Joseph with all his family around him.'

Brendon cleared his throat and rested his hand on Betty's entwined fingers. 'It's my mother,' he said flatly. 'We've been here since last night, and she didn't exactly welcome the news of our marriage – or that our son was born before it.'

'Good grief,' gasped a shocked Peggy. 'What's the matter with the blessed woman?'

Brendon shrugged. 'She feels we've let her down by doing things the wrong way round, and is absolutely seething over the fact we got married without inviting her.'

He gave a short, exasperated sigh. 'You know what she's like, Aunt Peg. She takes umbrage at the slightest thing, and has decided we got married behind her back in revenge for her complaining about me going to Devon on that last leave instead of coming home. Which, of course, is ridiculous.'

'Have you tried reasoning with her?' Peggy asked.

'She refuses to listen to a word I say, and I'm very much afraid she's working herself up to having a go at my poor Betty next, and will blame her for turning me against her.'

'Oh lawks, what a horrid and hurtful situation you've both found yourselves in,' Peggy sympathised.

'It's certainly unpleasant,' said Betty, 'made more so by the fact that she's incandescent about her sister Carol and their mother, Dolly, being Joseph's godparents, and witnesses at our wedding. When Brendon let it slip about Dolly she just clammed up completely and hasn't spoken to us since.'

'Some might say that was a blessing,' muttered a furious Peggy.

'Some might,' agreed Brendon, 'but it makes for a poisonous atmosphere. We would have booked into a hotel if it wasn't for Dad. He's delighted to have us home and has completely fallen in love with Joseph, so it didn't seem fair to abandon him while Mum's in that foul mood.'

'Probably best you stay there for as long as you can stand it,' said Peggy. 'The poor man will probably be in the doghouse with Pauline, and he'll need all the support he can get.' She took a deep breath and let it out on a sigh. 'I always knew Pauline was tricky and saw a personal slight in everything people said or did, and her relationship with Dolly was never an easy one, but never in a million years did I think she'd turn on you like that.'

She clasped their hands. 'Oh, my dears, I'm so sorry this homecoming has been such an ordeal. If you ever need to escape, you know where I am, and you'll be welcome at any time. If I'm out, just go in and make yourselves right at home. There's only Cordelia and four girls there now – and one of them is leaving next weekend – so if you need some space to yourselves, the big top room is free.'

Brendon got out of the deckchair and hugged her. 'Thanks, Aunt Peg,' he said softly. 'And if things get too bad at home, would it be all right if we moved in up there until we find our own place?'

'But of course,' she exclaimed, instantly dismissing the thought of how much trouble that might cause with Pauline. 'So, does that mean you'll stay in Cliffehaven despite your mum?'

'It's my home town, Aunt Peg, and we want Joseph to grow up surrounded by those who love him. Given time, I'm hoping Mum might come round to the idea of me being married with a son, but until then we're putting up a united front with Dad which she'll find very hard to break.'

He shrugged and gave Peggy a smile. 'We've got each other as well as you and Dad and Grandad – and with so much love and strength between us, we'll muddle through somehow.'

'Indeed we will,' said Betty, struggling out of the deckchair. 'We'd better go and fetch Joseph,' she said to Brendon. 'It's getting late and he'll need a nappy change and feed before we take him back to Tamarisk Bay.'

She turned to Peggy and gave her a hug. 'We've only just met, but now I know why Dolly and Carol love you so, Peggy. Thank you.'

'There's no need to thank me,' Peggy replied, feeling rather emotional. 'Now go and see to that baby, and please call in tomorrow so I can have a cuddle and get to know him.'

They assured her they would, and then strolled away arm in arm towards the fishing boats, their togetherness plain to see.

Peggy watched them enviously, remembering how she and Jim used to take evening strolls along the promenade before the children came along. But inside she was fuming. Pauline Reilly needed a sharp slap and a damned good talking to for being such a bitch – and if things didn't improve very quickly, she'd see to it the bloody woman heard exactly what she thought of her.

21

Burma

The orders had finally come through to the camp and, for the past couple of weeks, the mixed brigades of the 14th Army had been driving hard to push the Japanese back along the two roads that led into the main north–south axis from the east.

Jim and his brigade of engineers had been sent south but, crammed into the trucks, armoured cars and jeeps like sardines, or hanging onto the sides, it was hard going, and the drivers found it almost impossible to keep up with the leading tanks of the Indian Army's 7th Light Cavalry. These advance tanks moved so fast that they often came upon Japanese rearguards marching along the road and machine-gunned them down without losing speed.

As Jim and his brigade advanced south with the determination of a herd of buffalo scenting water, the petrol supply was stretched to the very limits. Maintenance of the vehicles became an urgent necessity, and breakdowns caused more delays than the enemy. Half-rations were once more put in place to allow the airlifts to be used for petrol and ammunition, but despite the desperate need to stop and see to the battered vehicles, the orders came down the line to keep advancing.

They'd arrived at Toungoo to find the Japanese bunkers heavily fortified with roofs of logs, steel bars and corrugated iron, and only a direct hit from a shell or bomb would destroy them. But the shells burst far too high into the trees and it soon became clear that they needed air support – and the infantry were desperate for the heavy American mortars if they were to make any headway.

Jim huddled in the back of a truck with Jumbo as they took a breather from the hard and terrifying task of clearing the mines under heavy fire and even heavier rain, so the tanks could advance and get closer to the enemy. Both men were soaked to the skin with rain and sweat, their uniform shirts and shorts stiff with mud as the endless rain gleamed on the gun-barrels and tin hats of the enemy. They were too miserable and battle-weary to try and talk above the noise of the tank guns which were throwing sudden orange flashes into the dark jungle, but there was comradeship in that silence as they shared a nip of rum ration, and smoked damp roll-ups.

Jim didn't want to look at the horrific sight just on the other side of the bridge, but despite his abhorrence, his gaze kept returning to it, making his stomach clench. The burned-out British armoured car lay on the edge of a bomb crater, the lump of charred meat and bone inside it all that remained of the driver who was still there after several days because no one had had the chance to get him out.

He turned away, looking back down the road, and nudged Jumbo as he saw the familiar jeeps with their red crosses come hurtling around the bend. There was a

British tank burning in the middle of the road, with two more firing into the jungle less than fifty yards behind it. Dead Japs were strewn beside their overturned field gun, and injured colleagues of the 14th Army were trying to crawl to safety beneath the hail of enemy machine-gun bullets that ripped and whined through the trees and thudded into the earth all around them.

And through all this mayhem came the American Field Service in their specially adapted jeeps which had double-tiered steel bed structures to accommodate two or three casualties at a time. They passed the firing tanks and stopped by the burning one to leap out in their Red Cross emblazoned uniform and, with not a gun between them, lifted the wounded from the tank, scooped up those in the road, stacked them in the beds, turned the jeeps and shot off the way they'd come. The whole exercise had taken less than three minutes.

'Considering the fact they're a bunch of pansies, Quakers and conscientious objectors, they're actually bloody marvels and have certainly won my respect,' muttered Jim who'd always been firmly against such men. 'I wouldn't be brave enough to do that without at least a bazooka to fire back with, let alone go in unarmed as they do.'

'Och, Jim, ye dinnae ken what ye'd do if the occasion called for it,' rumbled Jumbo. 'Although that particular lot were lucky to miss the bullets with so many flying about.' He shook his great head and then spat into the mud. 'The Japs have no respect for the sign of the Red Cross.'

Jim nodded, for he knew that many of those young men had been killed just as the armed fighting men were being blown up or shot to pieces. He picked up his gun, cleaned the firing mechanism and barrel of muck and reloaded. The short respite was over. It was time to return to the battle.

It had taken thirty days to push the Japanese back twenty miles from Toungoo. Jim was very aware of the number of casualties they'd suffered amongst the engineers who'd had to advance with the leading infantry to clear the road, but the tank squadrons could also count heavy losses, with every squadron depleted through direct hits, tracks being blown off by a hidden mine, and crews who were often machine-gunned down by the Japs as they tried to escape their burning tank through the turret or front hatch.

To the delight and huge relief of the battle-weary men of the 14th Army, the monsoon had washed away any last chance of the Japs being able to plan or execute a counter-offensive, and the enemy on the Mawchi Road broke into full retreat, heading for the border with Thailand. However, the fighting was not yet over, for they were soon informed of HQ's plans to send in the mixed brigades to get ahead of them by using air and sea transport.

The Japs' only hope of escape would be to cut through the Allies' line and head east to Thailand, but first they'd have to come out of the Yomas on one of the very few passable tracks. Then they'd have to cross several miles of open paddy fields which were now under deep water, forcing them to use the narrow, unstable paths formed by the raised bunds above the flood. Finally, they would have to cross the Sittang

River which was now in full, torrential flow, about as wide as the Thames by London Bridge and almost impossible to swim across. At every point along the route the Allies would be waiting for them.

Jim had been horribly airsick and was still feeling the effects of the extremely rough series of short flights from Toungoo to the Yomas as he and his brigade hunkered down in their sector of the thirty-mile-long line to wait for the Japs to emerge. Despite the teeming rain, swarms of mosquitoes, leeches and stinking heat, there was an almost tangible atmosphere of tense expectation for, if successful, this could prove to be the final battle of the Burma Campaign, and their ticket home.

Their machine guns covered every track out of the Yomas as well as the paths between the flooded fields. Infantry and barbed wire protected the machine guns which were dug in on the only ground above water. More field guns stood ready behind them, and waiting behind them were yet more infantry. All the boats had been removed from the Sittang River; tanks stood at road junctions and in the villages while others patrolled the road. Fighters and bombers waited on the few all-weather airfields, while patrols and scouts in the Yomas passed on information well in advance as to how many enemy were on their way, and by which route.

It was like a turkey shoot as they came screaming out of the Yomas brandishing what turned out to be empty guns, for the machine guns, Brens, rifles and tanks mowed them down. They drowned in their hundreds in the racing yellow waters of the Sittang River, their corpses floating in the fields and amongst the reeds. The brigades showed little mercy for what had proved to be a pitiless enemy, and by the time the guns fell silent, the 14th Army had killed and captured over eleven thousand Japanese.

The long, exhausting and bloody Burma Campaign was finally over.

Jim had now been on leave in Rangoon for two weeks, but most of that had been spent in the military hospital being treated for yet another bout of malaria, courtesy of the mosquitoes in the Yomas, and the suppurating jungle sores he'd gained from knocks and cuts whilst servicing the vehicles. He'd finally been passed fit enough to join his fellow officers at their comfortable billet in a seaside hotel, and was now sitting on a veranda, sipping tea and admiring the view of several pretty nurses who were playing ball on the sandy beach in their skimpy swimsuits.

'That's a glorious sight after all that jungle,' he murmured to Jumbo who was making a ham-fisted effort to patch up the bullet holes in his bagpipes.

'It is that,' the big man agreed, glancing up from his work to give the girls an appreciative once-over. 'It's quiet too, thank God. Ye ken me ears are still ringing from all that gunfire.'

Jim's were too, and although he'd been resting for two weeks, he was still weary to the bone and troubled by the memories of that final one-sided slaughter. The mixed brigades had given no quarter and shown no mercy, but then, he reasoned, if the boot had been on the other foot, the Japs would have been just as merciless. It had been a case of kill or be killed, so there really had been no choice.

'So what's next for us, do you reckon, Jumbo?' he asked through a vast yawn.

'Malaya probably,' Jumbo replied dourly. 'There's already a rumour going round that the Parachute Regiment are getting ready to go in there as soon as the monsoon ends in August or September. From there it could be into Thailand – or even an assault on Japan itself. It'll all depend on whether or not the Japs see sense and admit they've lost.'

'I won't hold me breath,' said Jim. 'From what we've seen of them, they won't give up until every man in Japan is dead.'

Jumbo set aside the hopeless task of repairing his bagpipes and gave a deep sigh. 'Och, Jim, I've had enough of Burma and even Rangoon, although it's very pleasant here. I'm weary, and sick of the heat, the flies, and the stink of the jungle. I want to be back home amongst my own people, at peace in my glen to tend the deer and be free to roam.'

'Aye, I feel the same about Cliffehaven,' agreed Jim. 'The brass talk about demob plans but nothing seems to come of them, and my poor Peggy must think I'm never coming home. I hope to God we don't have to fight again, because I've seen enough bloodshed and horrors, and I don't have the stomach for any more.'

Jumbo nodded in agreement with that sentiment, and stuck his large hands into the pockets of his baggy khaki shorts as he went to stand by the veranda railings. 'I ken you draw great comfort from your family, Jim, but I'm glad I didn't have anyone to worry about during this war,' he confessed. 'Marriage and a family is not something I've ever really wanted or needed, you see. I'm content with my own company out in the glen with the animals where I can play the pipes and disturb no one.' He glanced down at the ruined bagpipes and sorrowfully tugged his beard. 'Though I ken I won't be playing that set again.'

Jim had heard enough of Jumbo's stories of his life in the Highlands to be able to imagine him tramping through the heather like a modern-day Moses in his sturdy boots and kilt, his fiery beard flowing freely as he tended the deer, went fishing in the burns and lochs, or sought the shellfish on the rocky shores to cook over a fire on the beach with only the moon and stars for company.

In a way Jim envied him, for he was free to do as he pleased and cared nothing for what people might think of him. And yet, despite Jumbo's protests to the contrary, it must be a lonely existence, and the thought of not having Peggy and the rest of the family around him made Jim shudder. They were his life's blood; his reason for fighting this damned war was to keep them safe.

He idly watched the nurses laughing and splashing in the water. They reminded him of his Anne and Cissy, and the longing to be with them again was a physical pain in his heart. And yet he was stuck here in Burma with no choice but to wait for the army to decide where it would send him next.

If only the Japs would surrender, then they could all go home.

22

Somerset

Anne climbed back into the rickety old bus and sat down next to her headmaster, George Mayhew, as the driver ground the gears and they set off with a burp from the exhaust and a groan from the engine. It was the last Friday in June and they'd just accompanied the few remaining evacuee children to Taunton railway station. George's wife, Belinda, was travelling with them to make sure they were all safely collected by their families and would then make the long journey home again. Anne had offered to do it, but with things the way they were with Martin, it was decided she should stay close to home.

Some of the families who'd hosted the children had come to see them off, and there was a sorrowful silence in the bus as they started for home. The youngsters had become a part of the village community since the start of the war, and the men and women who'd taken them in had come to love them – and were loved in return – so it had been a very emotional parting, with tears on both sides when the train had pulled away.

Anne wondered how the children would adapt to life with their estranged families in war-damaged London after the gentle, welcoming years they'd spent in the heart of the quiet countryside, and could only hope that the lessons learnt and the assurance gained during that time would sustain them for whatever lay ahead.

Many of them had stayed on until the end of term because their parents had still to find decent accommodation, but it seemed that as time had gone on, the need to have their children home became greater than any inconvenience or hardship. Anne could understand that, for if it had been Rose or Emily in the same situation, she'd have moved heaven and earth to have them with her after so long, even if they did have to get to know each other again.

She gazed out of the window as the bus trundled along country lanes where the hedges were high and the fields golden with rippling wheat and barley. She'd heard about Ivy and her young siblings from Peggy, and although the whole thing was rather tragic, she admired the girl's good sense and courage in agreeing to them being adopted. From what Peggy had told her, the children had been so young when they'd left home that of course they felt no attachment to Ivy, or the parents who'd been killed, and had formed a close bond with the couple who'd taken them in.

Anne gave a deep sigh, thankful that she'd kept her children with her throughout, but her thoughts returned inevitably to Martin, and what they might have been up to whilst she was away. The girls were being watched over by Aunt Vi and Sally, and would no doubt be pestering young Harry, Charlie and Ernie to let them join in whatever games they were playing, but if Martin had decided for once to stay at the farm and not go wandering, she could only hope he wouldn't become morose through drink and frighten the life out of them when they made too much noise – or, God forbid, bump into Claus and start another long, distressing diatribe against all Germans.

She'd found Martin's secret stash of whisky at the back of the linen cupboard this morning and had been tempted to pour it down the sink, but doing so would have caused another furious row, and she simply hadn't had the energy to risk it.

George seemed to be aware of her troubled mood. 'How are you coping at home, Anne?' he asked.

She knew it was pointless to lie, for nothing stayed secret in a village and everyone had seen Martin wandering the hills and fields on his own, and it had soon got round that he was staggering drunk when he finally returned to Owlet Farm each night. 'It's getting harder each day,' she confessed. 'But it's Martin I'm really worried about. He's not the man I married, and isn't coping at all.'

'Has he told you anything of what he went through?'

'I wish he would,' she replied, thinking of those long, lonely nights when they lay beside each other like strangers in dreadful silence. 'Then I might be able to help him through this. But he clams up at the slightest mention of his time in that POW camp.'

She bit her lip. 'All I do know is that the death of so many of his friends has hit him very hard. Like Freddy Pargeter – he was such a livewire. He could turn a girl's head with just a smile, and he had that devil-may-care sort of panache. His wife had twins whilst he was in captivity, but he only lived just long enough to see them fleetingly. He'll be dearly missed by every-one,' she said sadly. 'Not least of all by Roger, his brother-in-law and Martin's wingman. Roger's always been a sturdy, dependable sort of man, and I know Martin relied on his companionship throughout their time in the camp, and they became very close.'

'Have they been in touch since being demobbed?' George asked.

'Martin writes to him nearly every day, and Roger replies, but I have no idea of what state of mind Roger's in, or how he's coping, for Martin never lets me see his letters. Mum doesn't tell me much of what's going on with Kitty and Roger, and I don't ask, because then she'd know that all is not well with me and Martin.'

'But why not confide in your mother, Anne? She sounds eminently sensible and caring, and I'm sure she'd be a huge help in easing that heavy burden you're carrying.'

There had been many a time that Anne had wanted to tell her mother what was happening, but if she did she'd be admitting defeat by passing the burden on to someone who really couldn't do anything about it. 'She has enough on her plate already, without me adding to it,' she said flatly. She gave a sigh. 'I'll muddle through somehow and keep faith that Martin will eventually come out of this and be his old, lovely self again.'

George sat in thought as the bus wheezed its way up a hill. 'I know that when I was shot down and burned, I found it impossible to talk to anyone, let alone my poor mother who was beside herself with worry – and of course the girl I was engaged to took one look at me and shot off before I could even blink my good eye.'

He gave Anne a self-deprecating smile before carrying on. 'The fear of what the future held for me, looking as I did, was overwhelming, and I kept having nightmares about the moment my Spit caught fire and I couldn't release my harness to get out.' He sighed deeply. 'I couldn't share those horrors with my poor little mother, so I existed in a silent world of pain and tortured thoughts until I was transferred to East Grinstead and discovered I wasn't alone. The men there understood what I was going through, and I found I could talk to them, cry with them, rage against what fate had brought us, and finally let all that horror and fear pour out. We used a great deal of black humour to get us through the painful treatments and deal with what was going on in our heads, but the more I talked, the easier it became to let go of those dark memories, and when I left the hospital, I was at peace and ready to face the world again.'

He turned to Anne and rested his hand on hers, his scarred face lit cruelly by the bright sunlight coming through the window. 'Martin needs desperately to talk to someone, Anne, and he's clearly trying to protect you from whatever demons he's fighting. That's understandable, and you shouldn't feel hurt by his lack of communication, even though you must find it hard not to be. But if he goes on bottling it up like this he'll send himself mad with it all.' He briefly squeezed her fingers and then took a breath. 'I'd be very willing to listen. He has only to ask.'

'I did suggest it,' Anne replied. 'But he refused point blank, saying you'd never experienced what he had and couldn't possibly understand.' She gave a sigh. 'I even hinted he might talk to the vicar, but of course that poor man would have meant well, but he knows so little of the real world he'd have been of no use at all.'

George patted her hand and then tugged at his jacket lapels – it was something he always did just before saying something the listener might not like to hear, and Anne steeled herself.

'You say that Martin writes most days to his Wing Commander – Roger, is it?' At Anne's nod, he continued thoughtfully. 'It seems to me that if they shared the same experiences, he would be the ideal person for Martin to talk to – face-to-face.'

'That's not possible,' said Anne. 'They're on opposite sides of the country.'

'I realise that,' he replied. 'But they don't have to be if you took Martin home to Cliffehaven.'

'I can't,' she replied. 'I'm too involved with the election which is only days away, and there's a lot of clearing up to do at school. Besides,' she added, realising they were flimsy excuses, 'Martin isn't fit enough to make that long journey, and it would be a complete nightmare if the children play up and he loses his patience.'

George regarded her evenly. 'Belinda and I can manage the school, and even at this late date, I'm sure there are plenty of people to take your place at the polling station and the count. Martin's quite well enough to walk for miles over rough country, and if he knows that his wingman is waiting for him at the end of the journey, he'll stay calm.' His steady gaze bored into her. 'Why the excuses, Anne? What are you afraid of?'

'They are excuses,' she conceded, 'but I'm not afraid of anything.' This was a lie: she knew deep down that she was dreading having to cope with Martin and his moods on her own. And yet there was a very valid reason for not returning to Cliffehaven, and she couldn't think why she hadn't mentioned it.

'The fact is, our cottage is rented out until the end of August so we'd have to move in with Mum at the boarding house. There are three lodgers still living at Beach View along with Grandma Cordelia and little Daisy, so it's already a bit of a squash. Now Mum's told me there's been some sort of trouble in the family, and she's asked my cousin Brendon and his wife to move in with their baby, so the crush would be even worse.'

She returned George's steady gaze. 'Although Mum would welcome us with open arms, Martin simply wouldn't be able to cope with the noise of four small children in the house, let alone a clutch of strangers going in and out all day.'

George nodded. 'I do see your point,' he murmured. 'But even so, I still think Martin would fare better in Cliffehaven than he is here.'

Anne had already come to that conclusion. She'd been so fixed on her ideas for his homecoming that she had not been prepared for its reality. The isolation and peace she'd thought would help him heal had had the opposite effect, and Martin was really struggling.

'If we had our own home to go to, then I'd agree,' she said. 'I'll try and talk it over with him tonight if he's back from the pub and sober enough for a proper conversation. But I really don't think it's wise to take him to Beach View. He's simply not ready for it.'

The ancient bus rattled down the hill and spluttered into the village, finally coming to a halt outside the schoolhouse with a sigh and much squealing of brakes. Everyone alighted and said their goodbyes, then went their separate ways to the homes which would now feel so empty without the children.

Anne stayed by the school gate, reluctant to go home just yet. While George had a conversation with the bus driver, she let her gaze drift over the small schoolhouse with its pocket-handkerchief playground, and then along the huddle of cottages and shops that lined the village street. She felt a great affection for it all, especially today when the thatched roofs glowed in the sun and the gardens were full of colour.

'I shall miss this place when I do leave,' she said after the bus had left in a cloud of exhaust fumes. 'Everyone has been so kind and welcoming to us over the years that it really does feel like home.'

'Belinda and I feel the same way,' said George, 'but unfortunately things are about to change and we might not be here much longer.'

Anne was startled from her thoughts. 'Why? What changes?'

'I wasn't going to say anything until the staff meeting tomorrow, but I suppose it doesn't matter.' He took a breath as if to steel himself for what was to come and clutched his jacket lapels. 'I received a letter from the Education Board yesterday morning telling me that once the evacuees have left, the numbers will be too low to sustain the cost of running the school, and if we don't increase our intake come September term, it will be closed down.'

'No!' Anne gasped. 'But where will the village children go?'

'They'll go by bus to the bigger school in the next town, I suspect,' he replied sadly. 'Of course they won't get the same close attention to their educational progress in those large classes and will have to learn to adapt to being just a number amongst so many.'

He gazed at the small brick building with its plaque declaring its foundation in 1856, and gave a deep sigh. 'It's awful to think the school has been here for almost a hundred years and it'll be closed on my watch.'

'You mustn't blame yourself,' she said firmly. 'It's not your fault the Education Board are being so short-sighted. The numbers are bound to rise again now the men are home.' She eyed him with concern. 'But what will you and Belinda do if it does close?'

'Find a position in another school, I suppose,' he replied. 'I can't pretend that Belinda and I won't find it an awful wrench to leave, but we both agree we'd rather avoid the larger city schools and try to find another village where we can settle down and become part of the community as we have done here.'

'Then I hope you'll find it, George.' Anne squeezed his arm. 'And wish you both all the luck in the world. You deserve it.'

George reddened and avoided looking at Anne. 'I don't know about deserving anything in particular,' he murmured bashfully, 'but it is quite important we find the right place to live and work. You see, Belinda and I are expecting a baby in December.'

Anne threw her arms round him and gave him a quick hug, aware they could be seen by half the village and would no doubt set tongues wagging. 'Oh, George,' she breathed. 'That's the very best news I've heard in ages. Congratulations.'

He went a deeper scarlet and dug his hands into his jacket pockets. 'Yes, it is rather. We're both thrilled, but the notice from the Education Board couldn't have come at a worse time.'

Anne chuckled. 'Then we'll just have to hope that the rest of the village follow your example and start having lots and lots of babies.'

She left him with a cheerful wave at the gate of the headmaster's cottage where he lived with Belinda, and began the walk home. Despite the threat of the school closure, it was wonderful news about the baby, and she could only hope she could keep up her high spirits long enough to face whatever awaited her at Owlet Farm.

Violet was affectionately known to all as Auntie Vi, even though she was aunt only to Sally and no relation whatsoever to Anne. She was now sixty, with a thick mop of silver hair and a comfortably rounded figure, but was still taking an active role in running the farm with Anne's brother Bob. Dressed in her usual wellington boots and many layers of clothing despite the warm day, she was herding the last of the cows into the milking shed. She looked round with a beaming smile as Anne came into the cobbled yard and waved.

'It's all been happening today,' she said, following the last cow into the shed and cleaning its udders before attaching them to the milking machine. 'We've got a new dairyman at last, and two more farmhands to help Claus and Bob.'

Without pausing for breath, Vi hurried on. 'And Claus has been with his young Lily to see the vicar, and arrange their wedding for mid-July. Her parents have finally come to realise she's determined to marry him, and although they're still a little frosty at the idea of her marrying a German, they've given their permission.'

She chuckled. 'The fact she's expecting probably had a lot to do with it,' she added with a wink. 'But don't say anything; he told me that in confidence.'

Anne grinned. 'My lips are sealed. And I have news for you too,' she said. 'George and Belinda are also expecting a happy event, but I'm not sure that's for public consumption just yet. It's still very early days. On a sadder note, the school is on the brink of being closed.'

Vi clucked her tongue and shook her head. 'We'll have to fight against it,' she said firmly. 'That school is an intrinsic part of the community and, with babies bound to be on the way now the men are home, we're going to need it. Perhaps, if your Conservative candidate gets in, he'll support our fight. Have a word with him, dear. You can be very persuasive, so he might listen.'

Anne didn't really think he would, but nodded anyway. 'How has Martin been today?'

'I haven't seen hide nor hair of him since the morning milking. He left the house shortly after you did, and he's not back yet.' Vi gave a deep sigh and grasped Anne's hand. 'I am sorry, dear – for both of you. It can't be at all easy, and I do wish there was something I could do to help.'

344

Anne told her about the long, difficult conversation she'd had with George. 'I was hoping he'd be here so we could talk about what to do for the best,' she said finally. 'But it seems the only real option I have is to take him home as soon as the election's over.'

'I think you're right,' murmured Vi. 'Although it will be horribly quiet around here once you've all gone.' She gazed across the yard to the row of small cottages where Sally lived with her younger brother, Ernie, and her little boy, Harry. 'I've got used to the sound of the children's voices,' she said sadly.

'You could always come with us, Auntie Vi.'

She shook her head. 'Bless you, dear, but this is where I belong, and where I'll stay until I turn up my toes. Bob, Claus and I can carry on now we have extra help, and in time there will be other children playing in the fields.'

She looked up at Anne and patted her cheek. 'The world keeps turning, Anne, and we adapt to the changes it brings – just as we do to the seasons. The things that worry us now are eventually resolved, the fears fade and what we once thought was important becomes insignificant as life's adventure carries us on. I know you're finding life very difficult at the moment, but with love and a good deal of patience, that will change, I promise.'

Anne could feel tears prickling as she kissed the rosy cheek. 'I do want to believe that,' she managed. 'Thank you for being so very kind to us all over the years. I don't know what we'd have done without you.'

'Oh, you'd have managed,' Vi said with breezy dismissal. 'You're a very capable young woman, Anne.'

She cocked her head at Bob's shout from inside the milking shed. 'It seems I'm needed,' she said cheerfully. 'The children have been bathed and fed, and there's a bottle of my parsnip wine in the kitchen. Forget your troubles for a while and just enjoy Sally's company on her last evening here.'

Anne gave a rueful smile as the small round figure bustled away. Vi's parsnip wine was famous all over the county for its deceptive honeyed notes, for it was a lethal concoction which slipped down far too easily and left the drinker with a blinding hangover the following morning. But, despite their very different backgrounds, Sally had become a close friend over the years they'd lived at Owlet Farm, and Anne could think of no better way to relax and set aside her cares than to spend the evening in her lively company.

Cliffehaven

It was Saturday and the very last day in June and Peggy was sitting in the front row of the wedding room in the Town Hall with Cordelia, watching the guests arrive.

Despite the fact Ivy had no family to speak of, it was a marvellous turn-out. The men from the local fire station had just come in looking very smart in their black uniforms, and they cheerfully greeted John Hicks, who was acting as best man today, and went on to tease the groom, who was similarly dressed, and waiting nervously by the registrar's table.

Doris was wearing a fancy hat and smart navy two-piece as she arrived on John White's arm, and Rosie looked terrific in a scarlet dress and enormous black hat. Not to be outdone, Gloria's hat was even bigger, and her dress was an eye-watering orange. It was skin-tight and far too short, but Gloria carried it off with her usual aplomb. With jangling bracelets and earrings, she approached an ashen-faced Andy and ordered him to take a nip from her brandy flask before he fell down. This achieved, she plumped down next to her sister in the front row and passed the flask amongst the firemen.

Stan from the station was in his best suit, and firmly gripping Harvey's lead as the dog slumped beneath his chair, sporting a red ribbon bow on his collar. Peggy smiled, for she knew there had been a bit of a rumpus between the registrar and the Mayor following Ruby's wedding, but it seemed the Mayor had decided he pre-ferred the quiet life and had given Ron belated permission to have the dog with him during such ceremonies.

Sarah, April and Danuta were in their pretty sum-mer frocks and straw hats; Peter Ryan was in his uniform and Jane looked extremely sophisticated in a figure-hugging pink dress and broad-brimmed cream hat as she arrived on the arm of her young man, Jeremy Curtis.

Jeremy had arrived that morning from London and had been a very pleasant surprise for Jane who hadn't thought he could take time off from his work. He was tall, slim and brown-eyed, with a lick of dark hair which, rather boyishly, fell over his forehead. Quietly spoken and rather shy behind those tortoiseshell-framed glasses, he reminded Peggy a little of Fran's

Robert, but he soon revealed a marvellous sense of humour which had clearly captured Jane's heart, and certainly endeared him to Peggy and Cordelia.

Peggy had just managed not to ask about any future wedding plans, or enquire after what sort of work he was doing in London, but by the look of him, she suspected he was something important in one of the government offices.

She glanced across to make sure that Daisy was behaving herself on the other side of the room with April and little Paula; then checked that Cordelia had enough handkerchiefs, and that Andy's mother, Beryl, wasn't being squashed by her sister Gloria's bulk.

Beryl was the very opposite of Gloria, small, skinny, quietly dressed, but a bag of nervous energy. She'd come down from London this morning, arriving at the Crown in a bustle and fluster, fearing she was late as the train had been delayed. Peggy had met her only briefly outside the Town Hall, but she seemed very pleasant, and it would be lovely to get to know her better during the reception.

Peggy breathed in the heady scent of the roses and lilies that Stan had arranged in vases about the room. She glanced at her watch, shot Andy a look of encouragement and sympathy, and gave a sigh. Ivy was in danger of being late – as usual – and with the Town Hall being so busy with weddings, she could lose the slot if she wasn't careful.

Peggy had fretted over Ivy's seemingly gung-ho attitude to it all, and therefore had been amazed to discover that despite her fears, Ivy had organised everything wonderfully well – although she suspected the involvement of Doris, Rosie and Gloria had had a great deal to do with it.

The party two nights before had been held at the Anchor, and Rosie had done Ivy proud with an excellent buffet supper and some of Gloria's black-market gin. The reception would be at the Crown. Ron would give her away, and Rita was to be her bridesmaid. The cake, the dresses – even the train tickets and going-away outfit had been organised. And earlier that morning, Ivy had made Peggy's day by asking her to help her get dressed. Everything was set for a wonderful day. All they needed now was the bride.

All talk faded, the registrar looked again at his pocket-watch, and Andy was going quite green about the gills as he anxiously watched the closed doors – as if by sheer will alone he could open them and find Ivy there.

And then the double doors slammed open and Ivy burst in, barefooted, shoes in hand, veil askew and cream lace dress rucked up at the hips. 'Ow Gawd,' she wailed. 'I'm ever so sorry, Andy, but Bertie's bleedin' car broke down and I 'ad to run all the way 'ere.'

The whole party collapsed into laughter, and even the po-faced registrar managed a slight twitch of his thin lips as a very embarrassed Bertie Double-Barrelled slid into one of the back rows.

'Don't yer worry, gel. I can wait as long as yer like,' Andy replied, his face now alight with humour and relief.

Ivy held Ron's arm to keep her balance as she shoved on her high-heeled shoes and then fidgeted impatiently as Rita adjusted her dress and veil and tried to bring a bit more order to her hair. 'That's enough, Reet,' she muttered. 'It's time we got on with this before my Andy decides he don't want a bride what looks like a dog's dinner.'

'You look bloody marvellous, gel,' called Andy from the front of the room. 'Get yerself down 'ere before they throws us out.'

'Blimey,' giggled Ivy, taking her bouquet from Ron and putting her hand through his arm. 'Givin' out the orders already, eh? Have to watch that.' She turned back to Rita who was wearing the same lovely dress she'd been given for Ruby's wedding. 'You ready?' At her nod, Ivy took a deep breath. 'Let's get on with it then.'

Peggy's laughter turned to tears of love and affection as Ivy walked purposefully down the aisle towards her future husband. The pale cream lace dress was a sheath over her slim figure and reached to just below the knee, showing a surprisingly good pair of legs that until now had always been hidden by dungarees. Her usually tangled hair was smooth and gleaming beneath the small coronet of flowers, and the veil drifted to just beyond her narrow shoulders. She carried a spray of perfect cream roses in which nestled her mother's brooch; on her wrist was her father's fire-damaged watch, and the slender chain around her neck held her mother's wedding ring.

'Beautiful,' sniffled Cordelia. 'Who'd have thought our little Ivy could turn into such a princess?'

Peggy smiled through her tears. All brides looked beautiful on their wedding day, even tomboys like Ivy.

Her gaze drifted to Rita who'd gone to sit next to Peter as the ceremony was conducted. It would be her turn next, and she too had evolved from tomboy to beauty in the last few years – although the pair of them were still capable of getting into mischief.

The newly-weds had said their vows and signed the book, and were now coming back down the aisle with beaming smiles. Everyone followed them out to the landing and waited at the top of the stairs as a photographer fussed about taking one picture after another. It seemed Ivy was no longer impatient or flustered, for she smiled and posed with Andy as if accustomed to all the attention, and then the couple went slowly down the sweeping staircase to the Town Hall's front steps.

The firemen formed a guard of honour with their fire axes and as Ivy and Andy walked between them, they were showered in confetti before being swamped by hugs and kisses from Gloria. More photographs were taken; Daisy and Paula got bored and decided to gather up the fallen confetti that now lay in drifts along the pavement and in the gutter, and Harvey bounced around in great excitement, his inquisitive nose going up skirts as his tail thudded against legs.

'Right, you lot,' shouted Gloria once the photographer had finished. 'Let's get on with the party.'

Ron held carefully onto Cordelia's arm on one side, Bertie on the other as the gathering trooped down the hill to the Crown. Sarah hitched Daisy onto her hip, while April went off with Paula to man the station until Stan came to relieve her in an hour's time. As they all arrived at the Crown, Doris suddenly looked unsure and held back on the doorstep.

'It's all right, love,' said Gloria on a laugh. 'We don't bite. Anyways, the reception ain't in the bar but in the function room, so yer won't 'ave to rub shoulders with the common folk.'

Doris reddened, held her breath, and stepped over the threshold to hurry through the large bar and into the function room. 'Oh,' she said in surprise as she stood in the doorway and took in the white linen cloth on the long tables, the flowers, candles, smart china and gleaming silverware. 'I didn't expect ...'

'What did yer expect, Doris?' asked Gloria with a gleam in her eye. 'Paper plates, jellied eels and cheap bottled beer?' She laughed at the other woman's discomfort. 'We do things proper 'ere,' she said, putting an arm around Doris and steering her towards the bar laden with champagne, spirits and cordials. 'Especially when it's a family wedding. Now, what can I get you to drink?'

They were presented with a veritable feast, for there was roast beef with all the trimmings followed by trifle and a slice of the delicious iced fruit cake Gloria had somehow managed to persuade the local baker to supply. No one dared ask where it had all come from, but Peggy suspected that Gloria and Ron had used all their black-market contacts to make it happen. The champagne toasts were made; everyone applauded the speeches which were mercifully short and then got down to the serious business of drinking and having a dance to the three-piece band which proved to be surprisingly good.

The party went on until five and then the newly-weds disappeared upstairs to get changed for their journey to Walthamstow. There would be no honey-moon, for Andy had already started working at the fire station, but they planned a trip to Margate in August when he had a couple of days off.

Peggy had managed to resist drinking too much, but Cordelia was definitely tiddly and Doris was showing signs that she too had over-indulged, for she was laughing at Gloria's off-colour jokes. Ron was studi-ously ignoring Rosie's withering looks as he matched drink for drink with the firemen, and Harvey was snaf-fling the left-over trifle which Gloria had left in a bowl on the dresser.

Looking at her watch, Peggy clucked her tongue. 'What's keeping them up there? Surely they must know what time it is,' she muttered.

Rita giggled. 'I don't expect they've given time much of a thought,' she replied. 'I know I wouldn't if it was my wedding day.'

Peggy blushed and realised how silly she must have sounded. 'Oh, I see what you mean.' She took a sip of champagne, lit a cigarette and shrugged. 'I don't sup-pose it matters,' she said to cover her embarrassment. 'There'll be another train in an hour.'

She watched Gloria stagger her way up the stairs and heard her yelling at the young couple to get their arses in gear and hurry up as everyone was waiting to see them off.

Ten minutes later they appeared rather bashfully with their suitcases and a large bag containing their wedding presents. Ivy was wearing one of Solly's smart skirt suits in navy pinstripe, and Andy had changed out of his uniform into grey trousers and a navy sports jacket with a white shirt and plain tie.

Andy went to his mother and, after kissing and hugging her, called for silence. 'We want to thank you all for making our day so special,' he said. 'But in particular, I'd like to thank John for getting me the job in Walthamstow, and keeping me calm when my wife' – this was greeted with cheers and whistles – 'when my wife was late.'

He grinned at the assembly. 'It's one of her most endearing 'abits, so I suppose I'll have to get used to it.' He hugged Ivy to his side. 'We'd like you to stay and enjoy the party, and not come to the station to see us off, if that's all right. We don't want no fuss or tears, 'cos it will only set Ivy off, and I don't want 'er crying on our wedding day.'

The gathering surrounded them to say their goodbyes, and Ivy eventually pushed through them to get to Peggy. 'Thanks for all you done, Auntie Peggy. I 'ope you enjoyed the day as much as me, 'cos that's what I wanted more than anything. You been so good to us all, and it were the only way I could think of to repay you.'

Peggy held her close, fighting back the tears, and kissed her cheek. 'It's been a wonderful day and you're a beautiful bride. Don't leave it too long before you come down to see us.'

'I promised Rita I'd come for 'er wedding if she don't leave it too long, so you ain't got rid of me entirely just yet.' Ivy hesitated and bit her lip. 'I got something to tell you, Auntie Peggy. Promise me you won't go off the deep end.'

Peggy smiled. 'I already know, Ivy, darling,' she murmured. 'I heard you being sick again this morning.' She hugged her once more. 'Your secret's safe with me,' she whispered. 'Just take care of yourself and that precious baby, that's all I ask.'

'Ow Gawd, I'm gunna miss yer,' Ivy breathed, on the brink of tears, before pulling herself from Peggy's arms and joining Andy who was waiting for her at the door.

Everyone trooped out to watch them go back up the hill, past the Town Hall where another wedding party was emerging in a hail of confetti, and then with one last wave they walked over the bridge and went out of sight.

Peggy stood on the pavement long after everyone else had gone back inside to carry on with the party. Another chick was on her way, and soon it would be Rita's turn to leave – and then if the war with Japan ever came to an end, she would have to say goodbye to Sarah and Jane. Her shoulders slumped and her heart felt heavy. It was like losing her own children all over again, and in that moment she wished with all her heart that Anne would come home.

23

Somerset

It was early Sunday morning and Anne was roused from a heavy sleep by the sound of drawers being opened and shut with great vigour and little thought. She opened her eyes and winced at the shaft of light coming through the gap in the bedroom curtains. 'Martin? What on earth are you doing?' she asked thickly.

'I'm packing,' he replied tersely.

Anne sat up, her head pounding from the effects of the parsnip wine she'd consumed the previous evening. 'Packing? Whatever for?'

'I'm going back to Cliffehaven with Sally.'

'But you can't,' she protested. 'Sally will have enough on her plate with Harry and Ernie without ...' She bit her lip, realising what she'd almost said.

He regarded her sourly. 'Without having to deal with me, you mean,' he said flatly. 'Look, Anne, I know you don't think much of me, and I can't blame you, but I want to go home – and I'm mature enough to make the journey without causing Sally any trouble.' He began ripping things off coat hangers and stuffing them into a case.

Anne hauled herself out of bed, staggering a little as she went giddy, and then grabbed his arm. 'Martin,

please don't do this. I know you want to go home –
and we will – but at the end of the week, not today.'

'I want to go today,' he said stubbornly, shrugging
off her restraining hand. 'Besides, I'd have thought
you'd be only too delighted to see the back of me.'

It was like a slap in the face. 'Oh, Martin,' she
breathed. 'Do you really think I'd wish that?' She
blinked away her tears, determined not to break down.
'I'm sorry if that's the impression you've got, but I'm
worried sick about you – need you to talk to me – need
some sort of acknowledgement from you that you still
love me and the girls.'

He stopped stuffing clothes into the case and stood
with his arms limp at his sides, his head bowed. 'Of
course I still love you,' he said hoarsely. 'It was only
the thought of you and the girls which kept me going
when …' He heaved a great breath and finally looked
at her. 'But I can't be the husband and father I was – or
the man you need. I can't talk to you the way I can talk
to Roger – and have no desire to.'

'But I'm more than willing to listen,' she replied,
taking his hand and kissing the stumps of his frost-
bitten fingers. 'Please, Martin, trust me enough to tell
me something of what you've been through so I can
help. I so desperately want to understand.'

He gently removed his hand from her grasp. 'It's not
a matter of trust,' he said sadly. 'And if I stay here,
things will only get worse between us. I'm sorry, Anne,
but I've inflicted enough pain on you and the children
and have lost my way. I need to go home.'

Anne saw his set expression and knew that no
amount of arguing would change his mind, but she

was filled with dread that this separation might be the beginning of the end for her marriage. 'Then we'll go together,' she said. 'We can catch a later train once I've tried to organise someone else to take my place at the polling station, and packed the children's things. Of course I'll have the devil's own job of trying to persuade Charlie to come with us, and ...'

Martin silenced her with a soft, brief kiss. 'No, Anne. That's too much to do in a couple of hours. It's better you stay, fulfil your election duties and take your time packing up and saying your goodbyes. The children will be less fractious and Charlie might be more amenable to the idea of going home to Cliffehaven if you don't force the issue all in a rush.'

'But I don't want you to go without me,' she managed through her tears. 'We promised on our wedding day that we would stick together through thick and thin.'

He drew her into his arms. 'It's not a case of what you or I want, Anne. It's what we both need. There are moments, even in the strongest of marriages, when it helps to spend time apart – to give each other breathing space to work things out.'

He held her tenderly at arm's length. 'I have to do this, Anne, not only for my sake, but for you and the children.'

Anne realised then that he was right, for if he stayed nothing would change between them, and the state of mind he was in would only worsen. She nodded and turned away, the tears rolling down her face as she emptied the case and folded the clothes more neatly so she could close it. She could only pray he would see things in a clearer light once he was back in Cliffehaven. 'Just promise me you'll telephone when you get to Mum's,' she managed.

'I promise,' he replied, picking up the case and kitbag. Anne's head was pounding and she felt nauseous as she grabbed her dressing gown and swiftly dug her feet into slippers before following him into the boot room. 'Aren't you going to say goodbye to Vi and the girls?' she asked fretfully.

'I did that earlier while you were sleeping off Vi's parsnip wine,' he replied, stepping out into the cobbled yard where Bob, Sally and the little boys were waiting in the Land Rover. 'I must say, you were dead to the world when I got in.'

Anne thought that was a bit rich after his drunken performances these past weeks, but let the thought go. This was not the time to start an argument. She tamped down on the nausea and tried to ignore the thudding in her head as she followed him and watched him swing the kitbag and case in the back. She noted with surprise, and some hurt, that his drawn face seemed less careworn, his step a little more jaunty as he prepared to leave her. However, she reasoned, if this was a sign of how quickly he might heal in Cliffehaven, then he was right to go, and she shouldn't see his departure as yet another rejection.

She went to him as he opened the back door. 'Take care, my love,' she murmured, kissing his cheek. 'I'll ring Mum and let her know you're on the way.'

He nodded, climbed into the truck and slammed the door. Sally blew Anne a kiss and the boys bounced up and down in excitement. Anne saw that Sally looked as rough as she felt, and didn't envy her the long journey with two lively boys for company. Bob engaged the gears and the truck rumbled over the cobbles towards the gate which Vi was holding open.

Anne ran to join Vi as Bob drove down the track, and they waved until the truck was out of sight. Vi closed the gate firmly and then squeezed Anne's hand. 'It's not really saying goodbye,' she said comfortingly, 'because you'll be seeing them all again in a few days' time.'

'I know, but it's still hard to see him go, and I have no idea what the future holds for us,' she replied, the bright sunlight hurting her eyes as an entire regiment of drummers marched in her head. 'And it will be harder still to ring Mum, because then she'll know that my plan for Martin's recovery has backfired spectacularly, and I failed him.'

Vi shot her a knowing look, and tutted. 'Now you're just feeling sorry for yourself, and that won't do at all,' she said briskly. 'I prescribe some hot, strong coffee and a couple of aspirin to deal with that hangover. And a dose of hard work to stop you moping. You and the girls can help me and Claus weed the south field so the cows can have fresh grazing. Moping about all day won't butter any parsnips, and it's time you all got some fresh air and exercise.'

Anne accompanied her back to the farmhouse, her heart heavy. Aunt Vi was nothing if not practical, and although weeding the field was one of the least enjoyable tasks on the farm, it would at least go some way to ease the guilt and stop her from worrying about how Martin was coping on that long journey. But she certainly wasn't looking forward to the conversation she'd have to have with her mother.

Cliffehaven

Peggy had been woken by the sound of baby Joseph's crying. Peering at the bedside clock, she groaned. It was barely six, which meant she'd had less than four hours of sleep. She checked that Daisy was still asleep in her small bed and then snuggled back down beneath the covers, hoping she could return to the pleasant dream she'd been having about her and Jim swimming in the tropical blue waters off Burma. But it wasn't to be, so she reluctantly left her bed and headed upstairs to the bathroom to prepare for the day.

The wedding party had continued long after Ivy and Andy had left for London, and Peggy had stayed on to help Gloria and Beryl clean up before fetching a sleeping Daisy from one of the bedrooms and wheeling her home. Daisy might still be asleep, but it was doubtful that would last, for Joseph was now yelling fit to bust and would soon wake the entire house.

Peggy felt a dart of sympathy for Betty and Brendon as she closed the bathroom door on the racket. It couldn't be easy for them living here and out of suitcases with a young baby, but as Pauline was still being a cow, they really had nowhere else to go. Brendon had been out every day this past week looking for somewhere to buy or rent, and had put their names down for one of the new houses which were being built on what had once been Chumley's estate, but it wouldn't be ready for another month.

Peggy decided on a strip wash this morning as running the bath would only further disturb Cordelia and the girls on this floor, and as she scrubbed herself with a soapy wet flannel, her thoughts turned to the disgraced Chumley. His conviction for fraud had earnt him a long prison sentence, and the estate had been seized by the taxman to pay off his massive debts. Lord Cliffe had bought some of the land, and a property developer had taken on the rest. The manor house and stable block were being turned into very smart flats, and a series of terraced, semi and detached houses would take up the rest of the estate grounds. Sarah, who worked in the council offices, had told her that the waiting list for these homes was growing by the day, but she'd managed to place Brendon's application near the top. She was risking her job by doing so, but felt so sorry for him and Betty, and thought the risk was worth it if they could finally have a home of their own.

Peggy finished washing and brushed her teeth before getting dressed. She had few plans for today other than going up to Briar Cottage to see if she could help in any way. Poor Charlotte was still in pieces, Kitty was struggling to keep her focused on their business plans, and Roger was usually out, wandering Cliffe airfield or drinking in one of the pubs.

She was brushing her hair when she heard Brendon's heavy tread on the stairs, followed by Betty's lighter, less confident one. The poor lambs weren't getting much respite, she thought, unlocking the bathroom door. But then what new parents ever did?

She hurried downstairs to find them in the kitchen. Brendon was pacing the floor with Joseph draped over his shoulder as Betty warmed a bottle of formula. 'Is there anything I can do to help?' she asked above Joseph's wails.

'I'm so sorry we woke you,' said Brendon fretfully. 'He's not usually so demanding at this time of the morning.'

Peggy waved away his worries and reached for the squalling baby. 'Come on, big boy, let's go out and look at the chickens while Mummy warms your breakfast.' She carefully carried him down the concrete steps and out into the garden. 'There,' she soothed. 'Look.' Squatting down so he could see the hens fussily parading in their pen, she held him close to the wire netting.

Joseph stopped crying and stared at the chickens, reaching towards them with his tiny chubby fingers. Enthralled by the sight of them, he forgot his hunger and gave a beaming smile.

'It seems you have a way with babies,' said Betty, coming to stand beside her.

'I've had enough of them to know what to do,' Peggy replied, handing the baby over.

Joseph opened his mouth to protest and it was swiftly plugged by the rubber teat. 'I'm still learning,' Betty said and giggled as her baby drank hungrily. 'But Joseph is like all other males, and the answer to most of their woes is usually food.'

Peggy cocked her head at the sound of the telephone. 'Oh lawks, I hope that's not Pauline at this time of the morning,' she muttered and hurried indoors.

'Hello, Mum. I'm so sorry for ringing this early, I didn't realise the time. I hope I didn't wake you.'

'Not much chance of that with a baby in the house,' Peggy replied warily. She sat down on the hall chair, prepared for bad news. 'What's the matter, Anne?'

'Nothing's the matter,' Anne replied. 'Everything's fine here. It's just that I felt I should warn you that Martin's on his way home with Sally and her boys.'

Peggy didn't like the sound of that at all. 'But why aren't you with him? There hasn't been trouble between you, has there?' she asked anxiously.

'Not trouble exactly,' Anne said hesitantly. 'He's found it very hard to settle here, that's all, and when he discovered Sally was going home today, he decided to go with her.'

'That still doesn't explain why you aren't with him,' said Peggy. 'What is it that you're not telling me, Anne?'

Anne let out a long sigh. 'It's a very long story, Mum, which I'm not prepared to go into right now. But Martin was determined to leave today, and I couldn't stop him. Also, it would have been impossible for me to go with him at such short notice. We parted on good terms, because I realised it was for the best. But Martin isn't well, Mum, so you'll need to keep a close eye on him.'

Peggy knew how it was for Roger and her heart ached to think that her lovely son-in-law was similarly afflicted. 'Why didn't you tell me how hard things were down there, darling?'

'Because I didn't want to worry you and I thought I could cope.' Anne's voice became choked, as if she was trying not to cry. 'You know me, Mum. I've always been so sure that my decisions are for the best. I got it so wrong this time, and instead of helping him, I think I only made things far worse. It's all been so difficult, Mum, and now I don't know what's to become of us if he doesn't get better.'

Peggy gripped the receiver, longing to be able to embrace her daughter and soothe her as she'd calmed little Joseph. 'Tell me what I should do to help him,' she said softly.

'Let him be with Roger,' Anne said. 'He needs to talk to someone who's been through the same thing and understands.'

Peggy listened as Anne recounted her conversation with the headmaster. 'Oh, my darling,' she breathed at the end of the tragic story. 'I can't begin to imagine what those poor men have been through.' She paused to light a cigarette and give herself time to absorb what she'd been told. 'Roger isn't coping either. He's wandering the hills and haunting the aerodrome like a lost soul, and poor little Kitty is beside herself with worry.'

'I can fully understand that,' said Anne. 'Martin's been doing the same, only his wandering has led him to a pub, and he's been drinking heavily.'

'Then let's hope their reunion will begin the process of healing for them both – and, in time, for the two of you,' said Peggy. 'I'll make up a bed for him in the big front room that Rita and Ivy used to share. What time is he due in?'

'At around six o'clock if there's no delay and the connections go smoothly. But don't worry if he doesn't turn up straight away. I suspect he'll go looking for Roger the minute he arrives.'

Peggy closed her eyes at the thought of how desperate both men must be to talk to one another and vanquish the demons that beset them. 'I'll keep his supper warm, and put a hot water bottle in his bed. He'll be safe here with me,' she soothed.

'Thanks, Mum. And I'm sorry I didn't tell you what's been going on, but to be honest, I was ashamed of the mess I've made of everything.'

'You made your plans with the very best of intentions, my love, so please don't feel guilty. But will you be coming home soon?'

'I'll be leaving straight after the count in Taunton. It would have been sooner, but I couldn't find anyone to replace me at such short notice.'

Peggy's heart lightened, for her prayers had been answered at last. 'And will you be bringing Charlie?' she dared to ask.

'Kicking and screaming if necessary,' said Anne flatly. 'I'll see you next weekend, Mum. And thanks for being so kind and understanding.'

Peggy was about to reply, but Anne had quickly finished the call and there was only a loud buzzing coming from the receiver. She stubbed out her cigarette and thought about the big double bedroom at the front of the house. It was directly beneath the one Brendon was sharing with Betty and the baby, so it was doubtful if Martin and Anne would get much sleep. And then there was Rose and Emily to consider. They were too young to be put into the basement room, so would have to sleep in with their parents.

She picked up the receiver and asked April at the telephone exchange to connect her to the Anchor. She knew Ron could lay his hands on most things; surely he could find a spare cot at short notice?

With Ron's promise to see what he could do, she checked on Daisy who was still asleep, then went into the kitchen to find Joseph peacefully asleep in his mother's arms and Brendon drooping wearily over a cup of tea. 'Why don't you both go back to bed? I can keep an ear open for him and entertain him when he wakes.'

'Thanks, Peggy,' said Betty, shooting her a soft smile. 'I think we will snatch a nap until he wakes again, but we don't expect you to be running about after us.'

'I really don't mind,' she replied, fondly regarding the baby. 'Besides, I'll have virtually an empty house for the day once Jane and Sarah leave with Jeremy for London. Danuta will be on duty this afternoon, so there's only Cordelia and Daisy to worry about.'

Brendon kissed her cheek. 'You really are the most lovely of aunts,' he murmured before helping Betty to her feet and guiding her towards the door into the hall.

'How very cosy.' The sneering voice came from the doorway leading down to the basement.

'You should learn to knock, Pauline,' said Peggy sharply, 'and not creep up on people like that.'

'I have every right to be here, considering you've stolen my family,' she retorted.

Peggy gestured to the young couple hovering uncertainly in the doorway. 'Go and have your sleep. I'll deal with this.'

'This?' Pauline hissed. 'I'm not an object, but Brendon's mother.'

Peggy closed the door behind the departing couple. 'Perhaps you should have remembered that when you turned your back on him and his little family,' she snapped.

'He shouldn't have betrayed me the way he did by not asking me to his wedding to that creature, who's clearly turned him against me by cosying up with Dolly and Carol.'

'The reason he didn't ask you is because you're inclined to cause a scene if you take umbrage,' said Peggy, barely holding on to her temper. 'And Betty is not a creature – she's your grandson's mother and your son's very much loved wife. If the reason you've come here is to cause trouble, then you can just turn round and sling your hook.'

'I'm not going anywhere until I get my son back,' Pauline said, folding her arms.

'You'll have a hard time of it if you're going to go about it in this fashion. Brendon isn't going back to Tamarisk Bay unless he's absolutely certain he and his wife and son are welcome there.'

'I can't believe he let that woman force him into marriage by getting pregnant,' Pauline said crossly. 'Surely, Peggy, you must understand how ashamed I am that my son has fathered a child out of wedlock? And to a cripple of all things.'

Peggy slapped her; the hard, flat sound echoing in the silence.

Pauline clutched at her reddened cheek in shock. 'How *dare* you strike me,' she gasped.

'I'll do it again if you don't shut up, sit down and listen to a few home truths,' growled Peggy. 'Go on. Sit down.'

Pauline sat, still clutching her cheek, her eyes wide with fear as she looked up at Peggy. 'You have no right to talk to me like that.'

'I have every right to say as I please,' Peggy said with deceptive quietness. 'This is my home and my kitchen and you came here uninvited.' She leaned a little closer. 'Others might not be willing to tell you how they really feel about you, but I hold no such qualms,' she said, her emotions now tightly under control.

Pauline cringed back into the chair, speechless as Peggy continued.

'You are the most unpleasant, whining, whingeing woman I've ever had the misfortune to know. The world is not against you, and neither is your son – it's you who puts everyone's back up and makes their lives a misery. You see insults and slights where none were intended. You've alienated your sister with your jealousy; you don't speak to your mother because she doesn't spend every day of her life feeding your extraordinary need to be the star attraction in the show that is Pauline. As for Frank, you're damned lucky he hasn't found another woman who will love him and admire him for the wonderful, caring man that he is.'

Peggy finally drew breath, but she wasn't finished. 'And now you've hurt your son by hounding him out with your silences and disapproval. He came home with his wife and son to settle here close to his family – but he and Betty are on the very brink of going back to Devon. And if they do, Pauline, you'll probably never see them again.'

She leaned even closer until she could feel the warmth of Pauline's breath on her face. 'Is that what you really want? Because you're going the right way about it, and I wouldn't blame them a bit.'

'He wouldn't do that,' Pauline moaned. 'He knows how much I mourned for his brothers and wouldn't be so cruel as to deny me my only surviving son.'

Peggy stepped back and folded her arms, her furious gaze fixed steadily on Pauline's ashen face. 'He wouldn't want to, certainly. But if things don't improve, he very well might, and then you'll have lost all your sons – and I doubt Frank would ever forgive you for that.'

'Frank is a man and doesn't feel things as deeply as I do,' she muttered, reaching into her jacket pocket for a handkerchief.

'Tosh!' exploded Peggy. She gripped Pauline's skinny shoulders and shook her so hard her headscarf fell off and her handbag hit the floor. 'Wake up and grow up,' she snapped. 'Frank cares much more than you could ever imagine. It's why he stays with you. And the same goes for your mother and sister and son. Though God knows why they still love you after the way you've treated them over the years.'

She stepped back again to coldly regard this loathsome woman who'd made her lose her temper.

Pauline's face was almost translucent but for the bright red finger marks on her cheek. There were tears in her eyes and her bottom lip was trembling like a toddler's.

Peggy felt no pity, just exasperation, so left her to stew over what she'd said while she poured them both a cup of tea.

'I didn't realise how nasty you could be,' Pauline said eventually. 'You put on that smile and come over all warm and lovely, when in reality you're a complete bitch.'

'It takes one to know one.' Peggy pushed the cup and saucer towards her as she plumped down in a chair. 'Drink your tea, Pauline, and give some serious thought to what you're going to do next.'

'That's very wise advice, Pauline. I should take it, if I were you.'

'Dolly! Where did you spring from?' asked a delighted Peggy, going to hug her.

'What are you doing here?' Pauline demanded belligerently.

Dolly sat down at the table and crossed her slim legs. 'I came to see you and your adorable little family before I left for America,' she replied. 'Frank told me what's been going on, so I left Carol with him, did a bit of business in the town and drove over.'

'You've brought Carol with you?' asked Pauline. She sneered and her eyes hardened. 'Is she going with you to America, then?'

Dolly took her time to remove her gloves and light a cigarette. 'That has always been the plan,' she said coolly. 'But then you knew that.'

'Hmph. I don't know why I'm surprised,' Pauline muttered. 'She always was your favourite.'

'She's certainly more pleasant company than some I could mention,' said Dolly, her gaze steady on her eldest daughter. 'And if her husband and baby had survived, she definitely would have loved and cherished them – not given them the cold shoulder and hounded them from the family home because they'd displeased her in some very minor way.'

'It's none of your business,' snapped Pauline. 'If you've only come here to poke your nose in and interfere, then you might as well leave. Take Carol to America, for all I care. That general isn't my father, after all.'

Dolly smoked her cigarette and glanced across at Peggy. 'I'm so sorry you've had to deal with all this,' she said on a sigh. 'I've spoken to Frank, and the poor man is worried sick over how to resolve the situation.'

'Hmph. You always were on Frank's side,' muttered Pauline sourly.

Dolly ignored her and continued her conversation with Peggy. 'I understand it won't be too long before their house is ready for occupation, so I'm in the midst of negotiating with the property company to rent one of their newly finished flats in the next village for the interim. I have to go back in an hour to finalise things.'

'Oh, but you didn't have to do that,' gasped Peggy. 'I'm very happy to have them here.'

'I just bet you are,' snapped Pauline.

Dolly dismissed her interruption with a wave of her hand. 'The flat has three large bedrooms, and if Brendon agrees, Frank will move in with them until he can find somewhere else to live.'

Pauline stared at her in shock. 'What! But he can't leave me. He's my husband, and has a duty to look after me.'

'You've left it rather late in the day to remember that,' said Dolly. 'I did warn you the last time I came down you were in danger of losing him, but it seems you took no notice. As for his duty to you – he's served that sentence quite long enough, and has earnt his freedom.'

'How *dare* you talk about our marriage as if it was a prison sentence,' gasped Pauline.

'He'd have got a shorter term if he'd committed murder,' retorted Dolly. 'This disgraceful carry-on over Brendon and his wife and baby was the final straw. Frank's had enough, Pauline, and if you don't change your attitude very quickly, he means to leave you.'

'But he can't; he mustn't,' she wailed. 'How will I cope on my own?'

Dolly reached for her hand. 'You're the architect of all your troubles, Pauline, and I very much wish you could have learnt to see things from others' points of view and be thankful for all the blessings you have. As it is, you're in danger of losing your entire family.'

'I must go home and sort this out,' said Pauline, gathering up her scarf and handbag.

Silence fell in Peggy's kitchen as she clattered down the steps and slammed the back door. Peggy and Dolly regarded one another sadly.

'Will Frank really leave her?' asked Peggy.

'He's threatened before, and not quite had the nerve to do it. But this time, I think he might,' said Dolly on a sigh. 'He's heartbroken that his only surviving son had little choice but to take his family away from that house, and although Frank is the most loyal of men, I do believe there is very little love left in him for Pauline, who seems so determined to wreck everything.'

Peggy reached for her hand in sympathy, but made no comment.

'Oh Lord, Peggy, I so wish my daughter could see the damage she does. And there are times when I seriously fear for her sanity – for surely no right-minded woman would carry on as she does?'

'I've often wondered the same thing,' murmured Peggy. 'It's all so very sad, for things seemed to have improved between her and Frank since your last visit. She got a job that interests her and Frank is back at sea again, and it was all fine until Brendon turned up.' She gave a deep sigh. 'The poor boy doesn't know what to do for the best, for whatever decision he makes will end up hurting someone.'

Dolly stubbed out her cigarette and took a sip of the tea Peggy had placed before her. 'There's nothing more any of us can do,' she said sadly. 'Pauline can have no illusions as to what we think of her or of where she stands regarding her family. Even if Frank stays it will only be out of a misplaced sense of duty. As for Brendon, he and his little family will settle into the flat and get on with their lives, with or without Pauline.'

Peggy nodded, feeling quite depressed about it all. 'Let's talk about something more pleasant,' she suggested. 'I'd love to hear about your plans for your American trip.'

Dolly visibly brightened. 'Carol and I are going by ship to New York where Felix has booked us into a hotel right in the heart of Manhattan. We plan to shop until we drop, and see all the sights before we fly across to Los Angeles. Felix will meet us there and drive us down to his home in the orange and lemon groves.'

'It sounds heavenly,' sighed Peggy. 'Lucky you, and lucky, lucky Carol.'

Dolly smiled. 'Yes, we're both aware of how blessed we are, Peggy.' She took another sip of the rapidly cooling tea. 'Carol will be with me in the States for a couple of months, and if she likes it out there she may even decide to stay. There's nothing much left for her in Devon, and she certainly didn't fancy keeping her job on the farm. She's renting out the two cottages while she's with me, so has an income to tide her over.'

'And what about you, Dolly? Will I ever see you again?' Peggy asked.

Dolly reached for her hand. 'I'm sorry, my dearest friend, but this is my farewell trip, and I'm not planning to return. I've sold up in Bournemouth and all my worldly goods are already on their way to the States.'

'Oh, Dolly, I will miss you,' said Peggy wistfully. 'But I do understand why you must go.'

Dolly nodded. 'Felix and I have already wasted too many years apart, and now I've found him again, I'm never letting him go.' She smiled, her face softening and lighting up at the mere mention of his name. 'He's the love of my life, Peggy, and now we've got a second chance to be together, we're going to grab it with both hands.'

'I'm so pleased for you, Dolly – and for Carol. It will be a wonderful chance for her to really get to know her father and see something of America. I'm just sorry that your trip down here has been ruined by all the goings-on at Tamarisk Bay.'

Dolly shrugged and tried to appear nonchalant about it all, but the sadness in her eyes told another story. 'I felt really guilty about leaving Pauline behind, so was going to surprise her with the boat and plane tickets so she could join us for a few weeks. Now I've been presented with the aftermath of her truly appalling behaviour, I've decided she doesn't deserve to be rewarded so will cancel the tickets. It's a great shame, Peggy, but she's brought it upon herself.'

'You'd better keep that to yourself,' warned Peggy. 'Or there will be a massive bust-up again.'

Dolly nodded, then looked at her slender wristwatch and got to her feet. 'I have to see the estate agent and then rescue Carol from what I suspect will be an unpleasant scene between Frank and Pauline.' She took Peggy's hands and kissed her cheek. 'We'll be leaving this evening, so would it be all right if we call in later to say our goodbyes to everyone?'

Peggy hugged her fiercely. 'Of course it would. You and Carol are welcome any time.'

Peggy realised that she would now have very little time to go to Briar Cottage, so she telephoned Kitty to apologise for changing her plans and to tell her that Martin was on his way home. The poor girl had been quite tearful with relief that, at last, someone was coming who might help raise Roger's spirits and see him through this awful time.

Peggy was feeling quite emotional too as she disconnected the call, and went to see where Daisy had got to. She found her with Cordelia, chattering away nineteen to the dozen. The child had clearly dressed herself this morning, for she wore her favourite dungarees over a back-to-front jumper, with pink socks and her shoes on the wrong feet.

'Come on, Daisy, let me sort you out so you can have breakfast. You must be very hungry by now, and there's a lovely brown egg waiting for you downstairs.' Peggy managed to change the shoes over as her daughter fidgeted impatiently.

'Wanna ride with Gan-gan,' she protested when Peggy tried to lead her out of the room.

Peggy glanced at Cordelia who nodded. 'I'll see to her, Peggy, dear. It sounds as if you've had quite enough to contend with this morning as it is.'

'That would be a help,' said Peggy. She explained what had been happening with Pauline and Dolly.

Cordelia tutted and shook her head. 'That woman's got bats in the belfry, if you ask me,' she muttered. 'I'm not surprised poor Frank's had enough.'

Peggy left Cordelia to it and went upstairs to Brendon and Betty's room. Hearing the murmur of voices, she tapped on the door and went in. They were sitting in the chairs on either side of the gas fire, looking thoroughly miserable, so Peggy told them the news about the flat – but didn't want to depress them further by telling them about Frank's threat to leave Pauline and move in with them.

'That's very clever of Grandma Dolly,' said Brendon, looking far more cheerful. 'Though how she's managed it, I can't imagine. Those flats are like gold dust.'

'Dolly has always had a way of getting what she wants,' said Peggy, giving them a fond smile. 'She and Carol are coming over later to say their goodbyes before they leave for America.' She looked at her watch. 'Now, I must get on and prepare the room downstairs for Martin.'

The morning seemed to disappear as she swept and polished and made up the big double bed. Hauling Daisy's cot out of the cupboard under the stairs, she carried it up and put it together, ready for when Anne and the girls arrived at the end of the week. She was being a bit previous, she knew, but it was better to get as much done as possible now so there'd be less of a disturbance later.

Peggy stood in the doorway, pleased with her work, and then went back downstairs to find Cordelia and Daisy having a very late breakfast with Danuta.

'Where are Jane and Sarah?' she asked, putting her cleaning things back under the sink and washing her hands. 'Surely they aren't still asleep?'

'They left about half an hour ago to meet Jeremy at his hotel. Sarah said not to bother about their supper as they'd be back very late,' said Cordelia. She eyed Peggy over her half-moon glasses. 'Sit down and take a breath, dear. The tea's still hot, although it's very weak.'

Peggy sat down, took a sip and grimaced. 'These tea leaves have been used so many times we might just as well be drinking hot water.' She added a few grains of sugar, but they didn't make much difference, so she lit a fag and tried to relax. It had been quite a morning, and the row with Pauline still resonated, but at least the act of cleaning and bed-making had been an outlet for her pent-up fury, and she felt a little calmer.

Dolly and Carol arrived shortly after two, laden with all sorts of goodies they'd brought from the West Country. There were pots of lovely home-made jam, cream and scones, biscuits, a packet of tea, another of sugar and two jars of potted fish paste as well as half a Madeira cake. Carol had emptied out her larder, it seemed, and Peggy was very grateful for the gifts, for her own larder was sadly lacking in everything.

Dolly looked her usual elegant self in a silk two-piece, high heels and discreet jewellery. Carol, who Peggy hadn't seen for years, was youthfully pretty with her wavy blonde hair and clear complexion, the light flowery dress enhancing her trim figure. They were a breath of fresh air to Peggy, and as Ron and Rosie turned up to wish them bon voyage, the after-noon tea turned into quite a party.

Dolly explained about the flat as she handed the key over to Brendon and took charge of baby Joseph. 'The lease begins in three days and is just for a month, which the agent promised me would neatly coincide with the date your house will be ready to move into.'

'How did you leave things at home?' he asked fretfully.

Dolly held Joseph in her arms and lovingly stroked his soft cheek. 'Carol and I managed to calm your mother down when she stormed in all set to rant at your poor father. We stayed long enough to ensure they could conduct a civilised conversation without it turning into a full-blown row, and left them to it.'

She looked up from the baby and regarded Brendon with great affection. 'I'm sorry, dear boy, but that's all we could do in the circumstances. It's up to your parents now to decide what happens next.' She reached for his hand. 'You just concentrate on your own little family. Things will work themselves out eventually. They always do.'

A short while later, Dolly reluctantly handed the baby back to Betty. 'We have a long drive ahead of us, so we must leave,' she said sadly. She wrapped her arms about Brendon and kissed him before turning to Betty. 'I'm so delighted you married our boy, and your baby is simply beautiful. Take care of yourself, dear, and should you ever decide to come for a visit, you'll be very welcome.'

Kissing Cordelia's soft cheek, she then hugged Rosie before being swept into Ron's arms. 'Good heavens,' she managed as he lifted her off her feet in a bear hug. 'That's one heck of a hug, Ron.' She giggled as he carefully released her. 'Goodbye, you old rogue. Don't do anything I wouldn't do.'

'Ach, to be sure, Dolly, that gives me a wide scope for mischief, so it does,' he replied with a wink.

Peggy hugged her, breathing in the familiar flowery scent. 'I wish you all the luck in the world, Dolly,' she murmured. 'Try not to forget us, and write sometimes.'

Dolly's eyes were suspiciously bright as she eased from the embrace. 'I'll never forget any of you,' she said gruffly. 'Now, we really must go before I make a complete fool of myself and ruin my make-up.'

She gathered up her things as Carol was hugged and kissed by everyone, and then dug in her handbag. 'I almost forgot,' she said, handing an envelope to Peggy. 'This is for Danuta. Tell her I'm sorry I didn't have a chance to see her again.' With that, she quickly made her way to the front door.

Everyone gathered on the steps and tearfully watched them climb into the smart black Austin parked at the kerb. And then, with a wave and a blown kiss, Dolly drove away into the glow of the late afternoon sun.

Martin ached all over from sitting down for so long, and he eased his back and neck to unlock the stiffness before helping Sally down from the train and swinging young Harry out and onto the platform.

John Hicks was there to meet them, and as the couple celebrated a joyous and loving reunion, Martin strode down to the luggage compartment and helped the guard lift down the numerous cases, boxes and bags and stack them onto a trolley. With just a nod in response to Stan's cheerful greeting, he dumped his kitbag and suitcase in the left-luggage, shook hands with John, said goodbye to Sally and the boys and hurried out of the station.

Instead of going down the hill and making his way to Beach View, he began the long, steep climb towards Cliffe aerodrome in search of Roger. It felt good to be on the move again – wonderful to smell the salt in the air and experience the familiar swish of the long grass against his trouser legs.

He breached the brow of the hill and paused to catch his breath and take in the view, revelling in the sight of the familiar sprawl of Cliffehaven below him: the curve of the horseshoe bay, the white of the cliffs and the way the low sun gilded the tips of the seabirds' wings. This was home, and his spirits rose as he set off again, his sights now set on the airfield he knew was in the far valley.

As he got nearer he could see that the runway was pitted and weed-infested, the grass on the side in need of cutting, although it looked rather lovely with the colourful wild flowers swaying in the light breeze. The control tower was in desperate need of a coat of paint, and the Nissen huts were showing rust patches and signs of decline.

Martin paused and looked out over the scene of his wartime exploits, remembering those who'd shared the sleeping quarters, sat in deckchairs waiting for the order to scramble, and caused havoc in the mess on their return. They'd partied hard to drown their sorrows when the list of missing and dead became ever longer, and to pluck up enough courage to do it all again the next day – and the next – until the weeks blurred into months, and then years. They'd all been so young and naïve to believe they were leading charmed lives where others had not been so lucky. But Martin had to admit that despite everything, those years had been the best of his life.

He slowly walked through the gap someone had forced in the wire fencing and wandered over to the ops room hut. There was nothing left of the large desk where the girls had moved toy planes about to signify enemy and Allied positions, but he thought he could hear their voices, and still detect a hint of their scent in the air.

Martin moved on past the accommodation huts and mess hall, the memories flooding back with every step. He finally came to the hut that had once housed ancient couches and chairs where the flight crews had restlessly awaited their orders when the weather had been too cold to be outside. The furniture was still there, but covered in dust and cobwebs, the stuffing bursting out at the ripped seams; and he suspected the field mice had made use of it for nests. Then he spotted a couple of deckchairs leaning against the wooden wall. They seemed to be in reasonable condition, so he dusted one down with his handkerchief and carried it outside to test it thoroughly before he sat down.

He could see the whole airfield from here, and if he closed his eyes he could hear the planes landing and taking off – see the enemy air raids which sent everyone scurrying for shelter – recall the death-defying heroics of men like Freddy who'd managed to steer his shot-up kite away from the huts and come screeching down on one wheel – and the bravery of the fire crews who raced alongside to put the fire out and drag the pilot and crew to safety.

Martin opened his eyes, not wanting to see those images any more, or hear those long-remembered sounds of a busy RAF base. He lit a cigarette and gazed over the abandoned field which now seemed so much larger than he'd remembered, and then a movement in the distance caught his eye.

He stilled and watched as the familiar, lonely figure emerged from the deepening shadows of the trees and began to wander unsteadily down the runway, clearly over-refreshed and lost in his own thoughts.

Martin felt as if a great weight had been lifted from his shoulders at the sight of his friend, yet he didn't call to him, but went to fetch the second deckchair. He brushed it down before setting it up beside his, then sat and waited for Roger to notice that he wasn't alone.

Roger eventually caught sight of him and, after a momentary hesitation, squared his shoulders and strode towards him. Eyeing the deckchair, he gingerly lowered himself into it, and took a sip from his hip flask. 'I wondered when you'd turn up,' he said, handing the flask to Martin. 'Nice view from here, isn't it?'

Martin nodded, at ease for the first time since he'd set foot back in England. 'The best in the world, old chum.'

24

Ron was tramping the hills with the dogs racing ahead of him, his cap pulled low over his brows, his little great-grandson nestled snugly in a blanket against his chest in a sturdy hessian bag he'd adapted for the purpose. He was at peace with the world and himself as he breathed in the soft, warm air of this summer day, for this was how he'd introduced his sons and grandchildren to the wide open spaces that surrounded Cliffehaven. And now, with this new generation, and the imminent arrival of Anne with Charlie and her two little girls, the old rituals could be carried out once more.

Ron peered down at Joseph's downy head and smiled. The boy would have the thick black hair and blue eyes of the Reilly family, and as he grew he'd learn their traditions of fishing, foraging and poaching – the last of which had to be done without his mother's knowledge, of course. Women didn't seem to approve of such things, but they rarely turned down the chance of a juicy salmon or a nice plump pheasant.

Harvey came bounding over to jump up and sniff at Joseph to make sure he was all right, before lolloping off again to join his pup, Monty, who was digging about in great excitement beneath a clump of gorse.

Ron carried on walking and when he reached the ruined farmhouse, he sank onto the grass and eased the straps from his shoulders. Cradling the sleeping baby, he gazed at him in awe. Joseph was a wonder he couldn't get enough of – he'd never imagined he'd be blessed by such a treasure that reminded him so very much of his namesake. Ron puffed on his pipe, letting his thoughts just drift for a while until he realised the morning was fast disappearing. Joseph was still asleep, so he bundled him back into the sack, made sure his blanket was wrapped tightly around him and then shrugged on his coat. Whistling up the dogs, he headed for Tamarisk Bay to check on Frank.

He reached the steep, rutted driveway that led down to the three wooden cottages overlooking Tamarisk Bay. Frank had spent time and effort to keep his weather-proofed and sturdy, but the other two looked rather care-worn, for they'd been left to rot over the war years. The original inhabitants had decamped back in 1939 and not returned, so Frank had bought them for a song, cleaned them up to make them habitable again, then rented them out to desperate families who didn't mind the fact he still had work to do on them.

Ron grinned at the two barefoot children who were watching him wide-eyed from a doorway. Letting the dogs race ahead, he trudged down the slope past Frank's utility truck and across the shingle to the small fishing boat which had been hauled above the waterline.

Frank seemed to be lost in his thoughts as he sat in the wheelhouse staring out over the sea, his broad shoulders drooping as he cradled a tin cup in his large hands.

'Everything all right with you, wee boy?' asked Ron, clambering on board.

Frank was startled out of his reverie and almost dropped the cup. 'Sorry, Da,' he muttered. 'I was half asleep and didn't hear you coming.'

'If you were out all night you should be in bed catching up on your sleep,' replied Ron, helping himself to a mug of tea and lacing it with whisky. He jerked his head towards the cottage. 'How are things?'

Frank heaved a sigh. 'Quiet for now. She's gone back to work.' He regarded his father from beneath his thick brows. 'She's not well, Da, and it worries me.'

'Aye, it would.' Ron had always suspected that Pauline had a screw loose, for no sane woman would carry on as she did, and this latest bout of illness was no doubt her way of seeking attention. 'What's the matter with her this time?' he asked neutrally.

'She's been suffering from sick headaches which have affected her eyesight, giving her blurred vision. I told her to go to the doctor's, but she refuses to listen, and blames her bad heads on the stress everyone has caused her lately.'

Frank heard his father's soft grunt and met his cynical gaze. 'I know what you're thinking, Da, and I agree that she has only herself to blame, but I really do believe she isn't putting it on this time.'

'If it's as bad as she says, then she'll do something about it,' said Ron, adjusting the straps of the hessian bag to a more comfortable position on his shoulders. 'Pauline has been running back and forth to that doctor for years. I don't see why she should suddenly change a habit of a lifetime.'

'Aye, you're right.' Frank brightened and ran a gentle hand over Joseph's head. 'I'm going over to see

Brendon and Betty later. They actually asked me to move in with them, you know.'

'Why didn't you?' asked Ron flatly.

'I couldn't leave while Pauline's feeling so ill. Besides, they're newly-weds and don't want me playing gooseberry.'

Ron sipped the stewed tea and came to the conclusion that Pauline's illness was very timely – but then that was entirely predictable. She certainly knew how to keep Frank under her thumb, and it made him dislike her even more. But Frank was a middle-aged man, and his marriage was his own business. It was just a pity he didn't have the gumption to see his wife for what she really was, and leave her to stew.

He decided to change the subject. 'Have you managed to find enough crew to man the boats?' he asked.

Frank shook his great head and grimaced. 'There's plenty willing to be taken on, but most of them don't know one end of a boat from another, and haven't the slightest idea of how to work a trawler.' He chuckled. 'I took a couple of men out the other day when it was as flat as a mill pond, and they spent the entire time throwing up over the side.'

'What about the old crew? Haven't they come looking to take up their jobs again?'

Frank's expressive face showed his sadness. 'Five never came back from the Atlantic convoys, two were wounded in France and won't work on boats again, and another two have decided to retire.' He heaved a deep breath and let it out on a sigh. 'There are just enough of us to man the two trawlers, but the rest of the boats are lying up idle.'

'At least the trawlers should bring in enough to pay the wages,' said Ron. 'And of course, you've got the rents from those cottages. You made a good move there, son.'

Frank nodded. 'The rents certainly help, but there's still a lot of work to be done to get those cottages how I want them.' He sipped his tea and lit a cigarette, watching the dogs cavort in the shallows. 'I hear Rosie's got involved with the local election. I never took her as someone who was interested in politics.'

Ron grinned. 'I don't think she ever was really, until bread and potatoes were rationed for the first time, and the prices shot through the roof. She hears a lot from behind the bar, and realised things had to change for the better, so started going to the candidates' meetings. Now she's all fired up and even talking about standing as a Labour candidate in next year's local council elections.'

Frank's brows lifted and he stared at his father in disbelief. 'Labour?'

'Aye, it surprised me too,' admitted Ron. 'Her family were all staunch Tories, and that's where I thought her loyalties lay, but she's swallowed Labour's promises hook, line and sinker, and has joined up with them. She's now spending every spare hour handing out leaflets and knocking on doors. The bar has become a meeting place during closing time, and election fever is high.' He gave a sniff of disapproval. 'I stay out of the way as much as I can, because airing my Tory opinions only causes heated arguments.'

'Oh, Da,' groaned Frank. 'You and Rosie haven't fallen out, have you?'

Ron shook his head before draining the mug of tea. 'We leave politics outside the bedroom door, and have agreed to disagree on the matter. To be sure, I'll just be glad when it's all over and done with and we can go back to a peaceful life.'

'I'm with you there,' said Frank, shooting him a wry smile. 'More tea?'

'No thanks, son. I've got to get back to Beach View, check on the tiler and hose down Harvey.' He looked towards the dog which was now rolling in the pile of discarded fish guts by the water's edge. 'Ach, to be sure there are times I could cheerfully murder that heathen beast,' he muttered without real rancour.

He squeezed Frank's shoulder. 'Chin up, son. Have a sleep, and when you've been to see Brendon, come to the Anchor for a pint.'

Frank's smile was weary. 'Thanks, Da. I might just do that.'

Solly's new enterprise on the factory estate was in full swing that afternoon, the production running as smoothly as a well-oiled machine. The cutters, machinists, checkers and packers were busy working at their stations on the array of maternity clothes and babywear in an atmosphere of pent-up excitement. It was the day of the election, and everyone had an opinion as to which party would win, so there had been a bit of argy-bargy when things had grown heated, but Peggy had managed to cool things down enough so it didn't come to blows.

She kept an eye on the less experienced machinists she'd placed close to an old hand and saw that most of them were getting along well, so went to see how the girls on the checking tables were doing. It was here that the work was assessed and either passed or set aside as seconds which would be sold on market stalls. She noted with pleasure that the seconds pile was smaller than of late, but having checked the machinist's number on the tag inside each piece, her spirits fell. Marge Sherman's work was still well below an acceptable standard.

She gathered up the maternity dresses and took them into the small office which had been partitioned off from the factory floor. Dumping the dresses on her desk, she pulled Marge's file from the cabinet and read through it even though she was familiar with the woman's background and work history.

Marge had been working in the armaments factory when her soldier husband had been killed during the beach landings, and she'd been left with three small children to raise. Both her parents were frail and unable to help, and her husband's family had been wiped out during the bombing raids on Coventry. The armaments factory had closed, and like so many others, Marge was out of work.

Peggy closed the file and sat back with a sigh of deep regret. Marge had begged her for this job and Peggy rather foolishly had let her heart rule her head and taken her on even though she'd had no previous experience of sewing. The poor woman had tried hard to learn but she was still making too many mistakes, and with all the unpicking and resewing, the garments ended up looking rather grubby.

Looking through the large window to the factory floor, Peggy spotted Marge struggling to clear her machine of the tangled cotton caught under the needle. Fanny Rawson stayed her hand and took over with her usual neat efficiency, and the blockage was cleared again.

Peggy was warmed by Fanny's seemingly endless patience as she once again showed Marge the correct way to thread the machine. Peggy had asked Solly for the girl to come with her to help oversee the new intake of sewers, and she'd proved to be very reliable.

However, this state of affairs couldn't be allowed to continue, and it was down to Peggy to do something about it. This was the part of the job she hated the most, especially when it involved someone who was desperate for work – and, it had to be said, a keen trier.

She examined the maternity dresses again in the hope they could be rescued from the seconds pile by a bit of judicious resewing. But the hem dipped at the sides, one of the seams gaped, and the armholes were rucked up where the material had been turned inexpertly and missed the needle altogether. It simply wouldn't do.

Peggy pushed the dresses to one side and mulled over what she could arrange so the woman wasn't left entirely without work. She let her gaze trawl the factory which was about a third of the size of the one in Camden Road, but still employed over sixty people.

The cutting tables were definitely not for Marge, and there were enough checkers at the moment, so that was out too. Work in the warehouse meant shifting heavy bales of material and loading and unloading the delivery lorries; the three finishers were nimble-fingered and experts at hand-sewing the final touches to the garments, and the canteen which served the whole estate was already fully staffed.

'But there might be something in the packing department,' she muttered, and reached for the list of employees. There were three girls and two men involved in packing the clothes for transport, and she remembered suddenly that one of the girls was pregnant. She placed the list on her desk, checked the time and hurried down the lines of machinists to the partitioned area that housed the packing department.

Returning a while later, she approached Marge who was close to tears of frustration as she tried to unjam the material from beneath the needle. 'It's almost the end of the day, Marge, leave that and come with me to my office.'

The blue eyes widened and a large tear beaded her lashes as she left her machine. 'You aren't going to sack me, are you?' she whispered fearfully.

Peggy's heart went out to her but she didn't reply as she gently nudged her towards the office. Once the door was closed behind her, she took Marge's hand. 'I'm sorry, my dear, but I can't keep you on the machines.'

Marge burst into loud sobs. 'But I need to work,' she managed. 'Please give me another chance.'

Peggy pressed her down into a chair and gave her a clean handkerchief. 'I do have another position for you, but it will pay less.'

'I'll take it,' Marge replied eagerly.

Peggy chuckled. 'You don't know what it is yet. But I think you'll be happier in the packing department, even if the pay isn't as good. The hours are the same, nine to five, and you'll still share in any bonuses rising from the sales orders.'

'Thank you, oh, thank you,' Marge breathed tearfully. 'I won't let you down, I promise.'

'Clock off at the usual time today, and start in packing tomorrow morning. Come in a bit early so Cathy can show you what the job entails.' She smiled at Marge who was looking a great deal more cheerful. 'It's her you should thank, really, because instead of handing her notice in next week as she'd planned, she'll leave once you're settled. She's heavily pregnant, and finding it very hard to be on her feet all day.'

Once Marge had left her office and she'd returned the dresses to the seconds pile, Peggy dealt with the seemingly endless paperwork which came across her desk each day, and then checked the order book.

Solly was a wise old owl, she thought fondly, noting how the orders were flooding in. He'd known there'd be a baby boom and had dived in before his competitors and was now reaping the benefits – as were the staff since he'd decided to reward them a monthly bonus from the profits. It was an innovative idea which encouraged the workers to greater efforts, and was no doubt making Solly a very rich man.

Peggy closed the order book, checked the time, then went to see if the warehouse was prepared for the large material order that was due to arrive the next morning.

All was as it should be, and on returning to the factory floor, she clapped her hands for silence.

'I know you're all in a rush to get home, but before you go, there's something I'd like to say.'

There was a general groan and shuffling of feet, but she had their attention. 'I just want to remind you to cast your vote,' she said. 'Not so long ago, other women died and were imprisoned so you could have a voice in the running of this country, and it would be disrespectful to their memory not to use your vote and have your say.' She smiled. 'Go on, get out of here, and I'll see you tomorrow.'

There was a stampede to clock off, and within minutes the factory was still and empty.

Once she'd picked up Daisy from the crèche, Peggy went to the Town Hall to cast her vote, then made her way home. When she arrived, she found Cordelia, Danuta, Jane and Sarah in the kitchen which was full of the delicious aroma of warming shepherd's pie. As usual there was no sign of Martin, who'd taken to leaving early and coming home long after dark during the past week, moving so quietly about the house that Peggy quite often had no idea if he was in or not. But there had certainly been no sign that he'd been drinking heavily, and according to Ron, he spent most of his time at the airfield with Roger. She could only hope that being together and talking things over was doing both of them some good.

'There are several letters for you, Peggy,' said Sarah, placing a cup of tea in front of her. 'And, going by the writing, I suspect one of them is from Ivy,' she added with a grin.

Peggy settled Daisy onto the cushion and tucked her chair closer to the table so she could reach the bowl of pie Cordelia had been cooling for her. Unable to resist looking through the tempting small pile of letters, she felt her spirits rise. There were two from Jim, one from Ivy – whose writing had not improved – and one from Fran.

'You go ahead and eat,' she told the others. 'I'll just have this cup of tea for now while I read my post.' She set Jim's letters to one side to savour them slowly after tea, and opened Ivy's, knowing it would be short, but fearing it would prove hard to decipher.

The single page had been scrawled on both sides with Ivy's appalling writing and bad spelling, but Peggy managed to work out that the girl was very happy with Andy in their lovely flat, and although she was suffering horribly from morning sickness, she'd managed to get a part-time job behind the counter at Woolworths.

Andy was working long, busy shifts, but his fellow firemen were a jolly bunch and he felt very much part of the team. She asked if anyone had heard from Ruby yet, and if there was news of Rita's wedding, because if she left it too long, she'd be too fat to get into anything decent. Almost as an afterthought, she mentioned the fact that George and Elsie's adoption had now gone through, then signed off with an unreadable signature and a row of kisses.

Peggy smiled and left the letter for Cordelia to read once she'd finished her tea, and then opened the one from Fran. It was four pages long and neatly written in a looping copperplate that was a pleasure to read – the nuns in Ireland had clearly taught her well.

Dear Aunt Peggy,

I'm sorry I haven't written much before, but I've been very busy settling in and getting used to a large, busy London hospital again. I'm back at St George's where I did my training, and working in theatre. The surgeons can be quite rude and very brusque at times, but the work is fascinating and I'm learning a lot as well as making new friends among the other nurses. None of us know what changes there will be, and how they will affect us if Labour gets in, but it's clear to us all that if they do, this promised National Health Service will be a godsend – especially for those poor, desperate people living in the devastation of what remains of the East End. The damage up here is quite appalling and serves to remind us both how lucky we were to spend the war years in lovely Cliffehaven.

Robert has settled into his new posting, and leaves every morning in his three-piece suit and bowler hat, carrying his briefcase and rolled-up umbrella, for all the world looking like a real London gent, which makes me giggle a bit, because he isn't at all pompous or grand like so many of the others he's working with. I have no idea what he's doing in that office, but he seems excited about it, and that's all that really matters.

We've joined an orchestra, which practises every Wednesday night in the rehearsal rooms of the Palace Theatre, and although we can't always make it because of our work commitments, we're finding it wonderfully relaxing to be playing again, and I can't thank Doris enough for letting me keep the violin.

The flat is very grand and furnished in the style of how I imagine a terribly smart and expensive hotel would be.

There are two large bedrooms, a drawing room, dining room and even a small book-lined office, which Robert has taken over. There's a lovely balcony which catches the evening sun, and we've taken to sitting out there to watch the world go by.

It's far too big for us, but being in the heart of the city, it's convenient for getting about easily, and I'm slowly learning which tube or bus to take, for it's all very different to my student days.

We have started looking for a place of our own, but the rents are extortionate and there's not much choice to be had, so we'll probably stay here for a while until we find the right place. Neither of us wants a long commute every day, but it looks as if we'll have to spread our search further afield to one of the London suburbs, and rely on the trains. The damage up here is awful to see, and my heart goes out to the poor people who have no choice but to camp out in the ruins, so I feel very guilty about rattling around in this palatial flat which could house an entire family, if not two.

I expect you've heard from Cissy, but I thought you'd like to know that I bumped into her the other day. She looked very glamorous in the skirt suit and little hat that is the company livery, and was positively buzzing about her partnership in the business and all the fun she's having mixing with the London society set. She told me she's still living with her friend in Mayfair until she finds somewhere else, and has certainly adopted the glossy look of a very well-to-do young woman about town. I felt quite dull beside her in my nurse's uniform, but then she always did have the knack of looking good in anything she wore.

As you warned me, our trip to Ireland was not a success. All doors were closed to us and my family refused to even hold a telephone conversation with me. The local priest was hostile, and even the shopkeeper I've known all my life refused to serve me. The whole thing was horribly dispiriting, especially when my mother ripped up the letter I put through her door, and scattered the pieces very deliberately into the gutter before slamming the door in my face. We didn't stay after that, and the next day we were on the ship to Liverpool. I can't pretend that I wasn't heartbroken, but I've vowed not to look back and to concentrate only on my new life with Robert, for I have far more important things to occupy me now.

Our baby is due at the end of December, so I'll have to give up work at the end of the summer – but I've been told on good authority that I'd be welcomed back should I wish to return in the New Year. It's certainly something I will consider as long as I can arrange suitable nursery care.

Robert's lovely mother has got so excited at the news she's begun to bombard us with the most exquisite layette, and a positive zoo of cuddly toys. I do believe she's raided Harrods as well as Hamleys and must have left their shelves bare!

I hope all is well with everyone at Beach View. Cissy told me you've been attending quite a lot of weddings lately, and that Ruby had finally married her Mike and set off for Canada. I suspect Ivy's now married Andy, and hope Rita and Peter have come to an agreement over where they'll live once they've tied the knot. Beach View must feel very empty now with so many of us gone, and I've kept a close eye on the news in the hope that Jim will soon be coming home. I expect Anne and the children are with you now, so they must be a comfort to you, and I very much hope that Martin and all the other fliers made it home in one piece.

I'll finish now, for it's late and I'm tired after a long day in theatre. Please pass on my very best wishes to Sarah, and tell her I'm keeping my fingers crossed that good news is waiting for her once the Japs surrender.

Do write to me with all your news, Auntie Peg, because I miss you and Ron and Cordelia so very much, and want to stay in touch. I promise to be a more regular correspondent from now on, as I'll soon have plenty of time to write while I wait for the arrival of this baby.

With lots of love,

Fran xxx.

PS Please pass on my congratulations to Doris. I met her son and Suzie at a government function the other day, and they're expecting a brother or sister for little Teddy! Suzie looks marvellously well, and it was quite like old times to be able to chatter away with her while the men pontificated over their port and cigars. But more of that in my next letter. X

'Whew,' breathed Peggy. 'Fran's expecting and is very happy in London, and our Suzie is also expecting at around the same time. I get the feeling this Christmas could turn out to be very exciting. Doris must be over the moon about it all. Here, read it for yourselves. Fran won't mind as long as you remember to write back. She's missing everyone, I think.'

She was about to fetch her meal from the warming oven when she remembered her earlier conversation with Rita. 'Oh, by the way, Rita and Peter will be setting the date for their wedding this weekend. It'll be at St Andrew's, where Suzie married Anthony, and Fran brought us all to tears with her divine violin playing.'

'Golly,' breathed Cordelia. 'I'm going to have to buy a new hat at this rate. The straw one is looking decidedly tatty.'

'We'll go to the shops on Saturday and see what we can find,' promised Peggy, eagerly tucking into her shepherd's pie.

Having staved off her initial hunger, she looked across at Danuta who'd been almost silent throughout. 'Why don't you come with us, Danuta? A new outfit will cheer you up no end. You must be sick of wearing the same old things.'

'That would be very nice,' she replied. 'But I am saving my money for the journey to Poland.'

Peggy experienced a dart of concern. 'Oh, I thought you'd given up on that idea, what with Europe being in such turmoil at the moment.'

Danuta nodded. 'For a while I will stay here, but Solly Goldman is planning to go to Warsaw at the end of the summer to try and find out if any of his family have survived the camps. I have agreed to travel with him.'

Peggy reached for her hand. 'I knew Solly had been talking of going, but I hadn't realised he was already making plans. I do wish you'd reconsider, Danuta. It's chaos over there, and probably quite dangerous.'

'I need to go home, Mamma Peggy,' she replied softly. 'I understand the risks and know there will be no one left of my family in Warsaw, but the hospitals and clinics are being overwhelmed, and they need every nurse they can find.'

'How long will you stay?' asked Peggy, fearful that once she'd gone they'd never see her again.

Danuta smiled. 'I do not know. But I promised Aleksy and baby Katarzyna that I would not abandon them, so I will return if you'll have me.'

'But of course I will,' breathed Peggy, going to give her a hug. 'This is your home and we're your family now. There will always be a place for you here.' She kissed her cheek. 'Just promise me you'll be careful, and won't take any silly risks.'

Danuta returned her kiss and chuckled. 'I think I have learnt my lesson about taking risks, Mamma Peggy, and with Solly by my side, I'm sure I'll be perfectly safe.' She pushed back from the table to wash her dishes. 'Now I must go to the clinic and begin my shift. I am hoping for a quiet night, but with so many babies on the way, I don't expect it will be.'

Barely mollified, Peggy finished her plate of food, her heart heavy at the thought of Danuta travelling through war-torn Poland. It was good that Solly would be with her, but despite his size and daunting appearance, he was no longer youthful or terribly fit, and would be unable to defend Danuta should they run into trouble. But then Danuta had gone into Europe during the war to work with the underground and had managed to escape the clutches of the SS before they'd tortured her to death. She might be small, but she had the heart and courage of a lioness.

Sarah seemed to be thinking along the same lines, although she had no knowledge of Danuta's war exploits. She patted Peggy's shoulder in sympathy. 'Danuta's a very capable girl, Aunt Peggy. Please try not to worry about her.'

Jane handed Sarah her jacket and handbag, and Sarah stood up. 'Jane and I are going to vote, and then take a stroll along the seafront before we go to the pictures at the Drill Hall. The chap in charge has managed to get hold of *Brief Encounter*, and from what I've heard, we're in for a jolly good cry.'

'Bertie's taking me to see it tomorrow afternoon,' said Cordelia happily. 'I do so enjoy a good cry at the pictures.'

Jane giggled. 'Yes, we did notice, Aunt Cordelia. You manage to cry at the drop of a hat, it seems.'

'Or the wisp of a wedding veil,' added Sarah on a chuckle.

'Cheeky girls,' Cordelia said cheerfully. 'Be off with you.'

They went down the cellar steps and quietly closed the door behind them, and Peggy cleared the table and did the last of the washing-up. There was still no sign of Martin, but hopefully his time-keeping would improve once Anne and the children came home at the weekend. Her heart did a little skip at the thought of seeing them all again, even though Bob wouldn't be with them – but he would come eventually, and so would Jim, God willing.

She was about to tear open his letters when she noticed that Daisy was drooping in her chair, so she gathered her into her arms and carried her upstairs for a wash before bedtime. The child was asleep before Peggy had finished reading a story, so she snuggled her beneath the bedclothes with her favourite toy rabbit, kissed her forehead and switched on the night light. With a loving smile at Jim's photograph on the bedside table, she hurried back into the kitchen to fetch his letters and join Cordelia in the back garden.

Cordelia was sitting in one of the deckchairs wrestling with her knitting. It was supposed to be a matinee jacket for Ivy's baby, but was a tangle of wool interspersed with holes where she'd dropped the stitches.

Peggy quickly unravelled it for her, knitted a couple of rows to start her off, and then settled back in the other chair to enjoy the evening sun and open the earlier of the two letters from Jim.

To her disappointment it was very short and full of moans. He couldn't tell her where he was, why he hadn't written for so long, or much about what he was doing, but it seemed he'd left the comfortable quarters on the coast and was back in a tent somewhere. The monsoon was the worst Jim had ever experienced, the rats were as big as dogs, the mud was up to his knees, and everything was constantly sodden and stinking. According to Jim it was a filthy place, and it would have been cleaner living in the jungle. There was no entertainment, and it seemed to him that the troops in Burma had been forgotten by ENSA as well as the rest of the world.

Peggy gazed across the sunlit vegetable patch and lit a cigarette. Jim was obviously feeling very low. She gave a sigh and returned to the rest of his letter.

Their camp had been set up near the shattered remains of a village pagoda, and he expressed his disgust at the fact that the beautifully carved alabaster figures of Buddha had been all but destroyed by the Jap invaders. Life was made completely miserable by the wet, the humidity and the swarms of mosquitoes, and he was down with yet another cold.

They were now all on standby again, which meant another round of packing, but he hoped it meant they'd either be sent somewhere decent, or finally receive their orders to board ship for home. He finished off by sending his love to everyone and his hope that this purgatory would soon be at an end, and he could be back in the cool of a Cliffehaven autumn.

Peggy tore open the second letter to find that he'd got part of his wish, for he was now stationed somewhere more comfortable in huts rather than tents, with proper beds to sleep in.

I've just got back to my workshop base after going 300 miles by air to clear a three-ton lorry out of the mud which was up to its chassis. It took hours to shift it, but the blessed thing started straight away, so it was a job well done, and we celebrated with one of the hottest curries I've ever had. One of the natives cooked it, so we weren't sure what was in it and didn't ask, but it certainly made my eyes water, I can tell you, and my tongue felt like it was on fire! Unfortunately, it proved just as hot on its way out, and I had gut ache for two days after.

There's a rushing river running past the workshop, and I have to be careful in this humidity not to knock my hands or scratch at the mozzie bites again. The sores can turn septic overnight out here, and as I was pretty banged up last time, I know how painful that can be, so I don't want a repeat of it.

At least now we can get Bob Hope and Jack Benny on the wireless, and last night we were treated to the Crosby film, Going My Way, *which we all enjoyed. The rum ration is very welcome, and when it stops raining – which it does for a while each day now – the coastal drive is quite beautiful, and reminds me of home. There are wonderful sandy beaches with the jungle rolling right down to the shore where there's good bathing to be had, so we go down there at every opportunity. It's hard to believe we once fought a long battle in this area and that there's still a war going on, for it's very peaceful down there.*

I got my Burma star today, and Jumbo's feeling very full of himself, because he's just been awarded the Oak Leaf Medal for gallantry, which he thoroughly deserves.

I'll write again when I can, but the workshop is overwhelmed with vehicles needing repairs and maintenance, and now the airdrop has brought the necessary supplies, I have no excuse but to get on with it.

I do miss you, Peggy, and wish with all my heart I could leave this place and be with you and our children. But it seems the army has other ideas and there are still things for us to do here. Keep writing, for wherever we're sent, the mail will follow us – it's about the only sure thing in this damn war – other than the rain.

Much love and many kisses,

Jim

25

As the train left Somerset behind and puffed and panted busily towards the London terminus on that Saturday morning, Anne gave up on the book she'd been trying to read and gazed out of the window. She was tired but elated, for her Conservative candidate, Victor Collins, had won the Taunton seat despite the fact he was a born and bred London businessman. The past week had been frantic with all the packing up, and on the night of the election she'd been kept for hours in Taunton for the count and then the jubilant party that followed, and hadn't arrived home until well after midnight.

The final result of the election wouldn't be in until 26th of July to accommodate the time it would take for the votes to come in from the far-flung constituencies in Scotland, but from what she'd gleaned at the party, and during the two following days, it sounded as if Labour was making huge inroads into the Conservative heartlands, which was bitterly disappointing and to her mind a rather shocking betrayal of Churchill.

Anne's thoughts turned to the last sad moments she and the children had spent on Owlet Farm. Charlie had disappeared into the machine shed, only to emerge at the very last minute to give Vi a brief hug and shoot a glower of fury at Bob who'd shoved him into the

Land Rover with little ceremony. Rose and Emily were too young to really understand what was happening, but Anne had found saying goodbye to Vi very painful and the tears had flowed on both sides, for Vi had been mother and grandmother to them for almost six years, and it was an awful wrench to leave her behind.

They'd wished Claus well on his forthcoming wedding, and there had been more tears when Anne had said her final farewell to George, Belinda and the dear little schoolhouse earlier that morning. Just thinking about it made Anne sad, for she'd come to love the farm, the village and its people, and knew she would hold the memory of it all in her heart for many years to come.

She took a steadying breath, for enough tears had been shed today and she was on her way home to Cliffehaven, her mother and Martin, and must prepare herself for whatever awaited her there.

Having telephoned Peggy the previous evening to tell her the time her train would get in, she'd asked to speak to Martin. But it seemed he was out with Roger somewhere and her mother had no idea when he'd return. Peggy had assured her that he knew she was coming home, and would no doubt be at the station to welcome them all.

Anne hoped with all her heart that he'd be there, and that although it had only been a week, the time they'd spent apart would have helped him come to terms with things. But how would they rebuild what they'd had if he still couldn't engage with her and the children? Where could they start when they'd been apart for two years and were almost strangers on his return? And then there was the future to consider. What were his plans? This had been a niggling worry ever since Martin had been released from his RAF duties, for her income as a teacher certainly couldn't support them all, and she very much doubted if he would fly a plane again.

Anne dismissed this worry as something to deal with later and looked across the carriage at Charlie and her two young daughters. Rose and Emily were quietly playing with their dolls, but her younger brother was ignoring everyone as he sat with his arms tightly folded across his broad chest, his dark expression warding off any approach. He'd refused point blank to wear his school uniform for the journey, and was dressed in his brother's old corduroy trousers and a jumper that had definitely seen better days.

Anne let him simmer, suspecting he couldn't keep it up for the entire length of the long journey, but it had been a tremendous struggle to force him to get on the train in the first place, for at fourteen, Charlie was big and brawny, and far too strong for her to be able to force him to do anything. Bob had eventually taken charge by hauling him aside to give him a stern ticking off before clipping him none-too-gently around the ear. Whatever he'd said had had the desired effect, but it was clear the boy resented every single mile of the journey.

Anne had been grateful for Bob's help, for Charlie was behaving extremely badly for a boy his age. She regarded her brother's sullen expression and gave an inward sigh. She could only hope he would buck up, and at least show his better side when he arrived in Cliffehaven – and he did possess such a thing, for he had a smile to lighten your heart and an enthusiasm for life which knew no bounds. And yet today, none of that was in evidence and Anne began to fret over what their mother would make of it if he didn't pull himself together and at least try to look pleased to be home.

Charlie was still looking quite surly as they pulled into the London station, but he stirred himself enough to help with transferring their luggage from the train onto a porter's trolley. By the time he'd had a bottle of pop and a sandwich at the railway refreshment room, he started to take an interest in his surroundings, and wandered off to talk trains with one of the off-duty guards.

Anne kept an eye on him, for once Charlie started talking about engines he'd be lost in another world, and she didn't want to miss their connection and have to wait another hour for the next train. Emily was grizzling because she was tired, and Rose was fidgeting through boredom. Pulling Emily onto her lap, she rummaged in her bag for a picture book to entertain Rose, and then made the rather stewed cup of tea last as long as she could until she heard the announcement blaring out that her train was arriving on platform four.

Hoisting Emily onto her hip, she slung her handbag strap over her shoulder and took Rose's hand. Charlie saw her and came across the concourse to pick up Rose and carry her on his shoulders. It seemed the interlude with the guard had cheered him up no end, for he was grinning, and there was a spring in his step as he organised their luggage and helped them all on board.

Anne breathed a soft sigh of relief and listened intently as Charlie animatedly told her all about the train they were on, where the engine had come from, when it had been built, and how it would soon be replaced with new rolling stock. She found it all rather boring, but anything was better than having him sullen and uncommunicative, and she could only hope this mood would last for the rest of the journey.

Cliffehaven

Doris eyed her reflection in the dressing-table mirror and nervously patted her freshly washed hair into place before applying her lipstick. She'd dressed carefully as usual, and because it was quite a warm day, had chosen a plain linen skirt to go with the sprigged cotton blouse she'd bought for a snip in the sales. Fastening her single strand of pearls round her neck, she fixed pearl studs into her earlobes and studied the effect dispassionately. She couldn't do much about the lines on her face that no amount of cream or lotions would iron out, and despite the hairdresser's efforts, there were definitely glints of silver showing through.

She heaved a sigh and turned away from this unedifying sight, then slipped her feet into low-heeled sandals for the walk to the Club. The strain of the past few weeks was beginning to tell, for although she'd done her best to put Michael at ease and make him feel at home, all her efforts had been met with a polite but cool detachment which hadn't changed throughout his long leave. John hadn't noticed, of course, so she'd said nothing and simply accepted that his son still found it hard to come to terms with his father's plans to remarry.

Michael had bought a car and was leaving today for Catterick where he would stay for his retraining and then be assigned a posting. He and John had gone for a game of golf straight after breakfast, and she planned to join them at the Officers' Club for luncheon before Michael set off.

She had to privately admit that she'd be relieved to see him go, for she'd lived on tenterhooks throughout his leave, wondering if his attitude towards her meant he would try to turn his father against the idea of marrying her. Not that she had any evidence to prove such a thing, and John had certainly been as loving and thoughtful as always despite being distracted by Michael's presence, but the lack of any warmth from the young man really bothered her.

Plucking a lightweight jacket from the wardrobe, she was about to leave for the Club when there was a knock on the door. She gave a tut of annoyance and went to see who it was.

The annoyance fled as Anthony smiled back at her. 'Hello, Mother,' he said cheerfully. 'I thought I'd pay a surprise visit.'

Doris fell into his arms and hugged him. 'Oh, Anthony, darling, how lovely to see you,' she gasped in delight. She glanced round him to the car at the kerb. 'Are Suzie and Teddy with you?'

'Not today, I'm afraid,' he replied, stepping into the hall and closing the door behind him. 'Suzie's not feeling the full ticket at the moment, and Teddy's got a rotten cold, so you'll just have to put up with me.'

'I'll put up with you any time,' she murmured, fondly patting his smooth cheek, and noting that although he was still her handsome son, he was looking a little drawn and tired. But as delighted as she was to see him without Suzie in tow, she was hugely disappointed he hadn't brought her grandson with him, for she hadn't seen Teddy since he was a babe in arms.

'So this is your new home now,' said Anthony appreciatively as he poked his head around the doors on the way to the kitchen. 'I must say it looks very cosy.'

She smiled. 'If by cosy you mean small, then yes, it is. But it's easy to run and suits me now I've returned to work. I've come to love living here, and don't really miss Havelock Road at all.'

'I expect a lot of that has to do with your neighbour,' he teased, jingling the change in his trouser pocket just as his father used to do. 'Will I get a chance to meet him, do you think? Give him the once-over to see if I approve of this match?'

Doris gritted her teeth at the annoying racket of those jingling coins. 'I don't know about giving him the once-over, but you'll certainly be able to meet him.' She glanced up at the clock. 'Have you had lunch?'

He shook his head. 'I was rather hoping to take you out. Didn't want to bother you with having to cook.'

'That's very thoughtful of you,' she replied. 'But I already have a luncheon engagement with John and his son at the Officers' Club, and was about to walk there when you turned up.'

'Jolly good timing, then, as I can drive us over there and save you the long walk,' he said, peering through the window into the back garden. 'I say, Mother, you have been busy. I didn't know you liked gardening.'

'It's mostly John's work,' she admitted, coming to stand beside him. 'I just do a bit of weeding and pruning and harvest the vegetables and fruit.' She reached for his hand. 'Tell me about Teddy,' she pleaded. 'It's been so long since I've seen him.'

Anthony put his arm around her shoulders and smiled with pride. 'He's growing fast and becoming a bit of a menace, climbing on things and getting into cupboards. He and Suzie have coped with the move to Cambridge very well, and we've found an excellent nursery school which is just round the corner from our new house.'

He reached into his inside jacket pocket and pulled out an envelope. 'I brought lots of snapshots which you can keep.'

Doris grabbed the envelope greedily and spilled the black and white photographs onto the kitchen table. She pounced on those of Teddy before turning to the ones of him and Suzie in the garden of a very smart detached house. 'It reminds me of our old house,' she said, peering at the snapshot more closely. Suzie was laughing at the camera, her hand resting protectively over her stomach. 'Oh,' she breathed. 'Oh, I see.' She turned to Anthony in bewildered hurt. 'Why didn't you tell me Suzie was expecting again?'

'It's the main reason I came down to see you, actually,' he replied, going a little pink. 'I know I should have written and told you earlier, but Suzie hasn't been at all well this time, and to begin with it was all rather uncertain as to whether she might actually miscarry.'

He put his arm around her again. 'Sorry, Mother, but we didn't want to tell you until we knew for certain she and the baby would be all right.'

Doris wondered fleetingly if Suzie had brought all this on herself by going to work in that hospital instead of staying at home as any proper mother and wife would do – but of course she couldn't say that to Anthony. 'You poor darling,' she soothed. 'It must have been a ghastly worry.'

'It was rather. She's had to give up her work at the hospital and rest quite a lot, although we did manage to spend a weekend in London to attend one of the MOD functions. Of course Robert and Fran were there, so we had a very jolly time catching up. Fran's also expecting, though it is still early days, and she told us all she'd bumped into Cissy in Oxford Street. I hadn't realised Cissy was even in London, let alone driving a taxi about. I take it things didn't work out with that American flier?'

'Peggy told me he survived the internment but went straight home to America. It seems his fling with Cissy had been just that, and he hadn't harboured thoughts of them getting together again. Cissy was terribly cut up about it, but she's tough like all the women in our family and has made a new life for herself in London.'

Doris looked at the kitchen clock again, and quickly tucked the precious snapshots back into the envelope. 'We'll be late if we don't leave now,' she said, gathering up her jacket and handbag, 'and if there's one thing John is a real stickler about, it's time-keeping.' She grinned up at her handsome son. 'I've learnt that you can take the man out of the army, but never the army out of the man – and that goes for his son Michael, too.'

He followed her down the narrow hall and waited for her to lock the front door. 'What's Michael like?' he asked as they headed for the car.

'A little stiff and formal, but pleasant enough,' she replied, sliding into the passenger seat as Anthony held the door for her. 'But I think he suffered quite an ordeal in the POW camp, so it's understandable,' she added, not wanting her son to be influenced by her opinion. 'I'll be interested to see what you make of him.'

Anthony took his place behind the steering wheel and started the engine. 'I've met a lot of chaps like that,' he murmured. 'The poor devils are finding it awfully hard to return to normal, everyday life.'

'Michael's actually returning to his regiment today,' said Doris as they left Ladysmith Close and motored down the hill. 'I think he'll be relieved to be back in familiar surroundings after being faced with me and his father's new life.'

'It can't have been easy for him to absorb all the changes,' said Anthony, concentrating on driving over the hump-backed bridge and heading up the hill to the Club.

'No,' she replied thoughtfully. 'I don't think it was.'

Anthony parked the car outside the Club entrance and hurried round to help his mother out. He offered her his arm. 'I get the feeling you found it rather trying too, but let's put on a united front and enjoy our lunch. I'm starving after that long drive from Cambridge.'

Peggy had spent most of the day in a lather of excitement and expectation. Her Anne and the children were at last on their way home, and she wanted everything to be perfect for them, right down to the very last detail. She'd made an enormous Woolton pie for tea, and to follow there was an apple cobbler she'd put together from the fruit she'd stored last summer, which would be accompanied by a tin of evaporated milk. She'd changed the sheets on the big double bed Martin had been sleeping in, dusted and polished the furniture until it gleamed and then placed a vase of flowers on the dressing table to welcome Anne and the girls home.

Jane, Sarah and Danuta had caught her excitement and done their bit by hoovering the carpets, cleaning their rooms and washing all the bedlinen. Danuta had scrubbed and polished the bathroom until it gleamed, and Cordelia, bless her, had taken a damp mop to the hall's floor tiles. Daisy had been told that Anne's children were coming, and she'd very sweetly selected a couple of cuddly toys to put in the cots so they wouldn't be lonely in the night.

After an early lunch of soup and toast, Sarah and Danuta accompanied Cordelia into town to look for a new hat, while Jane took Daisy off for a play on the beach so Peggy could get on and clean the basement bedroom for Charlie.

Peggy had to stop and almost pinch herself to believe that he really was coming home. She could have put him in the other large double room now that Brendon and his little family had moved into the flat, but she couldn't be certain that the agent's promises would hold water, so if their house wasn't ready by the time their lease was up, she would have somewhere for them to sleep.

Peggy reasoned that Charlie would be too big for the bunk beds now, so the double in what had once been Ron's room should suit him just fine. Having cleaned the windows, swept the floor and made the bed, she smoothed the colourful eiderdown over it and then attacked the rather decrepit old chest of drawers with polish and a duster. Once she'd lined the drawers with fresh paper, she remembered the collection of medals Ron had hidden on top of the wardrobe, so she checked they weren't still there, then dusted that inside and out as well.

It was finally ready, but as she stood in the doorway she saw how bleak and bare it all looked, so she went into the second room that Charlie and Bob had shared before being evacuated, which felt like a lifetime ago. Peggy gave a deep sigh, remembering how young they'd been when they'd left. Rummaging through the collection of boxes that had sat on the bunk beds ever since, she discovered they mostly contained very battered toy cars, old comics and annuals, worn slingshots and tarnished toy guns that Charlie must surely have grown out of by now. But digging deeper, she found a slightly soft football, a cricket bat, and a junior fishing rod, complete with a tin of flies, hooks, weights and spare line. She didn't know if they'd be of any interest to him now, but at least they'd make the room look more homely and welcoming.

She placed everything neatly at the bottom of Charlie's bed, and on her return to the other room in search of more treasure, spotted the large box which contained Bob's precious clockwork train set. The boys had fought over it, she remembered, and had wanted to take it with them to Somerset, but Jim had been very firm about it staying here so the pieces wouldn't get lost. Peggy smiled. It was just an excuse really, for it was Jim and Ron who'd played with it the most.

She hauled it down to find it was covered in dust and clinging cobwebs which made her sneeze as she dusted them away. But the trains and tracks, signal boxes and carriages inside were still as good as new, so she carried it into the other room and placed it on the bed with all the other bits and pieces. Bob had jealously guarded his train set when he was younger, but as he seemed to be more interested in cows and girls now, he probably wouldn't mind passing it on to Charlie. Or at least, she hoped he wouldn't.

Feeling pleased with her day's achievements, she went up to the kitchen to make a cup of tea and savour the delicious excitement of knowing her family would soon be home. Glancing at the kitchen clock, she realised it was now almost five, and wondered if Martin had slipped indoors without her hearing him. She rather hoped he had, for there was only an hour before Anne's train was due and he would need to shave and change into some decent clothes instead of those baggy old things he'd taken to wearing lately.

Peggy made the pot of tea and left it to brew while she went upstairs to get washed and changed. She couldn't hear anyone moving about up there, and prayed that Martin would turn up at the station and not lose track of time as he so often did when he was with Roger.

Having changed into her favourite yellow frock, she slipped on sandals and dabbed on some make-up.

A quick spray of scent, the addition of earrings and another brush of her hair completed her preparations, and she grinned at Jim's photograph. 'They're coming home, Jim,' she said excitedly. 'They really are this time, and I'm so happy I could burst.'

Chuckling at her silliness, she went back into the kitchen to take the tea into the garden and share it with Cordelia who was dozing in a deckchair after her shopping trip.

Peggy poured the tea, then quickly gathered in her dry washing, folded it neatly into the basket and carried it inside. The ironing could wait until tomorrow. She plumped down in the deckchair and gently patted Cordelia's hand. 'Wake up, Cordy. I've made tea.'

'Three already?' she asked with a frown. 'But we've only just had lunch.'

'No, Cordy, it's five o'clock and there's a cup of tea for you.'

'Do make up your mind, Peggy dear. It's either three or five – it can't be both.' She reached for her cup. 'Ah, tea,' she sighed. 'Just what I need after all that shopping.'

Peggy smiled indulgently but didn't ask about the hat, for it would have involved another convoluted explanation as Cordelia had clearly left her hearing aid turned off.

Jane returned with Daisy fifteen minutes later, and the other two girls came back from their brief trip to the bakery for more bread. Peggy left Cordelia twittering away to the girls and quickly took Daisy upstairs to wash chocolate ice-cream from her face and hands and change her into her best dress before she checked if Martin was at home.

To her consternation she found his room was empty, with no sign that he'd been in to get changed, but there was no time to dash off and try and find him, for she could hear Ron impatiently tooting Rosie's car horn outside.

The three girls had decided to stay at Beach View and see to the supper since they'd yet to meet Anne, and this was the family reunion Peggy had waited for so longingly over the years. Yet it was still a bit of a squash with Harvey taking up most of the back seat as Ron drove Peggy, Cordelia and Daisy to the station. It was also rather unpleasant, for Harvey's excited panting steamed up the windows and filled the car with doggy breath.

Peggy wound down the window so Harvey could stick his head out and the fresh air would clear the smell. She glanced back and waved at Bertie who was following them in his repaired and highly polished car and wished she'd elected to go with him instead. Bertie had been very good to offer to help today, for Rosie's car wouldn't be able to accommodate so many people on the drive home – and she couldn't expect any of them to walk all that way after such a long journey.

Ron pulled into the station car park, switched off the engine, and climbed out to help Cordelia. Peggy was trampled by Harvey in his eagerness to follow Ron, and when she managed to get out of the car, she discovered her dress had been horribly creased, and his claws had pulled a couple of threads. Smoothing them out as best she could, she refused to let anything mar this special day, and cheerfully took Daisy's hand to walk to the platform.

There was no sign of Martin, but Stan was there as always, beaming in delight. 'It's a big day for the Reilly clan,' he boomed, shaking Ron's hand and then making a fuss of Harvey. He winked at Peggy. 'I bet those six years apart will feel like nothing once they're home.'

Peggy very much doubted it, for those lost years were etched into her heart, but she smiled back at him. 'Is the train on time?' she asked anxiously.

'Aye, it is, and it won't come any faster for all your wanting,' said Ron, keeping a tight hold of Harvey's collar to stop him from watering the tubs of flowers Stan had placed along the platform.

Anne felt the first stir of excitement as the scenery outside the carriage window became ever more familiar. Everyone would already be at the station by now, and she suddenly couldn't wait to see them all again. But would Martin be there? She prayed that he would, for she'd missed him despite everything, and hoped he felt the same and would be eager to hold her again and welcome her and the children home.

She set aside these worries over Martin and concentrated on getting the girls ready to meet their grandmother. Rose had been only months old when she'd left Cliffehaven and Emily had been born in Somerset, and although Peggy had come down to the farm to see her shortly after the birth, she knew that neither child would remember her.

Anne tried not to think about the sadness that would cause her mother, and felt a wave of guilt wash over her as she wrestled the girls into cardigans. 'It'll be cold at the seaside,' she said, remembering the chill even in the summer if the wind was coming off the sea. 'Now do sit still, you two, and let me sort out these hair ribbons.'

Rose enjoyed having her hair brushed and sat patiently as Anne retied the ribbons, but Emily squirmed and whined, and the simple task took much longer. 'Good girl,' she said finally. 'Why don't you kneel up next to Rose and look out of the window? There are lots of things to see.'

She looked at Charlie and handed him the hair-brush. 'Your great mop could do with a brush too,' she said. 'Mum won't see how handsome you are with all that hair flopping over your eyes.'

Charlie ran the brush haphazardly through the dark tangle and handed it back. 'Will Grandad be there to meet us?' he asked with the now familiar adolescent break in his voice, and the hint of the soft burr of Somerset.

'I expect so,' said Anne. 'He'll probably have Harvey with him too. Do you remember Harvey?'

'Of course I do,' Charlie replied indignantly. 'He and I had great adventures with Grandad in the woods and on the hills, but I expect they're both too old now to get up there any more,' he added wistfully.

'I think you'll be pleasantly surprised to find that both are still in fine fettle, and could probably walk you to a standstill,' Anne replied with a wry smile. She eyed his jumper and old corduroys. 'I do wish you'd worn something smarter,' she sighed. 'You look as disreputable as your grandfather in that get-up.'

Charlie grinned. 'That's better than looking like a stupid schoolboy in a cap and blazer,' he retorted. 'And if I look like Grandad, then I'll take it as a compliment. He was always my hero.'

'More than Dad?' asked Anne with a frown.

Charlie bit his lip. 'Dad was terrific in a different way,' he replied. 'And now he's out in Burma fighting the Japs, he's a real hero too, with medals and everything, and when it's my turn to go to war, I want to be just like him.'

'God forbid,' breathed Anne, horrified by the thought of her little brother going to war – or the idea that there could ever be another.

She saw that they were turning slowly off the main line to the spur which would take them into Cliffehaven, so she gathered up the books and dolls and stuffed them into her large shopping bag. 'Stir your stumps, Charlie. We're almost there.'

Peggy could barely contain her fury at Martin's absence at the station, but when she saw the train slowly come round the bend, excitement took over. She walked down the platform, looking in every carriage window as the train slowly and rather majestically drew to a halt at the buffers with a snort of steam and smoke.

She peered through the foggy, sooty swirl as carriage doors opened, and Stan bustled down the platform with Ron to collect the luggage from the guard's van. And then Anne emerged from the thick haze with Emily on her hip and Rose clinging to her hand.

Peggy burst into tears and ran to them with open arms. 'Oh, my darlings, welcome home.' She kissed

Anne and tearfully smiled as Emily shyly buried her face in Anne's neck, and then bent down to kiss Rose's soft cheek. 'Hello, darling,' she murmured. 'Remember me? I'm your grandma.'

The little girl shook her head and plugged her thumb into her mouth as she leaned against Anne's leg.

'Never mind,' said Peggy, swallowing her disappointment. 'We'll get to know each other soon enough. And look,' she said to Rose, drawing Daisy to her side. 'This is your niece, Daisy, and I just know you're going to have a lot of fun together.'

The little girls eyed one another warily for there were only months between them, and then Daisy put her arms around Rose and gave her a rough hug. 'I got lots of toys,' she said in her piping voice. 'You can play with them if you like.'

Peggy met Anne's gaze as Daisy continued to chatter on nineteen to the dozen and Rose slowly lost her shyness. 'They'll be fine,' said Peggy. 'But where's Charlie got to? Surely you didn't have to leave him behind?'

'He's helping Stan and Grandad with the luggage,' replied Anne, peering over her shoulder in search of Martin.

Peggy looked down the platform and stared in disbelief at the sturdy, dark-haired youth who was hoisting bulky cases and bags onto the trolley as if they weighed nothing. He was almost six feet tall and had the striking good looks and strong build of all the Reilly men. 'That can't possibly be my little Charlie,' she gasped.

'I'm afraid it is,' said Anne, 'and I had a devilish job of getting him here, so don't be fooled by his size; he can still act like a four-year-old at times.' Her face showed her bitter disappointment at Martin's absence as she put her free arm around Peggy and held her close with Emily between them. 'It's good to be home again, Mum,' she murmured. 'I'm sorry it's taken so long.'

'And I'm sorry Martin wasn't here to meet you,' said Peggy. 'I don't know what's got into him. He was fine about things this morning and looking forward to having you all home.'

'Was he? Really?' asked Anne. 'It feels to me as if he doesn't care about us at all.'

'I'm sure that's not true,' Peggy replied, determinedly drying her tears as Anne was bombarded with hugs and kisses from Cordelia and Ron, whilst trying to fend off an over-excited Harvey, who'd been dashing back and forth not knowing who to greet first.

She watched him charge back to Charlie, who got down on one knee to make a fuss of him, and caught her son's eye as he looked back at her over the dog's head. Slowly walking towards this tall stranger who bore little resemblance to the nine-year-old boy she'd last seen, Peggy didn't know whether to laugh or cry.

'Hello, Mum,' he said, getting to his feet so he towered over her. He shot her a bashful grin. 'I'd forgotten how small you are.'

Peggy giggled. 'I've always been this size,' she managed. 'It's you who's grown so tall and strapping,' she teased. 'Vi clearly fed you well in Somerset.'

As he shifted from one foot to another, she looked up into bright blue eyes, noted the lock of dark hair falling over his forehead just as his father's had done

426

and felt her heart melt. He was the spitting image of Jim. 'Are you too grown-up for a hug from your mother?' she asked, not wanting to embarrass him by throwing her arms around him.

He shook his head and shyly gathered her to him in a swift, hard hug and then released her. 'I've got to help Grandad get the bags and things loaded into the cars,' he mumbled before hurrying off.

Peggy followed his progress down the platform and immediately began to fret that perhaps she should have set him up in the big room and not the basement. He was clearly no longer a little boy, but on the very cusp of manhood, and the toys she'd put out would be laughably inadequate. With a tremulous sigh she went to join the others.

The two cars formed a convoy and took the long route home, down the High Street and along the seafront, so Anne and Charlie could get their bearings and see the changes in the town. It soon became apparent to them both that Cliffehaven hadn't escaped from the war, for there were signs everywhere of the damage – some of it dangerously close to Beach View.

They finally drew to a halt outside the front of Beach View, and Anne noted sadly that there was no sign of Martin waiting for them on the steps. He clearly had no intention of welcoming them home. Whilst the men saw to the luggage, Anne climbed out of the car with the girls and looked up at the house that had been her home for most of her life. She noted the scars left in the brickwork by shrapnel and bullets; the missing lanterns that had once graced the plinths at the bottom of the steps; and the weed-filled rubble at the end of the cul-de-sac which had been someone's home.

She'd seen the bomb site two streets away and shuddered to think how close her mother and little sister Daisy had come to being obliterated by that V-2, and now she realised with shame how little thought she'd really given to the terrors her mother must have gone through these past few years. But then Peggy's letters had lightly skimmed over the reality of her war, and were filled instead with local gossip and the adventures of her evacuees.

Feeling sick at heart over Martin's lack of care, Anne followed her mother into the hall and set Emily down so she could run about with Daisy and Rose who seemed to have become best friends. Noticing the tired woodwork and scuffed wallpaper, she realised very little had been done to the house since she'd left, but the innovation of the stairlift was quite marvellous.

'I'm taking the girls for a ride,' chirped Cordelia, her little face flushed with pleasure. She plonked down into the chair and strapped herself in. 'Pass me Emily first,' she ordered Anne.

Anne hesitated, but a nod from Peggy told her it would be quite safe, so she placed Emily on Cordelia's lap.

'Thank you, dear,' she said briskly, clasping the child to her as she lowered the lever and set the chair going slowly up the stairs.

Emily clapped her little hands, squealed in delight and begged for more as they descended back to the hall.

Cordelia handed the protesting child back to Anne and did the whole thing again with Rose – and then with Daisy. 'That's enough,' she declared. 'I need a cup of tea – or a nice glass of sherry if you've got any, Anne,' she added hopefully.

'Sorry, Grandma Cordy. I didn't pack any.'

'Oh, well,' she sighed. 'Tea it will have to be then. Come along, girls. Let's find a nice biscuit.'

Charlie brought in the last of the large cases and dumped them down in the hall as the others drifted into the kitchen. 'Who is that old woman?' he whispered to Anne. 'She's not really our grandma, is she?'

Anne shook her head. 'That's Cordelia,' she whispered back. 'Surely you must remember her reading you bedtime stories, and helping with your homework?'

'I do remember someone,' he murmured, 'but …' He gave a deep sigh. 'It's all a muddle, Anne,' he confessed. 'Everything looks smaller and older than I remember – even Grandad.'

'That's because you're bigger and don't see things in the way the little boy you were when you left here did,' she replied gently. 'And of course everyone's older. You've been away for six years and all of us have changed.' She reached up to push the lock of hair out of his eyes. 'Especially you. Now let's have that tea and start settling in.'

Charlie felt adrift as he sat and listened to the chatter going on around the table while the three little girls played on the rug with Harvey who didn't seem to mind them dressing him up in doll's blankets and bonnets. He'd been introduced to Jane and Sarah who

429

looked very sophisticated and made him feel awkward, but Danuta seemed all right, even though she spoke in the same funny way as Claus. He vaguely wondered if she was German too, but when she started talking about going back to Poland, he realised his mistake.

He surreptitiously looked around the shabby kitchen, remembering it well, right down to the Kitchener range in the chimney breast and the dresser strewn with all sorts of discarded letters and bits and bobs. It was a far cry from Auntie Vi's spacious farmhouse kitchen with its large scrubbed pine table, vast dressers and tiled floor, but it felt the same – homely and welcoming.

He watched his mother who was in animated conversation with Anne and wondered where all her softness had gone, for he remembered snuggling up to her as a little boy and nestling his head in her pillowy chest. Now she looked thin and very small, and he could only suppose the strict rationing must have been the cause.

Auntie Vi had warned him about the lack of milk, eggs, honey and butter he'd find here, and in that moment, he wished he'd thought to bring some to help feed his mother up. Auntie Vi was very hot on feeding people and provided lashings of everything. He would miss Vi, and suspected he'd have to get used to smaller portions from now on.

His gaze moved on around the table to be met by his grandfather's. Ron winked at him and Charlie winked back. Ron hadn't really changed except his hair was tidy and laced with silver, but he still wore old trousers tied at the waist with garden twine and a jumper that had more holes in it than a colander – and that ancient, smelly old poacher's coat was still in evidence.

Charlie was glad he was the same, and just as robust as he remembered, and was impatient to go onto the hills with him and Harvey again, and perhaps even go down to the beach beneath the cliffs to inspect Uncle Frank's marvellous new fishing boats that he'd seen moored there. The summer holidays stretched before him with all sorts of glorious possibilities, and he firmly ignored the dark clouds that waited for him when it was time to return to school, because he would have to get used to a new one that in all probability didn't have a rugby team. Thinking of the loss of his hard-won place in the Somerset County junior fifteen took the shine off his summer plans, and he pushed back from the table, making the chair scrape against the worn linoleum. 'Am I still in the same bedroom?' he asked Peggy abruptly.

'I've put you in Ron's old room,' she replied, suddenly looking flustered. 'I hope it will be all right.'

'It'll be fine,' he replied shortly.

Collecting his bags from the hall, he felt the curious eyes follow him in the enveloping silence as he stomped back through the kitchen and down the concrete steps, slamming the kitchen door behind him. Stepping into the room he closed that door too, dropped his bags on the floor and stared at the toys on the end of the bed.

His mother clearly thought he was still a kid, for what on earth could he possibly want with these old things?

His interest was piqued by the train set which he remembered very well, but he gathered everything else up and dumped it all in the bottom of the wardrobe.

Charlie slumped down onto the bed and sadly regarded the bare, impersonal room before nudging the boxed train set away. He felt a tightness in his chest and the unfamiliar sense of loss and despair. An overwhelming wave of longing swept over him and a tear rolled down his cheek to be angrily brushed away. He wanted to be back in his comfortable bedroom at Owlet Farm, and to be with lovely Auntie Vi, for he missed her dreadfully. He also missed his friends and the other boys in the rugby team, and wondered if they'd already forgotten him.

Charlie curled up on the bed and buried his face in the pillow so they couldn't hear him crying.

'I should go down and see if he's all right,' said Peggy fretfully.

'Leave the boy be,' rumbled Ron. 'I'll take him out with the dogs after tea and he'll feel better for a long walk. The lad has a lot to contend with, and he'll deal with it all in his own time without you fussing over him.'

'I think I'll go and freshen up,' said Anne, who thought her grandfather's advice was wise. 'I'll take up the children's things with me; the rest can stay in the hall until after tea.'

'Do you want a hand?' asked Peggy.

Anne shook her head. 'I can manage.'

'Are you sure you're all right?' Peggy asked. 'Only I know how disappointed and hurt you must be that Martin isn't here.'

432

Ignoring the pain in her heart, Anne gave her mother a hug. 'It's something I've become used to, Mum. I'm fine – really I am.'

She left the kitchen and slowly went up the stairs until she reached the top floor. Charlie was miserably homesick, she could tell, and she could sympathise with him. But despite her brave words to her mother, she was feeling utterly betrayed. The fact that Martin hadn't come to the station or been at the house to welcome her and the girls had hurt her profoundly, and the disappointment lay heavy in her heart. Their time apart had evidently not changed a thing – and after his no-show today, it was doubtful they could come back from this and rebuild their marriage.

She walked along the landing and came to the bedroom door. Hesitating, she wondered if he'd come home at all tonight – and if he did, would she be able to hold back the hurt, and climb into bed with him as if everything was all right between them? She very much doubted it, for he'd gone too far this time and she was hurting too much to forgive him.

Pushing the door open, she lugged the case inside and then dropped it in shock as she saw Martin rise from the fireside chair. He looked well enough, she noted distractedly, certainly better than when he'd left Somerset. 'What are you doing up here?' she managed.

'I've been waiting for you,' he replied, coming towards her with his arms open to hug her.

She edged away, unwilling to be held. 'You should have met me at the station,' she said flatly. 'Not hidden away up here without telling anyone.'

He let his arms hang by his sides as he dipped his chin. 'I didn't want to go to the station. There would have been too many people and too much noise.'

'Then you should have waited downstairs for when we came home,' she retorted.

'I didn't want to welcome you in front of an audience,' he admitted softly. 'I really thought you'd prefer our reunion to take place in private.'

'But it wouldn't have been, would it?' she snapped. 'Grandad could have been bringing up the cases for all you knew, or Mum might have come with me and brought the girls. Whatever would they have thought to find you lurking up here when everyone assumed you were out?'

'I don't know,' he replied, rubbing his forehead and looking distraught. 'I hadn't thought of that.'

Anne was tired and not in the mood to appease him. She folded her arms and glared. 'Well, it's obvious you've given a lot of thought as to what *you* want, Martin, but there seems to have been precious little consideration for me. I really believed you'd be at the station – or at least here to welcome us home – instead of which you chose to hide up here and wait for me to come to you. Well, it just isn't good enough.'

'I'm so sorry, Anne,' he said. 'You're right. I didn't think it through properly, and I can't bear to see you upset.' He tentatively reached for her hand. 'Please say you'll forgive me.'

Anne's fury and hurt could not be swept away by the sorrowful look in his eyes, and she edged back from him. 'Do you realise how disappointed and hurt I was by what you did? Can you even begin to imagine how it was for me and the girls when you didn't show at the station? I've been waiting for today with such eagerness and hope that this might be the start of us repairing our marriage – but it felt as if you didn't care about us at all.'

'Oh, Anne, I'm so sorry,' he said. 'Please don't cry. I can see that it was selfish and thoughtless of me, and I didn't mean to hurt you, really I didn't.'

Anne could see that he was deeply touched by her reaction and in a quandary as to what to do about it. In that moment she realised their situation had been immensely difficult for both of them, and in their own way each of them was struggling to find a solution. Being bitter wasn't going to help ease anything, and the thought of not finding a way through this was unbearable. They would both have to be patient – her especially – and now it was up to her to take that first step towards repairing the damage caused by the war.

She took his hand and stepped into his embrace. 'Of course I forgive you,' she said against his chest. 'How can I not when I love you so?'

26

Upon entering the Club, Doris had spotted John and Michael sitting in the bar, and immediately sensed something was wrong. Neither man looked at ease, and the short exchange they were having appeared to be quite hostile. She'd hesitated in the doorway, unsure of what to do, but then John had seen her, and the angry lines in his face smoothed out into a warm smile.

It had been an awkward and embarrassing lunch, despite John doing his best to be solicitous to Doris and keep up a conversation with Anthony whilst virtually ignoring Michael who ate in brooding silence and then, very rudely, lit a cigarette before everyone had finished dessert.

Doris had been uncomfortably aware of Michael watching her throughout, his gaze quizzical and faintly resentful, so the end of the meal had come as a huge relief. She had no idea what Anthony must be thinking, but she could see from his expression that he hadn't taken to Michael at all. There had been plans for them to remain at the Club to take coffee in the lounge, and Doris had been dreading the ordeal dragging on. She could see Anthony was just as reluctant to carry on with this farce, and she'd been on the point of asking him to take her home when Michael abruptly announced his immediate departure.

Nobody had tried to delay him, and after stiffly shaking his father's hand, he'd ignored Doris and Anthony, run down the steps to his car and driven away at speed.

John had been profuse in his apologies, clearly deeply upset by his son's behaviour, but unwilling to discuss what had happened between them to cause such enmity. They'd had coffee in the lounge although no one really wanted it, and then John went off for a long walk while Anthony had driven Doris home.

'I'm sorry lunch was such a disaster,' said Doris, trying to relax in her sitting room as she lit a cigarette. 'I can't imagine what got into Michael to behave like that.'

'Whatever it was certainly rattled his father,' Anthony replied. He stood with his back to the fireplace, his hands in his pockets, the coins once again jingling through his fingers. 'But I do like your Colonel. He seems to be a very upright sort of man, who's clearly greatly enamoured of you.' He regarded his mother thoughtfully. 'You don't think their falling out had something to do with that, do you?' he asked worriedly.

'The thought had occurred to me,' she admitted, twisting the engagement ring around her finger in agitation. 'You see, I've had the awful feeling over the past three weeks that he doesn't approve of me or our engagement, and after today, I very much fear that John could be having second thoughts.'

'But he was so attentive,' protested Anthony, 'and there was no mistaking how much he adores you. It was there every time he looked at you.'

'I know,' she managed. 'John has always been attentive and caring; it's why I love him so. But if his son is
set against us being together, the poor man is caught in
a cleft stick.' She blinked back her tears and looked up
at him. 'I promised myself I would walk away from
him should this happen, but now I don't think I can.'

Anthony reached over and rested a consoling hand
on her shoulder. 'Poor Mother,' he said softly. 'It's
such a difficult situation to find yourself in, and I do
sympathise. But surely it doesn't have to lead to you
splitting up?'

'I have no idea of where it might lead. John's not
here, and I won't know how he feels until he returns.'
She stubbed out her cigarette and yanked a handkerchief from her bag. 'Oh dear,' she sighed. 'At my age
you'd have thought I'd have learnt by now. I do feel
foolish.'

'Do you want me to stay with you tonight?'

Doris would have loved him to stay, but the situation was so uncertain with John, she didn't want her
son to witness an embarrassing row. 'Thank you, dearest boy, but you must go home. It's a long drive and
I'm sure you'll be needed to help look after little Teddy.
I'll be fine, really I will.'

'I really don't like leaving you like this,' he murmured. 'What if I telephone Aunt Peggy and ask her to
come up to be with you?'

Doris shook her head. 'Anne, Charlie and the children are returning today, and I have absolutely no
intention of ruining it for her.' She got to her feet,
dabbed at her nose and straightened her shoulders.
'I'm just a silly woman who's allowed her imagination

to run away with her,' she said purposefully. 'I'm sure that John is not a man to be swayed by anything his son has to say and can make his own mind up about things.'

'Well, if you're sure …' he replied uncertainly.

'As sure as I can be,' she said with brisk determination. 'I'll come and see you off.'

He gave her a long, reassuring hug before kissing her cheek and heading for the front door. 'We'd love you to come and visit once we're straight and Suzie feels up to entertaining,' he said, turning at the gate. He handed her a business card. 'I've put our new address and telephone number on the back. Promise me you'll ring and let me know how things go with John.'

Doris nodded and then quickly kissed his cheek before he climbed into the car. 'Try and get down again very soon,' she said through the open window. 'And bring Teddy and Suzie with you next time.'

Standing on the pavement, she returned his cheerful wave and watched him drive away. As the sound of the car engine faded, the stillness and silence settled around her and, for the first time in many months, she felt bereft and very lonely.

Charlie was disgusted with himself for crying like a stupid baby, and he went to the scullery sink to wash his face and pull himself together before returning to his room and hauling his bags onto the bed. He could change nothing with tears and wishful thinking, and was quite old enough to accept the situation and make the best of it. The summer holidays were still ahead of him, and he would throw himself into whatever adventures came his way.

He began to unpack, and quickly stowed away his clothes in the drawers and wardrobe. Finding his rugby club pennants, he hunted about for the box of drawing pins he'd packed and stuck them to the wall. He lined his sporting trophies along the dresser, and placed the framed photograph of his team in pride of place at the centre. The room was looking better already. Diving back into the bag, he stacked his books on the floor next to the dresser and decided he would put up a shelf tomorrow to store them properly.

His reading was an eclectic mix of engineering and aeroplane manuals, and military biographies which he found endlessly fascinating and absorbing – as he did the books on nature and fishing. There were a couple of Western paperbacks; a thick tome called *A Treasury of Adventure for Boys*, which he still liked dipping into occasionally; very tattered copies of *Treasure Island*, *Twenty Thousand Leagues Under the Sea*, *A Journey to the Centre of the Earth* and *Black Beauty*, all of which he'd had since childhood and still loved, and a collection of Biggles books which he'd started collecting two years ago.

In with all these were school textbooks and a well-thumbed atlas in which he'd charted his father's progress through India and Burma, although he couldn't always be certain of exactly where he was as his letters didn't reveal much. But Charlie had used Jim's clues and newspaper reports and articles to guess the location, and thought he'd made a fair stab at getting it right.

Charlie looked at the three stacks on the floor and went back to the wardrobe to retrieve the comic annuals his mother had left out for him. Adding them to the pile, he thought it might be interesting to see what had amused him as an eight-year-old. But not right now, for he could hear his mother calling him to his tea.

Hungry as a bear, he closed his door and hurried upstairs to sit down eagerly to the large plate of Woolton pie his mother placed in front of him. Perhaps it wouldn't be too bad living here, he decided, and gave his mother a warm smile of thanks before he tucked in.

An hour later, he'd gone to the Anchor with Ron to meet Rosie, who he didn't really remember, and to pick up the dogs. Rosie turned out to be all soft curves and cushion-like bosoms which were very cuddly indeed, and she was extremely pretty for a woman of her age, which made him horribly shy, and he knew he'd gone bright red when she kissed his cheek and told him and Ron to get out from under her feet so she could run the bar without distraction.

Now he was tramping up the long steep hill, barely able to keep up with Ron as the dogs dashed off. The old man was amazingly fit, he realised, but then he supposed he had to be as he was married to a lively woman like Rosie. Charlie reddened again as he thought of the books Bob had lent him when he'd turned fourteen. They'd been about sex and how babies were made, with quite graphic pictures and drawings, and he'd found it very embarrassing, really, but rather exciting.

'Come on, wee boy,' shouted Ron. 'I thought you'd be fit after all those years on a farm. Are you to be letting an old man beat you to the top?'

Charlie was out of breath and had a stitch in his side after that long haul up the hill, but spurred on by his grandfather's challenge, he pushed himself harder until he passed him and reached the crest.

Ron arrived at his side barely out of breath. 'Ach, wee boy, I'll soon have you fit for the next rugby season,' he rumbled, digging his pipe out of his poacher's coat pocket.

Charlie was aware of Ron watching as he struggled to hide the fact he was too out of breath to voice his surprise.

Ron gave a chuckle once his pipe was lit satisfactorily. 'To be sure, I'm thinking you didn't know about the club that started up during the war on the old recreation field. They're big lads of eighteen, most of them, but going by your size, you should have no bother fitting in.'

'But it's not rugby season,' Charlie managed, his heart rate now slowly returning to a normal pace.

Ron smiled round the stem of his pipe. 'I'll take you down there tomorrow and introduce you. They meet most Sunday mornings and train every Monday night, regardless of the season, and actually won the county cup this year.'

This was all news to Charlie and his spirits soared as he set off shoulder to shoulder with his grandfather, a definite spring in his step. 'Are we going to Tamarisk Bay to see Uncle Frank?' he asked.

Ron took the pipe out of his mouth and shook his head. 'He'll be down with the trawlers by now, getting them ready for the night's fishing, and I doubt your Aunt Pauline will welcome a visit from us.'

Charlie frowned at this, but as Ron seemed reluctant to say anything further, he shrugged it off and began to take pleasure in his surroundings. These hills were very familiar, and he even had the vaguest memory of having been carried up here by his grandfather when he could only have been a baby. 'Did you used to bring me up here when I was really little?' he asked.

Ron stopped abruptly and looked at him in surprise. 'Aye, I did that, and now I'm bringing Brendon's young Joseph up.' He grinned, his blue eyes twinkling. 'Carried you in the dispatches case I brought home from the trenches, so I did. Cut holes in the bottom for your wee legs to poke through, and you kicked me all the way up and down.'

Ron chuckled and started to walk again. 'I did the same for your father and uncle before you, and every generation since.'

'Even Daisy?'

'Aye. Even Daisy, and now Rose and Emily are home I shall bring them here too. This is their heritage,' he said, waving an arm towards the sweeping landscape that ended sharply at the chalk cliff-edge. 'And they need to know this is what we fought for, and learn the family traditions.'

'I doubt if Anne will let them go poaching or hunting for eels, Grandad,' Charlie said with a laugh.

'Maybe not,' he conceded, 'but to be sure it will do them no harm to see where they come from, and to take in this clean, salty air.'

Charlie tramped beside him, listening to his familiar voice as he told him about the day he'd rescued a young British airman who'd been shot down and injured; how he'd been trapped underground following the explosive crash-landing of a troop carrier which had killed all on board; and of how he'd once stood on this hill and saluted the swarms of Spitfires and bombers as they'd thundered overhead on their way to the other side of the Channel.

'I wish I could have stayed here to see it all,' Charlie said. 'We hardly knew there was a war on down in Somerset until a rogue German fighter plane took pot shots at us all in the fields. That was scary, but exciting too,' he added.

Ron grimaced, tapped the spent tobacco from his pipe and glanced at his watch. 'There's no excitement in war, wee boy,' he rumbled. 'Just death and destruction and the awful waste of young lives. You were better off in Somerset.'

With that he made a sharp turnabout, whistled to the dogs and began the steep descent back towards Beach View. 'Frank won't be leaving until the tide's full, so we'll go down to see him for a cup of his good tea and whisky.' He eyed Charlie from beneath his thick brows. 'Just don't tell your mother.'

Charlie had tasted the whisky he'd found hidden in the linen cupboard back at Owlet Farm and hadn't liked it at all. But the idea of sharing such a thing in secret with Ron and Frank and being thought old enough to do so was something he couldn't resist. He'd just have to get used to the taste.

*

Peggy had been surprised to see Martin come down with Anne for tea, for he'd never eaten with them all since coming back to Beach View. She realised he must have been upstairs all the time, which was very odd behaviour. But then, she'd become used to him floating in and out unobserved, and it seemed Anne was unfazed by it all.

She'd watched them surreptitiously throughout the meal and noted with enormous relief that they seemed to have found some sort of tentative harmony, although she doubted everything was as rosy as they were making out. Anne was certainly looking a bit brighter, and Martin had really put an effort into making conversation, and helping her with the children who were rather fractious after their long, tiring day.

Daisy was just as temperamental, messing about with her food and demanding to be allowed to sleep upstairs with Rose. In the end, Peggy bundled her away from the table to wash and change her for bed, and by the time she'd brought her back downstairs, Daisy was fast asleep on her shoulder. She tucked her in, smoothed the dark curls from her forehead and kissed her softly before switching on the night light and leaving the door ajar. Life was certainly going to be hectic with such young children in the house.

Peggy returned to the kitchen to discover it was deserted, the table cleared, the dishes washed, and everything tidied away. She was on the point of going back up to see if Cordelia was all right and that Anne didn't need help with her two little ones, when Anne appeared in the doorway looking rather frazzled.

'Whatever's the matter, love?' Peggy asked, reaching for the kettle.

'I've just got the girls into bed after a real tussle in the bathroom,' she replied. 'They're both overtired, and Martin didn't really help by making bath time a game, but they were asleep by the time I'd put them in their cots.'

She fetched cups and saucers from the shelves and milk from the marble shelf in the larder before she perched on a kitchen chair. 'I have no idea where everyone else has gone, but I checked on Cordelia before I came down,' she said with an affectionate smile. 'She was exhausted too, and is now snoring away very happily. I took her glasses off and turned out her light.'

'Where's Martin?' Peggy asked, pouring the boiling water into the large brown teapot and giving the leaves a good stir.

'He's gone for a walk, but promised not to stay out too late.'

'How are things between you?'

Anne offered her cigarette packet and box of matches to Peggy. 'Not perfect,' she admitted, blowing smoke, 'but certainly a little less fraught than before. It's going to take time for both of us to get used to each other again, and I think being with Roger has helped him tremendously.'

Peggy poured the tea and came to sit with her at the table. 'I expect it will be the same for me and your father. We've experienced such different wars and must have been changed by them. Has Martin told you anything of what he and the others went through?'

Anne shook her head. 'I don't think he ever will, and I'm not sure I want to know after you told me about the state Freddy was in before he died. I'm just thankful he's home and starting to heal.'

Peggy squeezed her hand. 'You'll both muddle through, Anne,' she soothed. 'And your marriage will be stronger for it. But he can't mope about forever, and must start thinking about what he'll do for a living.'

Anne smiled. 'He and Roger have already started planning something, although Martin's being very mysterious about it, and trying hard not to show how much the idea excites him. We're due to go to Briar Cottage tomorrow morning when all will be revealed, and as it concerns Kitty and Charlotte as well, I suspect it might be something to do with flying.'

She grinned happily. 'I never thought Martin would get in a plane again, so if I'm right, this could be a real step forward in his recovery.'

Peggy knew exactly what the plans were, for she'd discussed them with the girls many months ago when they'd thought Freddy would be a part of their business plan – but she wouldn't spoil Martin's surprise.

Doris had switched on the electric fire to chase away the chill of evening as she waited for John to return. The thoughts and anxieties were churning in her head along with the conflicting ideas of what she should do if John ended things between them.

Unable to sit there doing nothing, she went to the window and closed the curtains even though it was still quite light outside. She then went into the kitchen to make a pot of tea and pore over the lovely snapshots Anthony had brought for her.

There was one in particular that stood out. It was of little Teddy in the sweetest romper suit, sitting on a metal rocking horse in the garden, and smiling up at whoever was taking the picture. Doris decided she would go to the shops at lunchtime on Monday and find a frame so she could display it on the mantelpiece with the others.

Carrying her tea back into the warmth of the sitting room, she sat down, looked nervously at her watch and lit a cigarette. She'd smoked too much this afternoon, but her nerves were in shreds, and there was still no sign of John even though it was now after seven.

'Where on earth have you got to?' she muttered fretfully. 'You must realise how worried I'd be.'

She sipped from the teacup and clattered it back in the saucer as the most awful possibility occurred to her. He might already have returned to the next-door bungalow without coming to see her first, and was sitting in there avoiding her because he wanted to break off their engagement and didn't know how to tell her. She knew he hated confrontation, and whatever had gone on with Michael earlier must have really upset him, but that was no excuse, and if he was hiding from her, then he wasn't the man she'd thought he was.

Doris stubbed out her cigarette and got to her feet. She would discover for herself the sort of man he was, and make him tell her the truth about what had gone on between him and his son today – even if it did mean the engagement was over. Going to her bedroom to fetch her jacket, she heard the key turn in the lock of

the front door and stepped into the hall, ready to con-
front him.

'Doris, my dear girl,' he said in a fluster. 'I am sorry
I'm so late back. You must have wondered where on
earth I'd got to.'

She let him take her hands but wasn't ready quite
yet to forgive him. 'I was beginning to worry that
something had happened to you,' she murmured.
'You've been gone for four hours.'

He ran his fingers through his thick silver hair, his
blue eyes troubled. 'Goodness me; time really does fly,
doesn't it?' He reached for her hands again. 'Oh, my
dear girl, I should have telephoned you. Will you ever
forgive me?'

She nodded warily and let him kiss her cheek. He
didn't look like a man who was about to break her
heart, but what on earth had he been up to all this
time? 'You must be cold after that very long walk,' she
said quietly. 'Come into the sitting room and warm
yourself. I've made a pot of tea, but I'll need to get
another cup.'

'I don't want tea,' he said firmly, leading her into the
sitting room and pressing her down into a chair. 'And
I haven't been walking all this time either,' he admitted, not quite looking her in the eye.

'Then what on earth have you been doing, John?'
she asked evenly.

'I did walk for a bit to clear my head after Michael
left. Although I love my son, I couldn't admire his
behaviour today, and certainly wouldn't stand for the
way he tried to ...'

He faltered and Doris finished the sentence for him.

'Tell you to finish with me,' she said. She saw the distress in his face and touched his arm. 'It's all right, John. I guessed some time ago that that might be the case.'

'Doris, darling, I never realised how difficult these past weeks must have been for you, and after the disastrous lunch at the Club I knew I had to take a stand and defend my right to be happy with the woman I love.'

She could feel the prick of tears and the thudding of her heart as she watched him reach into his jacket pocket for a slip of paper and then drop at her feet on one knee.

'I do hope you won't be too cross,' he said shyly, 'but I've been to the Town Hall to arrange our wedding ceremony for the end of August.' He placed the notice on her lap, his gaze never leaving her face. 'Please say you'll still marry me, Doris.'

Doris cupped his face in her hands and kissed him. 'You silly, dearest man,' she managed through her tears. 'Of course I will.'

Charlie burrowed beneath the blankets and eiderdown and gave a sigh of contentment. After all the concerns he'd had over this homecoming, it had proved to be all he could have hoped for – and more.

Grandad had told him his stories as they'd walked with the dogs – just like he'd done all those years ago. And when they'd gone down to the beach, Charlie had drunk the whisky-laced tea and asked for another as he'd sat enthralled by his Uncle Frank's reminiscences of the days when Charlie had gone out with them at weekends and school holidays.

The whisky had made him feel a bit light-headed, so he hadn't complained when Ron had silently removed that second cup from his hands and finished it off himself, and the bag of hot, vinegary chips they'd bought to eat on their way home had gone some way to filling the gap that lately always seemed to be there no matter how much he ate.

Charlie's head buzzed a bit, but it felt quite pleasant, and he was ready to sleep now. He turned off the bedside light and snuggled into the pillows. Tomorrow promised to be even better. In the morning, Grandad Ron would introduce him to the Cliffehaven rugby side, and after lunch, Frank had promised to take him out on the small boat to see if he still had his sea legs and could remember his way around it.

On the very brink of tumbling into sleep, Charlie smiled and wondered why he'd ever dreaded coming home.

27

Peggy had been shocked to hear about Michael's behaviour, but thrilled to learn that Doris and John had fixed a date for their wedding despite him, and had happily gone with her sister to Plummer's department store in search of an appropriate outfit.

She hadn't been quite so happy about the election results, for despite all that Churchill had done for the country, Labour had swept in with a huge majority and Clement Attlee was now the Prime Minister.

Rosie was cock-a-hoop, of course, and already planning her campaign to be voted onto the council in the local elections at the end of the year – though how she'd find time to run the pub and be a councillor, Peggy had no idea. Ron had been phlegmatic about it, bless him, for he was quite happy to let her spread her wings whilst he took charge at the Anchor, but Peggy suspected it wouldn't be long before they put the pub up for sale.

As July had slipped into early August, Peggy had come to the conclusion that only time would tell if Labour's radical social changes would come to fruition, but she had far more important and exciting things to deal with than politics.

Peter and Rita would be getting married on the eighteenth, and would then move in with her father until it was safe for them to leave for Australia. Ivy was over her morning sickness now and planning to come down with Andy to stay at Beach View for that weekend so she could be Rita's bridesmaid; and when Doris and John tied the knot a week later, their younger sister, Doreen, would be coming with her two girls and young Archie to help celebrate the occasion.

Peggy sat in her factory office and watched the women at their sewing machines, but her thoughts were still on the sleeping arrangements at Beach View. It wouldn't be too much of a squash, for there was still that double room on the first floor for them to sleep in since Brendan and Betty had now moved into their lovely new house, and Charlie was very content to stay where he was in the basement. However, the thought of five small girls and a little boy rampaging about the place was a daunting prospect. Daisy and Anne's two made enough noise with their screeching and squabbling, and it had become almost a pleasure to come into work where it was a good deal quieter and more orderly.

She snapped from her thoughts and noticed the women were packing up for the day, so she quickly collected her handbag, just as eager to be home. The atmosphere at Beach View had improved enormously now Martin was fully involved in setting up the air transport business which they'd decided to call PMB Air, using the initials of their last names. Martin was almost back to his old self, Anne was looking radiant, and within a few short weeks they'd be moving back into their own little house just in time for Anne to start her job at the new junior school with young Betty.

Peggy checked everything was locked, and headed across the estate. She'd barely seen Charlie these past few weeks, for he was always busy. His voracious appetite was quite a problem, though, and it seemed that no matter how much she fed him, he was constantly hungry. And yet it was hardly surprising, she reasoned as she approached Jack's lock-up, for he went with Ron onto the hills each morning to walk the dogs, and again at night if he wasn't on the rugby field with his new friends training for the next season.

He'd spent hours with Ron, who'd been a terrific and steadying influence, and with Frank on his boat, and had even gone out night-fishing in the trawler to make up the crew numbers when one man had fallen ill. He'd loved it so much he'd hardly stopped talking about it, and Frank had been full of praise, even suggesting he might take him on permanently once he'd left school.

Peggy had been dubious about that idea, for although Charlie came from a family of fishermen, he was academically very bright, with an aptitude for mechanical engineering that had impressed Jack Smith no end. Her hope was that when he passed his school certificate, he'd go to technical college and hone those skills so he'd have a stable, well-paid job in the future.

Peggy had been relieved that he'd settled back home so well, but still couldn't quite get over how much he'd grown – and how quickly he'd lost the burr of his Somerset accent. She'd quite liked it, but understood that Charlie had deliberately toned it down because he didn't like being thought of as different to the other boys.

She arrived at Jack's workshop and grinned. Charlie was in his element as he leaned beneath the bonnet of a car alongside Peter discussing what should be done with the engine.

'He's a clever lad,' said Jack appreciatively, sliding out from beneath another car as Rita continued to hammer something metal at the back of the workshop. 'I wouldn't mind taking him on when these two skip off to Australia.'

'Thanks, Jack, but he's got to finish school first.' She looked over at her son who was so involved beneath that bonnet that he hadn't seen her. 'Charlie. I want you home by six for your tea,' she said. 'It's toad in the hole, so don't be late.'

He replied with a wave of a filthy hand and a broad grin then disappeared beneath the bonnet again.

Peggy clucked her tongue and left him to it. She would pick up Daisy from the factory crèche and go straight home tonight to listen to the early newscast.

The fighting in the Far East was still raging, with the Americans now bombing mainland Japan itself. Several days ago, Truman had sent a stern and very threatening message to the Japanese, warning them he would bring death and total destruction to their country if they didn't surrender immediately. Peggy prayed with all her being that the Japs would see sense and give in, for it would mean Jim could come home at last, and her family could spend their first Christmas together in six years.

Beach View was quiet for once, with only Cordelia waiting for her in the kitchen, the wireless already switched on in the corner.

'Anne has taken the children to Briar Cottage, and will be back for tea,' she said, the silk flowers bobbing merrily on the sunhat she'd forgotten she was wearing. 'They were inspecting the airfield today, as they're hoping to get government permission to use it again.'

'From what I've heard it's not in a very good state at all,' replied Peggy, letting go of Daisy's hand so she could go into the garden and play in the makeshift sandpit Ron had made for her. 'Where are the three girls?'

'Danuta's gone to see Rachel and Solly to talk over their Warsaw plans, and Jane and Sarah have decided to buy fish and chips for supper before they go to see *Brief Encounter* again.'

The wireless hummed and spluttered with static and Peggy twiddled the knobs until the children's programme came through clearly. There were still a few minutes to go before the news. 'This could be it, Cordy,' she said excitedly. 'The Japs might have taken Truman's threats seriously and surrendered. Oh, just think, Cordy. Jim could be home for Christmas if that's the case. Wouldn't it be wonderful?'

'I wouldn't count your chickens, dear,' she replied. 'The Japs have proved time and again they can't be trusted to do what the rest of the world expects of them.'

Peggy sat down at the table next to her and lit a cigarette, fervently hoping that this time the war really would be over.

The announcer was introduced, and his solemn tone did not augur well.

'The President of the United States of America, Harry Truman, has delivered a statement from the White House.'

There was a pause and Peggy tensed.

'"Following the refusal of the Japanese to surrender immediately, I have had no recourse but to carry out my determination to bring an end to the war in the Far East, and to save the lives of millions.

'"Sixteen hours ago an American airplane dropped one bomb on Hiroshima, an important Japanese Army base. That bomb had more power than 20,000 tons of TNT. It had more than two thousand times the blast power of the British 'Grand Slam' which is the largest bomb ever yet used in the history of warfare.

'"The Japanese began the war from the air at Pearl Harbor. They have been repaid many fold. And the end is not yet. With this bomb we have now added a new and revolutionary increase in destruction to supplement the growing power of our armed forces. In their present form these bombs are now in production and even more powerful forms are in development.

'"It is an atomic bomb. It is a harnessing of the basic power of the universe. The force from which the sun draws its power has been loosed against those who brought war to the Far East."'

Peggy and Cordelia exchanged looks of horror as the news reader carried on talking about the secret scientific work that had been carried out since the very start of the world war, with Churchill and Roosevelt agreeing that the production plants should be based in America and as far from the war in Europe as possible.

As Charlie, Anne and Martin came quietly into the room and slid into the other chairs to listen, he continued reading the statement which extolled the achievements of the scientific brains which had put together infinitely complex pieces of knowledge held by many in different fields of science into a workable project. The Americans had spent two billion dollars on the greatest scientific gamble in history – and won.

'"We are now prepared to obliterate more rapidly and completely every productive enterprise the Japanese have above ground in any city. We shall destroy their docks, their factories, and their communications. Let there be no mistake; we shall completely destroy Japan's power to make war.

'"It was to spare the Japanese people from utter destruction that the ultimatum of July 26 was issued at Potsdam. Their leaders promptly rejected that ultimatum. If they do not now accept our terms they may expect a rain of ruin from the air, the like of which has never been seen on this earth. Behind this air attack will follow sea and land forces in such numbers and power as they have not yet seen and with the fighting skill of which they are already well aware.

'"The Secretary of War, who has kept in personal touch with all phases of the project, will immediately make public a statement giving further details."'

Peggy switched the wireless off and turned to look at the others through her tears. 'I'm sorry, but I can't bear to hear any more.'

'Let's hope that really is the end of it,' said Anne, taking her mother's hand. 'And please don't worry about Dad. He'll stay in Burma, I'm sure, and not get involved in any of this new bomb or fighting.'

But their hopes were dashed when the news came three days later that the Japanese had still refused to surrender, and President Truman had ordered a second atomic bomb to be dropped, on the city of Nagasaki.

Peggy managed to get through six endless days of fear and rising hope, before the glorious news came that Japan had finally surrendered, and would sign the agreement on 2nd September.

Having never known such joy, Peggy decorated the house with flags and bunting and threw a party which lasted until the early hours of the following day. She was so excited and happy that her Jim would soon be coming home that she'd gone out and spent a fortune on a new outfit, which had taken most of her clothing coupons, and then gone to have her hair cut and styled in the local salon. But she didn't care that she'd spent money on herself for a change. Jim was coming home at last, and soon, very soon, they would be a family again.

It was now the eve before Rita's wedding, and the house was alive with chatter and running feet as Rita and Ivy dashed about with Sarah, Danuta and Jane to prepare for their evening party at the Anchor. Anne, Cordelia and Peggy would follow later, as Ron and Martin had promised to babysit the children.

Peggy was just putting the finishing touches to her make-up when she heard the knock on the door. Everyone else was still upstairs getting ready, so, with a cluck of annoyance, she went to find out who on earth it was.

The sight of the telegraph boy standing there with a brown envelope in his hand sent a wash of cold dread through her. This was the moment she'd feared all through the war – for telegrams rarely brought good news.

Her heart skipped a beat and began to thunder and her hand was trembling as she took it from him and closed the door. She stumbled over to the chair, feeling unsteady and faint, and had to pause for a moment to recover before she was able to tear it open and read the few stark words which shattered all her hopes and brought a cry of anguish.

*New orders * not home for Christmas *
letter to follow * Jim*

WELCOME TO

Cliffehaven

ELLIE DEAN

A Map of Cliffehaven

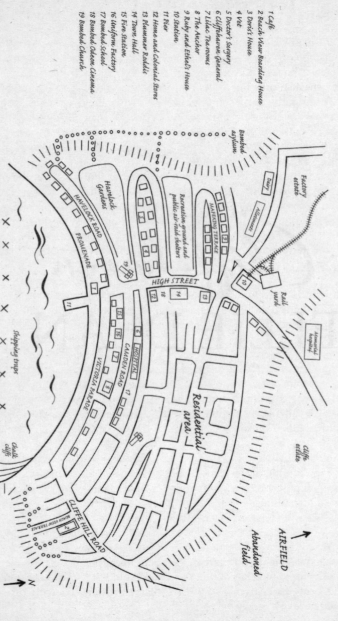

1 Café
2 Beach View Boarding House
3 Doris's House
4 Vet
5 Doctor's Surgery
6 Cliffehaven General
7 Lilac Tea-rooms
8 The Anchor
9 Ruby and Ethel's House
10 Station
11 Pier
12 Home and Colonial Stores
13 Plummer Roddis
14 Town Hall
15 Fire Station
16 Uniform Factory
17 Bombed School
18 Bombed Odeon Cinema
19 Bombed Church

Bombed asylum

Factory estate

Dairy

Allotments

Havelock Gardens

Recreation ground and public air-raid shelters

MAFEKING TERRACE

Rail yard

Memorial hospital

HAVELOCK ROAD

PROMENADE

HIGH STREET

Cliffe estate

Shipping traps

Chalk cliffs

Residential area

CAMDEN ROAD

VICTORIA PARADE

HOSPITAL

Abandoned field

AIRFIELD

CLIFFE HILL ROAD

BEACH VIEW TERRACE

N

MEET THE CLIFFEHAVEN FAMILY

PEGGY REILLY is in her early forties, and married to Jim. She is small and slender, with dark, curly hair and lively brown eyes. As if running a busy household and caring for her young daughter wasn't enough, she also runs the local uniform factory and still finds time to offer tea, sympathy and a shoulder to cry on when they're needed. She and Jim took over the running of Beach View Boarding House when Peggy's parents retired. When war was declared and the boarding house business no longer became viable, she decided to take in evacuees.

Peggy can be feisty and certainly doesn't suffer fools, and yet she is also trying very hard to come to terms with the fact that her family has been torn apart by the war. She is a romantic at heart and can't help trying to match-make, but she's also a terrible worrier, always fretting over someone – and as the evacuees make their home with her, she comes to regard them as her chicks and will do everything she can to protect them.

JIM REILLY is in his mid-forties and was a young Engineer in the last days of the First War, where he served alongside his elder brother, Frank, and father Ron. Now he's fighting for King and country in India and Burma.

Jim is handsome, with flashing blue eyes and dark hair, and the gift of the Irish blarney he'd inherited from his Irish parents; which usually gets him out of trouble. He enjoys the camaraderie of being a soldier, but the conditions and dangers he's encountering in the jungles have somewhat dampened his enthusiasm, and he treasures the letters and cards from home.

RONAN REILLY (Ron) is a sturdy man in his sixties who often leads a very secretive life away from Beach View now that his experience and skills from the previous war are called upon during the hostilities. Widowed several decades ago, he has recently married the luscious Rosie Braithwaite who owns The Anchor pub.

Ron is a wily countryman; a poacher and retired fisherman with great roguish charm, who tramps over the fields with his dog, Harvey, and two ferrets. He doesn't care much about his appearance, much to Peggy's dismay, but beneath that ramshackle old hat and moth-eaten clothing, beats the heart of a strong, loving man who will fiercely protect those he loves.

ROSIE REILLY is in her fifties and has recently married Ron, after her husband died following many years in a mental asylum. She took over The Anchor pub twenty years ago and has turned it into a little gold-mine. Rosie has platinum hair, big blue eyes and an hour-glass figure – she also has a good sense of humour and can hold her own with the customers.

HARVEY is a scruffy, but highly intelligent brindled Lurcher, with a mind of his own and a mischievous nature – much like his owner, Ron.

DORIS WILLIAMS is Peggy's older sister and for many years she has been divorced from her long-suffering husband, Ted, who died very recently. She used to live in the posh part of town, Havelock Road, and look down on Peggy and the boarding house.

But her days of snooty social climbing and snobbishness are behind her. Having lived with Peggy at Beach View Boarding House after bombs destroyed her former neighbourhood, Doris has softened and although she's still proud of her connections to high society, she's also on much better terms with her sister and the rest of the family. But despite all this, Doris is still rather lonely, especially with her only son now married and moved away. Could her recent change of heart also lead to a new romance?

FRANK REILLY has served his time in the army during both wars, but now he's been de-mobbed due to his age and is doing his bit by joining the Home Guard and Civil Defense. He's married to Pauline and they live in Tamarisk Bay in the fisherman's cottage where he was born.

CORDY FINCH is a widow and has been boarding at Beach View for many years. She is in her eighties and is rather frail from her arthritis, but that doesn't stop her from bantering with Ron and living life to the full. She adores Peggy and looks on her as a daughter, for her own sons emigrated to Canada many years before and she rarely hears from them. The girls who live at Beach View regard her as their grandmother, as does Peggy's youngest, Daisy.

ANN is married to Station Commander Martin Black, an RAF pilot, and they have two small girls. Ann has moved down to Somerset for the war, teaching at the local village school.

CICELY (Cissy) is a driver for the WAAF and is stationed at Cliffe Aerodrome. She once had ambitions to go on stage, but finds great satisfaction in doing her bit, and is enjoying the new friendships she's made. She has fallen in love with a young American pilot, Randolf Stevens, but now he's been sent to Biggin Hill, they rarely see one another.

BOB and **CHARLEY** are Peggy's two young sons, who are also living in Somerset for the duration. Bob is serious and dedicated to running the farm, whilst Charley is still mischievous, and when not causing trouble, can be found most of the time under the bonnet of some vehicle, tinkering with the engine.

DAISY is Peggy's youngest child, born the day Singapore fell. She can sleep through air-raids and simply adores pulling Ron's wayward eyebrows. She and Harvey are best of friends, but she has yet to truly know her father, or her siblings.

RITA SMITH came to Beach View after her home in Cliffehaven was flattened by an air-raid. Rita is small and an energetic tomboy who is a fully qualified mechanic, having been taught from an early age by her father. She can usually be seen in heavy trousers and boots, and a WW1 leather jacket and flying helmet.

FRAN is from Ireland and works as a theatre nurse at Cliffehaven General. She has been living with Peggy since before the war, and has become an intrinsic part of the family. She plays the violin at the Anchor for the sing-songs, and has fallen in love with Robert – an MOD colleague of Anthony Williams.

SARAH FULLER and her younger sister, **JANE**, came to England and Beach View after the fall of Singapore. They are the great-nieces of Cordelia Finch who has welcomed them with open arms. Sarah works for the Women's Timber Corps, and Jane has now left Cliffehaven for a secret posting where she's deciphering codes.

IVY is from the East End of London and was billeted for a time with Doris where she was expected to skivvy. She's stepping out with Fire Officer Andy, who is the nephew of Gloria Stevens who runs the Crown pub in Cliffehaven High Street. She and Rita are best friends and the untidiest pair Peggy has ever met – other than Ron and Harvey.

Lose yourself in the

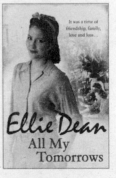

Find Love. Find Hope.
Find Cliffehaven.

world of Cliffehaven

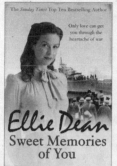

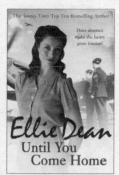

Hear more from

ELLIE DEAN

SIGN UP TO OUR NEW SAGA NEWSLETTER

Stories You'll Love to Share

Penny Street is a newsletter bringing you the latest book deals, competitions and alerts of new saga series releases.

Read about the research behind your favourite books, try our monthly wordsearch and download your very own Penny Street reading map.

Join today by visiting
www.penguin.co.uk/pennystreet